THE AMAZING
SNEAK RYERSON

THE AMAZING SNEAK RYERSON

A Sunday School Detectives Mystery

No. 1

Pep Stiles

Author's Note
This is a work of fiction. Names, characters, places, and inci-
dents are the product of the author's imagination or are used
fictitiously, and any resemblance to actual persons, living or
dead, events or locales is entirely coincidental.

Trade Paperback ISBN-13: 9780999096109
ePub ISBN: 978-0-9990961-1-6
PDF ISBN: 978-0-9990961-2-3
ISBN-10: 0999096109

Ordering/Contact Information:
Website: TheSundaySchoolDetectives.com
Email: TheSundaySchoolDetectives@gmail.com

INTRODUCTION

The sounds raced toward him, startling the boy from a prolonged and quiet meditation. They were loud and crunching. *Like hastily eaten crackers*, he thought. But the boy remained silent, hidden behind a cemetery monument making certain he would not be seen. *Men's moon boots on untrodden snow*, he said to himself identifying the noise.

Then, almost as quickly as the noises began, they stopped.

Slowly and quietly, the boy looked around the corner of the cold stone monument to see what he had long expected. In the near darkness of the early evening, less than twenty-five feet away, a young man – probably in his mid-twenties, face obscured by the darkness and the collar of his dark brown winter coat – was reaching behind a nearby gravestone.

Adorned with a newly placed bouquet of bright purple and white plastic flowers, the gravestone where the young man stooped, stood out among the many plain and unadorned markers in that section of the cemetery. The young man bundled in the brown winter coat, however, was not there to pay his respects or add another bouquet. Instead, he knelt, drew his body close to the stone, and ran his bulky gloves along the back of the headstone. Fumbling for a moment, the young man soon located the object he was seeking and quickly stood up, grasping tightly to a small white envelope in his right hand. Studying it in the near-darkness, the young man looked first at the front of the envelope and then the back.

"Got you," the boy said under his breath as he observed the young man in the distance.

Hearing the faint noise, the young man turned quickly and – still grasping the envelope – ran towards his car that was parked nearby.

"This may be the best chance I have to catch him," the boy said to himself as he stood – his legs aching from an hour of crouching in the cold of the night – and raced from his hiding place toward the car, hearing in quick succession the car door slam and the car's engine start.

Soon, to the boy's dismay, grey clouds of exhaust fumes lifted from the car's tail pipe as the car slowly accelerated along the icy cemetery road. *I was too far away*, the boy thought. *I should have been closer.*

Running as fast as he could – just before the car was out of reach – the boy lunged forward, grabbing the back bumper of the car with his fingertips. Dragged for a few moments, the boy quickly swiveled his feet so they were under him and crouching down, let the car pull him across the icy road. "Bumper hopping," he said to himself, remembering what the older kids called the technique. "I hope this works."

Clinging to the cold metal bumper with both hands, the boy's body shook with every bouncing movement of the car as his black Chuck Taylor sneakers, like ice skates, raced above the icy pavement.

"He threw the envelope in the passenger seat when he jumped in," the boy said to himself, as his photographic mind recalled how the young man had entered his car. "If I can open the passenger door and grab that envelope, the case will be over."

The car slowed as it reached the cemetery exit and the boy exerted all of his energy to move from the back of the car to the car's passenger side and quickly grabbed the cold metal handle of the car's back door as the car slowly passed the heavy green gates of the cemetery.

"Almost there," the boy said to himself.

An instant later, however, the car accelerated as it turned onto a busy road and began to increase in speed, every second going faster and faster.

Knowing that he had only moments remaining before the car sped away, the boy lunged toward the front door – his feet racing to keep pace with the car – hastily grabbing the silver handle of the front door with his right hand.

"I made it!" he said to himself.

But just before his thumb could press the oval button and open the door, the boy's feet hit a patch of ice and then just as suddenly found dry pavement again, making the boy's body crash into the car door and his face slam hard upon the window.

"What the heck?" the driver said loudly, surprised by the noise.

The impact was too great for the boy to keep his grip on the handle and moments later, looking into the car's side mirror, the driver watched as the boy fell into a snow covered yard and roll several times before coming to a stop. The car briefly slowed then continued its journey into the night.

"I was so close," the boy said dejectedly as he looked down at his knuckles, bloodied from his fall from the car.

A woman was nearby taking groceries into her house.

"Are you okay son?" she asked, concerned and confused at the sight of the boy sitting in a pile of snow in her front yard.

"Yeah, I'm fine," he replied. "I'm okay."

Rising slowly, his left leg sore from the fall, the boy walked back into the cemetery to retrieve his bicycle.

Twenty minutes later, after biking cautiously over ice and snow covered sidewalks, the boy arrived home and was greeted by his mother who was taking warm peanut butter cookies out of the oven.

"You've been out late Steven, you had me worried," she said as he entered the house.

"I was just over at Pep's," he lied. He felt bad for not telling his mother the truth, but was unable to think of an easy way of explaining that he had been sitting in a cold cemetery between the hours of seven and eight o'clock that night – and every night for the past two weeks.

"You better get ready for bed now, honey, it's getting late," his mother said warmly.

"K," the boy replied dejectedly as walked rapidly through the kitchen with his head down, avoiding his mother's gaze.

His thoughts on that cold evening were far from the pleasing aromas of the warm freshly baked cookies and the boy hastily went to the nearby stairs – taking two at a time – to quickly make his way to his upstairs bedroom. He was deep in thought, focused on the case – knowing now that it would be even harder to solve since he failed to get the envelope from the car.

Grabbing the salmon colored touch-tone phone off of his desk, the boy quickly dialed his uncle's phone number – he needed to warn him that tonight someone would be starting a fire.

CHAPTER 1

Jennie Ryerson was the first of the siblings to see their uncle's police car the following afternoon. A few moments earlier, the elementary school dismissal bell had rung and Jennie had rushed from her classroom to be one of the first in line to board Bus Four. While in line, she noticed her uncle next to his patrol car – parked behind the last bus waiting in front of the school. "Uncle Charlie!" she yelled as she rushed towards him, her blonde pigtails bouncing back and forth across her small head.

Her uncle, a tall man with wide shoulders, who had played college football and had served in the Vietnam War, stood next to his police car reading from a small black notepad, his navy blue police hat slouched low over his close cropped brown hair and forehead. Although the weather was bitterly cold, Jennie quickly noticed that he wore his blue police captain's uniform without a winter overcoat.

"Hey, it's my favorite first grader!" Her uncle said with a smile, as his breath made clouds in the cold air under his bushy mustache. "How ya' doin *Cindy*?" he questioned as the big blue jacket of his uniform enveloped the girl with his hug.

"I'm not Cindy, Uncle Charlie," Jennie said with a smile. "You know that."

"Oh, sorry, I got you confused with that girl on *The Brady Bunch*."

"Come on," she laughed.

"Or, maybe I was thinking of Buffy, from *The Family Affair*."

"I don't even know who that is Uncle Charlie," Jennie giggled.

"I guess that was before your time," her uncle said with a grin.

"Aren't you going to say anything to Mr. Knick Knack?" the young girl asked.

"Of course, it's good to see you again Captain Nick Nack," he said, giving a quick salute with his right hand in the direction of Jennie's imaginary friend.

"It's not *Captain*," Jennie corrected. "It's just *Mister*."

"Oh, right, sorry for the promotion," her uncle said, speaking again in the direction of Jennie's imaginary friend. "I guess I was thinking of Captain Crunch...or Captain Kangaroo."

"Mr. Knick Knack likes the *Captain Kangaroo Show*," Jennie replied enthusiastically.

"That's great, so do I," her Uncle added.

"Since he likes dogs, he mostly likes watching when Mr. Green Jeans is in the barn with the animals."

"That makes sense, I guess?" her uncle said, looking somewhat perplexed.

"You know give the dog a bone?" the girl said with a smile. "You remember that song, right?"

"Oh, right…Knick Knack Paddywack, give the dog a bone," her uncle replied.

"That's him!" the girl exclaimed.

"Sorry," her uncle said with a smile, "I was thinking of Nick Nack from the James Bond movie."

"What?"

"The actor was that short fellow, the guy who's on *Fantasy Island* now. He wears a white suit. I can't pronounce his name…Herve something or other. I think the movie was the *Man with the Golden Gun*…or maybe *Thunderball*."

"Well *my* Mister Knick Knack isn't short," Jennie said looking upwards in the direction of her imaginary friend.

"No, I can see that," her uncle said with a smile. "He definitely isn't short."

"Can you give me a ride home, Uncle Charlie?" Jennie asked, quickly changing the subject.

"Sorry kiddo, not today. I need to talk to your brother about some police business," her uncle said seriously.

"Oh, come on. I won't be a bother," the girl pleaded.

"I'll take you home next time I'm here, okay? I promise. It's just really important that I speak with him today. Could you go find him for me?"

"Okay," she said with her head down, turning to walk to the back of the line. Then, quickly, she turned again towards her uncle and asked, "Maybe you could take me home tomorrow?"

Her Uncle Charlie laughed. "You sure are persistent," he said.

"It doesn't hurt to ask," Jennie replied with a smile.

"Maybe tomorrow, but I can't make any promises."

Jennie beamed.

"Okay, maybe tomorrow," she said, still smiling.

"I'm not making any promises," Uncle Charlie said again. "But hey, I do promise the next time I'm here, I'll drive you home. And I'll even take Mr. Knick Knack home too."

Jennie grinned again, showing her missing tooth.

"That would be perfect!" she said. "He doesn't like to ride the bus without me."

"Looks like the kids are getting on your bus now, you better get going," Uncle Charlie replied. "Go find your brother for me, okay?"

"I'll find Sneak for you," the young girl said as she walked away.

Returning to the back of the line, she saw her brother approaching from the elementary school's front door.

"You're in *trouble*," she said almost singing the words. "Uncle Charlie's here for you."

"Ah man," her brother replied when he saw their uncle standing next to the black and white police car. "I think I'm in *big* trouble this time."

CHAPTER 2

"Hey Uncle Charlie," the boy said unenthusiastically as he approached the police car parked behind three long yellow buses in front of his school.

"Hey Sneak," his uncle replied with a similar demeanor.

That's a 1979 Ford LTD Crown Vic with a 302 cubic inch Windsor V8, the boy thought as he got closer to the police car. "Did you get a new car?" the boy asked his uncle.

"I did. Nice catch...my other car had too many miles."

"I like it," the boy replied looking at the four door sedan.

"Me too," his uncle replied.

"So, should I get in the front seat or the back?" the boy asked.

"You can sit in the front...for now," his uncle said earnestly. "Maybe you'll need to sit in the back on the way home," he added, without his typical grin.

The boy slid into the passenger side front seat of the car, swinging his gym bag full of books and detective gear onto the floor, while his uncle got behind the steering wheel. Although his uncle was a tall and fit man, for a few moments he had to awkwardly pull and tug at his walkie-talkie radio to get it out of his black gun belt before finally placing it between himself and his nephew on the front seat of the patrol car.

The two were quiet as the boy's uncle drove around the parked buses and passed the long one-story elementary school. They remained quiet as the older man stopped the car briefly at a nearby stop sign, then turned right, passing the gated entrance to the horse stables and the harness track of the County Fairgrounds. "So, I've got some good news and some bad news," the uncle finally said in a serious tone as they approached another stop sign and the car came to a halt.

The road where they stopped, the boy knew from pouring over area maps, was Blanchard Avenue – a street that ran southeast out of the city. On his maps it made an almost perfectly diagonal line, and for the most recent case, the boy had made a number of calculations as to how quickly the road – and many other major roads – could be travelled from different points in the city to different places throughout the neighboring countryside.

With no traffic behind them, they stopped for a few moments near the octagonal stop sign, located next to a store that sold cakes and baking supplies called *The Sugar Shack*. "Good news and bad news," the nephew said softly, first looking down at the gym bag he had placed at his feet and then looking out the car window at the small building painted white – with red trim around the store's doors and windows.

"First let's talk about the fire," his uncle said.

"Okay."

"The good news is we got it contained pretty quickly thanks to your tip last night. Once I got your call I was able to get a number of volunteer firefighters and auxiliary police to set up some patrols."

"Good," the boy replied positively.

"It really was good. But we'll need to talk about the bad news later, okay?"

"Okay," the boy replied.

"Want to go out to see where the fire was set?" his uncle asked.

"Sure," the boy said quickly.

"Alright," his uncle replied as he turned left at the stop sign. "I don't think Sheriff Bell would mind if we stop by. I was out there last night to take a look. We won't contaminate his crime scene if we just look from the side of the road."

"Was it pretty much the same as the others?" the boy asked quickly as they passed a bowling alley at the edge of town.

"Yeah, it had the same three burn patterns."

"Same size?"

"I think so," his uncle replied.

"Did anything other than a field get burned?

"There was a small building the farmer was using for storing seeds," his uncle explained. "We've been lucky these fires haven't spread to larger barns or farmhouses."

"Definitely," the boy replied.

They drove quickly out of town, and just before reaching Highway 15, turned onto a county road and soon came to their destination – a long and empty farm field. The terrain, the boy noticed, was flat in all directions and the areas untouched by the fire covered with small mounds of wind-whipped snow.

A sheriff's deputy sat in his black patrol car on one side of the narrow grey county road next to a line of yellow police tape that ran for a fifty yards in each direction of the vehicle, and he quickly exited his car when he saw the city patrol car approach.

"Hi Captain Foster, out to see things again?" the deputy asked when he saw Uncle Charlie exit his warm patrol car.

"Yep," the police captain replied as he shook hands with the deputy. "I brought my nephew out with me this time." Uncle Charlie motioned to the boy who had grabbed his gym bag as he was getting out of the car. "Deputy Curtis, this is my nephew Sneak Ryerson."

"Nice to meet you," the sheriff's deputy said while greeting Sneak, "I've read about some of your cases."

"Thanks," Sneak Ryerson replied as he walked toward the sheriff's deputy. The deputy was young, *perhaps twenty-two or twenty-three,* the boy supposed as he approached the deputy bundled in a heavy brown winter coat with a county sheriff's patch sewn on the shoulders. *Average looking, medium height, one hundred fifty pounds, blonde hair, brown eyes, coat smells like smoke,* the boy thought, as he shook his hand. "It's nice to meet you too."

"He was the one who called in the tip about the fire last night," Uncle Charlie explained motioning again to his nephew. "I thought he might want to take a look around."

"Wow, that sure is cool," the young deputy exclaimed as his eyes became wider. "Take all the time you need, sir."

Is the deputy faking an awe shucks approach, or is this how he always is? The boy wondered skeptically. *If he says 'Gee Whiz', I'll know it's an act.*

Turning to Sneak Ryerson, the deputy asked, "So, you knew it was going to happen, huh?"

"Well, the evidence pointed to it," Sneak explained.

"What evidence was that?"

Was that a smile I detected? The boy wondered. *Does he know more than he's letting on?*

"It's still pretty early in the investigation," Uncle Charlie interrupted. "But I've shared everything we know with the sheriff."

"That's good," the deputy replied. "It was quite a scene out here last night, with the flames and everything."

The three gazed for a moment at the empty field, blackened in the shape of three large circles while the smell of burned fuel lingered in the air.

Turning again to Sneak Ryerson, the deputy explained, "You can't go out there…it's still officially a crime scene, so you'll need to stay on this side of the tape, but you probably know that."

"Sure thing," the boy replied. "I can make some observations from here."

Uncle Charlie noticed that the boy was now looking at the field with a pair of black binoculars. "Where did you get those?" he asked.

"I had them in my gym bag," Sneak replied, looking down at the bag he had carried out of the police car.

"In your gym bag!" Deputy Curtis laughed. "Do you always carry stuff like that with you?"

"I never know when I might need them," the boy explained.

"What else do you have in your gym bag?" the deputy asked.

"I've got a few things that help at a crime scene, like evidence bags and a fingerprint kit."

"And probably some dirty gym socks," his uncle said as all three laughed.

The boy continued slowly scanning the field with his binoculars gradually moving them from one side to the other.

"So Sneak, what do you see?" his uncle asked after a few moments.

"Looks like the same pattern as before. Three large circles," the boy said pointing to the dark shapes in the field. "Looks to be about the same radius as the others and by the smell, I would guess it's the same accelerant, maybe a mix of kerosene and gas."

"We sent some samples to the lab in Columbus," the deputy added. "It will take a couple of days for all of the results to come back."

"Anyone come out here today?" Sneak's uncle asked.

"That's why my boss asked me to stay. He thought that maybe the perp...er, the arsonist would want to look at their work in the daylight."

"Anyone of interest?" Sneak's uncle questioned.

"Well, the farmer's been out a few times. He can't believe it. He said he didn't hear anything last night until the Volunteer Fire Department arrived. And a few neighbors have stopped to look. And of course, the F.E.E.T people have come and gone," the deputy added.

Sneak and his uncle both glanced at each other.

"How many of them were here?" the uncle asked.

"Five or six," the deputy explained. "They took a bunch of pictures and I had to be pretty stern with them to not go out into the field." He paused. "They were pretty excited about what they saw."

"I bet they were," Sneak added.

"I wrote down their license plate numbers," the deputy explained. "I can give those to you if you want them."

"Yes, definitely," the boy replied excitedly.

"I'll be the one to take them," his uncle interjected as he pulled out his notebook and quickly copied the license numbers from a piece of paper that the deputy gave him.

The three were soon quiet as they looked again over the burned field.

"Do you mind if we walk up the road?" Sneak asked.

"Sure, go on up as far as you'd like, there are train tracks about a half mile ahead," the deputy explained.

"I've got a theory about how the circles were made Uncle Charlie, I'd like to see if there is any evidence for it."

"Sure, let's take a look Sneak," his uncle affirmed.

"I'm going to wait in my car," the deputy added. "It's too cold out here for me."

"It is pretty cold," Uncle Charlie replied, as he and his nephew began walking along the narrow snow covered country road. They walked in silence, passing the last marker of yellow police tape and soon approached a railroad track.

"There! Look! " Sneak exclaimed as he pointed to tracks in the snow. "Those tracks are from a motorbike. That's how they did it!"

"But they could have been here before the fire," his uncle added.

"Right, there's no way to prove when they got here, but I'm pretty sure those are an exact match to tracks I found at the last two fires."

"Really?" his uncle asked.

"I think it shows that the arsonist is getting sloppy," Sneak added.

"Why's that?" his uncle asked.

"Well, at the first fire there was no evidence of any motorbike tracks. But I was able to easily detect the same tracks at the second and third fires," Sneak explained. "And now here they are at the scene of the fourth fire."

"That could be," his uncle said.

"I took impressions at the last two fires, and they were an exact match with each other. I'll have to compare them to this."

"You took imprints from the crime scene?" his uncle asked in a serious tone.

"Only after the scenes were cleared by the sheriff," the boy said smiling to his uncle.

"Oh boy," his uncle said shaking his head. "I thought you were going to get me in trouble."

"I'm pretty sure that's how they did it," the boy explained quickly, pointing from the road to the field as he spoke. "They drove the motorbike from the road over there and onto the field here. They were somehow able to muffle the noise of the engine so the farmer couldn't hear them from his farmhouse over there. After getting into the field, they went out and made their circles. They must have had some type of string or rope that helped them mark the center of the circle and the boundaries, so that the circles would be the same shape. And they must have had some type of barrel or container on the back of the motorbike to dump the liquid behind them. Then they exited the field and lit it up."

"It makes sense," his uncle replied. "A motorbike would explain how they could get in and out of the field quickly without anyone noticing them."

They paused to look closely at the motorbike tracks.

"It's going to be hard to figure out where this came from," Uncle Charlie stated, while looking at the faint tracks near the road.

"It's from a 1978 Yamaha DT 400," the boy said staring intently at the tracks in the snow.

"Now how did you figure that out?" his uncle asked, surprised at the detailed response.

"Just some elementary deduction," the boy replied in a serious tone, deciding not to tell his uncle about all the time he had spent bothering the mechanics at *Fornes* and *Findlay Auto Body* as well as the workers at three different tire distributors who let him look through greasy tire catalogs and motorcycle manuals.

"A Yamaha DT 400," his uncle said, as he wrote the information in his notepad.

"A *1978* Yamaha DT 400," the boy clarified.

"Got it," his uncle replied as he added the year to his notepad. "I'll have my guys be on the lookout for something like that."

"It's going to be tough to find," the boy added. "They probably used a truck or a van or some other sort of vehicle to get it here. I can't imagine being able to go too far without someone noticing a big oil drum on the back of a motocross bike."

"Yeah, that would be difficult to conceal. Shoot, it's probably difficult to drive."

The boy laughed.

"I'll put out a BOLO anyway," the uncle added, using the common police acronym for *Be On the Lookout*. "Maybe it will turn up."

"Maybe," the boy replied.

"Well, either that motorbike made these circles or a giant spaceship did it," his uncle exclaimed.

The two laughed heartily as they continued looking out into the field.

Soon they turned and began walking back to the police car.

"So there's something else I need to talk to you about," his uncle explained as he turned to a page in his black notepad. "An incident was reported last night near the cemetery."

Upon hearing these words, the boy immediately felt miserable. Earlier, he had hoped to avoid this conversation with his uncle, but now that it had started, his mood immediately changed and he walked with his head down, sadly looking at the snow covered road.

"Turns out someone matching your description was seen holding onto the back bumper of a moving car at the cemetery," his uncle explained as he read from his notepad. "After riding on the bumper, the person then jumped to the passenger side of the vehicle when the car turned eastbound onto West Main Cross Street. The person then appeared to try to open the front door of the moving vehicle before eventually being thrown to the ground when they slipped and fell on some ice on the road."

"Wow," Sneak said.

"The report was called in by a woman who was bringing in groceries from her car, she didn't get a good look at the driver, but saw the kid who was bumper hopping and trying to open the door of the moving car. She thought the kid was a High School hoodlum."

"Could be," Sneak replied. "There's a lot of High School kids that hang out over by the cemetery and *Bill Knapp's*."

"I doubt it!" His uncle said angrily. "The description she gave pretty much described you, down to your black Chuck Taylor shoes!"

Sneak was silent as his uncle continued.

"What were you doing out at the cemetery in the middle of the night?" his uncle asked.

"It wasn't the middle of the night," Sneak replied. "It was like seven thirty...or maybe a little before eight."

"I don't care when it was, you could have gotten yourself killed!"

"But I didn't," Sneak explained, "I'm here, right. I'm fine."

"But you could have really gotten hurt," his uncle said, sounding more and more exasperated as they continued their discussion. "I've visited a bunch of kids in the hospital who were doing the stuff you were doing last night! It's not fun having to call their parents and tell them that their kid got hurt messing around with a moving vehicle."

"But I had him dead to rights," Sneak replied.

"First off, don't say 'dead to rights'," his uncle scolded.

"I caught him," the young detective explained. "I'd been staking out the cemetery since the last fire."

"You've been waiting in the cemetery for over two weeks!" His uncle roared.

"Yes, but it's just…"

"Arg," his uncle protested, throwing up his arms. "Your Mom is going to kill me."

"But I caught him," the boy explained quickly. "He went to the section of the cemetery that I had been watching and he grabbed the envelope. Just like I thought he would."

"So?" his uncle asked.

"Don't you get it? That's how they communicate about the fires. It's perfect for them – a dead-letter drop. Because the details of the fire are in the envelope, Davis can make sure he has an air-tight alibi when the fire occurs, making sure he's miles away from the fire, when it starts. But, he still has enough time to get a letter into the newspaper before their eight thirty publication deadline. It's ingenious. I can't believe I didn't…"

"Ugh, no more!" his uncle yelled, loudly interrupting him. "I can't have you running around, risking your life for some arson investigation – with evidence that is circumstantial at best. You're going to get yourself killed chasing after these people who may – or may not even be – involved in the case.

You're off this case if I have anything to do with it! I'm going to talk to your parents and tell them about last night, unless you do!"

"But Uncle Charlie...," the young detective began.

Deputy Curtis, meanwhile, had been sitting in the warmth of his county sheriff's car, talking to his dispatcher and a few other deputies on his radio when he saw the boy and his uncle arguing. He was too far away to hear any of the words they spoke as they walked down the country road, but was wise enough to know not to interrupt them. The two were impassioned and heated and the exchange between the uncle and nephew lasted for several minutes, ending with the boy dropping his head as a sad look overtook his face.

When the two approached the captain's patrol car, the deputy quickly exited his car. "Did you see anything interesting?" Deputy Curtis asked.

"Maybe," the boy said softly, wiping away a tear from his eye.

"Well, okay," Deputy Curtis said awkwardly.

"Thanks for your help," Uncle Charlie replied somberly as he opened the door to his patrol car.

"Nice to meet you Sneak," the young deputy said with a smile. "Have a good one."

"Nice to meet you too," Sneak replied quietly as he got into his uncle's car – not looking at the deputy.

While his nephew looked out the window, Uncle Charlie started his car and slowly turned it around, following the same roads they had previously taken – and the two were quiet during the entire fifteen minute drive back into town.

CHAPTER 3

"I'll talk to you and your parents later," Uncle Charlie said solemnly to his nephew when the car arrived at the Ryerson's driveway.

"K, see ya'," Sneak Ryerson said in a clipped response, having already grabbed his gym bag and opened the car door even before the wheels of the patrol car had come to a stop. The boy exited quickly – not looking back for his uncle to see the distress on his face or the tears that were welling in his eyes.

After shutting the car's heavy door, the boy quickly walked to the back door of his family's house, opened it hastily and then loudly shoved it shut. From the doorway, he swiftly went up the three steps that led to the kitchen and angrily slammed his gym bag down hard upon the kitchen floor. The floor reverberated with the sound, while something cracked from within the bag. *Binoculars hitting nun chucks*, the boy thought as he identified the sound.

"Is that you Steven?" the boy's mother asked from the basement.

"Yeah," the boy said loud and angrily.

Mrs. Ryerson was downstairs in an area of the basement called *The Laundry Room* which was not technically a room, but rather a corner of the basement that held the family's washer and dryer – kept separate from the rest of the basement used by the children. Several years before, Sneak had converted most of the downstairs space into a crime scene investigation laboratory while his sister used the rest of the area for roller skating.

"Get a snack to eat," Mrs. Ryerson shouted from the basement. "We don't have long until Children's Choir tonight."

"Do I have to go to *Baby Choir*?" the boy asked incredulously.

"Don't call it that," his mother replied in muffled tones from the laundry room. "They are expecting you."

"But I'm really busy."

"You can do your schoolwork afterwards," his mother replied.

In what his mother would call "a huff", Sneak angrily went from the kitchen to the living room and found his sister stretched out on the green carpeted floor, her head resting on a stuffed toy giraffe, watching *Gilligan's Island* on the family's television.

Sneak marched to the television and turned the station to the *Munster's*.

"Hey, Mr. Knick Knack and I were watching that," his sister protested.

"Watch it some other time, I'm watching this," he said angrily.

"Mom!" Jennie yelled. "Sneak won't let me watch my show!"

CHAPTER 4

Forlorn and sullen – those are the two words that come to mind when I remember seeing Sneak Ryerson that night at Children's Choir. He was already there when I arrived, sitting by himself in the back of the small chapel at our church.

Sneak was a tall and thin eleven year old, who, for most of that night, kept his arms tightly folded across his chest while staring intently at the multi-colored linoleum floor. His long dark moppy brown hair fell frequently into his light blue eyes as he stared downward, forcing him to push his hair back up on his unruly head with his left hand. In his right hand, he held a thin and broken green rubber band that he twisted slowly back and forth, moving it between his thumb and forefinger. Twisting the rubber band in one direction and then another, I guessed, gave his hands something simple to do while his mind worked on an extraordinarily complex problem.

The boy's given name, as I should have told you earlier, was Steven Ryerson, but everyone, except for his mother and a few teachers, called him by his nickname: *Sneak*. He didn't receive the nickname because he was weird or sneaky, but rather because no one – and I mean no one – could sneak anything past him. This was a problem – especially for criminals – because Sneak, as you may have guessed, was driven to use his great mental abilities to figure out mysteries. Even as a child, he had one objective in life: to be a great detective.

For nearly all his life, Sneak had found he had a knack for solving mysteries that others could not. His family said that it had started out innocently enough when he was a very young child, barely able to walk around his parent's house. "Now where did I put the *Republican Courier*?" his father had asked, just before Sneak quickly found it.

"You found it!" was a common refrain at the Ryerson household when Sneak was young.

Then, a few years later, his gift was in full swing at school.

"Who stole the model train set?" our third grade teacher had asked us, in reference to a silver toy Amtrak engine and train cars that a student had brought to class for a school project – a shoebox diorama of "*The Railway Children*", that had been stolen only a few hours after it had arrived in the classroom.

Sneak raised his hand.

"It was you Sneak? I mean Steven," the teacher stuttered before correcting herself. "You stole the train?" she asked incredulously.

A few children gasped in amazement.

"No, I raised my hand because I know who took it," Sneak explained in a serious tone. "It was Roger."

Roger, a tall third grader who was seated across the room glared at the young detective.

A tense few seconds passed as Roger and Sneak stared intently at each other. Then, suddenly, Roger let out an exasperated sigh.

"Fine!" he angrily confessed as he pulled the model train from the deep recesses of his desk. "I took it. I don't know how he figured it out, nobody saw me do it!"

"It's elementary," Sneak said in a quiet voice, heard only to those seated nearby.

"Yeah, Whittier Elementary School," a boy seated next to him replied.

Even I had the pleasure – or discomfort – of discovering his gifts at an early age. You see, we had grown up going to the same church, both getting dressed up by our parents in tiny vests, petite bow ties and miniature sports coats and spending an hour together every Sunday morning in the Church's nursery and later in our Church's Sunday School classes. Then, at the start of second grade, we found ourselves in the same elementary school class. As a new student to the school, when I introduced myself, I told the kids that my nickname was *Pep* (in addition to telling them that I wanted to grow up to be a newspaper reporter).

"So Pep," Sneak said to me later that day when we were together on the playground for recess. "I'm sure it's hard having a nickname that was given to you because you are slow."

"What?" I responded, surprised by his statement. I had actually liked the nickname given to me by the kids at my previous elementary school.

"You're obviously not peppy," he replied seriously. "So there must be another reason for your nickname."

"Knock it off," I said angrily. "I don't know why the kids at *Wilson Vance* called me that," having just realized that perhaps the nickname might have been given in order to tease me.

"It's also got to be hard living in two houses since your parents separated," he added.

"Nobody knows my parents split up!" I said, shocked at hearing my family's biggest secret being spoken by someone outside of our family. "How did you know about that?" I asked, as I quickly looked around to see if any of the other kids had heard him.

"Elementary," he said matter-of-factly.

"Just shut up about it!" I yelled as I reflexively punched him in the stomach.

"I wasn't expecting that," the young detective replied weakly, bent over and crouching down on one knee. "I thought you would be impressed."

He later apologized for hurting my feelings. "I didn't mean to make you angry," he explained. "I was just saying what I had figured out."

"Just stop showing off," I told him. "And don't say anything about my family to the other kids."

"I won't," he replied.

Since then, Sneak and I became good friends.

Sneak had also used his gift for solving mysteries to help the city's Police Department. For several years, he had been calling his Uncle Charlie after reading about cases in the local newspaper. And after solving a number of cases by simply reading about them, his uncle, who was a captain in the Police Department, decided to officially bring him in to consult on a few of the department's "cold cases" – those cases that had gone unsolved for several months or sometimes even several years.

"I could really use a fresh set of eyes on these cases," Uncle Charlie had explained to his sister, Mrs. Ryerson. "Nothing major or dangerous," he had added. "It will be more paper-pushing than chasing bad guys. I just want to close these old cases out."

"Nothing dangerous," Sneak's mother had reiterated.

"I promise," Sneak's uncle had said.

Sneak officially started working with the police department the summer before we started sixth grade. He was so successful at solving some of the cold cases that his work was featured in articles in the *Courier*, the *Toledo Blade* and other area newspapers. One feature article had a headline that announced, "*The Amazing Sneak Ryerson*", while another article was titled, "*Young Detective Solves Case*". Still another article described him as a "consulting detective to the Police Department just like a young Sherlock Holmes".

And so, earlier that day, none of the children at our elementary school were surprised to see the police captain pull his patrol car behind the row buses and wait for his nephew – we were used to seeing him pick up Sneak after school. Seeing him enter the police car, we all knew that our classmate would somehow, in some amazing way, work to solve an important and baffling mystery.

And yet that evening, sitting on the hard wooden pew in the back of the chapel just before Children's Choir was about to start, young Sneak Ryerson did not feel amazing. He felt angry and confused because of his circumstances, and remained forlorn and sullen.

CHAPTER 5

"Hi Sneak," a few smiling children said as they took off their heavy winter coats and entered the small chapel.

"Hey," Sneak Ryerson replied, barely glancing to look up. The young detective's eyes, I noticed, when not studying the tiles on the floor, would sometimes turn their gaze toward the dark stained glass windows framed within the chapel's stone walls. During the day, the red, blue and green colors of the stained glass were cheery and bright but when we arrived, the evening had already turned to night and the unilluminated stained glass windows took on deep black and purple colors from the darkness beyond the chapel walls.

The night was a Thursday, and all of the church's rooms dedicated to choir practices were busy. While the elementary aged children practiced in the chapel, the Adult Choir met in a large choral room in the basement, while a teenage group practiced in a room nearby (followed by hand bell practice later in the evening).

As the time neared seven o'clock, more and more children filled the small chapel.

Our choir was led by Mrs. Willingham, who had served as the Children's Choir Director for a number of years. When she first arrived at the chapel that night – as she had done for years and years –Mrs. Willingham began organizing her music on her music stand at the front of the room, but as more and more children filled the small chapel, she walked around and greeted us – spending time with several parents who had walked in with their sons and daughters.

Mrs. Ryerson stood in the front of the chapel near a piano, talking to another parent before our practice started. At our Thursday night practices and at our monthly performances at the Sunday morning church services, Sneak and Jennie's mother played the piano while our choir sang.

As I recall, most of the kids who would later appear in many of my stories were at the Children's Choir practice that night. I remember Jennie – Sneak's sister – and her good friend Michelle being there, as well as our buddies Joel and Moscow, and Moscow's sister Hailey, along with Lisa and Cressida. It's funny to think that we were all there that night – oblivious to the events that were about to happen to us a few days later.

When I arrived, I too greeted Sneak, who, deep in thought, did not reply to me, and so I quickly took a seat next to Joel and some of the other older boys in the choir who were seated in the third row.

Soon the room was filled with over twenty children and Mrs. Willingham moved her black metal music stand to the middle of the chapel – where we could all see her.

"Okay, let's get started," she announced with a smile. "Take your seats, take your seats."

All of the children had designated places – the younger ones (like Jennie and her friend Michelle) sat in the first row of pews in the front of the chapel, while the older kids sat in the rows behind them.

Sneak, however, was still seated in the back of the chapel looking forlorn and sullen.

Mrs. Willingham, with white music baton in hand, gently tapped the metal music stand.

"Okay, let's begin," she said with a smile, her dark eyes beaming under her grey salt and pepper perfectly coiffed hair.

Some children still giggled and talked, ignoring our longtime Choir director.

She tapped again, this time louder over the cacophony of elementary school voices.

And then, "BAM!" came the noise from the baton.

Startled, we all looked up at our Director.

"Okay, now let's start," Mrs. Willingham said sweetly. "We haven't got much time before our next performance."

She paused and looked around the chapel, confirming that the children were listening to her and in their proper places. "Steven, you need to move closer," she said nicely.

Sneak, slowly looked up and saw his mother who was now seated on a leather piano bench in front of a dark black Kimball piano, glaring at him with her piercing blue eyes. With the thin index finger of her right hand, she pointed to Sneak's designated seat, which was currently the only empty space in the third row between Joel and myself.

"Now!" Mrs. Ryerson spoke firmly.

Sneak ruefully made his way to where I and the other sixth grade boys were restlessly seated.

"Okay, let's get our voices warmed up. Repeat after me," Mrs. Willingham said with a smile.

"Veesta," she sang.

"Veesta," we replied.

"Einey meany sally meany doo wop a donna meany," she sang.

"Einey meany sally meany doo wop a donna meany," we sang in response.

"Remember to smile. Smile!" She said encouragingly to us as we sang, pointing to her mouth.

"Very good," she said approvingly. "Let's do that one more time."

A groan came from the children.

"Veesta," Mrs. Willingham said again, smiling.

Sneak, I noticed, rolled his eyes as we heard this next set of instructions.

Hearing a different noise, we both looked over to a boy at the end of our row who had his thumb stuck in a small circular communion cup holder located in front of him — a holder used on those rare occasions when small communion glasses were distributed in the chapel.

"It's stuck," the boy mouthed the words as he turned in our direction. "I can't get my thumb out," he said in a loud whisper.

"Why do I have to be here?" I heard Sneak say to himself. "How is this going to get me any closer to solving the case? This is such a waste of time."

CHAPTER 6

The choir practice ended around eight thirty, and after gathering her music and purse, and saying goodbye to Mrs. Willingham, and then talking to more parents who had arrived to pick up their children, Mrs. Ryerson was ready to leave.

Darkness enveloped the three members of the Ryerson family as they made their way out of the church building and into the parking lot. As the cold air hit their faces, Sneak told me later that he was reminded that the weather matched his mood that night – dark and gloomy.

The three quickly arrived at the family vehicle parked nearby – a long red 1976 Chevrolet Impala station wagon, affectionately called *The Maroon Monster* by the family. The full-sized station wagon was wide and lengthy and could comfortably seat eight people in its three rows of seats.

Seven year old Jennie quickly "called" for the passenger side of the front seat for herself and her imaginary friend Mr. Knick Knack and bounded into the car with pigtails waving.

Sneak, being in no mood to argue about where to sit, opened the back door and quickly slumped down into the wide seat behind his mother and sister.

"Buckle up," Mrs. Ryerson told the children as she started the engine.

"Michelle told me about a new Holly Hobbie doll she got," Jennie said excitedly to her mother. "She got it last weekend at Franklin Park Mall."

"That's so stupid," Sneak replied quickly from his seat behind her.

"It is not," Jennie replied.

"It is too. How long are you going to play with dolls and talk to pretend people?" her brother asked unkindly.

"Maybe as long as you pretend you are a famous detective," the young girl replied.

"Hey!" Sneak objected, hitting his sister on the back of the head.

"Knock it off you two!" Mrs. Ryerson interjected. "Steven, stop hitting your sister."

"She started it," Sneak replied.

"No, she didn't start it, you did young man," his mother said sternly. "You've been acting horribly all afternoon and evening. You came home slamming your gym bag all over the place, then you yelled at your sister before we left, and now as we're leaving

Church you're arguing with her again. And to top it all off, I had to tell you to go to your seat between Pep and Joel. You looked like you'd rather have root canal than be at choir practice tonight."

"What's root canal?" Jennie asked.

"It's something that dentists do," Mrs. Ryerson explained.

"Ouch," Jennie replied.

Sneak remained quiet as they pulled out of the parking lot and turned onto East Lima Street and quickly passed Superior Cleaners.

"So, what in heaven's name is wrong with you?" his mother eventually asked, as they turned left onto a small street, near the YMCA. "You've been acting so strange today."

"I don't want to talk about it," Sneak replied dejectedly.

"Does this have something to do with a case you're working on with Charles?" his mother asked, having never been able to call her younger brother by the nickname most people used.

"I really don't want to talk about it."

"Well, if you're not going to talk to me about it, you'll be talking to your father about it when we get home," she explained. "Your uncle promised me that you would not be doing anything more than looking through old case files. I don't know how you could get so upset about that."

Sneak was silent.

"I saw Uncle Charlie at school today," Jennie inter-jected. "He said he'd take me and Mr. Knick Knack home the next time he's there. Maybe tomorrow."

"That's nice," said Mrs. Ryerson.

The three were quiet for a moment.

"So about that Holly Hobbie doll," Jennie addressed her mother. "Can I get one too?"

"We'll see," replied Mrs. Ryerson.

CHAPTER 7

When they arrived home, Jennie bounded into the house, while Mrs. Ryerson collected her piano music from the car as her son slowly plodded behind her.

"Let's discuss this with your father right now," Mrs. Ryerson told him.

"I don't really want to," Sneak answered gloomily.

"You don't *really* have a choice," his mother replied as they entered the house.

"Fine," Sneak said exhaling loudly.

Mrs. Ryerson dropped her music books onto the dining room table and the two entered the living room where they found Mr. Ryerson napping in a recliner, surrounded by newspapers and news magazines.

The year was 1980, and the crumpled news magazines that surrounded Mr. Ryerson – *Time* and *U.S. News & World Report* – were filled with updates on the struggling economy and upcoming Presidential primaries. A number of newspapers – recent copies of The *Courier* and *The Blade* – piled nearby, were also filled with articles about these important national concerns.

Mr. Ryerson was an average sized man who wore his hair in a short military style crew cut which, like his thick dark glasses, he had adopted from his time in the military – having served in the U.S. Army for two years after the Korean War. Now, many years later, he worked for a local oil and gas company, and next to the recliner in the living room, mingled in with his newspapers and national news magazines were a number of business journals on the oil industry: *Hart's Oil and Gas Journal, Offshore Drilling, Oil and Gas Reporter* and the *Rocky Mountain Oil Journal.*

"Hey, how was choir practice?" Mr. Ryerson soon asked after being awakened by the noisy trio.

"Great," Jennie said enthusiastically as she jumped onto her father's lap and gave him a hug. While Mrs. Ryerson and her son were slowly making their way into the house, Jennie had quickly gone to her room, changed into her pajamas and was ready for her usual Thursday night routine. While remaining next to her father on his chair she asked, "You didn't forget that *Rockford* is on tonight, did you?"

"Jennie, you shouldn't be watching that show!" Mrs. Ryerson exclaimed in mock indignation.

"It's really Dad that watches it while he reads his newspaper," Jennie explained. "I just fall asleep on his chair."

"Right," Sneak added. "You just pretend to be asleep, but you watch it too."

"I do not!" Jennie exclaimed. "You don't know what you're talking about."

"I do so know what I'm talking about," the young detective replied with a smile. "You pretend to be asleep while Dad pretends to read the newspaper, but you both watch the show! Jennie, you would hate it if Mom made you stop watching *The Rockford Files* with Dad."

"I would not," Jennie exclaimed.

"You would so," Sneak replied.

Jennie paused for a moment. "Just to show you that I wouldn't care," she added, after moving closer to her father and resting her head on his shoulder, "I'll fall asleep here and Dad can watch *Barnaby Jones* instead."

The three older Ryerson's laughed while Jennie offered a wide smile.

"Rockford is probably a re-run tonight," Sneak added after the laughter ended.

"I think it is." Jennie said softly.

The four paused for a moment and looked at the large television – the volume muted, while an episode of *Benson* was concluding.

"George," Mrs. Ryerson began. "Before you get too cozy, I need you to talk with Steven."

"Mom, do I have to?" her son asked in a whiny tone.

"Yes you do. You've been acting horribly today. You've been down in the dumps and you've been fighting with your sister more than usual. You need to talk to your father."

"Well, I've got to take some stuff out to the burning barrel," Mr. Ryerson said. "Why don't you come with me?"

"Fine." Sneak replied.

"Jennie, you still need to brush your teeth," Mrs. Ryerson said.

"I'll tuck you in later," Mr. Ryerson explained. "We can skip the T.V. detectives tonight if it's a re-run."

"Okay," Jennie replied sleepily, "I'll tell Mr. Knick Knack it's time to go to sleep too."

CHAPTER 8

For as long as Sneak Ryerson could remember, his father had taken the family's trash out to a rusted oil drum located behind their detached garage and lit the trash on fire. Mr. Ryerson had always called the oil drum "the burning barrel", but the name had always struck Sneak as somewhat funny because it was only burning on those evenings when his father lit a match to the trash, it was just an "old rusted barrel" the rest of the time, he thought.

Regardless of the name, Sneak enjoyed talking to his Dad around the burning barrel – hearing stories about his father's life and sometimes even asking his father for some advice.

I should have talked to Dad before now, Sneak thought as the father and son collected the trash cans in the house. *I wonder if Uncle Charlie has talked to Mom and Dad about last night yet?* Sneak wondered. *They'd be more upset if he had,* he concluded.

Soon, while father and son met in the kitchen, preparing to walk out into the cold darkness of the night, another thought came to the boy's mind – one that he had been thinking of during the afternoon and for most of the time in the chapel that evening: *When Mom and Dad find out about the bumper hopping and my time in the cemetery, they're going to make me stop doing detective work.* Dizzy, as the idea consumed his thoughts, the boy's stomach began to ache – as it had through most of the afternoon and evening. *They're going to ban me from working with Uncle Charlie and the police department and every single other case anyone asks me to investigate from now until I'm eighteen.*

He paused, dreading the possibility.

Or maybe until I'm twenty-one, he worried.

Soon, father and son put on their warm winter coats and boots and walked the short distance through the back yard with trash cans in hand.

"So have you watched many of the *Mrs. Columbo* shows?" Sneak asked weakly, knowing the great joy his father took in watching T.V. detective programs. "It comes on after *Rockford*," the boy added as he dropped his trash into the barrel.

"I've seen it a few times," Mr. Ryerson replied as he emptied the trash he had been carrying into the burning barrel.

"I guess the show isn't going very well," Sneak explained. "They started out having her be *Mrs. Columbo*, but Peter Faulk wasn't even on the show."

45

"Hmm," his father replied as he lit a match and threw it into the rusted metal drum.

"Then they changed the name of the show from *Mrs. Columbo* to *Kate Columbo*. Then they changed it to *Kate the Detective*. And then they changed her last name to something other than Columbo. Now, tonight's show is just called *Kate Loves a Mystery*."

"I think I read about that in the paper."

"It's just weird," the young detective concluded. "I thought it would be cool to see them together – Mr. and Mrs. Columbo – you know, like *McMillan and Wife*.

"Or *Hart to Hart*," his father replied.

"Exactly."

The two Ryerson's paused as they watched the orange flames dance through the family's trash and grow higher and higher above the barrel. As the smoke from the fire rose into the night sky and the flames cut through more and more of the debris, the smell became more and more unpleasant, burning the inside of their throats and nostrils with an acrid taste and smell – very different than burning a log at a campfire.

Sneak began feeling sick, not from the smoke of the burning trash, but from his thoughts that returned. *They're going to ban me from being a detective,* he thought again. *What other choice could they make?*

"So, I haven't told you much about my last case," Sneak finally said to his father.

"No, I don't think you have," his father replied.

"I should have said something to you and Mom about it earlier, but I didn't," he said quickly and passionately. "I am really close to solving it."

"Now what case is this?" his father asked.

"The Case of the Mysterious Circles," Sneak replied. *As if that were the official name of the case,* he thought. *It's like a name Dr. Watson would have given to one of Sherlock Holmes' cases, like the Adventure of the Speckled Band.*

Remembering the Sherlock Holmes case about a poisonous snake in a locked room, his thoughts turned briefly to one of his friends from church. *The Speckled Band,* he thought, *I need to tell Joel about that as a name for his music group.*

"Four fires have been set in the county," Sneak continued.

"The last fire was just last night, right? Somewhere south of town?" his father asked.

"Yeah, Uncle Charlie took me out there to see it today," Sneak explained.

"Oh really?" his father said, sounding surprised at the information.

So he hasn't heard from Uncle Charlie yet, Sneak surmised.

"I gave Uncle Charlie a tip that it was going to happen," Sneak explained.

"But I thought you were just going to be working on cold cases for him?" Sneak's father asked with a puzzled look on his face.

"Well, right, that's what we agreed to. But I figured this one out by just reading the newspaper. And I got really close to closing it out. But now I can't."

"What do you mean you can't?" his father asked.

"Uncle Charlie made me promise not to get any more involved."

"Ah," his father said. "That explains why you've been so upset today."

"Yeah, I'm just so angry," Sneak explained. "It wouldn't have taken me much longer to close the case, but now I'm not allowed to work on it. I'm really mad at Uncle Charlie and I'm really mad at God."

In the darkness, unseen by his father, Sneak began to cry and he quickly wiped away the tears with the palms of his hands.

"I can understand why you might be mad at your uncle, but why are you mad at God?" his father asked, not changing his demeanor.

"Well, you and Mom have always said that this thing I have – the way I can figure things out – is a gift from God."

"It is a gift," his father added, speaking now more quickly and animated. "He's given you a brain that works like a...like a computer. It can sort through lots of information and remember the smallest of details from an old case file or something you noticed, but no one else did. And how you can think about probabilities of behavior and think about scenarios....the math that you do in adding and subtracting potential scenarios and solutions is stunning. It's amazing. It's definitely a gift from God."

"So I'm wondering," Sneak continued, after his father had concluded. "If it's such a great gift from God, why isn't He letting me use it?" The young detective paused momentarily as he wondered again if that day would be the last day he would ever work for his uncle.

"That's a good question," Mr. Ryerson said as he paused a moment before answering.

Like many men of his generation, talking about his faith in God did not come easily to Mr. Ryerson. Having spent his teenage years during the 1940's and 50's, his adult models were mostly the stoic "strong and silent" types who rarely talked about their feelings or spiritual matters.

"Well, uh, I've seen what you're describing actually happen a lot," Mr. Ryerson continued as he adjusted his heavy black glasses. "When or, uh, where people have a really strong gift, sometimes they aren't able to use it like they want to. Sort of like Moses being a great leader, but God didn't let him lead the people into the Promised Land. It is something like that, right?"

"Yeah, something like that," Sneak said dejectedly. "I've got a gift to do something that not a lot of people can do, to figure out a case, but I can't. It's like I'm....like I'm Tony Dorsett, but I can't run with the football because Tom Landry is making me sit on the sideline."

"I don't have an easy answer for you," his Dad replied – appreciating that his son had used an example from his favorite football team. "We don't always get to know why God does what He does…or what He doesn't do. It's hard being in the hands of God sometimes. But we….we can trust that He's doing things for our good and for His own good purposes."

"Yeah, I've heard that somewhere before," the boy replied with a smile, remembering the many Sunday School teachers who talked about God's love and His control over His creation.

"Hey, I have an idea," Mr. Ryerson added brightly. "I may not be the smartest guy, but I was the smartest kid in the fourth grade!"

"Yeah, and the only one!" Sneak answered with a laugh, remembering Mr. Ryerson's youth in rural Wyoming, when his father had been the only member of his grade in a small three room elementary school.

"I remember you had some good discussions with Professor Telson. He's taught your Sunday School class a few times, right?"

"Yeah," Sneak replied. "I think he's going to be our teacher this Sunday too."

"He's only going to be in town for a few more months before he goes back to the school where he usually teaches. Why don't you see if he'd be available to meet with you? He might have some good ideas for you to think about. I'm not sure there's much more I can tell you."

"I can do that," Sneak replied optimistically, grateful for his father's suggestion of talking over spiritual matters with a seminary professor – and the fact that his father had not yet permanently suspended all of his investigations. "I'll try to meet with him," he added.

"I'll talk to your Mom about trying to get you over there to see him."

"That would be good," Sneak concluded. "Thanks, Dad."

CHAPTER 9

The next day, a Friday, was as cold and blustery as the day before, and in the afternoon, Sneak and his sister Jennie rode Bus Four home from their elementary school. After making a few stops on Fishlock Avenue near the County Fairgrounds, the long yellow school bus soon halted at the stop sign near the intersection of Decker and Osborne Avenues.

Once stopped, the kids leaped from their wide green seats and scurried through the narrow aisle before jumping down the steps of the bus's stairway, quickly passing the large silver handle that the driver had pushed forward only moments before to open the narrow glass panes of the school bus's front door.

The kids ran the short distance, lunch boxes waving in their hands, to their house, a white Cape Cod-style house, located only four houses away from the bus stop.

Once inside, the pair got a snack in the kitchen and moved quickly to the living room. Today there was no argument over what to watch on the family's large

Zenith television set – both agreeing to watch an episode of the *Munsters*, which was already in progress. The show was mesmerizing to both Sneak and Jennie. Set in a large Gothic mansion filled with dust and cobwebs – at 1313 Mockingbird Lane – the show featured a cast of monsters who were funny rather than scary. The kids' favorite character was Herman Munster, portrayed by the actor Fred Gwynne – who created a comedic version of a scary Frankenstein-type monster, popular in older black and white movies. The kids were enthralled by Herman's large chiseled forehead, bulky neck with bolts protruding from each side, huge feet clad with clunky black boots, and his wide smile as well as his outsized, large and booming laugh.

Mrs. Ryerson arrived home from the grocery store a few minutes after the kids began their television program and quickly encouraged them to get ready for their afternoon activities.

"Jennie, hurry and get your piano books together – you have your lesson this afternoon."

"Okay Mom, okay," Jennie said, still watching the television.

"Steven, get your shoes and coat on too. I scheduled an appointment for you to meet with Professor Telson this afternoon."

"Okay Mom," Sneak replied, who like his sister, continued watching the black and white television program.

A few minutes passed and an exasperated Mrs. Ryerson noticed that the kids were still engrossed in the television show.

"Come on you two!" she said, raising her voice. "You're going to be late."

A few moments later, Mrs. Ryerson walked into the living room and turned the large plastic knob on the T.V. to "Off", and soon the siblings grabbed their winter coats and scurried out the back door and into the warmth of the family's large station wagon.

Their first stop was at Mrs. Kulchar's house on Maple Street, near our church. Mrs. Kulchar was Jennie's piano teacher, who taught a group of children in the *Suzuki* piano method – an approach to learning music that focused on proper technique and memorization. Because memorization of the songs was so important, every night as she went to sleep (except for Thursday's when she was allowed to fall asleep on her father's chair watching T.V. detective shows), Jennie listened to the same music. Her teacher had explained that the repetition would help her and her fellow young piano students memorize the songs more easily. When Jennie snuggled in her big bed readying for sleep, Mrs. Ryerson would lean over a nearby red and black ladybug shaped turntable and play the same vinyl recording of classical piano music. The first song on the album was *Twinkle, Twinkle Little Star*, the second, third and fourth songs on the album were variations on *Twinkle, Twinkle Little Star*, which were followed by a short Mozart piano sonata called *Eine Kleine Nachtmusik*, which was followed by Beethoven's *Fur Elise*. Then the music would repeat.

Sneak said it drove him crazy listening to the same music over and over again, while Jennie explained that she thought it might have helped her memorize the songs.

That afternoon, after dropping Jennie at Mrs. Kulchar's house for her twice-weekly piano lesson, Mrs. Ryerson drove her son to his appointment with Professor Telson.

"I'm glad I was able to reach Professor Telson this morning," Mrs. Ryerson explained. "He said he was glad to meet with you."

"That's good," Sneak replied.

"So, how are you feeling today?" Mrs. Ryerson asked her son, who was seated next to her in the large station wagon. "You seem better."

"Maybe a little better," he replied thoughtfully. "It should be good to talk to Professor Telson today. It was good talking to Dad last night."

Sneak told me later that he was still feeling discouraged about the mystery. *I will never be able to solve this case*, he had thought throughout the day at school. *Plus, Mom and Dad will be so mad when they find out what I did at the cemetery, I'll be grounded for life.*

As the minutes passed and the pair drove north to the campus of the small seminary, Sneak did find some encouragement as he thought about explaining the case to Professor Telson – having really enjoyed the young professor teaching our Sunday School class. *He's only a seminary professor,* Sneak thought. *There's no way he could actually solve the case, but he might have some good ideas for me.*

Soon, Mrs. Ryerson and her son reached the campus of the small seminary.

"I've got to pick up Jennie from her lesson at Mrs. Kulchar's, then we'll come back to pick you up," she said as she stopped the car at the school's main entrance. "Maybe we can stop at Dietsch's for an ice cream treat afterwards?"

"Okay, see ya' Mom," the young detective replied as he quickly exited the car and walked briskly up the front stairs of the main classroom building.

"Think you can find where you're going?" Mrs. Ryerson was about to ask, before she remembered that her son was Sneak Ryerson. Finding things was what her son did.

CHAPTER 10

Around the same time that Sneak Ryerson was approaching Professor Telson's office, a young man was a short distance away nervously approaching a recently enclosed shopping center called the *Village Mall* – located on the east side of our city.

Earlier, the young man had become panicked by the sight of several people who had loitered outside of his apartment building throughout the day next to a parked *Purolator Courier* delivery truck.

I don't know any of those folks, he thought as he watched them discretely from behind drawn window shades in his bedroom. *They've got to be cops,* he concluded, imagining that each of the people were law enforcement officers. *But how could they be on to me?* He wondered, *I've been so careful.*

As the day wore on and the people remained outside of his apartment, the young man decided to make one final visit to the mall, in hopes of getting some vital information about his future.

I'm sure they are police or FBI, the young man thought. *And when I leave, they'll try to follow me, but I need to know what to do next.*

Leaving his apartment a few minutes later, the young man went quickly to his car parked on the street and left for the mall that was located a short distance away. Approaching the mall, he became more and more frustrated with traffic on Tiffin Avenue – as the congested four lane road slowed his progress.

Fearing that he would be pulled over at any moment and questioned by the police, he reasoned that it would be best to act as relaxed as possible. *Just play it cool. It's only a trip to the mall,* he thought.

"I just came out here to do some shopping," he quickly said out loud, practicing how he might respond to questions from a police officer – while also hearing his voice crack nervously. "Yeah, I needed a new dress shirt. I was thinking of getting one from Sears or J.C. Penny's."

He said the words again, hoping to sound more confident and less nervous if he were stopped.

"I just came out here to do some shopping," he repeated. "I needed a new shirt – a new *dress* shirt. I was thinking of getting one from J.C. Penny's....or Sears."

He paused as he thought of other questions the police might ask...and his possible answers.

"No of course not," he said with a laugh. "I didn't know anything about those fires before they were started."

He practiced again.

"Why no, of course not. I didn't know anything about those fires before they were started. Of course I know a lot about them now....from what I've read in the paper and heard on WFIN, but I didn't know anything *before* they were started."

That sounded good, he thought. *Emphasize how you didn't know anything before the fires started.*

As he got closer to the shopping center, the young man decided that it would be best to move from one parking spot to another – in hopes of losing anyone that might have followed him.

To get to his first location, he turned left at a Burger King, then after passing several larger stores connected to the mall, turned right into the parking lot on the north side of the shopping center. Stopping abruptly in a parking spot in an empty area close to the road, the young man waited – with his hands fidgeting on the car's steering wheel while his eyes darted anxiously from his car's side mirror to the rearview mirror as he looked for cars behind him.

After a few minutes he moved his car to another spot, this time near the mall's only barber shop. At this new location, he quickly turned off the car's engine and waited. His heart raced as he pondered the possibilities of what might happen next.

Arrest.

Trial.

Imprisonment.

His body shuddered at the thought. *They will catch me*, he concluded. *I'm sure of it.*

The nearby barber shop's large plate glass window made it easy for the young man to see the barbers at work – and he quickly turned his attention to the men in short sleeve blue barber jackets with their names embroidered in cursive above the front pockets. He first noticed Dan, a young and effusive barber, clipping the white hair of an older man. *Probably telling stories about his race car,* the young man thought as he saw the barber pause and demonstrate something to his customer with his hands. Dan, he knew, loved racing is old cars at the local speedway and smashing even older cars in the annual Demolition Derby – a popular event that marked the end of the week-long County Fair held every September in our town.

Next to Dan was Larry, a barber who was a little older and quieter than Dan. Larry, the young man noticed, was wearing new silver wire rimmed glasses and was busily cutting the hair of a teenager. The young man in the car smiled as he saw this barber, a man whom he had known since his youth, and guessed that he was talking about his family – perhaps chatting about his wife who was a local schoolteacher or their three girls who were in High School.

Watching the barbers work their scissors and clippers, served as a brief respite for the young man, taking his mind away from thoughts about being followed.

After a few minutes he looked around his car again, and to his relief saw nothing that looked like a marked or unmarked police car. Many of the people he saw were walking quickly – entering or exiting the mall from the nearby glass double doors of the mall's north entrance. There was only one person, he noticed, who was not moving quickly – a young woman who was bundled in a winter coat standing outside the barber shop who seemed to be helping a fussy baby as she leaned over a large blue baby carriage. *She must be waiting on someone*, the young man thought as he watched her rock the carriage back and forth.

Soon, several more uninterrupted minutes passed.

It doesn't look like anybody followed me, the young man thought confidently as he started his car and slowly navigated to the east side of the shopping center. Driving slowly, the young man eventually chose a spot near Sears and again waited anxiously, shifting his eyes from his side mirrors to his rearview mirror, checking once more to see if he had been followed. Here, the young man watched as several cars entered and exited the Auto Center and saw several people walk up to the store's nearby Pick Up desk to retrieve larger items they had purchased inside the store.

No one's on your tail, he thought.

After a few more minutes he moved his car to the south side of the shopping center. Once there, he parked his car as far away from the building as possible – right next to Tiffin Avenue – to provide him with as quick of a getaway as possible.

After parking, the young man walked as leisurely as he could toward the shops, casually looking around to see if he was being followed.

Look cool, he said to himself. *Look cool.*

Approaching the mall, he hammed it up a bit, first acting as if he might go to Britt's – a discount retailer located on the west side of the mall, but just before getting to that entrance, he acted like he wanted to go to J.C. Penny's instead, so he walked towards that store, located further east, but then, he acted like he had changed his mind once more and went to the mall's west entrance.

Entering the warmth of the mall, with the smell of kettle corn filling his nostrils, the young man's ears were quickly inundated by a multitude of noises as loud conversations between shoppers and beeping noises from video games filled the air.

The young man was initially surprised at how busy the mall seemed on that late Friday afternoon. *I guess this is a popular place to get away from the cold and the wind,* he reasoned.

The larger crowds bolstered the young man's confidence, giving him hope that he would not be noticed among the many people. *Plus the crowds might make it harder for someone to follow me,* he concluded.

Soon, the young man arrived at a blue metal bench located near the men's clothing store called The Toggery.

Yawning, he sat down as nonchalantly as possible on the metal bench.

I need to look laid-back, he thought to himself. *Just take it easy.*

But he couldn't.

His heart raced faster and faster and he looked down wondering if the thumping of his heart was actually visible to those who passed by.

He felt warm too. Even though he had just arrived from outside temperatures that hovered near a cold 25 degrees Fahrenheit, the young man could feel that his shirt and jeans were now drenched in sweat.

The bench where he sat was similar to many in the mall, and the young man panicked for another moment, thinking that he might have picked the wrong location.

No, the last note said I should go to this one, he said to himself.

He sat for a few moments at the bench and looked around one more time to ensure that he wasn't being watched. A few moments later, he quickly reached his hand under the bench to find a white envelope taped to the bottom of the seat.

He hastily grabbed it, and looked around again to see if anyone had seen him.

No one saw that, he said to himself.

Standing up, he yawned again before hastily shoving the envelope into the pocket of his brown parka and moved quickly toward the mall's exit.

I've made it, he thought confidently. *What was I worried about? Must have made up the whole thing...*

And then he saw her.

In fact, he almost ran into her as he was dashing towards the exit.

"Oh sorry, excuse me," she said hastily.

"Ah, no....problem," the young man replied in a low and deep whisper as his voice struggled to get out the words while his mind processed the shock of what was happening.

It's not possible! It can't be, he thought while he dashed passed her and quickly pushed open the cold glass exit door.

The cold air stung his face.

His vision seemed to become like a tunnel, his breathing was quick and short. Leaving the sidewalk and reaching the parking lot he quickened his pace into a near run to reach his car.

Hastily opening his car door, he slumped down into the driver's seat while his mind flooded with the significance of seeing the young woman at the exit.

It was her, he thought. *It was her! How could I have been so stupid?*

He had seen the woman before...only a few minutes before, he was certain...waiting with a large baby carriage outside of the barber shop. And now he had nearly knocked her over in his escape. Now she was carrying an armful of shopping bags – no baby carriage in sight.

CHAPTER 11

S neak Ryerson bounded up the stairs of the seminary building, breezing quickly past the first floor
that held a large auditorium and a second floor
where smaller classes were held. After reaching the
third floor of the building – a floor that contained a
number of offices for the school's professors – Sneak
was able to quickly find Professor Telson's office.

The door was open when Sneak arrived and
he noticed that the professor's office was small yet
brightly lit by a long rectangular dormer window
that brought in the late afternoon sun. The office,
he noticed, was filled with hundreds of books, some
piled atop a large messy metal desk in the center of
the room while others were crowded on metal and
wooden bookshelves that lined the office's four walls
while some books were even stacked in piles on the
floor.

In addition to being covered with books, the
large metal desk in the center of the small room

was swollen with stacks of papers and academic journals. When Sneak arrived, Professor Telson was sitting behind his desk holding textbooks open in each hand, carefully comparing the two tomes.

He's a study in contrasts, Sneak thought as he noted the professor's nice yellow Oxford cloth shirt and his narrow red striped tie worn under a dingy green corduroy jacket. His eyes, Sneak noticed were bright and warm on his wide round face, while the professor's auburn hair was unkempt and receding.

Sneak knocked twice on the open office door and quickly got the professor's attention.

"Mr. Ryerson!" Professor Telson exclaimed when he saw Sneak at his office door. "Come in, come in," he said warmly as he stood to greet the boy.

Sneak entered cautiously, unsure of where to sit or stand – with so many books in the small office.

"Good to see you again," said the professor, who dropped the two books on his messy desk and then reached out a large hand to shake Sneak's hand – a move that reminded Sneak of a large bear paw coming toward him.

"Sit, sit," the professor said, motioning to a blue chair located across from his cluttered desk. "Just move those books on the floor."

The blue cloth chair – where Sneak was directed to sit – was stacked with books and identical to the chair that Professor Telson had been sitting in behind his desk. Both chairs, Sneak noticed, had a thin covering of yellow chalk dust. *Probably from years of being in a classroom*, Sneak thought.

"Thanks for meeting me," the young detective said as he moved the books off of the chair and put them on the floor.

"Sure thing. It's not a problem, not a problem at all," Professor Telson replied.

The professor was a jovial man in his late twenties and his replies were frequently accompanied with a hearty laugh that echoed throughout the small office.

"Your mother said you might want to meet a few times before my time here at the seminary comes to an end," the professor said as he sat down in his chair behind the desk.

"Yes, that would be great," Sneak replied.

"Well, I'll be here until the semester ends in May. I'm more than happy to meet with you until then."

"That's terrific," Sneak added.

"After your Mom called, I called Pastor Thomas, just to get his blessing. You know, I don't want to step on any toes or anything like that...and he was fine with us getting together to meet."

"Oh, okay," Sneak replied, surprised that the professor felt the need to talk to our pastor.

Seeing that his comment had confused Sneak, Professor Telson added, "You see, I'm not your pastor,

I'm just an academic...a theology professor. So, in situations like this, I always want to make sure those in authority....those people with spiritual authority, like your parents and your pastor, are okay with me providing some Biblical counsel."

"That sounds good," Sneak replied.

"Your Mom and Dad, and the pastors at your church, they're the folks who will be your leaders as you're growing up. I'm just an encourager, a cheer-leader of sorts for the next few months."

"That makes sense," Sneak said, smiling as he imagined the large professor dressed as a cheerleader.

"Oh...ah....after I spoke to your mother and Pastor Thomas this morning, I also told one other person about our meeting....one of my colleagues from the theology department. I told him you were stopping by and he said he wanted to meet you. I hope that's okay."

"Sure, that's not a problem," Sneak replied – echoing the same words the professor had used a few moments earlier.

"In retrospect, I probably should not have said anything to him. I hadn't even asked if you wanted to keep this meeting confidential – outside of your parents and pastor. I'm sorry if that's a problem."

"No, it's cool," Sneak replied calmly.

"Okay, so, what did you want to discuss?" the young professor asked.

"It's about a case I've been working on," Sneak began.

Before he had a chance to continue, however, an elderly man, smiling widely, stuck his bald head into the small office.

"Guten Tag, Herr Professor," the older man said with a smile, his voice shrill and high pitched.

Sneak turned in his chair and looked at the man who was dressed in a checkered sports jacket, white shirt with a red bow tie and tan polyester pants. He saw too that the older man's eyes were deeply set but shone brightly behind wide, thick glasses.

"Guter Nachmittag, Herr Doktor," Professor Telson replied jovially in return.

"So this must be the young detective I've been reading so much about. Our own Young Sherlock Holmes!" the older man said.

"Yes Dr. Bayhill, this is Sneak Ryerson," Professor Telson explained.

Sneak stood up and shook hands with the older man.

"Nice to meet you Dr. Bayhill," Sneak said.

"Nice to meet you too young man," Dr. Bayhill said with a smile. "Has Professor Telson been filling your young mind with his ideas about presuppositional apologetics?"

Sneak gave a confused look and turned to Professor Telson for an answer.

"No, no," the young professor said. "Mr. Ryerson just arrived and he was about to fill *my* head with interesting things."

"Very good, very good," replied Dr. Bayhill. "You've got to watch out for this one," the older professor said pointing to Professor Telson. "He's dangerous."

The three laughed.

"Do you know my grandson Andrew?" Dr. Bayhill asked.

"No, I don't think so," Sneak replied.

"He's over at the High School," the older professor explained.

"I'm not that old yet. I won't be there for a few more years," explained Sneak.

"Ah, right, right," said the older professor. "A few more years until you are in High School."

"Yep," Sneak replied as the three paused.

"The newspapers say you're a young Sherlock Holmes," said Dr. Bayhill.

"Well I don't know about that," replied Sneak modestly.

"Can you believe it Nicholas, a famous detective coming to visit?"

"He's quite gifted." Professor Telson replied.

"Yes, so they say," the older professor said. "So they say." Then, turning to Sneak, he asked, "You know of course who wrote the Sherlock Holmes mysteries?"

"Sir Arthur Conan Doyle," Sneak replied quickly, unsure of where the older professor was taking the conversation.

"Yes, and did you know he had an inspiration? Did you know that? There was a certain Dr. Bell, who was a physician. Have you ever heard of him?"

"No, I haven't."

"They say," Dr. Bayhill continued, "that Dr. Bell's power of observation was so keen that he could tell a person's profession and even their recent activities within only a few minutes of meeting them."

"That's pretty good," Sneak added.

"The character of Sherlock Homes, you see, was based on a real person!"

"I didn't know that," Sneak answered.

"A real person, can you believe it, Nicholas!" Dr. Bayhill exclaimed excitedly. "Those famous stories, based on real-life?"

"That's quite interesting," Professor Telson added.

"Well, I don't want to keep you from your meeting. I better be going," Dr. Bayhill said as he slowly began turning to leave. But then, the older man stopped abruptly and turned back toward Sneak and the professor.

"Since we have a famous young detective here," Dr. Bayhill said addressing Professor Telson with a smile. "Maybe we could put him to a test of sorts."

"What do you mean?" Professor Telson asked.

"Well, since he has just arrived, maybe he could use his keen powers of observation and deduction to tell us what he's learned so far, like Sherlock Holmes might do. We could see if this young man's powers of observation are as good as the newspapers say they are."

"What would you like me to tell you?" Sneak asked.

"You could tell us what you've learned about the two humble professors who stand before you now," Dr. Bayhill explained.

"He's only been here for a minute or two," Professor Telson replied with a laugh. "Sneak, you don't have to do that if you don't want to."

"It might be interesting to see a young Sherlock Holmes in real-life," the older professor explained.

"You don't have to do this," Professor Telson said again.

"No, it's fine. I'll give it a go," Sneak replied thoughtfully.

"That's terrific," said Dr. Bayhill.

As the older man spoke, Sneak slowly looked at one man and then the other before turning is eyes toward the tile floor of the small office. His face showed a look of deep concentration while he stared downward for a few moments.

Soon, as his head moved further down, his brown moppy hair fell into his eyes and Sneak quickly pushed it back upon his head. Then, folding his hands together as if he was praying, he lifted his hands up to his lower lip as his mind focused on the many observations he had recently made.

"I will need just a few more moments of silence, please," Sneak said.

"Ah, a flair for the dramatic," Dr. Bayhill replied.

There was a moment of awkward silence as the two professors smiled at each other and Sneak looked down at the floor.

"Okay, I'm ready," Sneak finally said, while continuing to look down. "Professor Telson," Sneak said dramatically to the young professor – in a way that he imagined Sherlock Holmes might have said it. "You are from western Pennsylvania and recently returned to the United States after studying in West Germany."

He paused again, still looking down, while a faint smile came across his face – unseen by the two professors.

"If I'm not mistaken, you studied at the University of Tubingen."

"That's...I never told you," Professor Telson began. "How did you..."

"Silence, please. The silence will help me concentrate," Sneak interrupted in a serious tone.

Professor Telson laughed and Sneak paused again before continuing.

"Your hero in theology is a Dutch man who lived in Grand Rapids, Michigan, if I'm not mistaken."

The two professors smiled at one another as Sneak continued after another pause.

"You enjoy *Wilson's* hamburgers and you live alone."

"Wow," Professor Telson exclaimed, as he saw Sneak glance upward, indicating that he was done with his observations of the young professor. "That was amazing Sneak, you'll have to tell me how you did that."

"Did you notice anything about me?" Dr. Bayhill interrupted, cutting off any explanation that Sneak might have given.

"Yes, I did observe some things about you," the young detective answered, while he moved his gaze from Dr. Bayhill to the floor of the office.

"Dr. Bayhill," Sneak began dramatically, "you live on a farm outside of the city limits, whose value has increased considerably in the past few years."

"Incredible," the older man said.

"The soil on your farm is called *Pewamo silty clay loam*, if I'm not mistaken."

"What?" Professor Telson said as his jaw dropped. "You know the name of the soil on his farm?"

"Anything else?" the older professor asked smiling.

"Yes," Sneak continued, "Professor Telson has not yet obtained his Ph.D., so you like to tease him about that. And because he didn't finish his studies in West Germany, you like to tease him in German…"

"Yep," the young professor replied quickly.

"Which," Sneak continued, "Dr. Bayhill, is a language you learned during World War II….perhaps in a Prisoner of War camp."

The two professors turned to each other, both openmouthed, and then began to laugh.

CHAPTER 12

D r. Bayhill had been so surprised by Sneak Ryerson's words that he shuffled several steps backwards – nearly stepping completely out of the office after hearing Sneak's dramatic descriptions.

"Nick, you didn't tell him any of those things did you?" he asked Professor Telson.

"No Sam, I didn't." the younger professor explained. "I didn't tell him any of that. He just arrived in my office a few minutes ago. Before that, I led his Sunday School class a few times, but didn't tell him any of those things about me…or about you, for that matter."

"That was one of the most amazing things I've ever heard," Dr. Bayhill said enthusiastically. "Can you help us understand how you did it?"

"It was elementary," Sneak replied with a smile as he looked at Dr. Bayhill and then at Professor Telson.

"Of course it was!" Dr. Bayhill said with a laugh. "Elementary!"

"It didn't seem elementary to me!" replied a smiling Professor Telson. "Let's start with my studying at the University of Tubingen. How in the world did you know that?"

"That has a pretty easy explanation," Sneak replied. "When Dr. Bayhill arrived, I noticed that he spoke to you in German, so it was easy to deduce that you were both familiar with the language."

"Right, but that couldn't have told you were I went to school, I don't even talk with a Swabian accent like they do in Tubingen," the young professor insisted. "In fact, I've probably spent more time in Vienna, so I probably speak with an *oberösterreichisch dialekt*."

"I'm guessing that's an Austrian dialect?" Sneak asked.

"Right."

"Well, it wasn't your accent that told me where you went to school," Sneak continued his explanation to the young professor. "You see over the past couple of years I've taught myself how to read words upside down."

"Reading words upside down!" Professor Bayhill exclaimed.

"Right, so when I first walked into your office, I saw that top paper on your desk. It was facing towards you, but it told me you had studied there."

Professor Telson picked up a white typewritten paper that lay on top of his messy desk and read it carefully. "But this letter is in German and doesn't say anything about the University of Tubingen," he declared.

"Yes, but the heading says *Eberhardina Carolina* which, if I'm not mistaken, is the school's motto."

Sneak paused as the young professor examined the paper.

"It's another name used by the University of Tubingen," Sneak explained to Dr. Bayhill.

"What?" Dr. Bayhill exclaimed.

"Wow," said Professor Telson. "It's true, it's the school's motto. I wouldn't have guessed you would have known that."

"That's impressive," Dr. Bayhill added.

"It's...." Sneak began.

"Elementary!" Dr. Bayhill interrupted.

"Right," the young detective added.

"How did you know about the school's motto?" Professor Telson asked.

"I'm not exactly sure," Sneak replied. "I must have read that somewhere."

"Okay," Professor Telson continued, speaking quickly. "How did you know those other things about me, like being from western Pennsylvania and liking Wilson's hamburgers and living by myself?"

"Well that mustard stain on your coat gave away your favorite hamburger place," Sneak explained. "I've actually done a study of the condiments and sauces from local restaurants. Those stains actually show up a lot in crime scenes."

"That's a study I would have liked to help with!" the young professor said enthusiastically. "I love those Wilson's Specials."

"Me too," Dr. Bayhill added.

"And how about my marital status?" Professor Telson asked.

"Well, the fact that there are several older mustard stains on your jacket, and the elbows on the sleeves of your jacket are frayed, led me to deduce that you are a bachelor."

"Those are pretty good observations," Professor Telson laughed. "And all true. It looks like I'll need to get some patches for his old coat."

"And get it cleaned," Dr. Bayill laughed.

"And how about where I'm from?" the young professor asked.

"Well, that *is* where your accent helped me," Sneak continued. "The way you say your 'o's' definitely told me you are from western Pennsylvania. I'm guessing you'd pronounce the words cot and caught the same."

Sneak had first noticed this when Professor Telson taught our Sunday School class a few weeks before. The professor said words like *stock, gone, not* and *odd* in a way that sounded quite different than we did. So, a little research at the library the next day led the young detective to easily confirm the accent was the *Upper Ohio Valley Midland* dialect found primarily in western Pennsylvania.

"That's pretty good too," Professor Telson laughed.

"So, what about those things about me?" Dr. Bayhill asked excitedly. "How did you know I had a farm outside of town?"

"Well, I saw a bit of soil on the cuffs of your pants," Sneak replied.

Dr. Bayhill looked down at his shoes and pant cuffs.

"Well, I'll be. I must have got some of that dirt going out to the car this morning."

Although he had in fact seen the dirt on the man's cuffs, Sneak neglected to tell Dr. Bayhill that he had heard about the older professor from his grandparents who owned a nearby farm. His grandmother had referred to the older professor alternately as a "ding bat" or a "ding dong" for his strange and eccentric farming techniques.

"And how in the world did you know what type of soil it was?"

"I've studied that too," Sneak replied. "There are one hundred and thirteen soil types in Hancock County," Sneak explained. "But most of the county farmland consists of just two, *pewamo silty clay loam* and *blount silt loam*. The majority of the land is *pewamo*."

"I've never even heard of that," Professor Telson added.

"The boy's right," Dr. Bayhill concluded.

"Wow," said Professor Telson.

"And how about my being a prisoner of war?" the older professor asked quickly.

"Well, when I met you this afternoon," Sneak continued. "I remembered seeing you before."

"I don't remember meeting you." Dr. Bayhill replied.

"We didn't actually meet. I just remembered seeing you march with the veterans from the V.F.W. in the Fourth of July parade and the Memorial Day parade too. So, I knew you were a veteran. And I calculated your age by observing some common facial features, like wrinkles and hair loss, and your shoulder stoop and your gait as you walked into the room and deduced that you were in World War Two."

"Along with sixteen million other men and women who served," the older professor added.

"Right. So, then hearing that your German accent sounded very good, it gave me a clue that you'd spent some time there, likely as a prisoner of war."

"Yes, indeed. You're basically correct," Doctor Bayhill explained. "I don't talk about it much now, but I was in the U.S. Army Air Corps during the war. I flew B-26s and was shot down over Italy. My co-pilot and I hid in haystacks and haylofts for a few days before the Germans finally caught us and sent us to a camp...in Poland."

"Wow," declared Professor Telson. "I didn't know that about you."

"It wasn't easy," Dr. Bayhill continued. "It wasn't like *Hogan's Heroes*. It was more like *Stalag 13* or *The Great Escape*, if you've seen either of those movies. But we made it through. That's where I learned my German...it was helpful in talking to the guards. And that's where my faith in the Lord really developed. In those harsh conditions God really helped me."

"Wow Sam," Professor Telson replied.

"In those difficult times a lot of us turned to the Lord for help," Dr. Bayhill added.

The three paused.

Dr. Bayhill cleared his throat before continuing. "Son," the older professor said as he placed his hand on Sneak's shoulder, "you are one remarkable young man. You have a remarkable gift. I'll be praying that God uses it to bring Him glory and to help other people."

"Thanks!" Sneak said with a smile.

"I'll leave you two to your meeting," Dr. Bayhill said as he turned and left the office. "I've got a few things to do around the farm before it gets dark."

"Auf Wiedersehen, Herr Doktor," said Professor Telson.

"Auf Wiedersehen, Herr Professor," Dr. Bayhill replied.

CHAPTER 13

"Wow, that was something else," Professor Telson said after Dr. Bayhill left his office. "It was amazing…all of those things you were able to figure out."

"It's pretty fun to do," Sneak replied.

"Those things you observed about me were right on," the young professor said with a smile. "I can't believe you figured out Tubingen from its motto!"

"My accuracy has gotten better over time," Sneak added.

"And you were basically spot on with Doctor Bayhill too."

"Yeah, I was pretty close – I thought he was a Prisoner of War in Germany, but instead it was Poland."

"It was pretty close," the professor said encouragingly. "Since he was in German-occupied Poland at the time, you were technically correct."

"Well, I was thinking of the German country itself....not anywhere it took over."

They paused and sat quietly for a moment.

"Well, sorry for that distraction," Professor Telson finally said.

"It's okay, I get challenges and questions like that all the time. It's fun to solve mental problems."

"You came here to talk to me about something that was on your mind."

"Right, I wanted to talk to you about the most recent case I've been working on," the young detective explained.

"Go right ahead, we shouldn't get interrupted again," Professor Telson explained as he leaned back in his chair, before he bolted forward. "Actually," the young professor said, "Let me pray for our time together and then you can tell me what's on your mind."

"Sure," Sneak replied.

"Lord God and Heavenly King," the professor began as they both lowered their heads to pray. "Almighty God and Father. We worship You and give you thanks and praise. We are grateful for this time we have to talk about important spiritual matters. During our time together, I ask that you would give us clarity and insight as to who You are and the work that You have done for us. Give us wisdom to understand Your plans and Your purposes as Sneak shares what's on his mind this afternoon. In Jesus' Name. Amen."

"Amen," Sneak added.

"So, now, tell me what's on your mind," Professor Telson said as he leaned back in his chair.

"Well, I've been helping my Uncle Charlie," Sneak began. "He's a captain in the police department and a while ago he asked me to try to solve some of their cold cases."

"I think I saw that in the newspaper," the professor added. "Cold cases are the same as old cases right?"

"Well, basically," Sneak explained. "They are the old cases that haven't been closed."

"Got it, so you closed them out."

"Right....well I closed out a lot of them. They were mostly B&E's, but a few were...."

"What are B&E's?" the professor interrupted.

"Oh, sorry, Breaking and Entering crimes," Sneak explained.

"Thanks," the professor replied.

"So, it didn't take me too long to close a lot of the cold cases for him."

"That's great," the professor replied.

"Yeah, so, that's been going really well...I helped him close out a lot of cases..."

"But, I'm guessing there's more to the story," Professor Telson added.

"Right," Sneak said. "So, anyway, about two months ago someone, an arsonist, started making crop circles in some fields out the country."

"I read about that too, I thought it was a bunch of kids."

"Well, probably not." Sneak added. "The fires have all been very exact...almost scientific in their precision, so it doesn't seem like the work of kids."

"Interesting."

"There have been four separate fires so far, each happening about every two weeks. The pattern is always the same, three very large circles burned in a field. Each of the circles barely touching the other."

"So, like a nuclear radiation sign?" the professor asked.

Sneak paused to think for a moment.

"Well, actually a radiation sign has three triangles. With these fires, there are three circles barely touching each other. I think it's the sign for biohazards that you might have been thinking of," Sneak replied.

"Ah, a biohazard sign."

"Well, it might look something like that if you view it from the air. "

"I've read about crop circles before," the professor added. "But it seems like they are mostly in England, right?"

"They've been reported in a bunch of countries," Sneak explained. "But almost all of those were done by pushing down crops and making a pattern. Sometimes the pattern is a circle, but other times there are curves or other symbols."

"Hmm."

"The circles that have been happening here," Sneak continued, "were made in the middle of winter. The ground was frozen and covered with snow, so there weren't any crops to push down or destroy."

"That's interesting," the professor responded.

"And of course, the fires were set with an accelerant. Probably gasoline and kerosene. I haven't been able to see the lab results on that."

"It all sounds pretty strange."

"And it gets even stranger," Sneak added.

"Really?"

"What I think is the strangest and really the most interesting part of this case is that the morning after each of the fires, a letter has appeared in the *Letter to the Editor* section of the newspaper."

"What does it say?"

"Well each letter is about the fire from the night before."

"Wow, I think I missed those, I don't read the paper too closely."

"It's usually on the Editorial page."

"I start with the *Sports* section, then I look at the news," the professor explained.

"The first thing I read are the police reports in *The Docket* section," Sneak replied.

"I'm not surprised you start with that first!" Professor Telson said with a laugh.

"Anyway, each of the letters have been from a guy named Julian Davis. He's the President of F.E.E.T."

"Feet?" Professor Telson asked.

"Not like at the end of your legs with your toes. It's F...E...E...T. It's an abbreviation," Sneak explained. "F.E.E.T. stands for Findlayites Entertaining Extra Terrestrials."

"Extra Terrestrials?" the professor asked with a grin.

"Yes," Sneak added with a smile. "I'm not making this up. F.E.E.T. is all about getting ready for aliens. They think that aliens will be coming to create a colony on Earth. So they are getting ready for their arrival. The group claims that the fires have occurred because aliens are looking for an ideal landing site for their spaceships."

"What?"

"They think the circles are caused by the rockets from spaceships."

"So, they think we're becoming like an airport for UFOs?" the professor said humorously.

"According to the F.E.E.T people we are."

"So you probably think someone from the F.E.E.T group is starting the fires?" Professor Telson asked.

"I do," Sneak replied seriously. "It's pretty obvious that they know when the fires are going to start. How else could they get a letter into the newspaper exactly at the right time? It might have been a coincidence that a letter is in the paper after just one fire, but it's happened all four times now. The morning after each of the fires there's a letter. They're definitely in on it."

"Wow," replied the professor. "So how come your uncle hasn't arrested the people from F.E.E.T?"

"That's the hard part," Sneak explained. "All of the evidence is circumstantial, I don't have any proof. I've been mostly trying to follow the group's president – Julian Davis – but he's got air-tight alibis for each of the nights of the fires."

"So is he the one who's been writing the letters?"

"Yes, but he makes sure he's doing something else and seen by a lot of people on the night of the fires."

"That's pretty smart," the professor added.

"Definitely. There are several officers and group members in F.E.E.T, so any one of them could be the ones who are actually setting the fires," Sneak explained.

"So, there's a lot of people to track down and follow."

"Right, it's impossible for me to follow everyone."

They paused for a moment.

"So, are you pretty much stuck then, in your investigation?" the professor asked.

"Well, I was able to figure out how they communicate with Julian about the fires."

"Don't they just call him to tell him?"

"No, they are really sophisticated. They use what's called a dead-letter drop," Sneak explained.

"Sounds very spy-like," replied Professor Telson.

"It is. It's how spies communicate," replied Sneak. "What they do is the person who writes the letter drops it at a designated place. Usually they put it in a place that's somewhat hidden, where other people wouldn't be able to find it. Then, later, after they've dropped off the letter and left, the other person comes to get it. That way, they won't ever get caught meeting in person."

"That's pretty sneaky Sneak," the professor said with a smile.

"It is," the boy replied. "That's how Julian Davis can have an alibi on the night of the fires, but still be able to write about the fires in a letter to the editor."

"So why do Julian and the F.E.E.T people even want to start these fires?"

"Ah, the motive question. My uncle's been asking me about that and I've been thinking about that too."

"What do you think it is?"

"I think it's so they can get noticed."

"So, publicity?"

"Right. I think it's so that other people will join their group. They're not a very big organization, and I know that some people have made fun of them, so I think all these fires are being set so they can get more people to join the group."

"Hmm," the professor replied. "Seems like there could be easier ways to get people to come to a meeting."

"I know, but that seems like the most obvious motive to me."

"Well, okay, then," said the professor. "So how can I help? It seems like you've got the mystery all figured out."

"Well I have," the boy replied. "Or, at least I think I have."

Sneak paused before continuing. "It seems really obvious to me who is setting the fires, but my Uncle Charlie doesn't think so, he says I don't have enough evidence yet."

"Well, I guess you will need more to go on than the letters to the Editor."

"Yeah," Sneak continued, as his voice became quieter. "You see, I wasn't really supposed to be investigating this case. Like I said, I was just supposed to be helping him with the cold cases, that's what my Mom and I agreed to. But, then, I read about this case in the newspaper and began looking into it on my own."

"Ah, I see."

"And then I did some things that I shouldn't have, and now I've got to accept the consequences for that."

"What did you do, if you don't mind me asking?"

"Well I staked out a cemetery at night for almost two weeks."

"Wow," replied the professor. "Really?"

"Yeah, it wasn't like all night, it was just in the evening after dinner. But, it was there that I saw him… Julian…I'm pretty sure it was him, I just saw him from the back after he picked up the envelope from the dead-letter drop. Anyway, when I saw him, I grabbed onto his car as it was leaving the cemetery."

"Grabbed onto his car?"

"Yeah, I grabbed onto the back bumper of his car and rode it out of the cemetery, then I tried to open the car door to get the envelope to prove he was guilty, but then I fell in the snow," Sneak said dejectedly.

"Ah, I see."

"A lady reported me to the police," Sneak explained meekly. "And now my Uncle says I'm forbidden to work on the case anymore."

The boy paused.

"And…my uncle says I need to tell my parents about what I've done, because I haven't told the truth and I've broken their rules. He says if I don't tell them, he will." The boy paused again. "I was just trying to follow the evidence," the boy said as tears began to form in his eyes. "I know it was Julian, I was just trying to catch him. And now…" The boy paused once more. "And now, I can't catch him. I can't follow the evidence because my uncle thinks it's too dangerous. And I need to tell my parents what I've been doing…but I know if I tell them, they'll ground me and I won't be able to do any more investigating…not forever, but for a really long time…all the while this guy is getting away with setting a bunch of fires. He hasn't hurt anybody yet, but it won't be long before he does."

They sat in silence again for a few moments.

"So you're wondering if you should tell your parents?" Professor Telson asked.

"Yeah, but it's more than that," Sneak replied. "I'm wondering why God would even have put me into this situation. I don't understand why he's given me a gift for helping other people, for solving mysteries, and then all of a sudden He allows something like this to happen so it's all taken away. Why would God do that? It just doesn't seem fair."

The two were silent yet again as the professor began writing a few sentences on a long yellow legal notepad that he had taken from his crowded desk.

"Those are some really good questions Sneak," Professor Telson replied as he looked down at the yellow legal pad. "Let me think about where to start."

CHAPTER 14

While Sneak and Professor Telson were talking, the young man had arrived back at his apartment with the letter he had retrieved from under the bench at the mall.

To avoid prying eyes, he closed the blinds of his kitchen windows before taking the envelope from the pocket of his brown parka.

He opened the envelope and pulled out the contents: a single piece of white typewritten paper. He laid the letter flat on his kitchen table and noticed that the contents of the letter were surprisingly longer in length than the others he had received.

To anyone looking at it, the letter would have made no sense. The sentences contained only a number followed by a word followed by a comma followed by another number and then another seemingly random word.

For a moment, the young man stared intently at the incoherent text and wondered what mysteries they might reveal. He read:

62 with, 116 undiscovered, 241 it, 191 1917,
108 that, 98 inversely, 140 not, 314 Yiem, 271
was, 235 matter, V Canada...

Rising, the young man quickly roamed his apartment, finding a pencil, a piece of blank paper and
his worn copy of Isaac Asimov's *The Universe: From Flat
Earth to Quasar.*

"Time to decipher the encrypted letter," the
young man said to himself, sounding very scientific
and important.

Seeing the first number listed in the letter – *62* –
he quickly turned to that page in the worn book. *Page
62*, he thought to himself.

Then he searched to find the first occurrence of
the word next to the number.

"The word is *with – got it.*"

Then, using his index finger to follow the sentence
in the book, he looked to find the word that appeared
three words to the right of the word he had just found.

You.

After finding that new word he wrote it on his
blank piece of paper.

After some time, he finally deciphered the letter
and read the full text.

YOU WERE FOLLOWED OUT OF THE
DEAD ZONE BY YOUNG RYERSON. BE

CAREFUL. HE ALMOST GOT YOU. YOU MUST STOP HIM. AN ACCIDENT WOULD BE BEST. HE IS VERY DETERMINED. YOU MUST STOP HIM. WE NEED TO ACHIEVE OUR GOAL TO BRING AN INFLUX FROM OUTER SPACE. THE LANDING IS VERY COMPLEX. YOUR HELP IN PINPOINTING THE BEST LANDING AREA WILL BE HIGHLY KNOWN AMONG THE COMETS AND STARS AND GALAXIES. BECAUSE IT ALMOST WENT WRONG, WE WILL NOT SPEAK TO YOU FROM THE DEAD ZONE BUT WILL SPEAK TO YOU IN ANOTHER WAY INSTEAD.

The young man read the letter again, making sure he understood the contents.

"You have some work to do," he said to himself.

CHAPTER 15

"You've raised some really important questions," Professor Telson said, responding to Sneak Ryerson in his office. "You know, we could probably talk for hours about all of the implications of the things you've asked about. Maybe over the next few weeks we can get into a few more of the details."

"That would be great," Sneak replied.

"It's funny," the professor continued. "When people have scheduled meetings like this with me, I never know what they'll want to talk about. When your Mom called this morning to schedule our time together, I thought you'd be asking some vocational questions and my thoughts turned to a book we don't read too often as Protestants called *Bel and the Dragon*."

"Bel and the Dragon?" Sneak asked.

"Yeah, Protestants put the story in the *Apocrypha* – those books that we think were written in the intertestamental period – that time between the Old and New Testaments. But Orthodox and Catholic Christians include *Bel and the Dragon* in the Book of Daniel in the Old Testament."

"Wow, that's interesting, I don't think I knew that. I definitely haven't read it."

"You probably haven't. It's not in the Revised Standard Version that we use at Church....or the NIV that a lot of people are starting to use now. But anyway, I read somewhere that Daniel, as he's described in *Bel and the Dragon*, was likely the first detective ever described in literature."

"Really?" asked Sneak.

"Yes, it's really interesting," Professor Telson added. "I thought you'd be interested in hearing about that."

"Yes, definitely," Sneak replied.

"Well, the mystery in *Bel and the Dragon* surrounds a challenge that King Cyrus presented to Daniel. The King, who was the king of Persia, worshiped an idol named Bel. Every day, as you can imagine, with the ancient forms of worship, the king had large amounts of food and wine placed in front of the idol. The king assumed that every night the food and drink were consumed by the idol because every morning it was all gone. Daniel, as you probably know from reading the Bible, was a faithful follower of God, and he laughed at that idea because he was certain the idol wasn't real. He knew the idol wasn't the living and true God that is described in the Bible. Well, as you can guess, that made the King angry, so the king issued a challenge to Daniel saying that if he couldn't prove his theory, he would be killed."

"No pressure or anything, right?" Sneak said with a smile.

"Right," Professor Telson replied with a laugh. "No pressure to prove his theory! Hopefully you'll never be put in a situation like that."

"I definitely don't ever want to be in a situation like that! So, what happened with Daniel?" Sneak asked.

"Well, the King really wanted to prove that his ideas about the idol were true and that Daniel's ideas were false. So, on the day he decided to prove this to Daniel – after the servants had brought in all the food and all of the wine and placed them before the idol – the king had his servants lock the front door to the temple and then the King sealed it shut with his signet ring, to show that nobody was coming into the temple. And then, the next morning they unsealed the door and found that all of the food and drink were gone. And the King, of course, thought this proved that the idol had spent the night eating all of the food and drinking all of the wine."

"It's a locked room mystery!" Sneak suddenly exclaimed. "Like *The Adventure of the Speckled Band.*"

"That's Sherlock Holmes, right?"

"Right," replied Sneak. "And locked room mysteries are some of my favorite to solve. So what happened?"

"Well, Daniel, you see, was a good detective," Professor Telson continued. "And like all good detectives, he wanted to have some evidence. So, just before the door was sealed, he had his servant scatter ashes on the temple floor."

"That was a good idea," Sneak replied with a smile.

"Precisely," said the young professor. "And the following morning, after the King gloated for a moment and showed Daniel that all of the food and wine was gone, Daniel asked the King to look at the floor."

"Nice," Sneak replied.

"The ashes on the floor showed footprints from the priests and their families who had come into the temple through secret doors and had eaten everything offered to the idol," the Professor explained. "And Daniel, the first detective in history, had solved the case."

"That was an interesting story," Sneak said.

"I thought so too," Professor Telson replied. "It shows that detectives have been around for quite a long time. It's an important vocation. It's work that is valuable and can be helpful to others."

"So that's what you thought we should talk about?" Sneak asked.

"Well...uh...," Professor Telson said with a stutter. "That story just came to mind this morning, when I was thinking about your visit, I just thought it might be encouraging for you to hear."

"Oh, okay," Sneak replied.

"I thought too about how the word *mystery* appears often in the Bible. The word in Greek is *musterion* and Paul uses it a lot to explain the mystery of Christ."

"Oh," the boy replied again.

"But, really, what would be best with the time we have left is to address some of the questions you've asked," the professor continued as he looked down at his yellow legal pad. "I thought you might be asking some general career advice, but instead you've asked some really deep questions, like '*Should I tell my parents about breaking the rules*' and some other really deep questions like, '*Why can't I do what I've been gifted to do?*' and '*Why would God put me in this situation*' and '*It's not fair that God would not let me solve the case*'."

"Well...I guess they are deep thoughts," Sneak replied.

"Let's take a look at a passage in the Bible for some insight."

CHAPTER 16

While Sneak and Professor Telson were discussing *Bel and the Dragon* and some answers to
Sneak's questions, the young man was in his apartment pondering the message he had received.

The note said I was followed out of the "DEAD ZONE",
he reflected. *That must mean the cemetery,* he concluded. *That is definitely a DEAD ZONE. So, no more trips
there to get my messages.*

He paused.

*I wonder how he'll contact me next? It'd be great if he
could just pick up the phone and tell me what to do.*

The young man paused for a moment.

*It would be really great if they would just take me out
of here.*

After a few more thoughts like these, the young
man turned his attention to the words in the letter
that said that "Young Ryerson" had followed him out
of the cemetery.

The young man, like many in our city, was well
aware of Sneak Ryerson's reputation for solving

mysteries. He had read the many articles about Sneak in the local newspaper and had even had a personal interaction with the young detective. The fact that Sneak had almost caught him at the cemetery was disconcerting to the young man. In fact, he had been driving so quickly out of the cemetery that he hadn't even seen the young detective. He had heard a noise on the side of his car, but it was so sudden that he hadn't seen who or what had caused it – he simply saw someone fall into the snow as he drove away.

Now that he knew it was "young Ryerson" who had tried to get the letter from him, his thoughts turned darker and more malicious as he thought about the meddlesome detective.

He must be stopped, the young man thought. *The work has got to continue.*

The young man's eyes re-read the second line of the letter and he repeated the phrase multiple times.

"He almost got you," he said to himself.

HE ALMOST GOT YOU, HE ALMOST GOT YOU.

He continued reading the next line in the letter, *YOU MUST STOP HIM. AN ACCIDENT WOULD BE BEST. HE IS VERY DETERMINED. YOU MUST STOP HIM.*

I must stop him, but how? He wondered.

Soon an idea came into his mind and he quickly grabbed the phone book from a nearby table. Hastily, he turned to the "R's" and was relieved to find that the Ryerson's home address was published in the directory.

Rushing through his apartment he found a blank envelope and lined paper, and grabbed each carefully at the edges trying to avoid placing any fingerprints on them.

Grabbing the blank envelope first, he wrote Sneak's name and address with slanted upper case letters and numbers, being careful to make the handwriting appear much different than his normal penmanship. After a moment, he paused to look at his work:

SNEAK RYERSON
918 DECKER AVENUE
FINDLAY, OHIO 45840

Mrs. Willingham, his Junior High School English teacher, had drilled into him and the other students the proper layout of an envelope and letter, and so he had to remind himself several times not to put his return address on the front of the envelope.

Next, he composed the letter, again being careful to make the handwriting appear different than his normal script:

DEAR SNEAK,
I NEED YOUR HELP ON A VERY IMPORTANT CASE. ONLY YOU CAN

HELP ME. MEET ME AT RAWSON PARK
ON MONDAY NIGHT AT 7:00PM. COME
ALONE.
SINCERELY,
MR. X

Signing it Mr. X sounds so stupid, the young man said to
himself. *Maybe I should have left it blank?*

Just leave it, he thought after a few moments.

After quickly sealing the envelope, he put it into
the pocket of his brown parka and walked the short
distance to the Post Office.

To the young man's relief, there was no sign of
the delivery truck or the people who had been loiter-
ing outside of his apartment earlier in the day.

Arriving at the Post Office, the young man
quickly grabbed the envelope from his coat pocket
and held it by its edges as he opened the small metal
slot labelled *Outgoing Mail* and dropped the letter in
the bin.

Mailing the letter this afternoon, he was certain,
would ensure that it would arrive at the Ryerson's
house on Saturday – the following day – or at the latest on Monday afternoon – time enough for Sneak
Ryerson to know about the meeting and time enough
for the young man in the brown parka to set a trap.

CHAPTER 17

"So, you've asked some really important questions," Professor Telson said as he continued his discussion with Sneak Ryerson. "Why don't we spend some time looking at Scripture for some answers?"

"That sounds good," said Sneak.

The professor began to look through the stack of books on his desk. "I've got a Bible in English somewhere around here," Professor Telson said as he continued digging through his academic journals and papers.

"Yeah, I'll need one in English," Sneak replied.

"Here's a few Greek versions," the professor said as he went through the books on his desk. "...and a Septuagint," he added.

Moving to a bookcase behind him, he bent down to see more books.

"Maybe around these reference books....here's that B-D-B I've been looking for," he said referring to a Hebrew lexicon by the authors Brown, Driver and Briggs.

The professor continued looking.

"Okay, here's a few Bibles in German...*Die Bibel.* And a few in French...*La Bible.*"

Sneak enjoyed watching the professor navigate his vast library.

The professor continued, going next to another bookshelf.

"Here's some texts in Hebrew and Aramaic," he added. "I can't believe I'm having so much trouble finding a Bible in English."

Moving to another bookshelf, he exclaimed, "Here we go...oh, no that's Italian. And of course a Vulgate."

Sneak smiled.

"Ah, here we go," the professor said, after finally finding what he had been looking for. "Sorry about that," he said as he grabbed the red hard-covered book from the bookshelf and handed it to the young detective.

"That's okay," the boy replied.

"It's a King James version, so the English is going to be older than what you are used to at church, but it's English!" the professor exclaimed. "Is that okay?"

"Sure that's fine."

"I have a Greek New Testament here for me."

Sneak smiled as he saw the professor return to his desk and pick up a small and very worn red covered bible with a title in upper case Greek letters.

"Before we do some reading, I'm reminded of an important point," the professor said as he sat down. "I didn't really talk about many of my assumptions before we started. But maybe I should talk about those now."

"Sure," said Sneak.

"So, one of the things that I like to talk to my students about is what we call presuppositions."

"Pre-what?" asked Sneak, remembering that he had heard Dr. Bayhill mention the word earlier.

"It's a big word…presuppositions. It's the assumptions that we have about life…or about faith."

"Like what?" Sneak asked.

"Well, everyone has assumptions about life. Like, '*the future will be similar to the past*', or '*most other people have minds like mine*', or '*life is generally rational and logical*'."

"I definitely have that last assumption."

"Right, if you didn't think life was generally rational and logical, you couldn't figure out all of those mysteries like you've been doing."

Sneak nodded in agreement.

"Anyway, as Christians we are called to make certain assumptions about truth. We presuppose that the Bible is true – in my Theology classes we use big words like *inerrant* and *inspired,* and *sufficient* to describe the Bible. What those words mean is that the Bible is from God…and that it's true. We even call it God's *Word.* We believe that God wants to use it to speak to our lives, to be our authority on matters of faith and practice. And, from the Bible, we get *sound doctrine* – those things we believe."

"That makes sense," said Sneak, as he thought about the Bible stories his parents and Sunday School teachers read to him from the big illustrated *Children's Picture Bible.*

"And what's interesting," the professor continued, "is that there are presuppositions in the Bible too. The Bible presupposes that God is real. If you remember the very first verse in the Bible, in Genesis, the writer says, 'In the Beginning God...' You see the assumption is that God is real. That He is doing things. He is creating, He is sustaining. He is taking the initiative to reconcile people to Himself."

"That's pretty cool."

"It is, it definitely is."

The professor paused for a moment.

"So, why don't we take a look at a passage in Matthew," the professor said as he turned the pages in his Greek Bible. "I was thinking Matthew...chapter eleven....verse twenty-eight would be helpful for us to look at."

"Okay," Sneak said as he found the passage near the back of his English Bible as the professor found the passage in his Greek version.

"As you know, one of the main things that the Bible tells us about is Jesus," the Professor continued.

"Yeah, when we come home from Sunday School and Mom asks us what we learned about, Jennie and I always say *Jesus*, and then she says, 'You kids say that every week – what specifically did you learn about?'"

The professor laughed. "Well, it's good that you're learning about Jesus every week!"

"There seems to be a lot to learn," Sneak admitted.

"Well, there is a lot to learn. In fact I teach an entire class on the subject of Jesus!" the young professor said with a laugh. "We spend three months just talking about Christology and Soteriology!"

"Wow," the young detective replied – unsure of the meaning of the professor's words.

"Anyway," the professor continued. "Let's read from verses twenty-eight through thirty in Matthew chapter eleven. Do you mind reading that, Sneak?"

"Sure, no problem. I found it," Sneak said as he looked down at the Bible. "It says, 'Come unto me, all ye that labour and are heavy laden, and I will give you rest. Take my yoke upon you, and learn of me; for I am meek and lowly in heart: and ye shall find rest unto your souls. For my yoke is easy, and my burden is light.'"

"Thanks," said the professor. "So, this passage – I'm guessing you've heard it before in Sunday School – is a quote from Jesus. What He is doing is telling his followers that they can come to Him. The phrase in your version where it says *all ye that labour and are heavy laden* is sometimes translated as *all who are weary and burdened.* And that's the sense I was hearing in your voice and in your questions – you sounded burdened – you know, about the things that are happening in your life right now." The professor paused and looked down at his legal pad. "Especially as I heard you say how you wanted to be a detective and use your gifts but you can't. That sounded like you were carrying a pretty heavy burden. Does that sound about right?"

"Yeah, that's right. It is a heavy burden for me," Sneak replied. "I want to use my gifts but I can't. And I can't figure out why I can't."

"So here in Scripture," Professor Telson explained, looking now at his Greek Bible, "Christ bids us to come to Him and He tells us that He will give us rest. It's a great promise…to find comfort in the Son of God."

"I like that," said Sneak.

"I do too," the professor added with a smile. "I'm sure this is something your Sunday School teachers have said a lot of times before – but both of us need to be reminded of it, especially when times are tough and we are feeling weary and are carrying those heavy things in our hearts and minds. Jesus is saying in effect that He is trustworthy. He is faithful. He can be relied upon. Even when things seem darkest, we can turn to Him and find rest."

"Things seem pretty dark right now," the young detective admitted.

"Yeah, it sounds like it. But, this is essentially what I have to offer when we get together. Even though I've got bachelor degrees in linguistics and philosophy, and have two master's degrees from Yale and am finishing up an advanced degree at…well as you know, the University of Tubingen, as a Christian the ultimate thing that I can offer someone…like you… or anyone, is Christ. I can encourage them to turn to Him and trust Him with their burdens. I can encourage them to get to know Jesus as someone who is reliable and trustworthy. Does that make sense?"

"Yeah, that makes sense," Sneak replied, as his thoughts began processing the words that the professor was saying.

"If you don't mind, I'd like to give you a little homework," the professor added.

"Homework?"

"Well, not real homework like you have in school, but some work for you to do at home before the next time we meet again."

"Okay," Sneak replied tentatively.

"Here's a couple of other passages in the Bible that speak of God's faithfulness," the professor said as he turned to a blank page in his yellow legal pad and began writing. "Why don't I give you…five?"

"Sure."

The professor noisily tore the page from the legal pad.

"So, here are the passages," the professor said as he handed the paper to Sneak. "Why don't you read those and spend some time reflecting on what they say about God's faithfulness and trustworthiness, and then we can chat about it the next time you come back."

"There's no pop quiz or anything, right?" Sneak asked with a smile.

"No, no quiz," the professor said with a laugh. "It's homework without a grade."

"Cool, I like that kind of homework."

The professor then looked at his watch.

"So, I don't think we have too much time before your Mom comes to get you...I think she said she'd be gone for about an hour. Anyway, I did have a couple of other thoughts for you before you go."

"Sure, what are they?" Sneak asked.

"Well, in addition to looking to God for help, I'd encourage you to look to others as well," the professor continued. "From what you've told me, it seems like you've been wrestling with some pretty significant questions on your own."

"Yeah," said Sneak gloomily.

"So, in addition to talking to your parents, maybe there are some peers – some friends from Church you could talk to about these things. As you know, my visiting professorship ends in May, so I'll be going back to the East Coast then. But, maybe there are some kids you can process some ideas with…you want to be careful with who you pick, but it might be helpful. You never know, they might be going through some similar things too."

"Other kids," Sneak replied hopefully. "That's a great idea."

"And then the last thing I wanted to mention," the professor said as he looked down again at the notes he had taken on the yellow legal pad, "I'd encourage you to tell your parents about what happened. It would be better to have it come from you instead of your uncle. It sounded like you broke some of their rules or didn't exactly tell the truth about going to the cemetery, so you need to tell them that you messed up. In Church we call that *confessing*. It would be good to do that with your parents and with God – just tell them what you did and say that you are sorry – that's what we call *repenting*."

"Ah, I thought you might say that," Sneak replied with a grimace on his face.

"It's the right thing to do," the professor said confidently.

"I don't know," Sneak replied.

"The right thing to do is to tell the truth and then accept the consequences," the professor explained. "With the Lord, He is quick to forgive….that's one of the key things about Christianity that is so important and so different from a lot of other religions…that God is loving and kind and His grace is sufficient when we mess up and break His rules. But, there are still consequences for our mistakes. Sometimes the consequences are small and sometimes they are big…like your parents grounding you."

"Yeah, I'm pretty sure that's what will happened when I tell them."

"I think that's pretty likely too," the young professor said seriously. "But once that is over, you'll be back to solving your mysteries."

"If I'm able to solve mysteries when I'm eighty or a hundred," Sneak said as they both laughed.

The two were quiet for a moment, and then they heard footsteps echoing in the hallway.

"That will be my Mom," Sneak explained.

Soon, they heard a quick knock on the door and Mrs. Ryerson appeared in the doorway.

"Hey you two, I hope I'm not interrupting," Sneak's mother said with a smile.

"I think we were just wrapping up Mrs. Ryerson," Professor Telson replied as he stood to greet Sneak's mother. "Was there anything else you wanted to talk about Sneak?" he asked the young man.

"Nope not today. This has been really helpful," the young detective replied.

"Thanks so much for meeting with him," said Mrs. Ryerson.

"Not a problem," Professor Telson replied. "I just had a big stack of papers to grade, so meeting with Sneak was a great diversion, it wasn't a problem at all. Plus, I always like hearing about a good mystery."

"Thanks," Sneak replied as he stood and shook the professor's hand. "I appreciate it."

"Sure thing," the professor said. "You can call me anytime."

"Jennie's waiting for us in the car, so let's be quick," his mother said as the two quickly left the office.

"I had a hard time finding this place," said Mrs. Ryerson as they walked down the hallway. "Were you able to find it okay?"

"Yeah, I found it pretty quick," Sneak replied.

"So, how was your meeting?" Mrs. Ryerson asked as they descended the stairs to the lower floors of the building.

"It was good. Professor Telson was really helpful."

"I'm glad you had a good time talking with him," his mother replied. "You look a little tired, do you want to get some ice cream at Dietsch's on our way home?"

"Not tonight Mom," Sneak replied, "I've got some phone calls to make."

CHAPTER 18

Sneak Ryerson and I – as you may have already noticed – grew up in a community called *Findlay, Ohio* – a city in the American Midwest. In 1980, when our adventures began, the city had a population of 35,533 – which was a slight decrease from the previous census taken ten years before.

In 1980, Findlay was a hub of activity and commerce – the largest city in the area and home to a number of businesses – with a number of retail stores in its downtown shopping district and a large shopping mall to the east. The city, however, was in some ways also an isolated community, surrounded by miles and miles of farmland in rural northwestern Ohio. Larger Midwestern cities were quite a distance away: Chicago 300 miles to the west, Toledo and Detroit 50 and 100 miles to the north, Cleveland and Columbus over 100 miles away. Thus, in many ways Findlay was separated from some of the larger issues that affected urban cities at the time. In some ways that was good, and others not so.

For my father, the distance to larger cities was one of several things he said he was depressed about. In a moment of honesty earlier that year, he told me that he felt "stuck" because it seemed like "nothing was happening" in our town. More exciting things, it seemed, were happening in places far beyond where we lived – and he longed to be "there".

"Where?" I asked him.

"Anywhere but here," he told me in a moment of sadness.

I felt sorry for my father and would frequently try to make him feel better by pointing out some of the fun things we could do together in our town. On that Friday evening – after I had watched a few episodes of *Gilligan's Island* and my Dad arrived home from work – only a few hours after Sneak Ryerson had met with Professor Telson at the seminary – I tried to encourage my father once again.

"Hey, Dad," I greeted him happily when I found him absent-mindedly paging through an old foreign language textbook at his kitchen table. "Only a few more months 'til we can go fishing at the reservoir, right?" I said enthusiastically.

"Yeah," he replied with a sigh, sounding tired. "That will be good."

"Maybe this year we could borrow the neighbor's pontoon boat to go out on the water?"

"Yeah, maybe."

There was a long pause before I thought of another activity.

"Hey if you want to, maybe we can go roller skating tonight over at Ohio Skate – by the mall?"

"I'm pretty tired," he told me. "Plus, I'm not the greatest skater."

"Or ice skating?" I tried. "Out by the Dark Horse restaurant?"

"I've been on my feet all day," he explained wearily. "How about I take a rain-check tonight? Maybe we could go somewhere tomorrow night after I get off work? We close at six. Maybe the Y?" he suggested. "You like shooting baskets in the gym. And the pool will be open late, so we could go swimming. That would be fun, right?"

"Sure," I replied. "The 'Y', sounds great."

Seeing that he still seemed depressed, I suggested a restaurant I knew he would definitely enjoy. "How about Captain D's for dinner tonight?"

He looked up from his book and smiled.

Finally, he's smiling, I thought.

"You know I never turn down deep fried hush puppies," he replied. "Afterwards, why don't we just watch a little T.V. and call it a night."

"Can I stay up for the *Tonight Show*?" I asked, hoping to watch Johnny Carson's opening monologue or maybe even see an interview with one of his guests.

"The last time I let you do that, you fell asleep on the floor and I had to carry you up to your bed!" Dad replied with a smile.

"Well, maybe not tonight," I told him, wanting to keep things positive.

Maybe at a sleepover in a few weeks, I thought.

"Give me just a minute to finish this page and then we can go," my Dad replied as he returned to his book.

Soon, he finished reading the faded page of the old textbook and we went to the back door and pulled our black rubber galoshes over our shoes. After a few minutes of tugging and pulling the ill-fitting boots, we donned our heavy winter coats and made our way outside into the cold dark night. We drove quietly to the restaurant, ate our seafood, hush puppies and coleslaw with only a few words said to each other and returned home about an hour later.

The phone was ringing as we walked into the house – it was Sneak, his timing was amazing.

How can he always figure out where I'm staying? I wondered. With my parents separated, I stayed on alternate weekends at my Dad's house or my Mom's – but Sneak never seemed to check with either of my parents to find out where I was – he could just find me.

"Hey Pep," he said cheerfully when I answered.

"Hey," I replied, surprised to hear my friend's voice sounding uncharacteristically upbeat.

"Can you come over to my house tomorrow morning at eleven?" he asked.

"Let me check."

I quickly asked my Dad and then told my friend that I could be there.

"Okay, see you then," the young detective said and then immediately hung up the phone.

That was the entirety of our conversation. It consisted of about twenty-five words – to invite me to his house. Interestingly, I did not suspect anything unusual. After hearing his invitation, I assumed that once I arrived at his house in the morning we would play with his collection of *G.I. Joe's* or *Johnny West* guys, or if we had time, get out his massive box of *Army Men* – just like we had done many other times – and many other Saturday mornings – before. Maybe one or two of our friends might join us, I thought. After his brief call, I didn't give any additional thought to his invitation until the following morning.

Had I asked my friend any questions about what his plans were – or had he told me what he would be asking of me – I doubt I would have been able to sleep that night. I would have been so excited at the thought of working on a case – catching bad guys – maybe even being a hero who figured out a crime.

Twenty-five words – that was the extent of the conversation. Little did I know how those twenty-five words would change my life.

Not long after the phone call, I felt tired – well before the start of *The Tonight Show* – and decided to go to bed.

After changing into my pajamas and stumbling into bed, my Dad, in his kind and quiet way, came up to my bedroom to "tuck me in" as I was falling asleep.

I asked him if he could tell me one of his stories about France, but he hesitated.

"I'm pretty tired," he told me. "And it looks like you are too. Let's do that tomorrow," he told me quietly.

"Okay," I said with a smile as I rolled over in the bed to look up at him. "Don't forget 'zee stinky cheese."

"Don't you forget 'zee stinky cheese either," he replied as he turned off the lights in my bedroom.

"Bonne nuit Pep," I heard him say, just before I fell into a deep and peaceful sleep.

CHAPTER 19

While my Dad's house was tranquil and quiet that night, the mood at the Ryerson's was anything but calm and peaceful. The cause of the tumultuous evening turned out to be the diminutive Jennie Ryerson.

The problem – if you'd like to call it that – was that Jennie, although young and precocious, was a lot like her older brother. And although she wasn't featured in newspapers, nor was she compared to a "young Sherlock Holmes", she was still able to perceive nearly everything around her – and figure things out – just like her older brother.

As that Friday night got later and later, and the night's darkness fell deeper and deeper upon the Ryerson house, Jennie approached her mother who was working on a sewing project at their family's dining room table.

"I thought you had gone to bed a long time ago?" her mother questioned when she saw her young daughter – clad in flannel pajamas – approach her at their dark wooden dining room table.

"Mom, Sneak is starting a club and he's not going to let me join it," Jennie explained as she drew near to her mother.

"Of course you can join it," her mother replied half-listening while she focused on finishing a stitch with a small needle and thread. "You're his sister."

"That's what I'm going to tell him, but I'm sure he's going to say that I can't join," Jennie said with a pout.

"How did you find out about this club?" Mrs. Ryerson asked, directing more of her attention to her daughter. "Did he tell you about it?"

"Sneak's been calling people all night," Jennie explained.

"Calling people? Are you sure?" their mother asked, surprised by this new information.

"Yes, I'm sure."

Mrs. Ryerson soon stopped her sewing and then, angling her neck, looked at the ceiling. "Steven!" she soon yelled from her chair in the dining room.

Footsteps were soon heard and Sneak quickly came downstairs from his bedroom. "Yeah, Mom?" he asked when he reached the last step.

"What's this I hear about a club you're starting?"

"A club? I'm not starting a club," he replied quickly.

"I heard you talking to Hailey for a long time and that's what it sounded like to me," his sister explained.

"You were listening in on the line?" her brother asked incredulously.

Jennie was silent – trying hard to maintain a look of being wronged.

"Mom, she should get in trouble for that," her brother admonished.

"I'll talk to her about that later Steven," his mother replied. "But tell me more about this club or non-club you're making. Did you talk to your father about it?"

"No. I'm just having a few friends over tomorrow morning to talk about a case. It's not a club."

"Yes it is," his sister insisted while talking more and more rapidly. "Hailey's coming with Moscow and Sneak invited Joel and Pep. And he even talked to Uncle Charlie."

"Oh my gosh," Sneak said loudly, shocked by the extent of his sister's knowledge. "How many of my calls did you listen to?"

"I don't know, how many did you make?"

"Mom, this is totally not cool," Sneak said emphatically. "She shouldn't have been listening to my calls."

"Jennie, he's right. You shouldn't have been listening in," Mrs. Ryerson scolded. "But Steven, you should have told me if you were planning to have people over to the house."

"Yeah, I know. I'm sorry," Sneak said. "We were going to have the meeting in a few days from now, but all the kids are available tomorrow. We're just going to be out in my office in the garage. Will you and Dad be around?"

"Well, your father has bowling first thing in the morning, but he'll be back by eleven or eleven thirty."

"That's what I thought," Sneak replied. "My friends are coming over at eleven, but then I wanted to meet with you and Dad after that."

"Well, I was going to do some shopping, but that can wait until later," his mother explained.

"Thanks," Sneak said with a smile. "The timing should be perfect."

Sneak turned and began walking up the stairway to return to his room when he heard his sister's voice.

"I still want to join the group," Jennie insisted.

Scowling now, Sneak turned and descended the two stairs he had just walked up.

"Mom, it's mostly *older* kids," he began explaining to his mother. "She's too young. Plus, I've tried to keep the group small...there's only six kids, so there will be a sort of symmetry to the group."

His mother gave him a confused look.

"It's symmetrical," Sneak continued. "There will be three guys and three girls, so if they need to investigate something together they could go out as a big group of six, but not be too big of a group to draw suspicion. Or, if they want, they can go out in two groups of three, or three groups of two. The size of the group is perfect."

"But what about Uncle Charlie?" Jennie asked.

"What about Uncle Charlie?" Sneak replied.

"Well, he would make the group seven, so it's not really the-metrical."

"Symmetrical." Sneak corrected.

"Whatever," said Jennie.

"Uncle Charlie's not in the group," Sneak explained. "He's an advisor."

"Still," Jennie replied. "If you're going to have your uncle in the group you could at least have… your sister, right?"

"Oh my gosh," Sneak replied in an exasperated voice. "Mom, I just explained that Uncle Charlie isn't in the group. The group will have six kids…three girls and three guys…I'm not counting Uncle Charlie in the group because he's just an advisor."

"Okay," Jennie replied, quickly thinking of a new response. "Here's what I think we should do. I will join the group, so there will be four girls. And Mr. Knick Knack can join so there will be four boys. There," she concluded with a wide smile showing her missing tooth. "It's even."

"Mom," Sneak replied raising his voice. "Jennie just invited her imaginary friend! These are *older* kids who are coming over. They aren't going to want an imaginary friend in the group! It just shows that she's too young. She's just a little..."

Sneak paused as he searched for the right word that would create the most explosive emotion in his sister – to prove his point that she was unfit to join the group.

"...*crybaby*," he finally declared.

In writing this now, so many years later, the taunt seems like something that the Ryerson's grandparents might have said as children in the 1920's, instead of something said in more modern times. But even in the 1980s, the taunt was common on the elementary school playgrounds and after school at the Ryerson's house.

Jennie was shocked when she heard the word *crybaby*, and even took a step back. A slight, small teardrop appeared in one of her eyes, but she was careful not to let it fall and quickly blinked twice, hoping it would not be observed by her brother.

In a surprise to both her brother and her mother – and to many of our friends who heard about the drama afterwards – she did not let the taunt outwardly affect her. Instead, she looked calmly at her brother and in an even voice said, "I am not a crybaby. I just want to join the group."

"Oh my gosh," Sneak said again.

Seeing that his latest attack had failed, Sneak tried another tactic. "Mom," he whined, "There's another problem with her joining the group."

"Oh, what's that?" asked his mother calmly.

"She's not analytical. She doesn't use deductive reasoning," he explained.

This comment, unfortunately for Sneak, did not have the intended results he was hoping for. Instead, to his amazement, it sparked the interest of Mr. Ryerson who was laying back, nearly completely horizontal in his recliner, reading his newspaper in the nearby living room. After first noisily setting down the bulky newspaper onto his lap, he declared sternly, "Deductive reasoning isn't the only kind of reasoning, Steven."

This is not going to end well for me, Sneak thought.

"In addition to deductive reasoning there's inductive and abductive reasoning," Mr. Ryerson explained from his recliner, while Jennie looked up at her brother and smiled widely. "Inductive reasoning is probably how she processes information – coming up with a general answer after making only a specific observation," Mr. Ryerson continued.

"She just goes with a hunch," Sneak replied. "You can't convict someone of a crime because of a guess. That's not a good investigation....investigative.... technique."

"But I'm right a lot of the time," Jennie interjected. "Remember when I found the neighbor's contact lens *in the middle of the sidewalk* at the corner of Sandusky Street? No one else could find it, but I found it in like thirty seconds."

"Yeah, but that doesn't have anything to do with..." Sneak began.

"What was the name of those G.K. Chesterton detective stories I read a year or two ago?" their father interrupted – his voice coming loud and clear from the living room. Mr. Ryerson, it should be noted, not only liked watching T.V. detective shows, but he also liked reading detective stories and novels. "Those stories sort of remind me of how she figures things out," he added.

"Are you thinking of Father Brown?" Sneak asked.

"Well," their father paused. "G.K. Chesterton wrote the Father Brown mysteries, but that wasn't what I was thinking of. It was something else he wrote."

"Miss Marple?" Jennie offered as her brother scowled and shook his head "No".

"No, it was....I'll think of it....it was...uh, it's right on the tip of my.....got it, it was *The Man Who Knew Too Much*....that was it," their father explained.

Sneak shook his head, knowing now that he had definitely lost the argument. "You sound like the man who knew too much," he replied quietly.

"Steven!" his mother whispered, scolding him quietly while smiling at her son.

"In those stories," his father continued his lecture from his recliner. "The man that knew too much – Mr. Fisher, I think was his name – knows all the in's and out's of international politics. So, when crazy events happen, it all makes sense to him because he has all this other information, even if at first it doesn't make any sense to the reader or anyone else."

"So, it's deduction...he figures it out," said Sneak.

"Well, maybe that's not the best example," Mr. Ryerson said. "But it seems more like *induction* to me – seeing the big picture of what's possible – even though one only sees small, minute, little things."

The young detective rolled his eyes, careful this time not to be noticed by his mother. "I still don't think the big kids will want her to tag along," he explained.

"I won't be tagging along," Jennie replied confidently. "I'm going to figure stuff out."

"We'll see how good you are at that," Sneak replied while twirling his index finger in the air, mirroring Jennie's unconscious and constant twirling of her pigtails – something that she was currently doing – and frequently did throughout the day.

"I'll see you tomorrow at eleven," Jennie said with a smile, as her brother frowned.

"I don't even know what you'll be doing when your friends get here," his mother interrupted, wondering about her son. "You said it wasn't a club, we've got that much information. But, why did you invite your friends over? What are you planning to do?"

"I just want to talk to them," Sneak explained.

"It's more than that," Jennie interrupted confidently. "Once all the kids are here, we're going to work on a case together."

"It's just some kids from Church," Sneak tried again, ignoring his sister.

"Technically its kids from Sunday School," Jennie insisted. "And we're going to solve a mystery."

"Well, I don't know if everyone will...," Sneak began.

"So you're going to ask some kids from Sunday School to help you solve a mystery?" His mother asked, surprised that her son – the great and gifted detective – would entertain the idea of asking others for help.

"Yes," Sneak replied feebly.

"Well, I think that's a great idea," his mother concluded.

"We're going to be called *The Sunday School Detectives*," Jennie added.

"Oh brother," replied Sneak.

CHAPTER 20

The next day was Saturday – March 8th, 1980 – a day I hope to remember for my entire life, for it was on that cold grey winter day that I became a *Sunday School Detective.*

I started the morning by waking early in order to watch Saturday morning cartoons on TV. I watched *Super Friends* at eight and then *The Bugs Bunny Show* at nine o'clock, resting my head on my pillow as I lay on the floor in front of my Dad's large wood paneled Zenith television set. My imagination ran wild those Saturday mornings as I watched the exploits of Batman, Aquaman, Wonder Woman and Superman – my cartoon superhero friends. Part of the fun was waiting to see if some of my favorite minor characters – like The Green Lantern or The Flash – would appear in an episode and help the others fight against the evil plans of the *Legion of Doom.* Watching *The Bugs Bunny Show* – a rebroadcast of short cartoons from the late 1940s through the 1960s – gave me a chance to laugh at the gags of another cast of characters: Bugs, Porky Pig, Tweety Bird, Sylvester the Cat, Yosemite Sam, the Road Runner and many others.

I dressed before *Bugs Bunny* ended and my Dad dropped me off at the Ryerson's house around ten thirty on his way to work. Because Dad had to get to work, I arrived earlier than the time Sneak had asked me to come over, so I was the first of the kids to arrive.

I entered the Ryerson's house through their back door and after greeting Mrs. Ryerson and Jennie, quickly discovered that Sneak and I weren't playing *G.I. Joes*, or *Johnny West* or *Army Men* that morning.

"We're going to meet some other kids out in the garage," Sneak told me quickly. "But there's a few things I need to do in here first."

"Okay," I replied unquestioning. "I'll go out and start the heaters."

Sneak left me without saying another word and I soon made my way outside again – glad that I had not removed my bulky black galoshes that covered my shoes or my heavy winter coat – both of which would have taken some time to put back on.

Outside, I walked the short distance to the Ryerson's detached garage located behind their house – unsure of what the morning would bring.

The garage was a white aluminum-sided building located about forty feet behind the Ryerson's house and had, until the previous summer, been home to the family's two cars: their long red 1976 Chevrolet Impala station wagon – driven by Mrs. Ryerson – and their small four-door 1979 red Chevrolet Chevette, driven by their father.

Several months earlier, Sneak had convinced his parents that the garage would make a perfect location for his detective office, and now the garage contained a large metal desk with several office chairs and a wide green chalkboard for his meetings.

With Sneak's office taking over most of the garage, his parents parked their cars in the driveway between the house and garage – and the morning I went outside, the maroon and red exteriors of the family's cars were covered with a white layer of snow mixed with residue from de-icing road salt, while large chunks of ice and snow clung to the wheel wells behind each of the car's tires.

I quickly entered the garage through a door located on the side of the building – the top portion containing a large glass pane window with the words "SNEAK RYERSON DETECTIVE" engraved in upper case gold letters. Entering, I found the garage surprisingly bright, with morning light coming in from the large window on the side door, as well as three windows located on each side of the garage and several smaller windows located on the two closed wooden garage doors.

In addition to being bright, I also found the garage to be very cold and I quickly turned on two large space heaters to bring warmth to the large open space.

I was not bored being alone in the garage, because that morning I had brought a gym bag full of equipment. So, while I waited, I worked on the items within the bag – keeping busy until my friend arrived.

CHAPTER 21

A few minutes after I arrived, I heard a car door slam, and looking through one of the small garage door windows, I saw Hailey Cotton and her younger brother arrive. Hailey – wearing a purple ski jacket and matching multi-colored headband popular on the ski slopes – and her brother sped quickly from her parent's car to the Ryerson's house, avoiding the chill of the cold winter morning.

I knew Hailey from Sunday School and from spending time with her and her younger brother at the Ryerson's house. She was my age and went to my former elementary school, but had only moved back to the area a year or so before – having spent most of her elementary years out west.

For Sneak, Hailey was a long-time friend. And when I say long-time friend, I mean it. Hailey was literally one of the first people he saw after he was born, as their parents were very good friends. Hailey and Sneak's fathers had known each other in their early

20's, having gone to college together out west, while their mothers had been friends at their first jobs. And so, when Hailey was six months old and Sneak was only a few weeks old, their parents dressed them up in infant cowboy and cowgirl outfits for one of their first of many pictures together.

Interestingly, Hailey and Sneak actually looked a little bit alike, and sometimes, to their enjoyment, were sometimes mistaken for brother and sister. Like her *almost*-twin, Hailey was tall and thin and had a high forehead and cheekbones.

Although they were alike in some ways, Hailey and Sneak were very different people. Their hair, while both dark, was styled very differently. Sneak's dark brown hair was long and fell into his eyes, while Hailey's light brown hair was cut in the popular page-boy style – made famous by the singer Toni Tennille in the 1970s. Their eyes were also different. Sneak's eyes were light blue, while Hailey's eyes were light green with gold circles around each dark pupil – a trait, according to her grandmother, she inherited from their Native American ancestors. (Sneak had also noticed the interesting design in Hailey's eyes, and while reading through medical journals wondered if it wasn't caused by a mineral deficiency).

Hailey's personality was also quite different than her *almost*-twin. While Sneak would typically be moody and somber, Hailey was almost always upbeat and spunky, smiling even when things were difficult. She also enjoyed working with our friends to solve mysteries together – unlike Sneak, who enjoyed the solitude of adventuring out on his own. It wasn't a surprise for me to see – when I went to the Cotton's house a few months later to visit her brother – that Hailey's bedroom was filled with posters and mementos of a white cartoon dog named Snoopy, from the comic strip *Peanuts*. The character's winsome personality, self-confidence and focused determination were things that I identified with Hailey – and maybe she did too.

Interestingly, most people thought that Hailey was named after Hayley Mills, the star of *Pollyanna, The Parent Trap* and several other popular Walt Disney films from the 1960's. The story of her name, however, is actually more interesting than that. Hailey's parents, I learned, loved the American west. Her father had been born and raised in a small town on the high plains and after he and Mrs. Cotton were married, they lived in several western states. Just before she was born, her parents decided to name their firstborn after a town in the American west that they hoped to visit one day. (This was before the popularity of first names inspired by western places like Cheyenne, Cody or Dakota). So, the young couple poured over western maps at their kitchen table looking for baby names. Eventually the two chose Hailey for their girl's name – after Hailey, Idaho, a small town of several thousand people, near Sun Valley. Their choice for a boy's name would have some interesting consequences when Hailey's brother was born two years later.

CHAPTER 22

A few minutes after their car arrived in the drive-way, Hailey Cotton's brother joined me in the garage, having quickly grown bored of the conversations going on inside the house.

Like his sister, their parents had decided to name their son after a western town they hoped to visit one day – so they named their son Moscow, after the city of Moscow, Idaho – home of the University of Idaho. "People will think we are Communists!" Mrs. Cotton famously said to her husband. "Moscow isn't just in Russia," Mr. Cotton had told her. "There's a town of Moscow in Pennsylvania and another in Iowa. There's even a village in Ohio, too."

Moscow Cotton was two years younger and very different from his older sister. While Hailey was care-ful and cautious, her brother was – for want of a bet-ter word – a *daredevil*. I would frequently find him deep in thought, in a world all of his own, not think-ing of the case we were all working on, but instead, thinking up the next stunt he would do next. When discussions among the young detectives dragged on and on, Moscow would find something, anything, that looked dangerous and try it, usually saying the words, "I bet I can..." just before taking flight.

If a nearby object had wheels or no wheels, brakes or no brakes, if it was vertical or horizontal, dangerously high or claustrophobically narrow, if it was at all dangerous he would try to go as fast or as far or as perilous with it as possible with it. The list is too numerous to catalogue, but I remember his feats including: hand stands on a six-foot tall unicycle, juggling sharp knives while standing on ten foot high stilts, standing up on a speeding mini-bike, jumping from his parent's rooftop onto a nearby maple tree, diving into a swimming pool after jumping from a nearby trampoline, creating dangerous ramps to jump his bikes and skateboards, and building a zip-line to propel him at great speeds from a tall tree house down to a small stream in the woods behind his house – none of which are recommended for children to try. He was an extreme sports enthusiast before the X-Games were invented.

Moscow Cotton's inspiration and hero during this time was the stuntman and entertainer, Bobby "Evil" Knievel. If Moscow could have joined Evil Knievel in jumping nineteen cars at the Houston Astrodome with his motorcycle or being propelled in his

"Skycycle X-2" rocket over the Snake River Canyon, or jumping school buses at the King's Island amusement park – he would have done it in a heartbeat. Although he didn't talk about it much, I learned that Moscow had some Evil Knievel toys at his house and had even secretly hoped to acquire a white jumpsuit with a red, white and blue cape just like his hero.

Sometimes Moscow's parents were annoyed at his exploits. I remember one time his Dad angrily called him a "show boat" after Moscow had jumped from the roof of their house and into a maple tree. The branches where he jumped, it turned out, were dangerously thin, so Moscow had no way of climbing down. Instead of calling the fire department, Mr. Cotton decided to climb up and help his son down – which he did, but with much effort. Most of the time, however, his parents were supportive – paying for ski jump lessons or helping him buy multiple motorbikes and skateboards. They also paid the hospital bills when his exploits led to broken bones and bruised ribs. His risks may have resulted in injury, but Moscow was undeterred.

That morning, the young daredevil decided to enter the Ryerson's garage conventionally – through the side door, like I had – letting in a very cold blast of air, which was quickly dealt with by the two large dark brown space heaters that were pumping out warm air.

"Hey Pep," Moscow greeted me when he arrived.

"Hey Moscow," I replied as I fiddled with the items in my gym bag.

After Sneak's terse instructions for me to go to the garage and then seeing the Cotton's arrive, I had assumed that some sort of meeting was going to take place, so I found a place to sit – perched on top of a large pile of old newspapers that filled a wide wooden box near the back corner of the garage. Mr. Ryerson, being a prolific reader, used the wide wooden box to discard all of his of old newspapers and magazines. By the time I decided to use it for our meeting, the pile had grown to nearly four feet high, even spilling over the sides of the wooden box, while Mr. Ryerson waited for the weather to improve to load the papers into his maroon station wagon and take them to the Boy Scouts' recycling trailer.

"So, what's going on this morning?" I asked my friend. "I thought I was going to come over and play *G.I. Joe's* with Sneak, but instead I guess we're having a meeting or something? Are there a lot of other people coming over?"

"I don't know," said Moscow as he looked around the garage. "Hailey just woke me up and told me to come over."

"Oh," I replied.

"She said that she and Sneak are coming out here soon," Moscow explained, distracted now that his eyes had spotted the large wooden storage platform above my head. "Bet I can get up there," he replied looking up at the wooden platform that stood below the back half of the garage's roof and contained large outdoor lawn chairs. That winter, the wooden storage platform was especially useful to the family, now that Sneak had taken over most of the ground floor of the garage for his detective office.

"There's a ladder over there," I said pointing to an old wooden ladder that was spotted with flecks of paint. The previous summer, Mr. Ryerson had let me use the ladder to climb up to the wooden platform and explore the storage area. I had been in the garage with Sneak and Mr. Ryerson, when Sneak had told me his idea about using the garage as an office for his detective agency. Looking up, I told them that the wooden platform would make a perfect office – if only there was a stairway going up to it.

"Why don't you go up there and see for yourself," Mr. Ryerson said with a smile as he opened the wooden ladder and bid me to climb up.

While he held the ladder, I carefully walked up the narrow rungs and lifted myself onto the wooden platform.

"Whoa," I said as I began to stand up. "I almost hit my head on the roof!" I said kneeling over. Sneak and Mr. Ryerson chuckled as I explained, "It's a lot shorter up here than I thought. There's no way you could have an office up here, is there?"

"Looks can be deceiving," Mr. Ryerson added. "Be careful coming down."

I carefully made my way down the ladder and had not been up to the storage area since.

"So what should I use to get up there?" Moscow asked me, as he looked for a way to get up to the storage area.

"The ladder is right over there," I said again, pointing to the long wooden ladder.

"Come on Pep, that is so boring," he replied as he quickly began looking around the garage, looking first near Sneak's long metal desk in front of me, before quickly moving to the other side of the garage where Mrs. Ryerson had an old table covered with gardening supplies. Soon he moved to the back corner of the garage, opposite from where I was sitting, and sorted through a cluttered group of bikes and kids toys including a small red tricycle, a Big Wheel and an old blue wagon. Eventually the young daredevil found an orange plastic horse and lifted it from the pile of toys for me to see. The plastic horse, I could see was about three feet in height and had a red handle near the horse's head. Its four hooves, I noticed, once I got a better look, were made of tightly coiled springs, which made the plastic horse a fun and bouncy ride for younger kids.

"This should work," Moscow said as he placed the plastic horse below the front of the wooden storage platform.

"For what?" I asked.

He didn't answer. Instead the young daredevil first sat on the plastic horse, and then, in a flash he quickly stood on top of the horse's back, balancing himself by placing a hand against one of the wooden poles that held up the wooden storage platform.

In an instant, the young acrobat placed his feet on top of the two red handles near the ears of the plastic horse, allowing him to stand a few inches taller. And then he jumped, grabbing the end of the wooden platform with the ends of his fingertips and dangled in mid-air for a few moments.

Slowly he moved to the right, first a few inches and then a few inches more. "There's nothing to grab onto," he explained. "Can you give me a push?"

"I'm busy right now," I said, still working with the equipment in my bag.

"Okay," the young daredevil said as he moved to the left, still grabbing the edge of the platform and still looking for something more to hold onto.

"Sure you can't give me a push?"

"Uh uh," I responded to his request.

"Okay," he replied and instantly dropped from the edge of the platform and rolled several times onto the cold cement floor.

"Are you okay?" I quickly asked, hoping that he had not hurt himself.

"Ta-Da!" he said jumping up with arms extended. "That was my first trick of the morning," he said with a smile and then bowed deeply. Soon, Moscow Cotton eyed the tall wooden platform again. "For my next attempt, I need to get a little more distance," he explained. Quickly he jumped back onto the plastic horse, and then onto the red handles. He jumped up again towards the wooden platform, but this time he jumped higher and was able to get not only the tips of his fingers onto the platform, but his entire left arm as well as the palm of his right hand. In an instant, he quickly pushed his left arm down while at the same time pushing down on the platform with the palm of his right hand allowing the top half of his body to fall heavily upon the wooden platform with a loud thud while a small cloud of dust rose up to the rafters.

"Voila!" I heard him say as he rose onto the platform. "That wasn't so hard," he concluded.

"That's pretty impressive," I said.

Soon, I heard him moving around on the platform above me, ducking his head down low, I was sure, because of the closeness to the roof.

"Hey, there's some cool stuff up here," I heard him say.

"I think it's just furniture," I told him.

Soon we heard someone at the door.

"Hey someone's coming," Moscow observed. "Don't tell them I'm up here."

I looked up from my open gym bag and saw Jennie entering the carless garage.

"Wow, it's cold, cold, cold out there," she shivered.

"I'm glad there are heaters in here," I replied pointing to the two space heaters slowly warming the area.

"Yeah, it is starting to get nice and warm," Jennie said with a smile as she paused momentarily to look around. "I thought Moscow came out here," she said after she had looked around the room.

"I did too," I told her.

"Oh, well," Jennie continued. "He probably went to climb a tree or something. He won't be outside for very long, it's so cold out. Hey Pep, do you know when everyone else is 'posed to get here? I think it's after eleven now."

"They must be running late," I told her, still focused on the last piece of equipment in my gym bag.

Soon Jennie took off her winter coat and pulled out a Barbie doll from a deep front pocket of her tan corduroy jumper. Jennie was in a patriotic fashion phase during this time and enjoyed wearing red, white and blue colors. But today, however, her color scheme was tan and white – a white turtle neck and white tights under a tan corduroy jumper.

"Barbie, where do you want to sit while we're out here?" she asked her doll. "Do you want to sit on Sneak's desk?"

Soon she began looking for a location on her brother's desk to place her doll, but a moment later, a pebble was heard rattling against one of the windows of the closed wooden garage door.

"Hey, did you throw something at me?" Jennie asked me.

"No," I replied, still working on the contents of my gym bag.

"Well I thought...hey did you hear that, I thought I saw something," she said as another pebble rattled against the garage door.

"I didn't throw anything," I told her.

"Is someone else in here?" she asked.

"JE...NN...EEEE." a voice came behind some furniture on the wooden platform. "JE....NN...EEE."

"Who's up there?" she asked looking up at the rafters in the garage.

"It's God," Moscow said with as deep a voice as possible. "Who's down there?"

"It's me, Margaret." I replied with a laugh.

"It's me Jennie," the young girl replied with a smile. "Is there anything you want me to do, God?"

"Yes, jump up and down while patting your head in a circle."

Jennie began attempting the maneuver but soon began laughing at her failed attempts that had resulted in much stumbling and tripping.

"Moscow, you're crazy," she said looking up into the darkness. "Where are you?"

"I'm here," he said with a broad grin, sticking a head out from behind an outdoor lounge chair. "I got up here without a ladder."

"How did you do it?" Jennie asked.

"Horse," I replied as Jennie looked at me quizzically.

"Check this out. I found an old clothesline up here," Moscow explained, as he began lowering and raising the white rope from the platform. "Isn't that an empty flower pot over there? Throw it up to me."

"I'll hand it up to you." Jennie said as she took one of her mother's empty flower pots and reached up towards the platform as Moscow laid down flat on the platform and reached down.

The distance was too great, however, and even though he tried to grab only the top edge of the pot he couldn't reach it to bring it up to the platform.

"Can you just throw it?" he asked.

"Sure," Jennie replied as she threw the flower pot up. Fortunately, even though she did not throw it very far, it was high enough for Moscow to grab in mid-air and bring it back onto the wooden platform.

After hearing a few more noises, we heard Moscow explain, "It's not working."

"What are you trying to do?" Jennie asked.

"I thought I could tie the clothesline to the flower pot, but it's not working. I can't get the knot tight enough, it keeps slipping.

He paused to look again around the garage.

"Hey, how about that bucket?" he asked, after seeing a grey metal bucket on Mrs. Ryerson's old table with gardening supplies. "Could you send that up to me?"

Once again Jennie tried to hand it up, but the distance was too great.

"Just throw it," Moscow told her.

Soon, Jennie threw the bucket up, and again, although her throw was not very high, it was high enough for Moscow to catch in mid-air while lying flat on the platform.

In a few minutes, Moscow tied the end of the rope to the handle of the metal pail and lowered it down towards Jennie. "Hey, check this out," he said as he slowly moved the bucket up and down by pulling the rope of the white clothesline. "We have an elevator up to the top. It's just like a department store."

"Cool," Jennie replied.

Seeing that Jennie had carried a doll into the garage, Moscow implored her, "Hey, put the Barbie in there."

"No, I'm going to hold her for the meeting."

"Come on, come on, it will be neat," Moscow said enthusiastically.

"No…"

"Come on, it will be cool."

"I don't know if you want to…," I began.

"Okay," Jennie said while trustingly placing the doll in the metal bucket.

Soon, Moscow began to slowly raise the bucket up with the doll inside. "Ding! Second floor, women's dresses and hats," he said seriously as he continued pulling the bucket upward. "Ding! Third floor, kitchen stuff." He continued to raise the bucket higher and higher.

"Hey, be careful with her," Jennie demanded.

"Ding! Fourth floor, something else....what do they have on the fourth floor?"

"Maybe, more clothes!" Jennie replied.

Suddenly Moscow's voice changed to a more alarmed tone. "Oh oh!" he said. "Oh no, I didn't think this would happen. Watch out! Watch out!"

"What is it?" Jennie asked, concerned.

"The building where the elevator is located has caught on fire. And your doll is stuck in the elevator!" As soon as Moscow said these words he began to swing the bucket around in a circle above Jennie's head and she immediately began jumping up to try to reach it. "It's just like the Towering Inferno," Moscow explained – referring to the 1974 movie – "we need Steve McQueen to come to the rescue! I think I see him scaling down the elevator ropes. Do you see him Jennie? Say hello to Mr. McQueen."

"No, I don't see him." Jennie laughed as she jumped up several more times, her arms high in the air, trying to grab the bucket. "I almost got it that time!"

Soon, Moscow made the swinging bucket change directions, from clockwise to counterclockwise, and then a few moments later changed directions again in random herky-jerky up and down motions.

"I can't believe she's staying in there," Jennie replied.

"Me neither," said Moscow, "We need Steve McQueen to rescue her soon!"

Quickly, however, he brought the bucket to rest on the edge of the wooden platform. "Hey, I think I hear someone," he said, just as someone else was entering the garage.

CHAPTER 23

Hearing the door open, I looked up to see our friend, Joel Hemlinger, arrive. Joel was my age and went to the same elementary school as the Cotton's. He was average height, wiry, and wore his already thinning hair in the trendy curtained haircut style, parted in the middle. When he arrived, Joel was humming The Beatles' song "Good Day Sunshine", while looking intently at some words written on a piece of notebook paper. "Hey guys," he said, after closing the door and briefly looking up from his paper.

"Hey Joel," we said in unison.

"What cha' lookin' at?" Jennie asked as she saw Joel with his notebook paper.

"Casey Kasem's *Top Forty Countdown* will be on tonight and I'm trying to predict what song will be number one."

"Have you ever guessed right?" Jennie asked.

"A couple of times. I'm not really good at it," Joel said with a laugh.

"How about a Long Distance Dedication?" Moscow replied, hidden until then behind some lawn furniture on the wooden storage platform above.

"Moscow? I didn't even see you up there!" Joel exclaimed with a smile.

"I got up here without a ladder."

"How'd you do that?" Joel asked looking around the garage.

"Horse," I said, from the pile of newspapers in the corner of the garage.

"Ah, a horse!" Joel said as he walked over to the orange plastic horse, stopped and then looked up at the tall wooden platform. "That's a long jump!" he exclaimed.

"Yep," Moscow replied from above.

"Does this horse have a name?" Joel asked Jennie.

"Horsey, I guess," Jennie replied.

"I went through the desert with a horse with no name," Joel said seriously.

"What?" Jennie asked, confused by the song reference.

"Neil Young, right?" I asked.

"Actually, no," Joel explained.

"Neil Young's band?" I guessed again.

"Nope."

"Neil Young's brother?" I joked.

"Nope, it sounds just like him, but it's by *America*," Joel clarified. "People always think it's Neil Young, but it's not."

Joel – I had learned in Sunday School, many years before – was someone who loved music. He loved humming and singing music and collecting music on vinyl records, eight-track tapes and cassettes (and then many years later on CDs and downloadable digital music). He also loved performing music and eventually, he even tried out for *Ed McMahon's Star Search* – but was eliminated in an early round. Joel liked music so much, that a few months after our meeting in the garage and after an album called *The Stranger* was released, he'd introduce himself in a way that reminded me of a James Bond introduction, but only worse. When James Bond made an introduction, he would say, "The name is Bond, James Bond" and then cue the theme song music and maybe some explosions. When Joel introduced himself after the album was released, he would say, "The name is Joel, as in Billy." Most people would not get it, so he would frequently have to say, "As in Billy Joel – the singer and songwriter – the Piano Man. He just came out with a new album."

"Joel, I don't know how you keep everyone apart?" Moscow said from the rafters after hearing his clarification to my guesses regarding the song.

"What do you mean?" Joel asked.

"A lot of bands just all sound the same to me."

"Sound the same?" Joel asked incredulously. "I don't think they sound the same at all," he said looking down at his paper. "Like right now, a song by Queen is number one. But two weeks ago a song by Michael Jackson was number one. Queen and Michael Jackson don't sound anything alike."

"I love Michael Jackson," Jennie said sweetly. "… and his brothers. ABC," she said smiling.

"They're the Jackson Five," Joel reminded her.

"Right," Jennie replied.

"Well, I can see how you could tell those bands apart," Moscow continued. "But the singers? They all sound the same to me."

"Like who?"

"Like Neil Sadaka and Paul Anka," I interjected. "My grandma loves both of them but I can't tell them apart."

"Well Paul Anka is…" Joel began.

"That's the kind of coffee my grandpa drinks," Jennie added.

"That's *Sanka*," Joel explained.

"Oh," Jennie replied.

"Paul Anka's the guy that wrote the *Love Boat* Theme, right?" Moscow asked from the wooden platform.

"No, that's Paul *Williams*," Joel answered. "He wrote 'The Rainbow Connection' too."

"I love Kermit the Frog," Jennie added. "Kermie! Kermie!" she said smiling.

"Which Paul was that?" I asked, wondering if I had heard him correctly.

"Paul Williams," Joel replied.

"So who sings Moon River?" I asked. "My grandma likes that song too. That's Paul Williams too, right?"

"No, that's *Andy* Williams," Joel explained.

"So, which guy wears the white shoes?" Moscow asked from the wooden platform.

"That's not either one of them. That's Pat Boone!" Joel laughed.

"See, I don't know how you can keep them apart!" said Moscow. "I sure can't."

"That's not even the kind of music I listen to," Joel explained. "But I know enough to know they are different people!" He looked his paper again. "Okay, so the top song last week was *Crazy Little Thing Called Love* by *Queen.*"

"Like the Queen of England?" Jennie asked.

"No, that's just their name. Do you guys think they'll stay number one?"

"I'm not sure," I said honestly.

"Me neither," Moscow said as he hung upside down from one of the garage's rafters, where the roof of the garage slopped steeply downward only a few feet above the wooden platform.

"The song goes like this..." Joel said, and he began singing the song for us. He sang the first verse and then the chorus and then the second verse and chorus again.

Eventually, he finished the song and Jennie, Moscow and I clapped.

"That was really good," I said from my perch on the newspapers.

"I really liked it too," Moscow said from the wooden platform. "This garage has great acoustics. That song's pretty good, Joel. I'll bet it will stay number one, don't you think so Jennie?"

"Naw, I never even heard that song before," Jennie added, "I think Michael Jackson will be number one this week."

CHAPTER 24

Hailey Cotton arrived just as Joel was finishing his song and waited for him to finish singing before she started talking. "Wow, Jennie," she joked with the younger girl. "You're already getting guys to sing to you. That never happens to me!"

"Well, I don't think he was…" Jennie said, as she stopped twirling her pigtail, surprised by Hailey's comment.

"I wasn't singing *to* Jennie," Joel explained, appearing a little rattled by Hailey's words. "I was singing *for* her and everyone else here. They hadn't heard *Queen's* new song. It was the number one hit last week and might be the number one hit this week."

"I don't think I know it either," Hailey replied.

"I could sing it again," Joel said enthusiastically.

Moscow coughed loudly.

"No, that's okay, you don't have to sing it again," Hailey smiled. "But if you ever want to sing a song *to* me, or *for* me, that would be okay."

"Okay," Joel said seriously. "What would you like to hear?"

"Well, what was the number one song before the song from Queen?"

"*Rock with you*, by Michael Jackson," Joel explained.

"I like Michael," Hailey said with a smile.

"That's what I said," Jennie added. "ABC," she said with a smile.

"Unfortunately, I don't know all the words to that song," Joel confessed.

"Well, anything would do," said Hailey.

"I've got a good one that everyone can sing along with. It's from a couple of years ago."

He cleared his throat.

"Ready?" he asked, looking over to me.

"Don't look at me," I replied, shaking my head.

"Here we go," he began as he counted out the rhythm. And a few seconds later, Joel was singing *Isn't She Lovely* by Stevie Wonder. "Come on guys, join in," he implored Moscow and I after he had sung a few lines. Unfortunately, neither Moscow nor I knew any of the words. "You guys can join me," he said again half-way through the first verse.

"Oh brother," I heard Moscow say from the wooden platform above me.

Bored by the new song, Moscow slowly lowered the metal bucket with the Barbie doll inside. In a flash Jennie was jumping up, reaching for the bucket, trying to get her doll. But like before, just as it got closer to her, Moscow quickly pulled on the rope and raised the bucket up and out of reach. Not wanting to be out-performed by Joel, Moscow began singing a modified version of the song called *The Itsy Bitsy Spider* as he moved the bucket up and down. "The itsy bitsy spider went up the water spout," he sang as he lifted the bucket up. "Down came the rain and washed the spider out," he sang as he dropped the bucket. "Out came the sun and did something else." As he got to the chorus of the song he sang loudly, "Where is Jen's dolly? Will she get it back?" As he sang noisily, he swung the bucket in one direction and then another. "Here is the dolly, watch out for the whack!" As he sang those last few words, he swung the bucket right at Jennie, forcing her to duck to avoid getting hit in the head by the grey metal pail.

"Hey, give it back!" Jennie exclaimed. "Give it back to me now!"

"You'll have to guess the magic word," Moscow said, as he swung the bucket and started the song again.

"It's mine," Jennie pleaded. "It's for me." She began jumping up again and again, with arms reaching in the air, trying to get the bucket and retrieve her doll.

It was among this cacophony of noises: Joel singing all of the words to Stevie Wonder's song *Isn't She*

Lovely, Moscow swinging a metal bucket from the wooden storage platform while singing a modified version of *The Itsy Bitsy Spider*, Jennie jumping up, reaching for her doll and pleading *"For me! It's for me!"*, that Sneak arrived, opening the side door to the garage and walked in.

A surprised look immediately came over the young detective's face as he tried to determine why all of the activity was occurring. But after Sneak took two steps into the garage, we were the ones who were in for a surprise. Stunned, I saw that two girls followed closely behind him.

CHAPTER 25

In picturing their entrance over the years, my mind imagines the girls entering the garage in slow-motion, illuminated by a bright light – like California sunshine – the type of light that one frequently sees saturated upon actors and actresses in movies or on TV. But in thinking about their entrance now, I know that my memories cannot be correct. The early winter day was cold and grey and we were in Ohio, where the quality of light, even close to noon, is quite different than a sunny morning in southern California.

My mind, already fuzzy at being able to accurately describe the girl's entrance, doesn't remember any sort of loud verbal gasp made by any of us who were already in the garage, when the two entered, following Sneak. But as soon as we noticed the girl's arrival, there was an abrupt pause as we all hastily stopped doing what we had been doing. Joel stopped singing *Isn't She Lovely* in mid-verse, I stopped working on the stuff in my gym bag, Jennie stopped jumping up trying to grab her doll while Moscow stopped singing his modified version of *The Itsy Bitsy Spider*. In fact, Moscow was so surprised at seeing the girls, he released the rope that he was holding, and seconds later the grey metal bucket containing Jennie's doll fell to the floor with a loud crash. "BAM!" came the loud noise from the garage floor, making all of us momentarily jump at the startling noise that rang throughout the large space. "Sorry about that," Moscow said quickly.

"I didn't know any girls would be coming over," Joel said haltingly, staring at the girls that had just arrived.

"Hey," replied Hailey scornfully.

"Yeah, hey," added Jennie. "I'm a girl."

"Well – I meant any *other* girls. I know that you and Hailey are girls," Joel said with a nervous laugh.

"Yeah, we know," replied Hailey.

"Were you singing a song to Hailey?" the first girl asked Joel.

"No," Joel replied quickly. "I was singing *for* her… and the other kids. It's a song by Stevie Wonder." He paused, then nervously added, "…he wrote it when his daughter Aisha was born a few years ago."

"Alright then," Sneak interjected. "Now that those facts have been established," he said, turning to the two girls that had followed him. "Let me show you into the office."

The girls followed him for a few more feet and he quickly showed them to a wooden bench across from his desk where they could sit. *Are they new clients of the detective agency?* I wondered. *Do they have a mystery that all of us need to help them with?*

I knew the two girls from our large Sunday School class at church, but had never spoken to either of them – they always seemed to be at the other end of the table from me or talking with each other in another part of the classroom. They were the same age, best of friends as well as cousins (something more common than not in a small city like ours). They were alike in some ways, but also very different.

Lisa Lavin was the first girl who entered the garage following Sneak. She was short in stature with short dark hair and wide brown eyes. She was a spunky girl and full of energy, often compared to one of America's sweetheart's – first Dorothy Hamill, the American ice skating champion who won a gold medal at the 1976 Olympics and then a few years later, Mary Lou Retton, the great American gymnast who won the gold medal at the Olympics held in Los Angeles in 1984. Lisa was an ice skater and gymnast, but not on the level as those she was compared to. A great athlete, Lisa was also quick on the track – later setting school records on her Junior High School track and field team.

The girl following Lisa, her cousin, looked very different. She was tall for a girl of our age and wore her full blonde hair layered long on the front and the sides in the flip hairstyle of Farrah Fawcett, the famous American actress. The girl was Cressida Hudson, named by her parents after an unpopular Shakespearean play. Her mother, a devotee of the arts, loved the unique name she had chosen for her daughter. Her father thought it sounded nice, and said he did not mind that Toyota came out with a car model called the *Cressida* a few years after his daughter was born.

Incredibly shy, it was actually rare to hear Cressida speak. Instead, she would whisper to her cousin, who would then speak for her. The few times I did hear her, her voice reminded me of the breathy, lilting, soft tones of Jacqueline Kennedy giving a tour of the White House.

Interestingly, there always seemed to be some sort of rumor circulating about Cressida and her family. Once, one of my friends from school said that her family owned the local *Little Caesar's* pizza shop. A few days later another friend said that her family actually owned the whole company. And then, a few days after that, another kid said her Dad was a pizza delivery driver. The real truth about her family, I would learn later, would be even more interesting than any of those guesses.

CHAPTER 26

Our group greeted Sneak and the girls when they entered the garage, and I was surprised, when a few minutes later, the side door opened again, letting in another blast of cold air as well as two adults who joined us that morning: Sneak's Uncle Charlie and Professor Telson. They were joking as they entered.

"I think it was a Diet 7-up commercial," Uncle Charlie was saying.

"I haven't seen it," Professor Telson replied.

"Anyway, it's like a split screen, so Flip Wilson is on one side of the screen and he's talking to himself dressed up as Geraldine Jones on the other side, and she says '*What you see is what you get*' in that way she does. It was pretty funny."

"Sounds like it," the professor replied with a smile. "I'll have to look for it."

Jennie, upon seeing her uncle raced to him and gave him a hug. "Hey Uncle Charlie," she said happily.

"Hey Cindy," he said to her with a smile.

The two adults were carrying metal folding chairs from the Ryerson's house, and soon unfolded them near the door. Taking off their winter coats in the warm garage, revealed that they were both wearing white bowling shirts with their first names written in cursive script on the front with different company logos on the back.

"Turns out we are in the same bowling league over at the *Sportsman's*," Professor Telson said with a smile.

"Cool," Moscow Cotton replied.

"We're on different teams, but we play at the same time," Uncle Charlie explained. "I bowl on a team with Sneak's Dad, while Nick's on a team with some seminary professors."

"My team is not very good," the professor confessed. "But we have some fun together. We're called *The Four Professors. The Holy Rollers* name was already taken," he explained, laughing loudly, filling the space with his joyful noise.

All of the kids in the garage knew Professor Telson from Sunday School and greeted him warmly. Not everyone, however, had met Sneak and Jennie's Uncle Charlie, so he introduced himself to those he did not know.

The two men, as Sneak would say, were a study in contrasts.

Sneak's Uncle Charlie, the older of the two, in his mid-thirties, was tall with wide shoulders, a fit and strong man with a distinctive bushy moustache. I learned from his many stories that the police captain had played football in college and had served in the Vietnam War. When the weather was warmer, I remember him saying that he would drive to Toledo or Columbus to play rugby. Uncle Charlie seemed fastidious too. His bowling shirt and pants, I noticed, were ironed and may have even been dry-cleaned with heavy starch.

Professor Telson, not yet thirty, was very different. He was a large man, who did not fit well on the folding chair when he eventually sat for our meeting. He seemed physically out of shape and tired and I could see that dark tired semi-circles had formed below his warm and bright green eyes while the auburn hair on his uncovered round head was already receding. I had really enjoyed Professor Telson being our Sunday School teacher on the few occasions he filled in for our regular teacher. I was impressed by his deep knowledge of the Bible and languages. I spoke to him after our Sunday School class one morning and asked him all of the languages he knew. He said besides English, he could speak or read German, French, Italian as well as Greek, Latin, Hebrew, Ugaritic and Aramaic. Those last two languages, I had never even heard of.

Both of the men were friendly and warm and stood and spoke to each of us for several minutes after they arrived.

CHAPTER 27

Soon Hailey, Jennie and Joel found places to sit around the now crowded garage: Jennie on a small kid's folding lawn chair, Joel on a multi-colored adult folding chair and Hailey on one of the nice chairs that Sneak had borrowed from his parents to use for meetings with clients. Hailey had moved the chair when she arrived so that it was located next to Sneak's office chair behind his desk.

The kids and adults all faced the large metal desk that Sneak and Hailey sat behind and after everyone was seated, Hailey asked, "Do you want to begin, Sneak?"

"Sure," he replied quickly. "So, uh, you're probably wondering why you've been invited to come here."

"Yeah, what's going on?" Moscow asked, as his feet dangled from the wooden platform above us.

"So, I was..."

Suddenly, the side door to the garage opened again, letting in another burst of cold air, and Jennie's friend Michelle entered. "Sorry I'm late," Michelle said quickly as she found a place on the bench next to Lisa and Cressida. "My Mom thought she could run one more errand before dropping me off."

For a moment, Sneak stared angrily at his sister who was giving a "thumbs up" sign to her friend who she had invited earlier that morning.

Regaining his composure, Sneak continued.

"So I guess everyone knows everyone from Sunday School," he began, "so we don't need to do introductions." He paused. "So, I've been talking to Professor Telson as well as Hailey and my Uncle Charlie this week about some things going on in my life," Sneak began. "And I came to the realization that for some important investigations to continue, there needs to be more than just me doing them."

Sneak and I had not talked about his current cases, so I wasn't really sure what investigations he had been working on, but I was eager to learn more.

"So, I think everyone knows I've been helping out my Uncle Charlie with some investigations," Sneak continued.

"Cold cases," his Uncle added, with his arms folded across his chest.

"Right, some cold cases...those are cases that the police haven't solved. Plus, I get a lot of calls from people who ask me to help them. Since the articles came out about me in the paper, I've been getting a lot more calls....and letters too."

"That's cool Sneak, but why are we here," Moscow said impatiently from his perch above us.

"So, I wanted to see if all of you who are here – the kids – would be willing to help, to be part of a new detective agency."

"Now that sounds cool," Moscow said from the platform.

"I like it," said Michelle.

"Yeah, it sounds cool," Joel added as I nodded my head in agreement. The older girls, however, were more tentative and continued listening intently to Sneak's speech.

"Hey, if we do that, I want to be the Quartermaster," Moscow added suddenly, as Uncle Charlie and a few others laughed.

"What's that?" Hailey asked her brother.

"It's like in James Bond, they call him Q, and he's always coming up with cool gadgets and gizmos for them to use…like an exploding wristwatch."

"I don't think you'll be needing that," Sneak replied.

"…or miniature recording devices," Moscow added, as I shot a quick glance at Sneak.

"So, we'd be like the *Three Investigators?*" Joel interrupted.

"Except, there are….eight of us," I said as I counted the kids around me.

"Instead of this garage, maybe we could meet in like a junk yard like those guys…and have an office there," Moscow added.

His sister looked up at him sternly.

"Maybe we could drive around Findlay in a Rolls Royce, just like they do too," Joel added.

"Or have a light blue van that says 'Mystery Machine' on it?" I replied with a laugh.

"Scooby doobie doo!" Jennie howled as Joel began singing the *Scooby Doo* theme song.

"Yeah, someone's got to work on transportation," Moscow added.

"I think a pink jeep would be nice," Jennie replied as she looked at Michelle and her friend responded with another "thumbs up" sign.

"No, we need wheels, something that will go fast," Moscow explained.

"Like Rockford," I said.

"Yeah, a Pontiac Firebird," Moscow replied, "with copper mist paint."

"Or, like Starsky and Hutch," I added.

"A bright red Ford Gran Torino with a white vector stripe," Moscow replied enthusiastically.

"Well, I'm not driving anybody in any of those cars!" Uncle Charlie said with a laugh. "You'll have to get around on your bikes!"

A moment later Hailey interrupted, "Alright you guys, let's get back on track," she said firmly.

Cressida whispered something to Lisa and her cousin soon asked a question to the young detective. "So, what do we need to do exactly?"

"Well," Sneak explained. "You would be investigators…detectives. You'd work on a case just like I would. If Uncle Charlie wanted you to work on cold cases you could do that. Or, you could take cases that people ask you to take. When they come in on the phone or in letters, you could decide which one's you'd want. Really, it's just trying to help people who ask for your help."

"But what will you be doing?" Lisa asked quickly.

"So, that's the thing," Sneak replied as he looked at his long-time friend Hailey for support. "I've got to take a break from doing detective work for a while."

"What do you mean?" his sister Jennie asked, surprised by his words.

It was here I saw, that in spite of all their arguing, Jennie genuinely liked her brother and knew how much being a detective meant to him.

"Well, I might as well tell everyone," he said, this time looking over at Uncle Charlie and Professor Telson. "I've made some mistakes – some really big ones over the past few weeks. And I'm going to get in trouble for it."

"What do you mean?" Jennie asked again.

"Well, I lied to Mom and Dad and told them I was at Pep's, when really I was conducting a stakeout at a cemetery."

"What day was that?" Jennie asked.

"It was for like two weeks straight from seven to eight o'clock at night."

"Oh," his sister replied, shocked by the revelation.

"And then," Sneak added. "When I tried to follow the suspect out of the cemetery, I grabbed the bumper of his car and rode it out...so he wouldn't get away with some evidence."

"Whoa," Moscow said from above.

"You were bumper hopping...in the cemetery?" Joel asked.

"Yeah."

"And on the street," his Uncle added.

"Yeah, and on the street too," Sneak confessed.

"Wow," Lisa said, surprised – as we all were – at the information.

"I'm so glad you didn't get hurt," Hailey added in a concerned voice. "You really could have gotten hurt."

"Yeah, I guess I could have," Sneak replied as our entire group was quiet for a moment.

"That was really dangerous," his sister added.

"So," the young detective continued, "I've got to take a break for a while. I'm not sure how long my parents will ground me, but I'm pretty sure it will be for a long time. I'm going to tell them all about it right after this meeting."

"That stinks," Moscow replied. "Do you really have to tell them?"

"Yeah, I need to," Sneak said, looking at his uncle and then Professor Telson.

"What are you going to do?" I asked.

"I don't know," replied Sneak. "I'm not sure if they'll ground me from doing research in my crime lab in the basement, or not. If they ban me from the basement, I guess I'll have to pick up another hobby."

Jennie began to cry, as did her friend Michelle and tears welled up in the eyes of several of the older kids.

"Sneak that is so sad," Jennie said as she wiped away her tears. "I didn't know we were going to talk about sad stuff today."

Seeing how much his sister cared for him was something that profoundly touched the young detective and he went to her and gave his sister a long hug, wrapping her up into his long arms.

"It's going to be okay," he said softly. "It's not like I'm going away or anything. I'm still going to be here."

"Lo, I will be with you always," I heard Professor Telson say quietly.

Eventually Sneak turned to the rest of the group. "After today, I'm probably not going to be able to work on any of the investigations, but if you guys have questions about a case, you could always tell Jennie and she could find me and I could give her my thoughts about it."

"So, it's a good thing I'm in the group after all!" Jennie said smiling through her tears as she looked up at her brother.

"Yeah, it's a good thing," her brother replied.

"But you're like the best detective around," Joel said. "We can't do the stuff you do."

"Yeah," Moscow added. "We've never done investigations before."

"I'll try to help out how I can," said Sneak.

"So, can't you just take a break for a while, until your parents say you're not grounded anymore?" Lisa asked. "What do you need all of us for?"

"Now comes the time when I explain why I need their help, right Hailey?" he said turning to his old friend.

"Right," she replied with an encouraging smile.

"So, like I said," Sneak continued. "I get a lot of calls and letters from people asking for my help, and it would be great if there was someone – or several people – who were able to help them. Sometimes the cases are easy to figure out and sometimes they are hard, but it would be cool if you could try to help people if they called or wrote me."

"I like that," Michelle added. "That would be cool. You could just give us their names and we could talk to them."

"Right, and there are the cold cases for Uncle Charlie," Sneak added.

"Those can wait," his uncle interjected loudly. "I don't want a group of kids rifling through those records. Some have been there since before I joined the force."

"Okay," Sneak replied to his uncle, then turning to the group. "So it sounds like you don't have to worry about the cold cases. But, there's....well.... there's one more case I'd like you to help with."

"What's that?" Joel asked.

"It's the one I've been working on and it's officially – for now – technically – I guess you'd call it my last case. At least my last case for a while. Do you want to hear about it?"

"Yeah!" I said in unison with the others.

CHAPTER 28

"Okay, so let's talk about the case," Sneak said as he quickly moved to the back of the garage and retrieved a large green chalkboard – one identical to the portable chalkboards we had in school – that had been unnoticed by me next to the back wall of the garage. Pulling, then pushing it, he hastily moved the chalkboard to the front corner of the garage next to his desk for all of us to see. "Here are the basic facts, ready?" he asked.

"Oh, wait a second," Hailey interrupted. "I have notebooks for everyone. And pens!" Quickly, she pulled out a number of black covered notepads and blue ballpoint pens from a brown paper Great Scot grocery bag.

"Can I help pass them out?" Jennie asked while raising her hand.

"Sure Jennie," Hailey responded to her young friend with a smile.

Once we had all received our notepads and pens, Sneak continued. "Okay, so let's review the case," he began. "I've written a few important things about the case on the chalkboard," he said as he flipped the green chalkboard over, just has our teachers frequently did to start a new subject in class. "Can everyone see this?" he asked, while looking around the garage.

Most of us answered with a "yes" or "yeah'", as we tried to make sense of the board.

"This was a little tricky to create," Sneak explained as he stopped to admire the words and symbols that he had written on the board. "In order for you not to see it when you came in, I decided to write it all on the other side of the chalkboard. But, in order to be able to flip it, I had to write it all upside down."

"Impressive," I said.

"Nice," Moscow added.

Michelle gave a thumbs up sign to the famous young detective.

"Couldn't you have just written it normally on the back of the chalkboard and then pushed it out from the other direction?" Lisa asked.

We paused for a moment.

"Ah....yes. I guess I could have done that," Sneak replied with a grimace after looking at the chalkboard and seeing that Lisa was correct. "I hadn't even considered that approach. My mind's been pretty distracted lately. I guess it just proves I need more help, right?"

Many of us chuckled.

"So anyway," Sneak continued. "The last case I was working on is one that I've been calling, *The Case of the Mysterious Circles.*"

As we looked at the top of the chalkboard, we could see that Sneak had printed, in large upper case letters, the name of the case: **THE CASE OF THE MYSTERIOUS CIRCLES**. I noticed too that several of my fellow detectives were writing the name of the case in their notepads.

"When Hailey and I talked about this yesterday…"

"For like three hours," Hailey added with a laugh.

"Yeah, we probably talked that long!" Sneak replied, also with a laugh. "Not three hours consecutively, but I kept hanging up and calling other people, then calling you back!"

Sneak paused as Hailey smiled, looking up at her friend.

"Anyway," Sneak continued. "Hailey thought it would be good for me to not just go over the details of the case with you, but to also talk about the methods I follow when I conduct an investigation – so that you would know what to do when you're on your own."

"That's a good idea," Joel added. "I wouldn't even know where to start."

"So you're gonna' tell us what to do?" Moscow asked.

"Yes," Sneak answered.

"That's cool," said Moscow, as Michelle gave a thumbs up sign.

"So, in thinking about my methods," Sneak continued, "even though each case is different, here's generally what I try to do." As he finished saying these words he pointed to two words on the chalkboard with an arrow between them:

INVESTIGATE

DEDUCE

"What I try to do first is investigate. This involves asking questions and making observations. Then I deduce what has happened."

Michelle raised her hand.

"Yes," Sneak asked.

"What does *deduce* mean?"

"It's the process of reasoning or assuming things based on what you have observed," Sneak explained. "It's basically figuring out what happened."

"Oh," Michelle replied.

"To help you with this case," Sneak continued, "...or any other ones afterwards, I wrote down these questions," and he quickly pointed to seven questions that were written on the chalkboard:

What is the mystery?
When did it happen?
Who did it happen to?
What evidence has been gathered?
What really happened?
Why did it happen?
Who did it?

"Kind of like the reporter's questions we learned about in school...who, what, when, where and why," Lisa commented after reading the list.

"Yes," Sneak said encouragingly. "When you begin the investigation you'll want to gather the basic facts – just like a reporter would do to write a newspaper article. But there's one big difference between investigating a mystery and writing an article. In a newspaper article you might not know a lot of information when you start – right Pep?" he asked me.

"There's still some stuff I don't understand about some of the mysteries I've written about," I joked.

"But one of the things with detective work, is that from the very beginning of your investigation you'll probably have some theories about what happened.

And then, on top of your ideas, other people will usually tell you about *their* theories about what happened."

"Like what?" Joel asked.

"Well, maybe someone is accused of a crime – so everyone thinks they did it, and they'll tell you why they think the accused person is guilty. Or, maybe the accused person claims they didn't do it. So, there's at least two opinions, or theories, you'll have to sort out."

"That's interesting," Lisa added.

"So, from almost the very beginning of the case you'll have possible answers to all of these questions," Sneak said pointing to his list on the chalkboard.

"So," Moscow replied. "If it's like a fill-in-the-blank test, a lot of the blanks will already be filled in."

"Right," Sneak continued, now at a fast pace. "But what's important is that as you're gathering evidence through observation and asking questions, you're also confirming – or testing – each of the theories to see which one is correct. Some explanations to the mystery will seem completely improbable – they'll seem totally crazy. But you still need to check even the craziest of ideas to see if it could be true."

"I like crazy ideas," Moscow said with a laugh.

"As Sherlock Holmes once said," Sneak continued. " 'Once you eliminate the improbable…'" then he paused, stopping himself. "– well I can talk about that some other time, that actually might be a little too detailed for us this morning. Anyway, as you work your case, it's always important to look at the evidence and let the evidence inform your deductions about what *really* happened."

As Sneak explained his methods in excited and animated tones, some of us took notes, but most of his young friends, including myself, stared back at him blankly with expressionless faces. It was overwhelming to receive so much new information at once – on this, the first day that any of us had ever thought much about criminology or the proper investigative methods for solving a mystery. (Besides Sneak, I probably had the most experience among our young group with mysteries, but I had simply wanted to write about the mysteries *he* was solving, never imagining myself as an actual detective).

As we listened to the young detective, we could tell, even in those first few moments that he was, as my mother would say, "in his element". He spoke about his investigative methods and deductive skills with such an unusual vitality, vibrancy and intensity that it was easy for us to see his genuine passion and excitement for solving mysteries. He loved talking about collecting evidence, making observations and constructing deductions in order to unravel secrets and get to the truth – and he wanted to share his immense knowledge with us, so that we could be successful detectives as well. It was fun to watch him talk with such passion. As Sneak continued with his detailed explanation, my feelings of joy soon turned to sadness as I thought more and more about how his parents would soon ban him from working on the thing he loved doing most – solving seemingly unsolvable mysteries.

"Okay, let's go to the first question on this list. **What is the Mystery?**" Sneak continued as he pointed to the chalkboard. "It's important to remember that what *seems* to have happened may not *actually* be what *really* happened. But you have to start somewhere, so I'd recommend that you start here, with this question. This is the usual starting point, because it's usually the first thing people tell you when they ask for your help, they'll tell you what seems to have happened."

"What's happenin'!" Moscow said loudly – in reference to the T.V. show.

We laughed.

"Sometimes the mystery is a crime," Sneak continued, ignoring his friend on the wooden platform above us. "…like the one I'm going to tell you more about. But other times people might come to you and ask for your help when it's not a crime – like if they ask you to find something that went missing – like a missing pet or a long lost friend who moved away – it's not a crime but there still is a mystery to solve."

Sneak paused while some of us wrote in our notepads.

"Usually the person asking for help will be your client, but other times they may not. I guess in this case – in *The Case of the Mysterious Circles* – I'm sort of like your client, I'm the one asking for your help to solve the mystery." He paused for a moment. "I hadn't really thought of that before – I'm a client asking for help."

We were silent as his words echoed throughout the enclosed space. The only sounds – for several long seconds – came from the two space heaters as their orange glowing faces gently hummed and crackled while warming the garage. *Our friend, Sneak Ryerson, the great young detective, had just asked for our help. He actually needs us!* I thought, shocked by my friend's admission.

"Okay…," Sneak continued. "So let's talk about what's been happening in *The Case of the Mysterious Circles.*"

"Actually, let me jump in here for a moment," Uncle Charlie interrupted in a serious tone, while remaining seated on the folding chair next to Professor Telson by the door. "Sneak just brought up a good point that I want to make sure everyone is crystal clear in understanding. *He's* the one asking for your help in investigating this case….the *Case of* the…what did you call it, *Mysterious Circles,*" he laughed smugly as he said the name. "We don't actually refer to it as that in our police reports," he said, changing his voice to a serious tone. "Anyway, you may choose to talk about this case as a group and talk to your friends about it here, or at school, or read more about it in the newspaper, or do some research about crop circles from the encyclopedia or at the library...or you may not. You may decide *not* to investigate this case. It's up to you...you don't necessarily have to do what Sneak has asked you to do. Okay?"

All of us were silent, assuming his question was rhetorical.

"And there's another thing I want to make sure is crystal clear," he added gravely. "My presence here, even though I'm a captain in the police department, is in an entirely unofficial capacity."

"What does that mean, Uncle Charlie?" Jennie asked.

"That means," her uncle explained, "that I'm here because my nephew asked me to come here to serve as an advisor to your group. I'm an advisor, just like I might be an advisor for any other student group that asked for my help, like the Cub Scouts, or DeMolay or Junior Achievement."

"They made that cool penny hockey game that we play, right Sneak?" Moscow asked his friend.

"Yeah, I think so," Sneak replied.

"I just want to make sure," Uncle Charlie continued, "that it is perfectly clear to everyone here that the Police Department is in *no way* asking for your help. The County Sheriff and the city's Police Department have trained detectives and investigators who are working this case. We are not asking you to conduct an investigation. You can talk about it all you want. And what you decide to do individually or as a group is entirely up to you. But you have not been asked by the police or the County Sheriff to be part of an official investigation. Got it?"

"Yeah," many of us replied.

"Professor, do you have anything to add?" Jennie and Sneak's uncle asked.

"Well," Professor Telson replied in a serious tone. "I guess you could say I'm also serving in an unofficial capacity here too," he said before pausing dramatically. "In no way should my presence here lead you to believe that the seminary is asking you to conduct an investigation into this matter." By the time he got to the end of the statement he was laughing as many of us joined him.

"Sorry captain," the professor said turning to Uncle Charlie. "I honestly don't know why I'm here. The only investigations I do at the seminary are with ancient manuscripts. But, I'll try to assist...or advise – as you call it – the best that I can," he added with a smile. "If you need a handwriting expert in Ugaritic, I'm your man."

"Okay, well, thank you Uncle Charlie and Professor Telson for being here," Sneak responded. "There were some things Hailey and I talked about – about how you could help us as advisors – and we were going to talk about that later."

"Oh, okay," the professor said sheepishly. "That's fine, we can discuss that later."

"So, now that that is all cleared up," Sneak continued. "Let me tell you about the case."

"It's about time," Lisa replied impatiently with a smile. "Let's get going."

"So, *The Case of the Mysterious Circles* involves arson," Sneak explained as Michelle raised her hand. Anticipating her question, Sneak clarified, "Arson, is when someone starts a fire when they shouldn't."

Michelle put her hand down.

"With this mystery," Sneak continued, "someone – or multiple people – have been setting fires – specifically in farm fields – outside of Findlay. Each fire was set within the boundaries of Hancock County and except for being in different locations outside of town, they appear to be identical. There have been four separate fires…"

"Four different ones?" Jennie interrupted in a serious tone, as she wrote some words in her notepad.

"Yes, four fires," Sneak responded back in a similarly serious tone.

"What did you mean they were identical?" Jennie asked as a follow-up question.

"Well, good question. What I mean is that all four of the fires have the same pattern. What the *arsonist* – that's the technical name for someone who starts a fire – what they did at each of the fires was to create three large circles out in the fields. All of the circles at each location were exactly the same shape and size. They were made really close together, so that each circle barely touched the others. They all looked like this," he explained while pointing to three circles that he had drawn earlier on the chalkboard.

"Sort of like a bunch of upside down grapes," Michelle commented.

"Or, one bowling ball stacked on two others," Moscow added.

"Or, cannonballs," said Joel.

"Right, one circle stacked on two other circles," Sneak added.

"Do you think the pattern is important?" Hailey asked.

"It might be," Sneak replied.

"I'll make a note that we should look into that," Hailey added as she wrote in her notebook. "Maybe we could see if that pattern has been used in other fires, or in other crimes?"

"That would be interesting," said Sneak.

"How big are each of the circles?" I asked.

"I didn't bring my notes out here with me, but I can get you the exact dimensions," Sneak added. "I think the radius for each circle was thirty two feet."

"Wow, those are big circles," Joel commented.

Seeing that Jennie was about to ask about the word *radius*, Sneak began, "The radius is..."

"The distance from the center of a circle to its perimeter," Hailey interrupted. "The perimeter is the outer edge of the circle," she explained while quickly standing and pointing to the edge of one of the circles on the chalkboard.

"So, it's like half of the circle?" Jennie asked.

"That's right," Hailey replied. "The diameter is twice the radius, or the distance across the circle from one edge to another," she said while making a line with her finger across one of the circles.

"Nice explanation," Professor Telson added.

"Academic quiz team," Hailey replied with a brief self-effacing smile as she returned to her seat behind the desk.

"So if half the distance is thirty two feet," I concluded, "then the diameter is seventy four feet, that's one really large circle. And there's three of them."

"Yep," Sneak replied.

"Actually, sixty four feet," Hailey corrected.

"What?" Sneak asked.

"The diameter of each circle is sixty four feet," she clarified.

"Right," Sneak agreed, then continued quickly. "We're talking about three really large circles. So, in addition to knowing that they are really big, what else might you deduce after knowing that each of the circles at each of the fires has the same pattern and same dimensions? What might that tell us?"

"That the same people are setting the fires?" I answered.

"I think the evidence suggests that," Sneak agreed. "Anything else?"

"Wait a minute," Lisa interrupted. "What if someone was copying the first pattern?"

"Good point," said Sneak. "You always want to be careful when comparing multiple crime scenes, because there's always the chance of a copycat crime." Sneak then looked to his uncle who had remained in his seat near the door and was now impatiently leafing through *his* black notepad – a notepad that he had been using for several weeks to enter information about the case. "Uncle Charlie," Sneak asked, "has the sheriff released the details about the size and pattern of the fires?"

"What?" his uncle stammered. "Sorry, I was just looking back at something."

"Has the sheriff released the details about the size and pattern of the fires?" Sneak asked again.

"No, he hasn't released any of the specifics," Uncle Charlie replied dryly. "...so as not to encourage copycats."

"Okay, thanks. So, without the details about the crime being released, it would be hard for another person to copy the first crime because it would be really hard for them to get the exact measurements of the circles. So, I'd say there a high probability that each of the four fires were set by the same person... or the same group of people. Is there anything else you might deduce from what you've learned so far?"

"That they did some planning," Lisa said quickly. "It wasn't just some crazy High School kids who were bored after a basketball game, or something like that."

"Like your older brother," I heard Cressida say softly.

"Right, like my older brother, Brad, and his friends," Lisa added with a chuckle. "Whoever did this had to do some measuring to get the circles to be the exact same shape and size, right?"

"That's right," Sneak added. "I think that's a very good deduction – that planning was involved in each of these fires. They'd have to figure out where to start the fire, how to measure the field to get the exact distances, and then figure out how to start it. So, it probably took a lot of planning. It's a good deduction, but remember, for this deduction and all of your other deductions, we'll...or you'll...want to make sure it still makes sense after you get more evidence. But, for this one, I think it will."

"Was the fire just on the lines of the circle, or was it inside the circle?" Michelle asked while looking at Sneak's diagram of the three circles on the chalkboard.

"That's an interesting question," Sneak answered. "The fires were inside the lines of the circle."

"So, what evidence have you gathered from the crime scenes?" I asked in a serious tone – trying to sound as much like a smart young detective as possible.

"Let me get to that in a minute Pep," my friend replied. "I've found some really interesting things at the scene of each of the crimes, but first, let me talk about when and where the fires occurred. That's the next question on the list," he said while pointing to the next question on the chalkboard: **When did it happen?** "I guess I should have added the question 'Where did it happen?' as well."

As he said this, the young detective soon drew our attention to a list he had made on the chalkboard that described details for each of the fires. His chart listed the day of the week the fire occurred, the date it occurred, the approximate time the fire started and the location of each fire:

#	Day of Week	Date	Approximate Time	Location from Downtown
1	Wednesday	1/23	9:45pm	North
2	Tuesday	2/5	10:30pm	East
3	Thursday	2/21	9:30pm	South
4	Wednesday	3/5	10:00pm	East

"So in this chart," Sneak explained, "I list out *when* the fires occurred and their location." He paused for a moment as we read the details. "Now that you've had a chance to read the list, what kinds of things do you notice?"

"They're about two weeks apart," Hailey said quickly. "January 23rd, then February 5th, then the 21st then on Wednesday, March 5th."

"Right!" Sneak added energetically, "they are happening about every two weeks."

"They *have* happened about every two weeks," Uncle Charlie corrected while looking up from his notepad. "You know what's happened in the past but you don't know for certain that they'll continue with that pattern in the future."

"Okay, fair enough," granted Sneak. "As Hailey observed, they *have* happened about every two weeks."

"Also, they're not always on the same night," Joel added thoughtfully.

"Yes!" Sneak responded in an excited manner. "They were on different nights, one was on a Tuesday, two occurred on Wednesdays, and one was on a Thursday. Anything else?"

Cressida turned to her cousin, whispered something to her, and then Lisa said, "They did not occur on Mondays, Fridays or on the weekends."

I chuckled, thinking that this was a funny and completely irrelevant observation and I was just beginning to say, "Oh, that's *real* important...," when Sneak jumped in.

"Right! No weekends!" he answered her, much to my surprise. "That's an important fact! And I'll talk more about that later."

Cressida turned again to her cousin, whispered something else to her, and then Lisa said, "All of the fires began between nine-thirty and ten-thirty at night."

"Yes!" Sneak replied again, almost shouting – evidently very pleased with the deductions we were making. "I noticed that timing too, and that led to some of the conclusions I've drawn." He paused. "Do you notice anything else?"

"The locations are not consistent," Professor Telson added enthusiastically, as he sat on the edge of the folding chair, fascinated by the discussion that was occurring around him. "At least in this sample, they are not bunched up in any one location, but spread out around Hancock County."

"Good point Professor," Sneak added. "North, south and east of downtown."

We were silent for a moment as we studied the board.

"So, we've covered answers to the question of **When did it happen?**" Sneak concluded. "So, let's move on to the next question, **Who did it happen to?**" He said as he pointed to the chalkboard.

"Okay," I heard one or two of us say.

"So, in this mystery, I think I told you already, all of the fires occurred on farmland – and, all of the victims are farmers," Sneak explained. "If you're investigating multiple crimes – like this one – it's important to always check to see if the victims have anything in common or any kind of connection. So, what kinds of things do you think the victims of the fires might have in common?"

"Before we do that," Joel asked. "Could you tell us why this is important for us to know?"

"Well, let's say all the farmers were all part of the same club – maybe they were like the officers of a club. And then someone committed a crime against all of them to try to get them to quit the club – so that the criminal could then become the Club President. So, for that mystery, if you knew the common connection between all of the victims, you could solve the case."

"Ah," said Joel. "That makes sense."

"Can anyone think of any other examples of victims having something in common that would be important in solving a case?" Sneak asked.

"Like maybe a group of people were all related, and someone wanted to inherit the land they owned or something like that," Moscow suggested from his perch above us.

"Right, being related might be a connection between the victims," said Sneak. "Any other examples you can think of?"

"Or maybe," suggested Hailey, "all the victims went to the same school and someone wanted all of them to fail a test so that the criminal could get a good grade, or something like that.

"Oh right," Moscow said, scoffing at his sister's idea.

"That's actually a good example," explained Sneak. "So if all of the victims went to the same school – that would be the connection between them and important to know in solving that mystery. Does anyone have any other examples you can think of?"

"Maybe they were all supposed to testify against a mob boss," young Jennie added. "And the fires were a sign to keep them quiet."

"Woah!" Uncle Charlie replied spontaneously as our group burst into laughter.

Some of us were still laughing when Uncle Charlie asked his young niece, "Now, Jennie, where did you get that idea about mob bosses? I didn't know Hancock County had any mob bosses running around trying to keep people quiet! If we do, my weekend just got a whole lot busier!"

Many of us laughed at Uncle Charlie's comment.

"I think I saw it on *Rockford* once," Jennie explained.

"Oh brother," her uncle replied with a sigh. "I've got to talk to your Mom about the T.V. shows you're watching!"

"Jennie really loves *The Rockford Files*," explained Michelle.

"Yeah," Jennie confessed.

"And so does her Dad," Michelle added.

"So, with Jennie's example," Sneak continued, again unfazed by the added discussion and laughter around him. "...the victims were all targeted for *the same reason* - so the criminal could get something afterwards. That will be something to look for as you do your investigation of this case or any other ones," Sneak explained. "Any other examples you can think of?"

We were silent before Sneak continued.

"Okay, so, this is one of those areas of the investigation that can take a lot of time to research and not yield much of a result. You could spend hours going through old records downtown at the Library or staring at a microfiche screen at the county records office and not find anything connecting the victims. Sometimes you just have to ask the victims a bunch of questions and see if there's a connection between them."

"So, in this case, what's the connection between the farmers?" Lisa questioned.

"Were they part of the same club or something like that?" asked Michelle.

"Were they going to testify against a mob boss?" Moscow asked with a grin.

"I couldn't find anything that ties the victims together," Sneak confessed. "They aren't related. They don't know each other...other than by name. They go to different churches. They all attended different schools when they were younger and their kids don't go to the same schools either. They aren't in the same organizations. The only thing they have in common is that they all are farmers. I couldn't find any other connections."

He paused as many in our group wrote down this information on their notepads.

"How about the Fair?" Hailey asked suddenly.

"The Fair?" Sneak asked.

"Well, they would all probably go to the County Fair at Labor Day to show their animals, right?"

"Or show their crops," Lisa added.

"That might be a connection, right?" Hailey asked.

"Maybe," replied Sneak.

"Lisa mentioned crops," Hailey continued, talking quickly. "The Farmer's Market is at the fairgrounds too. Maybe they all bring their crops to sell at the Farmer's Market?"

"It's worth checking out," Sneak added.

"We go to the Farmer's Market sometimes," Jennie admitted. "Wouldn't it be funny if the person starting the fires was someone we knew from there?"

"I don't think it's very likely," Sneak replied, "I haven't told you everything I've learned."

He paused as several people finished writing notes on this part of the investigation.

"So, why don't we move to Pep's question about the physical evidence I've collected from the crime scenes," Sneak said when we were ready to continue. "This will help answer the question, **What evidence has been gathered?**" he said pointing to the chalkboard.

"Sounds good," I answered.

"Before you start, let me just jump in here," Uncle Charlie said sternly, leaning forward in his chair. "I want to make sure it's clear to everyone here that you can't take any evidence from a crime scene, that's called *tampering with evidence*. In nearly all cases, it's a criminal offense. So, it's a really bad thing to do and you could get into a lot of trouble for it. Got it?"

"Yeah," a few of us replied, as Uncle Charlie continued.

"An important idea in law enforcement is what is called *chain of custody*. That means that evidence is collected and handled and stored with care by the right people and not planted or tampered with. Got it?"

A few of us muttered affirmative words.

"Why don't we all say that phrase together, just so I know you've all heard it? *Tampering with evidence,* ready, one, two, three…"

"Tampering with evidence," we said dispassionately, but mostly in unison.

"So, that's what you want us *to do?*" Moscow asked with a laugh.

"No, no, no," Uncle Charlie smiled and laughed. "That's what I *do not* want you to do."

"Oh, okay," Moscow said smiling.

"So you can't take stuff for your own investigations," Uncle Charlie said. "It's our job to process the scene of a crime."

"Right," Sneak continued, undeterred by his uncle. "So, one of the things I observed – careful not to disturb the crime scenes – were some very distinct tire tracks in the snow and dirt near the circles. I didn't notice them at the first fire – but I did see them at the three fires that followed. I made a few impressions using gypsum plaster – most people call it *Plaster of Paris* – and discovered some interesting things." At this point Sneak walked to the back of the garage and pulled out several white molds from a cardboard box. The molds were relatively flat, each about two or three feet long and one foot wide. "I'll pass these around for you to look at. These came from the second and third fires."

"Can I help pass them out?" Michelle asked as she raised her hand.

"Sure," Sneak answered, "and don't worry about raising your hand, we're not in school."

"Okay," Michelle said with a smile as she grabbed the plaster molds and passed them to Uncle Charlie, Professor Telson and the kids near Sneak's desk.

"Be careful with these," Sneak warned. "They might crumble if you drop them."

"Hey toss one up here!" said Moscow.

"No," his sister said sternly. "You can come down here if you want to look at them up close."

"Okay, okay," Moscow replied dejectedly, remaining on the wooden platform.

"These tracks were in the snow?" Professor Telson asked.

"Yeah," Sneak answered. "And dirt."

"These are pretty good impressions," the professor commented.

"Thanks," said Sneak with a smile.

Soon, Michelle gave one of the molds to me and I ran my fingers over the bumpy treads. Turning it over, I saw that Sneak had used a black marker to print the words on the back: *The Case of the Mysterious Circles – Fire #2 – 2/5/80.*

"So, after I made the molds, I was able to figure out that the tire treads are from a motocross bike. A 1978 Yamaha DT 400."

"Whoa," Moscow said from his perch above us. "A Yamaha DT 400! Those things can fly."

"Right," Sneak answered. "I'm thinking that what the arsonist – or arsonists – did was to muffle the bike's engine, and put some type of barrel on the back of it to get the accelerant around the field."

"Makes sense," said Professor Telson.

"Okay, okay," Uncle Charlie said in an exasperated tone as he stood up and walked towards Sneak's desk so all could see him. "Let me jump in here again." Uncle Charlie soon arrived at Sneak's desk and sat down on it. "Sneak, again you've done a really nice job summarizing this case and explaining your investigative methods. But I have to point out that this evidence with the tracks and the motorbike is not definitive. You don't know *when* the tire marks were left there – it could have been sometime well before the fire even happened – it could have been a few days before or even longer. You have to be really careful about evidence like this. Plus, even if your theory is right about the motorcycle, we don't know if the driver swapped out his original tires with the Yamaha tires. So we might be spinning our wheels – so to speak – looking for a Yamaha DT 400, when it could be something totally different."

"Nice one," Professor Telson added, "...spinning our wheels."

"Oh, I get it, that's good." Moscow exclaimed.

"'Cause it's a motorcycle!" Jennie added.

"Well, you're right Uncle Charlie," Sneak replied as he moved to sit in his chair behind the desk, after standing next to the chalkboard for most of the discussion. "There are always questions with evidence like tire tracks, but these just might be the clues we need to find out who did this. And it's interesting that I found the same tire marks at each of the crime scenes."

"At three of the four crime scenes," Lisa corrected.

"Right, that's right, three of the four crime scenes," Sneak added. "I didn't notice the tracks at the first fire."

"These impressions of the tire tracks," Uncle Charlie said, still sitting, as he pointed to one of the plaster molds, several of which were now on Sneak's desk. "Sneak, you told me he didn't go into the crime scene to get these, right? You weren't just pulling my leg were you? You waited until the scene was cleared, right."

"Right," Sneak answered. "I made sure that each of the crime scenes was cleared before I went in. That's why I don't have anything from the fourth fire."

"Okay, good," said Uncle Charlie. "That's good. But you still had to go into the fields to get these impressions. Going onto someone's property is trespassing."

"Well, it's not if you get the owner's permission," Sneak explained. "After each of the fires I introduced myself to each of the farmers and conducted an interview with them. And then I asked them if it would be okay for me to collect evidence after the Sheriff cleared the scene. And each of them agreed. All three even took me out into their fields to help me look around. At the second and third fires – the two fields where I took the impressions – both of the farmers even helped stir the plaster and water with me."

"You talked to each of the...victims?" Michelle said as her eyes widened with surprise.

"Well sure," Sneak explained. "How else would I know if they knew each other, or had anything in common? The farmers were pretty excited to see how I was going to collect the evidence. And, at the two locations where I was able to see the tracks and get the impressions, they really liked that I was taking the plaster samples. One of the farmers even told me that if things didn't pan out for me as a detective, I could work as a vet, setting animal's broken bones with plaster casts!"

We laughed.

"When I talked to them," Sneak continued, "I asked them if any motorcycles had been in their fields before the fires. And they didn't know about any...at least they didn't give any motorcycles permission to ride in their fields."

"You sound pretty thorough," Uncle Charlie replied, smiling.

"I try to be," Sneak said with a smile.

"How about a snowmobile?" Michelle asked. "Could it have been a snowmobile instead?"

"No," said Sneak. "I was able to match the tire tread exactly to a Yamaha motocross bike.

"Okay," Michelle answered.

"Why don't you keep going," Uncle Charlie suggested as he left the desk and moved back to his chair near the door. "I told Hailey earlier that I couldn't stay all morning and I need to get going in a few minutes," he said as he looked at his silver wristwatch. "Marie's making some special Vietnamese noodles for lunch and I definitely don't want to miss those."

"Oh, those sound good," Jennie told her uncle.

"Well, I don't have much more to talk about," Sneak replied. "I should be able to wrap things up pretty quickly. The other physical evidence I collected was some residue from the accelerant used to start the fires."

"What's *accelerant?*" Michelle asked, raising her hand before quickly lowering it.

Jennie, I noticed, gave her friend an approving nod.

"Accelerant is what is used to start a fire. Because it's snowy on the ground, the arsonist can't just drop a match and start a big fire, they would need to use something that could catch fire. So, I collected samples from the first three fires – and, like I said, I haven't been able to get a sample from the fourth fire, yet. After I collected those samples, I tested them in the lab down in my basement and from what I could tell, the accelerant they used was the same in each location. It's a combination of kerosene and gasoline."

"Kasoline!" Moscow shouted.

"Right!" Sneak replied with a smile, "I guess you could call it that. I hadn't thought of that name."

"I can come up with all kinds of stuff!" Moscow added.

"Was it a special mix, or something?" Hailey asked, looking up from her notepad. "You know, like, could we track it back to a special gas station in town, or someplace like that?"

"That's a great question!" Uncle Charlie said encouragingly.

"Well," said Sneak. "Both gasoline and kerosene are pretty common, so the arsonist probably just bought them separately and then mixed them together."

"Ah," several of our group said.

"So, there's one more piece of evidence that we need to talk about that didn't come from the crime scene, but was in the newspaper," Sneak explained.

"Oh brother," Uncle Charlie replied as he rolled his eyes. "This wild idea of yours is going to take forever to explain."

CHAPTER 29

"Okay," Sneak said as he quickly moved from his chair behind his desk to the chalkboard. "This next part that I'll talk about will answer the question we were just looking at, **What evidence has been gathered?** And then, after I explain that, we'll move pretty quickly into my deductions about **What really happened?, Why did it happen?** and **Who did it?**"

"Sounds good," said Lisa.

"So, after the first fire," Sneak began. "I noticed something really interesting. The very next day, a letter appeared in the *Letter to the Editor* section of the newspaper that alluded to the fire."

"Really?" someone said.

"What's *alluded?*" Jennie asked. "And can you not use such big words?" she said in a tired voice.

"Sorry Jennie. What I mean is that the Letter to the Editor said *some very specific things* about the fire from the night before – but didn't explain all of the details about it."

"Well, it's the newspaper, you'd think there would be news about the fire in there," Moscow suggested.

"Right, there was an *article* on the front page about the fire, but I got to thinking about the newspaper's printing schedule, and how *Letters to the Editor* probably need to be turned in earlier in the evening. And guess what? They do!"

"Whoa!" Moscow exclaimed. "Busted!"

Sneak laughed.

"How did you find that out?" asked Joel.

"I called and talked to some of the editors to make sure I understood their deadlines," Sneak explained. "What they told me was that the newspaper doesn't go to print until midnight – and what they do is reserve a place on the front page for late breaking stories. Because the fires happened well *before* midnight – like Cressida noticed, pointing out that they were set between nine-thirty and ten-thirty at night – the reporters had time to hear about the fires on their police scanners, go out and see it and then write a short front page story – not a big story, but enough of a story to include on the front page before the paper went to print at midnight."

"That's interesting," I mumbled as several of the kids wrote some of the details in their notepads.

"Yes, but what's strange is that the Editorial Page deadline is eight thirty at night. They won't take any new *Letters to the Editor* after that. So, what can you deduce from those facts?"

"If someone wrote about a fire before eight thirty," Lisa explained, "they would need to know about it in advance."

"Right!" said Sneak.

"Because," Lisa continued. "The fires didn't start until after nine-thirty," she said pointing to the chart on the green chalkboard.

"That's what I deduced too!" Sneak said enthusiastically. "There's no way something could be in the *Letters to the Editor* section that describes the fire, unless the writer knew about it before it was started."

"So who was the writer?" Joel asked quickly.

"The writer of the four letters about the fires – and a whole lot of other letters – is a guy named Julian Davis. He's the President of a club – or organization – called F.E.E.T." Sneak said.

"Feet?" several of us asked.

"If he's the President of F.E.E.T," Moscow joked. "Do they call him *The Big Toe*?"

"I don't think so," Sneak laughed.

"They probably just call him *The Grand Poohbah*," Joel added.

"Like the Loyal Order of the Water Buffaloes!" I said, laughing about the men's club on *The Flintstone's* television cartoons.

"I'm not sure what they call him," Sneak continued. "But you're going to love this." He paused dramatically and smiled widely. "*F.E.E.T.* stands for Findlayites Entertaining Extra Terrestrials."

"Extra Terrestrials?" several asked.

"What's that?" I heard someone say.

"An extraterrestrial is like, well, something from outer space," explained Sneak.

Both Professor Telson and Moscow let out large laughs and smiled widely at each other and the others in the garage, while Uncle Charlie frowned and shook his head.

"When I heard we were going to be detectives," Moscow chimed in loudly from his perch above us, "I was going to make a joke about trying to have our first case be about investigating *The Lagoon Monster*, but now, instead of a Lagoon Monster, we're going to investigate *The Men from Outer Space!*"

"Hey, I like that Scooby Doo Lagoon Monster episode!" Jennie replied.

"Me too," Michelle added.

"Scooby Dooby Doo!" Joel sang out.

"Let's focus," encouraged Hailey.

"They really believe in aliens from outer space?" Lisa asked.

"They really do," replied Hailey. "I couldn't believe it when Sneak was explaining it to me last night on the phone, but my Dad had some old newspapers and I read the letters to the editor myself.

They say they're expecting a group of U.F.O's to arrive soon…like within the next few days."

"Oh my!" Lisa said shocked.

Cressida let out a short laugh while revealing a broad smile.

"That's totally crazy!" I said from atop the stack of newspapers.

"Greetings, earthlings!" Moscow intoned in a voice like Marvin the Martian. "I come in peace!"

Joel began singing – or rather loudly humming – the theme song from the movie *2001: A Space Odyssey.* "Bom, bom, bom….da dum!" He hummed, not telling us that he knew the name of the composer and the symphony: Richard Strauss' masterpiece *Also sprach Zarathustra.*

"Open the pod bay doors Hal!" Moscow intoned. "I'm sorry, Dave. I can't do that! Open the pod bay doors!"

"Okay, let's stay focused," Hailey encouraged us again.

"There's no need to get worked up about it," Uncle Charlie added as Joel stopped his humming. "There's absolutely no evidence that the fires were started by U.F.O's."

"But that's really what they think," explained Hailey. "They say that the fires are from the rockets of U.F.O.s – when they land and then take off again. Plus, they say that those four spaceships are just the beginning. They came to scout out a good place for all of their spaceships to land. They're expecting an invasion!"

"Cookoo, cookoo," Moscow replied twisting his finger near his head.

"Right, well that's the gist of the letters," Sneak concluded. "I don't know if everyone in the F.E.E.T group *really* believes all of it, but at least that's what their letters are about."

"So, did the F.E.E.T guy..." Lisa interrupted.

"Julian Davis," Sneak added.

"Did he start the fires?" Lisa asked.

"Well, that would be a good deduction – knowing that the writer of the letters would need to know about them in advance," said Sneak.

"He seems to be the most likely....uh, suspect," Lisa added, smiling at using the correct detective word.

"That's what I thought too, he was my prime suspect," Sneak explained. "So I checked him out."

"That sounds like a good idea," Lisa added. "What'd you do?"

"Well, after that first letter, I looked up Julian's address in the phone book and went to his apartment. He wasn't home, but someone in his building said he worked out at the *Twin Theaters* by the mall, so I went out there."

"You went to talk to him?" Sneak's Uncle asked incredulously.

"Well, yeah," Sneak said. "That was before there were four fires and I realized it was an active investigation by the county sheriff."

"Oh my," Professor Telson added.

"I started by telling him I was interested in joining F.E.E.T. but he could tell I really wasn't interested, especially when I started questioning him about the fire."

"What happened?" Cressida asked, in one of the few times she spoke out loud that morning.

"He said he didn't know who started the fire. And he told me that he arrived at the movie theater at eight o'clock to start his shift and worked there until twelve thirty that night."

"And we know that the fires all started after 9:30," Hailey said pointing to the chart on the green chalkboard.

"Right," Sneak continued, "I double checked with another usher I met out there, and he confirmed Julian's alibi. Julian was at the movie theater from eight until after midnight."

"Could he have sneaked out, Sneak?" Moscow asked with a laugh from his perch above us.

"I don't think so," Sneak replied. "The usher definitely remembers him being there all night. And, after the other fires, I double-checked with my usher friend again and he told me that Julian was working each of those nights too....from around eight until after midnight."

"So, if it wasn't Joel...." Lisa asked.

"Hey," Joel replied. "His name's not Joel."

"Sorry, I mean, *Julian*." Lisa corrected herself. "So, if it wasn't Julian. Who was it?"

"So here's where we get to talk about my deductions about **What really happened?, Why did it happen?** and **Who did it?**," Sneak said pointing to those questions on the chalkboard.

"Cool," said Michelle.

"So, my theory," Sneak explained. "Is that Julian is keeping his distance from the actual arsonist so he can't be accused of setting the fires."

"And he can't be accused of setting the fires because he has an alibi for the time of each of them," I said, trying to sound like a competent detective.

"Right," Sneak said with a smile. "His alibi's airtight. He definitely couldn't have started the fires, because he was working at the movie theater."

"Hmm," said Michelle with a perplexed look.

"So, Michelle," Sneak explained, seeing the girl's confusion. "It's a perfect crime if you think about it. Julian can talk – or write – all about the fires and make people scared of a U.F.O invasion and try to get people talking about his group – while at the same time, never be blamed for setting any of the fires."

"It is pretty tricky," I summarized.

"But, I got to thinking," Sneak continued. "Somehow Julian Davis has got to know the exact day when to drop off his Letter to the Editor, so that his timing matches with the night of the fire."

"Another good one," Professor Telson said.

"Matches!" Moscow said.

"Matches, 'cause it's a fire!" Jennie giggled.

"Right," Sneak continued, oblivious to the laughter of the others. "Somehow Julian needs to be informed when the fire will be set and get a few details about the fire, so he can write up a quick letter and drop it off to the editor at the newspaper. And that led me to the idea of the dead letter drop."

"What?" someone asked.

"A dead letter drop is something that's used a lot by spies," Sneak explained. "But it's perfect for this mystery too."

"What is it, exactly?" someone asked.

"A dead letter drop is when one person writes a letter and leaves it in a hidden place. Then, after they've left, another person comes along and gets it."

"That way they're not seen together," Lisa commented.

"Exactly," said Sneak. "And I think that's how Julian Davis his getting his information."

"But couldn't they have just called him?" Lisa asked. "Or just gone to his house and told him what was going on?"

"Right, there are other ways Julian could have gotten his information," replied Sneak. "But that would have opened him up to people listening in on the conversation. The police could put a wiretap on his phone," he paused before explaining more. "A wiretap is when a phone call is recorded."

A few of us nodded, having heard the term before.

"And even without a wiretap, maybe a neighbor or a roommate could have heard a phone conversation in his house," the young detective continued. "And if the arsonist came over and told him about the plans for the next fire, then he would be seen with the arsonist. That's why I thought a dead letter drop made the most sense," Sneak explained, before pausing briefly. "So, I thought if I could just catch Julian with that information – given to him by the arsonist – the case would be solved. There's no way he could have written those *Letters to the Editor* without that inside information. And with that proof, I figured Julian would be forced to give me the arsonist's name."

"Oh brother," I heard Uncle Charlie say from his seat near the door.

"So what did you do?" Lisa asked, interested in how the case had progressed. "How did you figure out where the dead...."

"Dead letter drop," Sneak added.

"Right," Lisa continued. "How did you know where the dead letter drop was going to happen?"

"Well," Sneak continued. "The night of the third fire happened to be the night of my sister's birthday," he said, pointing to his chart on the chalkboard.

"Oh yeah," Jennie said with a smile that revealed her missing tooth. Her friend Michelle smiled and nodded in return.

"So, for her birthday, our family went out for pizza at *The Rocking U* before *Baby Choir*...I mean Children's Choir practice," Sneak explained.

We laughed.

"Cattle Baron!" Moscow said from above, reminding us of his favorite style of pizza at the restaurant.

"I remember that night," Hailey said. "Your Mom brought cupcakes and we ate them after choir practice."

"Yeah, those were really good," Joel added.

"So, as we were leaving the *Rocking U*," the young detective continued. "I saw Julian Davis drive his car past us going down West Main Cross Street."

"So, where were you, exactly?" Lisa asked.

"We were in that narrow street next to Dietsch's," Sneak explained. "Ready to turn left on Main Cross Street."

"Oh, okay."

"Anyway, Julian flew by us going really fast, like he was headed toward the interstate. And I assumed he was going out of town. Anyway, we were in Mom's car..."

"Maroon Monster," Moscow added.

"...waiting to turn onto Main Cross Street, and after he passed us, we turned left, going in the opposite direction from where he was headed, but I asked my Mom to pull over in front of the Post Office by Great Scot, so I could see where he was going. Anyway, our station wagon has a really big back window, and as I looked out the back, it looked like instead of continuing on towards the interstate, Julian had instead put on his brakes and turned into the cemetery."

"Why would he go to the cemetery at night?" Jennie asked. "That's creepy."

"That's what I wondered," said Sneak. "Now, I knew I could have been wrong in seeing him turn – the cemetery's a long way from where our car was – but, I was using my binoculars and there weren't any other cars behind him. I thought for sure it was his car that turned into the cemetery. And that's when it hit me. He had to be going there for a reason...."

"He could have been paying his respects," Uncle Charlie added.

"Yes, but it was cold and dark, and the best explanation that I could think of was that he was going there for a dead letter drop....to get information about the next fire! At that point I pleaded with my

Mom to turn around and go towards the cemetery to catch him, but she said we were already late for Choir practice."

"Oh yeah," Jennie added. "I remember that. It's too bad we couldn't catch him on my birthday."

"Bummer," Moscow commiserated. "But those cupcakes were good."

"Well," Sneak continued. "Just like I thought, that night there was another fire. And the next morning...."

"There was a *Letter to the Editor* from Julian!" Hailey finished.

"Yep," Sneak persisted. "He must have dropped off his letter to the newspaper just before going to work that night."

"The newspaper's office isn't very far from the cemetery," Lisa noted.

"Right!" Hailey said encouragingly.

"So how can we catch him?" I asked.

"Well, that's what I tried to do," explained Sneak. "After seeing him that night at the end of February, I felt like I knew their schedule. I knew they wouldn't set a fire on the weekend..."

"Why's that?" Jennie asked.

"Because the paper has a limited edition on Saturday and doesn't come out on Sunday."

"That makes sense," Lisa said. "Cressida noticed that the fires were only during the week."

"Yep," Sneak replied, as Cressida nervously smiled.

"Nice job cousin," Lisa said as she patted her cousin on the back.

"So what I did next," Sneak continued, "was, I got Julian's work schedule..."

"Oh brother," Uncle Charlie said again.

"Well, that makes sense," Hailey mentioned. "Because the next fire would have to be on a night that Julian worked, so he would have an alibi."

"Right," Sneak agreed. "And I found out he was off on the weekends, but working every night during the week from eight to midnight. So, that's why I waited at the cemetery for two weeks."

"For two weeks?" Joel asked surprised.

"Well, it wasn't like I waited all night for two weeks straight, it was just between seven and eight o'clock."

"How did you decide on that?" Lisa asked.

"Well, for my seven o'clock *start* time...that was about the time I saw Julian going into the cemetery on the night of Jennie's birthday. I figured he would want to wait until at least seven o'clock so it was dark and nobody else was around. And for the eight o'clock *end* time, I knew he'd need time to pick up the note from the arsonist, write his own Letter to the Editor with some hints about the fire in it, then drop off his letter at the newspaper office and still get to work at the movie theater. Like you mentioned

Lisa, it would only take him a few minutes to get from the cemetery to the newspaper office. Then a few minutes to write his own letter and drop it off and then a few more minutes to get out to the theater. So he'd need to be at the cemetery at least by seven forty-five or so, to be able to make the cut off time at the newspaper and then, if he showed up a few minutes late at the movie theater for work nobody would probably notice."

"This story is amazing," Joel said astonished.

I felt my heart beating faster and faster – feeling nervous and excited – as Sneak told us more and more about the mystery. *It's a real case*, I thought. *This is a real mystery and there's a real bad guy out there and I am going to help catch him. I can't believe I'm doing this.*

In talking with the other detectives afterwards, they told me that they also had thoughts and feelings that were similar to mine. One of them said she kept thinking, *I can't believe I'm really doing this. This is so exciting!*

"Well, I guess that about sums up what I know so far," Sneak concluded. "As Uncle Charlie mentioned, you can decide to take the case or not take the case. It's funny to think that after I meet with my parents in a little bit, I won't be able to do any detective work for a while."

"I think it would be good for you to take a break," his uncle said.

"I don't think it will be very good," Sneak responded dejectedly.

We were silent for a moment.

"So, like I said earlier, I'm your client," said Sneak. "…if you choose to take the case for me."

"Wow, it just seems so weird that *we're* the detectives and *you're* the client?" Moscow replied to his friend. "That's crazy."

"It doesn't seem possible," I added.

"It's going to be really hard to do this without you," Lisa confessed.

"Well, I'm going to go and talk to my parents now," Sneak said as he moved from the chalkboard. He took several steps towards the door, but suddenly stopped and turned back to look at Hailey who was still seated behind his metal desk. "Oh, I guess I forgot to mention it," he added. "I asked Hailey if she'd be willing to lead the group. I think she'd be great, and she said yes."

"Alright!" Joel replied with a smile.

The girls nodded in approval.

"Hey, hold on," Moscow interjected. "Just wait a minute."

"What do you want me to wait on?" Sneak asked.

"I think we should vote on it," Moscow said dramatically. "Just because Sneak says that Hailey should be the President – or whatever – doesn't mean that it's a good idea….I mean, he's not even going to be around to see how she's doing."

"Well, I might be around...," Sneak began.

"Sneak, you're not going to be around," Jennie interrupted. "Mom and Dad are definitely going to ground you for a really long time when you tell them what you did at the cemetery."

"I don't think President is what I'll be called," Hailey explained to her brother.

"Okay Moscow," Sneak continued looking up at his friend. "Even though I'm not going to be around, I still think Hailey would make a good leader of the agency. She's trustworthy and dependable. Plus, she tries to get things done."

"Plus she likes to talk to people," I added, thinking of the many times I had witnessed Sneak lost in thought – like he had been two nights before at Children's Choir – melancholy and moody, unable to interact with others, his mind focused solely on solving a case. Hailey, I knew, wasn't like that at all, she was friendly and smiled a lot and would encourage us as we did our detective work. I thought Hailey would make a great leader of our group. And I was not alone.

"Well, I think Hailey would be great," Joel declared.

"I do too," added Lisa. "Hailey and I talked about it on the phone last night. She's got a lot going on – with the Academic Quiz Team and the Science Fair coming up – but she thinks she'll have time for this too."

"Alright then," Uncle Charlie interjected. "I've got to get out of here to get my lunch, so let's put it to a vote."

"Surely *we* won't vote?" Professor Telson asked Uncle Charlie with a surprised look.

"No, we're just *The Advisors*," he said making quotes with his fingers. "I meant the kids can put it to a vote."

"Oh good," Professor Telson responded.

"Alright then," Uncle Charlie said. "All those in favor of Hailey Cotton becoming the leader of this…. this…"

"Detective Agency," Sneak explained.

"The Sunday School Detectives," Jennie interjected. "We all know each other from Sunday School, so that's what I think we should be called."

"I like the sound of that," said Joel.

"Me too," Lisa agreed.

Cressida turned and whispered something in her cousin's ear. "We both do," Lisa added.

"Okay," said Uncle Charlie. "All those in favor of Hailey Cotton becoming the leader of *The Sunday School Detectives* say 'aye'."

"Aye," many of us shouted.

"I ask for a Roll Call vote," Moscow added.

"Alright," Uncle Charlie grimaced. "Someone has been watching too much *School House Rock*,"

We laughed.

"All of those in favor of Hailey Cotton being the leader of The Sunday School Detectives, raise your right hand." Uncle Charlie first looked over at me in the corner with my hand raised. "Pep, that's one vote." Then he turned his attention to Joel and Jennie who were sitting in folding chairs near his chair. "Joel, that makes two votes for and Jennie makes three."

Next, Uncle Charlie looked at the three girls who were sitting on the bench across from the desk. Not remembering all of their names, he simply said, "Girls, you're all raising your hands, so that's three more votes. So the total is six. Six votes in favor."

"I'm for it," Sneak said, with his hand raised.

"Okay, that's seven."

"Wait a minute. Sneak shouldn't get to vote," Moscow complained. "He's not even going to be in the group."

"Maybe eventually I will," Sneak said hopefully. "And maybe I can answer some questions to help you out while I'm grounded."

"I've really got to get going," Uncle Charlie said impatiently.

"He should get half a vote," Moscow replied.

"Okay, fine. Six and a half for Hailey," Uncle Charlie added.

"How about you Hailey? Will you vote for yourself?"

"Sure," Hailey said with a laugh. "I told Sneak I'd give it a try."

"Okay that's seven and a half votes for Hailey. How about you, Moscow?" Uncle Charlie asked.

"I've got my hand raised up here," Hailey's brother said from above us.

"You're voting for her after all of the fuss you've made?" Michelle asked incredulously.

"Well sure," Moscow replied with a smile from his wooden perch. "She's my sister."

CHAPTER 30

"Okay, the ayes have it," Uncle Charlie summarized. "Congratulations to Hailey on being the leader of this motley bunch."

"*The Sunday School Detectives*," Jennie corrected.

"...The Sunday School Detectives," said Uncle Charlie.

"Alright Hailey!" Michelle said as she gave a thumbs up to her older friend.

"Good luck!" I heard someone say. "You're going to need it," someone else added.

Many of us were congratulating Hailey as Sneak walked passed us on his way to the side door of the garage. He was only moments away from leaving, with his fingers on the door handle, when he was stopped by a question from Lisa.

"So Sneak," Lisa asked, over the chatter of other voices. "There's one thing I don't understand. If you caught Julian getting a note from the arsonist at the cemetery, why didn't the police arrest him?"

We were all suddenly silent once again, as we awaited Sneak's answer.

"Ah, that's a good question, isn't it Sneak?" Uncle Charlie replied loudly. "Why didn't we arrest Joel..."

"Hey!" Joel said, with a concerned look on his face, hearing Uncle Charlie mistake his name for the name of the prime suspect.

"...I mean Julian, sorry Joel. Julian Davis," Uncle Charlie clarified. "So Sneak, who exactly did you see at the cemetery?"

"It was Julian Davis," Sneak said adamantly.

"So, you got a good look at him?" his uncle asked with a serious look on his face as he began interrogating his nephew.

"Well, no, I didn't get a clear look at his face, he was wearing a big winter coat that blocked my view," Sneak said. "But it was him."

"Well, at least you got the license number from his car...while you were holding onto his bumper?"

"No."

"Then, you had to have gotten the make and model of the car, right? You were right there, almost wedged between the tailpipe and the back tire."

"No, it was too dark."

"So, at least you got the note from the arsonist he allegedly grabbed from the cemetery that night, right? That would at least be a basis for the police to question him."

"No, I couldn't reach it, his car was moving too fast."

"So you got nothing," Uncle Charlie said bluntly. "You put your life at risk, for what? You couldn't establish the identity of the person you were chasing...or even the car he was driving."

"But it had to have been him. Logically it doesn't make sense for it to be anybody else."

Uncle Charlie turned to the rest of the group, after scolding his nephew. "See kids, this is why you want to be careful not to get involved in an ongoing police investigation. Let the police handle it."

"Just like Rockford," Jennie added.

"What?" her uncle asked.

"Jim Rockford will lose his detective's license if he gets in the way of an open police investigation," Jennie explained in a serious tone.

We laughed at Jennie's solemn explanation.

"Right, right," her uncle said as the laughter continued. "Wow, I really need to talk to your Mom about the T.V. shows you're watching. Anyway," her uncle continued addressing the entire group. "Now, everyone here certainly has the Constitutional right to organize into a group, to meet together, to talk about a case and share your ideas. Those rights are guaranteed under our Constitution and I'm sworn to protect them – you'll learn more about that when you learn about the Bill of Rights in school..."

"Uncle Charlie we know a lot about the Bill of Rights already," Jennie interrupted, "we have *School House Rock.*"

"I'm just a Bill…" Joel sang attempting a low baritone voice.

We laughed as Joel continued singing.

"You just need to know, that you can get yourselves in trouble – big trouble – if you get involved in an open police investigation. Sneak could have really hurt himself by chasing that guy – whoever it was."

A few of us mumbled in agreement.

"Plus, he didn't even get the information that he needed. I can't arrest someone, or bring someone in for questioning, just because he *probably* was at a cemetery at night or just because logically it couldn't be anybody else."

"Well, it was past closing time at the cemetery," Sneak added. "You could have got him for that."

"Have you listened to one thing I've been saying?" his uncle said loudly. "I need proof! And you should have let the police handle it!"

We were silent for a moment.

"Kids," Uncle Charlie continued. "If you think you know something about a case you need to go to a trained professional. Don't try to get the evidence yourself. Don't try to chase the suspect. Don't try to interfere with what the police are doing. You know how to reach us right? We're at…"

"424 – 7150," we chanted, from the memorization drills given by our teachers in school to remember the police department's phone number.

"Or, if you forget that number you can always...."

"Dial zero for the Operator," Jennie added.

"Right!" Uncle Charlie replied.

"I did see his brown parka," Sneak added gloomily. "But I didn't see his face."

"You can end up causing a lot of problems if you do stuff on your own," Uncle Charlie continued his lecture, seeming not to hear his nephew. "If you think you've discovered any new information about this case or any other case – *please* just give me a call."

We were silent for another moment.

"Well, I'm going to get going," Uncle Charlie said as he stood and put on his winter coat. "Marie's got those Vietnamese noodles waiting for me...if the kids haven't eaten them all by now!"

"Say hey to the kids for me!" Jennie replied loudly, in reference to her two small cousins – Uncle Charlie and Aunt Marie's kids – who were a few years younger.

"Yeah, say 'hi' for me too," Sneak added.

"Will do," their Uncle Charlie said as he walked passed his nephew and opened the side door to the garage, letting in a cold burst of winter wind. "See ya' kids. Remember to call me if you find anything!"

"I'm going to go too," Sneak explained. "I told Mom and Dad that I'd see them after we met."

"See ya' Sneak." I replied. "I hope it's not too bad for you."

"Hang in there," Hailey said with an encouraging smile. "The hard part will be over soon."

"Not doing investigations will be hard," Sneak replied dejectedly. "It will seem like an eternity."

"We'll take care of things here," Joel told his friend with a reassuring look. "Don't worry about the case."

CHAPTER 31

Professor Telson stood when Uncle Charlie and Sneak left the garage. "Well, I'm not exactly sure why I was invited," the professor said after rising from his folding chair. "It certainly has been an interesting morning. I'll be praying that you get the answers to the mystery of those crop circles."

"Wait professor," Hailey said quickly – the first of many times she led our discussion. "Could you stay for a few more minutes? Sneak thought you could serve as an advisor to our group – because you had been so helpful when he met you at your office yesterday."

"Really?" the professor asked, surprised. "I guess I didn't realize I was all that helpful."

"You were, professor," Hailey replied. "Do you remember what you said to him?"

"Well, I think it might be best if my conversation with Sneak remain confidential."

"Oh no," Hailey insisted. "Sneak wanted everyone to know what you talked about."

"He did?" the professor asked with a laugh and another surprised look.

"He was hoping you could tell us the same things you told him."

"Well," the professor said before pausing, "that's going to be a bit of a problem." And then the professor then let out a booming laugh.

"Why is that?" Hailey asked. "What's the problem?"

"It's because I can't remember exactly what I told him!" The professor chuckled loudly. "I can be a bit of an absent-minded professor at times!"

"Oh, that's okay," Hailey said as she quickly looked at her notebook. "He told me there were three things you talked about and I wrote them down."

"Ah, that's good. That's very good," the professor replied as he returned to the folding chair.

"Sneak said the three main things were: presumptions, the faithfulness of God and working with other people."

"Ah, well, that sounds about right."

"Could you talk about those things?" Hailey asked.

"Sure," the professor replied. "Absolutely. Now what was the first thing? See how absent minded I am!"

"Presumptions."

"Well Hailey," the professor explained. "The word I probably used was *presuppositions.*"

"Pre-what!" Moscow asked, as he and the rest of the group gave the professor confused looks.

"Presupposition is the technical term I probably used – I use it quite a lot."

"What does it mean?" Hailey asked.

"Well, presuppositions are those foundational beliefs people hold to be true about God or their lives."

"And what does that mean, professor?" Lisa asked quizzically.

"Well everyone – not just Christians – holds some basic beliefs about life and God. For example, as Christians, we *presuppose* – or assume – that the Bible is true. That's one of our most basic and important beliefs. In Church you might have heard your teachers say that the Bible is inspired, and inerrant and infallible. We use those words to describe our belief – our presupposition – that the Bible is God's Word. Like the apostle Paul, we believe that Scripture is 'God breathed'."

"I think I've heard that before," said Jennie with a smile.

"I'm glad you have," the professor replied.

"Me too," Jennie said.

"Me three," Michelle added.

"What's interesting," the professor continued. "Is that God uses the Bible to shape our beliefs."

"Like what?" Lisa asked.

"Well, for example, the Bible presumes God's existence, declaring that God is living and true. It explains that He is Lord and is active in His creation and takes the initiative in reconciling and restoring people to Himself."

"That's cool," I heard Joel say.

"Yeah, definitely," the professor agreed. "But that's not all, there are lots of other descriptions of God in the Bible, describing how He is faithful and good, loving, kind and holy – among other things."

"So, the Bible helps us grow in our understanding of God," Hailey summarized.

"Right!" said the professor.

"I'm starting to get it now," Lisa said. "So basically, would you say that for Christians, we pre....we presume that there's a God, but non-Christians don't?"

"Well, I think you are essentially correct," Professor Telson replied. "For Christians, one of our basic assumptions – a fundamental presupposition, if you will – is that God is real and is Lord over all things. That description of God in the Bible – as Lord, full of power and might and glory are all things described in the Bible and are characteristics that – as Christians – we think are important to understand. For non-Christians, I'd say it's a little more complicated, but you're essentially right, if you asked them about their fundamental beliefs, they would say that their basic presupposition is that there isn't a God, and therefore life is caused by impersonal forces."

"It seems pretty easy to me," said Lisa. "They believe basically the opposite of what Christians believe, right? We presume there is a God and they presume there isn't a God. So why do you say it's complicated for non-Christians?"

"Well," the professor began with a laugh. "That may take some time to explain, but in a nutshell, here's why: they live in God's world, but they deny it."

"What?" I asked, confused.

"That doesn't make any sense," Moscow said from the wooden platform.

"Well, with most non-Christians, at least those who are atheists," the professor continued, "they'd say that because there is no God, life's causes are due to impersonal forces like matter, motion, time or chance."

"So just random things?" Lisa asked.

"Right!" Professor Telson said. "Without a Lord who governs all things, they would say that life starts and ends or happens all because of random chance – maybe it's because of a bunch of molecules colliding, or energy eroding…things like that."

"Hmm," I replied.

"But here's the point I was trying to make about non-Christians – and why it's complicated – even though they say they hold the view that God does not exist, they actually don't act from that presupposition."

"So they say it," Joel stated. "But they don't really believe it?"

"That's one way of putting it," the professor explained. "What I find, is that non-Christians actually make assumptions about life that are much more in line with what Christians believe – instead of their own non-Christian views. So in effect, they're actually borrowing a bunch of our beliefs and then denying that they've done it!"

"What do you mean by that?" Lisa asked, intrigued by the professor's conversation.

"Well...let me give you a few examples." The professor paused for a moment to think of examples that we would find helpful. "So, let's think about math for a few minutes," he began.

"Math?" Moscow complained. "On a Saturday?"

"Math might help you figure out the angles for your next stunt!" Lisa joked.

"Oh, well then, I'm all ears!" Moscow replied.

"We're not going to get too complicated," the professor said with a laugh as he walked to the chalkboard and wrote the equation: $2 + 2 = 4$, in an empty space, away from Sneak's notes about the case. "So, if I were to ask you the question, '*Does two plus two equal four?*' How would you reply?"

"Yes," Michelle replied quickly. "I would reply by saying 'yes'. Two plus two equals four."

Jennie smiled and gave a thumbs up sign to her friend.

"Okay," the professor said, "Does everyone agree with..."

"Michelle," Jennie's friend said.

"Right," the professor continued. "Does everyone agree with Michelle?"

Most of us muttered 'yes' or 'yeah' in agreement.

"Okay, so we're in Ohio," the professor continued.

"Last time I checked," Moscow said sarcastically, as several of us laughed.

"Okay, well, how about in Oklahoma? Does two plus two equal four in Oklahoma?" the professor asked.

"Yes," a couple people answered with a laugh. "Sure," I said.

"How about in Canada? Does two plus two equal four there?" the professor asked.

"Yes, two plus two equals four in Canada," Michelle said with a giggle.

"Okay, now how about on Pluto?" the professor questioned. "That planet is pretty far away. Does two plus two equal four there?"

A few of us laughed as Lisa replied, "Of course it does, professor."

"I could go on and on like this with different places, but you get the gist of it. What you're telling me is that this mathematical formula is true every-where, right?"

"Right," someone replied.

"So we might call it a *universal truth*, is everyone okay with calling it that?"

"Sure," someone answered, as the professor wrote the words ***Universal Truth*** on the chalkboard next to the formula. "What's interesting," the professor continued. "Is that both Christians and non-Christians would agree with all of those statements that you all just agreed to, right? Non-Christians would agree with you that *two plus two equals four* in Ohio and in Oklahoma and in Canada and on Pluto and throughout the universe, right?"

"I think so," Joel replied.

"So, here's another one," the professor continued. "How about an ethical issue, like hitting your sister?"

"Are you listening to this Moscow?" Hailey said looking up at her brother.

"You want me to hit my sister?" Moscow asked, pretending not to pay attention.

"No, no," the professor smiled.

"I wish Sneak was here for this," Jennie added.

"And my brother Brad too," Lisa commented.

"Sneak really doesn't hit me," Jennie confessed. "He just says mean things sometimes."

"Okay," the professor continued, "So would we say that it is wrong for brothers to hit their sisters here in Ohio?"

"Yes," Michelle was the first to say.

"And what about in Oklahoma?" the professor asked. "Is it wrong there?"

"Yes," a few replied.

"And how aboot in Canada?" the professor questioned, laughing as he tried to sound Canadian. "Is it wrong for brothers to hit their sisters if they lived there?"

"Yes," many replied with a laugh.

"Okay, how about in space. What planet did we use earlier?"

"Pluto," Hailey answered.

"Right, Pluto," the professor continued. "Is it wrong for brothers to slug their sisters in the arm on Pluto?'

"No," answered Jennie. "I mean yes, it's wrong."

"So, could we say that this is another universal truth, just like our math problem of two plus two?" the professor asked as he pointed to the words **Universal Truth** written on the chalkboard.

"Well, yeah, I guess so," Moscow replied.

"Yeah," said Michelle.

"I think so too," the professor said. "It's fair to say that in both of these examples, we're talking about things that are universally true. The math equation is true wherever you are, just like ethically, it's wrong for brothers to hit their sisters wherever they are. And again, everything we've talked about – all of those statements – would be agreed upon by both Christians and non-Christians."

"I would hope so!" Lisa exclaimed. "I don't want my brother to hit me – whatever he believes about God!"

We laughed.

"Okay," the professor continued, "Here's one more example, my last one – this is one that I shared with Sneak yesterday. How would you respond to this statement, true or false: *Other people's minds are like mine.*"

"So, you're wondering if *other people's minds are like mine*?" Joel clarified.

"Yes," the professor answered. "Would you agree or disagree with that statement?"

"Are other minds like mine?" Michelle wondered.

"Well, Moscow's mind is definitely not like mine!" Jennie said with a laugh as she looked up at her friend. "He does some really crazy things sometimes."

"Hey!" Moscow said looking straight down – his feet dangling high above Jennie who was sitting nearly directly below him. "Remember, what goes up must come down."

"What goes up….," Joel immediately sang in a funky, soulful voice. The words were from the pop song *Spinning Wheel* by the band *Blood, Sweat and Tears.*

"…must come down," a number of us joined him.

Joel continued singing more lyrics from the song, but the rest of us did not know the words.

"Okay, let's focus," Hailey chided the group. "Come on guys."

"So," the professor said as the cacophony of voices brought their singing and laughter to an end. "If we think about the statement, '*Other people have minds like mine',* I'm asking if you would agree that other people have minds that can think and reason like you can? Or, are other people's minds different?"

"Well sure they're basically the same," Lisa answered while a few others answered in agreement. "I mean basically, other people have minds that can think like mine," she added. "With, you know, some exceptions."

"Like Moscow's," Jennie said with a laugh as she looked up at her daredevil friend, who gave a brief scowl before smiling widely.

"Okay, okay," the professor replied with a laugh. "So, everyone agrees with that? That *other people have minds like mine.*"

"Yes," a few of us said.

"So, that would be true if we were together in Oklahoma or some other place?"

"Yeah," I heard someone say.

"So, would this also be a universal truth?" The professor asked as he pointed to the chalkboard.

"Yeah," some said in agreement.

"I think so too," he explained. "If you didn't hold the assumption that you can reason and think with other people, you'd have a hard time doing your detective work with each other, wouldn't you!"

"Right," I heard someone agree.

"And again," the professor continued. "It's interesting to note that the statement – *'Other people's minds are like mine'* – is something that both non-Christians and Christians would agree on. Both groups would say that we can reason together, that we can work with others to figure things out, because our minds are similar in many ways, right?"

"Right," Moscow said from the wooden platform. "But, how does this have anything to do with the differences between Christians and non-Christians?"

"Great question," the professor said. "And this is how I'll tie it in with our earlier discussion about why non-Christian views are complicated." He paused for a moment. "For Christians, in each of our examples, we would say that these universal truths show us something about a God who is Lord of the...."

"Universe?" Hailey hesitantly interrupted.

"Exactly!" Professor Telson exclaimed. "If there is a God who is Lord of the universe, it makes sense that in each of these areas we've looked at – like math and ethics and knowledge – there would be universal truth!"

"Hmm, that actually makes a lot of sense," Lisa affirmed.

"I'm glad you think so," the professor replied with a smile. "As Christians, we would say that these universal truths reflect God's wisdom and planning and thought and care."

"So not hitting your sister," Lisa summarized, "teaches us about God?"

"Right," the professor replied as a few of us giggled at the thought that prohibitions against hitting a sibling might help us learn about the Lord of the Universe. "Here's what I would argue," the professor said seriously. "Things in creation are a reflection of the Creator."

"Hmmm," Lisa said.

"I'm reminded of Paul's description," said Professor Telson. "That the 'invisible things of him from the creation of the world are clearly seen'."

"So what about non-Christians?" Moscow wondered. "What's up with them?"

"Ah, that's where it gets interesting...."

"Why's that?" Hailey asked.

"Well, what's interesting is that it seems to me that their beliefs are really inconsistent. Do you remember what I said earlier? For non-Christians, their fundamental assumption – at least what they'd say – is that life is caused or ended by impersonal forces like matter, motion, time and chance. So, your birth, or the birth of your friends, or the beginning of the universe or the earth...it's all just happenstance, it was just multiple molecules colliding together to make that happen. Or, when you die, it's just a random chance – you were just unlucky."

"That doesn't sound too good," I replied.

"Well, no it doesn't," said the professor. "But, what's really interesting is when you take their fundamental presupposition of random, impersonal forces and compare that with their other beliefs, like their use of universal truth in math or ethics…"

"Like how it's wrong for brothers to hit their sisters," Jennie added.

"Right," the professor continued. "…and their ideas about knowledge – how other people's minds are like their own, it doesn't stack up."

"How's that?" Michelle asked.

"Well, if life really were a series of random chances of molecules and electrons colliding, as they would have us believe, then it seems incredible that multiple minds would be similar enough to engage in logic – to figure out answers to really big questions, like the mysteries you will be doing! Can you imagine the odds of that happening?"

"Hmm," I heard Moscow say above us.

"Or having universal laws of math and science," the professor continued. "It seems incredible that would be the case. If the world were really random chance events, it seems like a lot of other things would be random too. Why wouldn't answers to math questions be different in different places? Or, ethical issues? If things in life really are random, why did we all agree that those things were universally true?"

"I can see your point," someone said.

"So again," the professor continued. "When you look at the beliefs of non-Christians, there seems to be a real inconsistency there. And that's what I meant when I said they are borrowing from us. Their views really don't support how things actually work in this world, so they need to borrow from Christians – but they usually won't admit to that."

"Wow, that is really interesting," Moscow added from his seat above us.

A few of us agreed.

"So again, for Christians," the professor concluded, "we'd say that all of these facts we've been talking about – like our minds being similar, so that people can reason together and figure things out – are facts in creation that point to a loving and wise Creator. It's really a miracle – if you think about it – that we're not all completely different from each other. But because of God's love and mercy, He allows us to work together to try to figure things out."

"That makes lots of sense to me," Hailey replied. "So, is what you're talking about, Professor Telson, similar to the idea that because God is wise, we can be wise too? We talked about that one time in Sunday School."

"Well, that's an interesting point," the professor answered as he sat on Sneak's desk. "It's not exactly the point I was making, but it's a good point to think about. The Bible explains that people are made in God's image. So, it makes sense that there would be some similarities between the attributes of God and the attributes of His creation. In theology, we sometimes call these the *communicable* attributes of God. These are things like love and mercy – and, like you mentioned – wisdom and knowledge. These are all God's attributes that He lets people have, although not fully or perfectly, of course, like they could be described of God."

"Nice, Hailey," Moscow added, smiling down at his sister.

"Then there are," the professor continued, "other attributes of God that could never be described of people – like being infinite or all-knowing or self-sufficient. Those would be attributes of the Creator but not His creation."

"But, I don't get it," Lisa began. "I mean, I get what you are saying and it makes sense, but what I don't get is how non-Christians don't believe what we believe. If Christians and non-Christians think that a lot of the same things are true, why doesn't everyone believe in God?"

"That's a great question," the professor said encouragingly. "And I've thought a lot about that myself. The best answer I've seen can be found in the Bible."

"That's not a surprise," Moscow added from above us.

"You're right, I find a lot of things in the Bible!" the professor replied with a laugh. "What Scripture says in regards to that question, is that non-Christians suppress the truth about God."

"What do you mean by 'suppress'?" Lisa asked.

"Well, the image in the Bible is that they push it down. They repress the truth of living in God's world – that's the sense you get when you read something like Romans chapter one."

"That's pretty wild to think about," Moscow chimed in.

"It is, it is. And it makes it challenging for us as Christians to try to understand. You see, the Bible doesn't just say that God is some ethereal ghost, or a cloud out-there-somewhere, or some unknowable force in the sky. Instead, the Bible says that God is *Lord*. That word, Lord, is used several thousand times in the Bible. And we learn that He's not just Lord over a few of the things in His creation, but He's described as being Lord over *all things*. Everything is under His Lordship. That means He is governing and ruling everything. As Lord, He's described as our Creator, Sustainer and Redeemer. So, God is actively involved in His Creation – sustaining us, redeeming us, uniting people with Christ."

"That's cool," I said.

"Definitely," Jennie replied.

"So for non-Christians," Hailey summarized. "They're living in a world where God is Lord, but acting like He isn't."

"That's it!" the professor said.

We were quiet for a moment as we reflected on the professor's ideas.

"So," the professor concluded. "I guess that's it on the subject of presuppositions, at least for now."

"So is that stuff mostly helpful to know about when we're talking to non-Christians?" Moscow asked from the wooden platform.

"Well, it definitely can be helpful when you're talking to non-Christians," the professor replied. "But, I think presuppositions are pretty important for Christians to understand too. I'd encourage you to look at your own beliefs about life and God. Maybe ask yourself, '*What authority am I trusting to hold those assumptions?*' For Christians, like I explained earlier, it's important that our assumptions be guided by God's Word – that's our Standard for Truth, so to speak. So asking yourself questions about your beliefs can be helpful." He paused for a moment. "Plus, understanding your assumptions can even be helpful with your detective skills, too."

"How's that?" Joel asked.

"Well, I think it would be important for you to look at your assumptions when you're making deductions about a case," the professor said as he pointed to Sneak's drawing on the chalkboard with the words "Investigate" and "Deductions" and the arrow between the two words.

"What do you mean?" Lisa asked.

"So let's say you assumed at the start of a case that an accused person is guilty. That assumption would influence your choices and decisions as you're gathering evidence and making deductions about what happened."

"That makes sense," Hailey replied.

"In my *Philosophy of Religion* course, I talk about this very thing and use the example of swans."

"Swans?" Cressida asked. "Like the ugly duckling?"

"Well, we don't use that story," Professor Telson replied.

"What about swans?" Michelle asked.

"You probably won't be surprised," the professor explained, "but I ask my students a question –about swans."

"Do two swans plus two swans equal four swans?" Lisa asked with a laugh. "…in Oklahoma?"

"Do all swans have minds like mine?" Moscow asked.

We laughed at Lisa and Moscow's questions – while the professor laughed the loudest at their funny remarks.

"No, no. I don't ask them *those* questions," he said. "I ask them the question, '*Are all swans white?*' and they usually answer by saying something like 'Yes, all swans are white.'"

"That's the right answer, right?" Jennie asked.

"How does this have anything to do with solving a mystery?" Moscow asked.

"Well, let's say you were working on a case about a missing swan," the professor continued. "And, when you took the case, you believed that all swans were white. During your investigation, you'd probably make all sorts of deductions about the swan you were looking for, based on your assumption that all swans were white, right?"

"Right," several of us replied.

"But you'd be in for a big surprise," the professor continued, "...if I told you that there are black swans in Australia."

"There are black swans?" Jennie asked, surprised.

"Yes," the professor added. "I've never seen one, but I've read about them."

"Wow, that's cool." Moscow replied as he looked down at the professor from the wooden storage platform.

"Back when I was learning Latin in school – many years ago," the professor continued with a chuckle, "We had to memorize a phrase about a black swan, '*rara avis in terris nigroque simillima cygno.*'"

"What does that mean?" Moscow asked.

"A rare bird, very much like a black swan," he said reflectively translating the ancient quote.

"Yeah," someone said.

"So, for your investigations," the professor continued. "It might be helpful to ask, 'What are my assumptions about this mystery? What do I think is true?'"

"We could write that on the board," Lisa suggested.

"Or, just in our notebooks," Hailey replied quickly – knowing that our meeting would need to conclude within a few minutes.

"So, what were the other things on your list Hailey?" Professor Telson asked as he prepared to move on to the next topic. "I'm sorry, I feel like I've talked about that first topic for a really long time."

"The faithfulness of God," she read from her notebook. "And working with others."

"Ah, right, so Sneak had some interesting questions for me when we met yesterday. Essentially he was asking, 'How could God be good, when all of these bad things seemed to be happening to him?' For Sneak, specifically, he knows he is a great detective – and we'd all agree on that, right?"

"Oh yeah," Joel replied.

"So, he was wondering," the professor explained. "Why would a good God take him away from walking in his God-given gifts as a detective and let him be grounded by his parents?"

"Wow, that's a tough question," I replied. "I've wondered about stuff like that before."

"I have too," the professor said. "Well, there's no easy answer to the question, but, the answer I would point to – and what I told Sneak yesterday – is that even in the midst of difficulty, God is faithful. I can say that with confidence because that's who God's revealed Himself to be in...where do you think Moscow?"

"The Bible?"

"Indeed! There are a lot of passages in the Bible that describe God's love and faithfulness to His people. I gave a few verses for Sneak to read this week. Many passages explain how we can take refuge in God – like someone seeking shelter from a storm. I'm praying that Sneak can find some peace and strength from God during this time."

"That's good," Jennie replied. "But what about the bad stuff? It doesn't seem fair that Sneak can't be a detective anymore because of his mistakes."

"Well, I know it doesn't seem fair," the professor replied. "But what we see in the..."

"Bible," Moscow replied.

"Yes!" the professor said with a smile. "...is that sometimes people suffer. It's a really hard message to understand – and to explain, quite frankly. But, sometimes our outward circumstances don't always seem very good. Sometimes really bad things happen to us and to our friends. Sometimes we feel sad and sometimes we suffer consequences due to the things we've done or things that other people have done to us."

The professor paused for a moment.

"So, I guess I would suggest a couple things to keep in mind. The first, is not to think that God is punishing us when bad things happen. If you remember from…" the professor paused as he looked up at Moscow.

"…the Bible," Moscow added.

"Correct!" said the professor. "Because Jesus has taken the punishment for our sin, we shouldn't feel like God is punishing us."

"That is really cool," I replied.

"Yes, it is," the professor added. "So it's not punishment, but we can try to learn some things during those times we're suffering."

"Like what?" someone asked.

"Well, like our dependence on God. One of the things I'm often reminded of when I'm suffering, is that I really need God and I'm not justified by my own performance."

"What does that mean?" Moscow asked.

"Well, so often we think that God will do things for us based on our own performance – if we are just good boys or girls, we think God is obligated to act a certain way towards us. But, God, as He's described in the…"

"Bible," Moscow added.

"…isn't like that. He's not like some talisman…"

"Talis-what?" Moscow asked.

"He's not like a lucky charm that you rub and get something good from," the professor explained. I winced a little as I heard this comment, because I carried a silver cross in my pocket and rubbed it and said a prayer before taking tests in school. "God's not like a gumball machine, where you put a penny in and a spiritual blessing comes out," the professor informed us.

"I think they cost a nickel now," Moscow added.

"Okay a nickel," the professor replied with a laugh. "You can't just put in a spiritual nickel and make God do something you want Him to do. In my seminary class, I have my students read the Old Testament to learn how other gods in the Ancient Near East were worshipped. And what I just described to you was essentially what people *outside* of Israel believed. They thought that if they did something, like bring an offering or a sacrifice to their idol, then their god would do something for them. One of their practices was to build a wooden idol called an Asherah pole."

"Ash... what?" Joel asked. "I've never heard of that."

"Me neither," Lisa said.

"It's in the Old Testament – mostly in *Kings* and *Chronicles*," the professor explained. "...but it's written about throughout the Old Testament – from Exodus to Micah. Anyway, it was used by religions outside of Israel. And God got really upset when the Israelites put the poles up in their towns. The common practice – according to most scholars – was for a person to approach the pole and ask the idol for something, then the person would promise to either bring something to the idol or do something for it."

"So, it was a pole – like a telephone pole?" Moscow asked. "They worshipped a telephone pole?"

"Gee," Jennie said.

"No G-T-E!" Joel replied as we all laughed loudly at Joel's reference to the computer and long-distance telephone company.

"Good one," Michelle added, smiling at Joel.

"'Cause it's like a telephone pole!" Jennie said.

"Well, we don't know exactly what it looked like," the professor continued, still smiling after he ended his laughter. "I guess it could have been as tall as a telephone pole. What we do in our class is to compare that religious approach, to the practices that are described in the Bible. In the New Testament, you probably know, God used pieces of wood in a really different way. Your Sunday School teachers have probably explained that the Cross where Christ died was likely fashioned from two pieces of wood. The way he was killed – called crucifixion – was a common way to put people to death in the Roman Empire."

"Yeah," came a few somber voices.

"We learn in the Bible that it was on the Cross that Jesus suffered and died – not just for a random reason – but for our sins. So, what we do in my class is compare these two very different approaches – one with the idol of the Asherah pole, supposedly giving blessing because of how people performed, and the other, the Cross, where Jesus gave great blessing because of what *He* did." The professor paused. Then he added, "It's because we couldn't save ourselves that Jesus, in His great love, made a way for us to be saved – by dying on the Cross in our place."

"That's cool," I heard someone say.

"So I say all this for a couple of reasons," the professor added. "One, is that as Christians when we suffer and feel sadness, we can know that our Savior – Jesus – knows what it's like to suffer and feel sadness too. He felt those same things, like the book of Hebrews explains, we have a High Priest who we can turn to for help. And do you remember what I said before?"

"About what part?" Moscow asked.

"The part where I said that God is faithful. How we are encouraged in the…"

"…Bible," Moscow replied as did several others.

"…to turn to Him in times of difficulty. God is our refuge." The professor paused again. "According to the…"

"…Bible," Moscow added.

"…God does things for His glory and our good," the professor continued. "So even though we suffer and feel sad, we can trust that God is always good and always working things for our good, even in the worst of circumstances."

"Hey, that's pretty cool," I said. "You should be a preacher Professor Telson that was a good message."

"No, no," the professor said modestly as he shook his head. "My place is in the classroom, I'm a little too absent minded to deliver sermons every Sunday or lead a church."

"Okay," Hailey said with a smile. "So that was the second thing on the list right?"

"Right," said the professor.

"The third thing was *'work with other people',*" Hailey commented, looking at her notebook.

"Well, that's really what you're doing now. When Sneak told me he was dealing with some pretty difficult things, I encouraged him to work with others, to share what he's been going through, and to ask others for help," the professor paused. "I just never expected he'd take my advice so quickly!" The professor said with a deep laugh.

"That's good advice Professor Telson," Hailey said with a smile. "I hope we can help him."

"Oh, I think you can. And just like I encouraged Sneak to ask others for help, I'd encourage you to do the same. If you're going through some difficulty, ask your friends to pray for you. Your friends can encourage you in your journey. You're going to have some bumps and tough times along the way – especially with this new detective work you're undertaking – but other people can encourage you."

"I like that," Jennie said.

"Me too," Michelle replied.

"Well, I think I covered all the topics – maybe more thoroughly than you wanted me to," the professor said with a laugh. "There wasn't anything else on the list was there?" he asked with a chuckle.

"No, that was everything," Hailey replied.

"If there aren't any more questions, I think I'll get going," the professor concluded as he stood. "I have a lot of papers to grade this weekend."

"Thanks for coming over professor," I said. "Your advice has been good for us to hear."

"Yeah, it was really encouraging," Lisa added.

"Not a problem, not a problem at all," the professor said with a smile, "Glad to be of some help."

While the professor was putting on his winter coat, Hailey asked him a question.

"Professor Telson, I'm not sure if Sneak asked you or not, but I was wondering…well we were wondering…Sneak and I…and I'm sure the other kids here would agree – if you would be willing to help us out if we needed your advice? I think we all really liked what you had to say – even though some of it was hard to understand."

"Yeah, like the part about those poles," Moscow said.

"Or the pre-sups," Michelle added.

The professor laughed. "Well, hopefully some of what I talked about was helpful!"

"Those things were really good for us to hear," Hailey insisted. "So, Sneak and I had hoped that you might be able to help us when you could – as an advisor to our group. I'm sure all the other kids here feel the same way."

"Yeah," many of us replied.

"Sure, just let me know," the professor answered. "Call me if you have any questions."

"I was thinking," Hailey continued. "If we got together on Saturday mornings, like we're doing today, would you be willing to stop by?"

"Oh," the professor said surprised. "Well, I'll think about it. I've got bowling for a couple more weeks and I don't know if you heard, I'll actually be leaving the seminary at the end of the semester – to return to the school where I came from, out on the East Coast. My work here was just temporary. But, I should be available until then."

"Oh," I said dejectedly.

"Maybe, after you leave, you could call in?" Joel wondered.

"Call in?" the Professor asked.

"Yeah, there's a phone extension out here in the garage," Jennie said eagerly.

"And it would be easy to set up a phone with a speaker on it, so you could hear us and we could hear you," I explained. "Just like…"

"Charlie's Angels!" the kids said in unison.

CHAPTER 32

After our laughter ended, Professor Telson reminded us that we already had someone named Charlie helping us – Sneak and Jennie's Uncle Charlie, our city's police captain – but he said he would consider calling us, and I had a feeling that with only a little more convincing the professor would be willing. We thanked the professor for joining us as he reached the door. "Not a problem, not a problem at all," he explained before leaving.

The garage was quiet for a few moments after the professor left, but soon Hailey stood up, and moved to the front of the desk to get closer to her fellow detectives. As she moved closer, I noticed the notebook she held in her hand – a black three-ring binder that contained a large number of pages, much bigger than the small notepads she had given to us earlier in the morning.

"Okay," she said in a serious tone as she looked at her notes. "I wrote down a few things about the case." She paused before continuing.

"Can we get going?" Moscow asked. "I'm bored."

"First," Hailey continued, ignoring her brother. "I was thinking I'd spend some time at the library this afternoon looking into those crop circle patterns. I'm interested in learning if there's any significance to that pattern – like maybe if it's an ancient symbol or something. Plus, I'd like to know if any other fires have been set in Hancock County or anywhere else that are like the ones we're investigating."

"Gee, spending a Saturday at the library – that sounds like fun," Moscow teased.

"No one else wants to go there, right?" Hailey asked.

Jennie and Michelle both grimaced at each other as they considered the prospect of spending a number of hours doing research in a book filled room at the library. "I don't want to go there," Jennie said to Michelle in a voice above a whisper.

"It's okay, I'll go by myself," Hailey said to the group with a smile. "I've done a couple of research projects there and I should be able to get the answers to my questions pretty quickly." She decided not to tell us that she had recently become friends with one of the younger librarians who would likely help her quickly find what she needed. "So, how about you guys? What else do you think we should be doing?"

"We should be dancin' yeah! Dancin' yeah," Joel began singing as he jumped up from his seat and began dancing. As he sang the lyrics and hummed the rhythm of the song, he pointed his finger up above his shoulder then down across his chest – a dance move recently made famous by John Travolta.

"Oh yeah!" Moscow yelled from the wooden storage platform, as he rose from his seated position on the edge of the platform and began dancing and stomping above us.

Everyone but Hailey began clapping in rhythm as Joel pranced around the garage singing the *Bee Gee's* song made famous in the movie *Saturday Night Fever*.

"Okay, come on guys," Hailey said, setting down her notebook on Sneak's desk and placing her hands on her hips as Joel continued singing and circled the bench where Michelle, Lisa and Cressida sat clapping and swaying in unison to the song. "Let's figure this out!" Hailey said sternly – her sharp words instantly silencing the dancing and singing and clapping.

Hailey's words that morning – or maybe it was early afternoon by then, I had lost track of time in the midst of all of the discussion – had a powerful effect on us, as they would many times again after that day. Our group, I would discover over the next few years, was typically high-strung, loud and unfocused – like a barrel of plastic monkeys falling over each other. With Hailey at the helm, however, we were able to stay focused on our tasks as young detectives: investigate and observe, ask questions, analyze our results and come to conclusions about cases, and amazingly, do all of that while still having some fun. Hailey was great in helping us stay focused on the important mission we had all chosen to accept.

"So does anyone have any other ideas?" she asked with a smile.

"Yeah, I do," replied Lisa in a serious tone. "I want to see this Julian Davis for myself. I wish we had a picture of him. Did Sneak give you one?"

"No," Hailey replied. "Why do you want to see him?"

"I was just thinking that Findlay really isn't that big, so maybe someone in our group has seen him around town or knows something about him, like who his friends are or where he likes to hang out."

"Probably at the library," Moscow joked, as the rest of us laughed.

"Hey," his sister replied while looking up at him with a smile.

"Good one!" Michelle said smiling up at Moscow.

"Plus," Lisa continued, "If we know what he looks like, we could follow him, like Sneak tried to do at the cemetery. My older brother Brad might help us with that – he's got a car."

"We can't just knock on his door and introduce ourselves and take his picture," Hailey replied.

"No, but that gives me an idea," Lisa said, and soon she and Cressida were making plans for some investigative work they could do later that afternoon.

"Oh, hey," Joel said, interrupting their discussion. "I know some people at the newspaper. I could stop by there today before everyone goes home for the weekend and see what I can learn."

"That would be great," Hailey responded enthusiastically. "If you can find out more information about F.E.E.T. or the fires, or anything else about the case, I'm sure it would help our investigation."

"I'll see what I can do," Joel replied.

"Maybe Michelle and I could think of something to investigate?" Jennie said.

"Okay," Hailey replied. "Let me know if you need anything."

"We'll have to discuss the case with Mr. Knick Knack too," Jennie explained.

"Of course," Hailey responded with a smile.

"Hailey," her brother interrupted from above us. "I'm really getting bored up here, can we get going?" During the morning's discussion, Moscow had spent a large part of the time thinking about how to reach the highest beam in the garage – one that stretched high above us, across the top of the garage – but had concluded there was no way to jump or crawl to it and he was now getting restless.

"Sure, just a few more minutes," Hailey replied, smiling up to her brother. "So, I'm thinking we should probably get back together soon to talk about what we've learned. Joel might have some information from the newspaper. And I might have something from the library. And Lisa and Cressida, you two seem to be working on a plan – who knows what you'll come up with. And Jennie…."

"I'll try to talk to Sneak when Mom and Dad aren't around and see if he as any more ideas for the investigation," Jennie explained.

"Okay, that sounds good. So, when should we get back together?" Hailey asked.

"How about we meet tomorrow at Church?" I suggested. "We'll all be there for Sunday School, right?"

"Yeah, but we'll need some time to talk." Joel responded. "I might have a lot of stuff to talk about and I'm not sure we could talk about everything there."

"We could call each other," I suggested as another option.

"That might be pretty hard to pass along all the evidence to everyone else in the group," explained Hailey.

Cressida whispered something to her cousin, who soon spoke.

"Why don't we all go out for lunch after Church," Lisa suggested. "That would give us a lot of time to talk about the case. Plus, if we needed to do more detective work tomorrow afternoon, we'd still have some time to do it. Does anyone have lunch plans with their grandma or family or anything?"

"I don't think so," Joel responded.

"I don't," I said.

"So, where should we go?" asked Michelle.

"I don't care," replied Joel.

"Well the Cotton's and the Ryerson's always go to the same place every Sunday after Church." Hailey explained.

"Where's that?" asked Lisa.

"*Friendly's!*" Jennie and Moscow said at the same time.

"Can we crash the party?" Joel asked.

"I don't think it would be a problem," Hailey replied.

"Okay, so it's settled," Lisa continued. "*Friendly's* after church – to talk about the case."

"And to get some ice cream," Jennie added with a smile.

"That sounds great!" replied Michelle.

A moment later, the door opened letting in a cold gust of air and Sneak entered the garage looking especially gloomy and downcast. His eyes were bloodshot and it looked like he had been crying.

CHAPTER 33

"Well, I was right," the young detective said weakly when he entered the garage. "I'm grounded, you'll all have to leave. My mom's already called your parents."

"I'm so sorry Sneak," Hailey said sympathetically.

"Me too," I added.

"Us as well," Lisa added, speaking for herself and her quiet cousin.

"I'm sorry," Jennie said as she approached her brother and hugged him. "You knew they would do that, right?" she added.

"Yeah, I knew they would ground me, but it's still sad."

"What exactly did they ground you from?" Joel asked.

"Everything," Sneak explained. "...the detective office here in the garage, the crime lab in the basement, taking new cases, talking on the phone about cases, going to crime scenes, working on cold cases, working with the police and Uncle Charlie, they grounded me from everything."

"Bummer," Joel said.

"Yeah, my life is going to be really hard for a while."

After hearing Sneak's words, those of us gathered in the garage instinctively began finding our winter coats and began the process of putting them on to meet the cold air outside. Moscow carefully began lowering himself off of the wooden platform, grabbing the edge of the storage platform with his fingertips and dropping down between two folding chairs while others found their scarfs and gloves located on tables and atop handles of nearby bikes stored in the garage. While the others were getting their coats on, I packed up my gym bag with the equipment I had been working with.

"Oh, Sneak," Lisa asked our friend before we left. "I had one more question about the case. Do you mind answering it as we're walking out?"

"Sure," said Sneak, his face looking dazed and disoriented. "I don't mind answering a few more questions."

"We didn't talk about who you thought is actually setting the fires and sending the notes to Julian Davis?"

"Ah, you're right we didn't," said Sneak. "I think it's got to be someone from the F.E.E.T. group. From what I was able to tell, there are about twenty regular members in the group and five or six officers. So, I think one of them is the arsonist who is working with Julian Davis."

"And one more question....what do you think the reason is?" Lisa asked. "I'm not sure if we got into that earlier – why is the person doing this?"

"Ah their motive," the young detective replied. "I guess we didn't talk about that either, did we?" Sneak said as he gave a short, melancholic laugh. "I think it's to...ah, what would be the best way to call it...I think it's to get other people to know about their group. Publicity, that's the word I was looking for. I think they're setting the fires so that more people will join their group. The stuff that's in the *Letter to the Editor* is just so farfetched, it's hard to imagine that any of them actually believe it – but maybe they do. I don't know."

"So, it's pub...publicity...that's the reason?" Lisa asked.

"Yeah," said Sneak. "Last week I talked to one of the reporters who wrote a story about me last summer..."

"The one who called you The Amazing Kid Detective or the one who called you the Young Sherlock Holmes?" I asked.

"One of them," my friend replied. "Anyway, he told me that some national news crews are coming to town – all because of the fires. He also said the rumor around the newspaper is that *Real People* will be here too."

"*Real People?*" Joel asked.

"Yeah."

"That's a funny show," Moscow replied. "I like that one guy....man what's his name? I can't think of it."

"So if the national news is coming to town," Sneak concluded, "you know that there's going to be a lot of interest in F.E.E.T. They could get a lot more members from Findlay, but they could even get people interested in their group from Lima or Toledo, or even farther away."

"Can I ask one more question?" Lisa asked as we all approached the door.

"Sure," Sneak replied.

"Is there anyone else we should investigate? I mean, is there anyone else besides the F.E.E.T. people with a – what did you call it – a reason to set the fires?"

"A *motive*," Sneak added.

"Right, is anyone making any money from the fires or anything like that?" Lisa asked.

"Well, there's one guy who lives near Defiance," Sneak explained.

"Oh?" asked Lisa.

"Yeah, he's going to start flying people over the fields in a little Piper Cub airplane."

"So, he's going to be making money off of the fires, right?" Lisa asked.

"Well, yes, but he doesn't seem like much of a candidate for the crimes," said Sneak. "I wouldn't look into him as a suspect."

"Why's that?" Lisa questioned.

"Well, he's an older guy, and I think the real arsonist is younger – to be able to haul around the fuel and measure the fields quickly. And he can't get many passengers into his plane, it's just a small Piper Cub. Plus, if he were the one setting the fires, why would he come all the way over here to set them? It would take him quite a while to drive here from Defiance. Wouldn't he want to set the fires closer to where he lives?"

"Ah, that makes sense," said Lisa.

"But, you could check him out," Sneak added. "There's a chance he's involved."

"Okay," Lisa replied.

"You know I thought it was kind of funny," Sneak continued in a morose tone with a slight smile on his gloomy face. "Maybe it was funny only to me, but I was thinking that maybe he'd turn out to be the *Napoleon Ohio of Crime.*"

"What?" Moscow asked. "Who?"

"The Napoleon Ohio of Crime," Sneak repeated.

"I don't get it," said Moscow.

"It's a Sherlock Holmes joke," Sneak explained. "You see, the guy with the airplane lives near

Napoleon, Ohio and Sherlock Holmes would call Moriarty, his arch-nemesis, the Nap....oh, never mind, I can explain it later."

By then we had put on our scarves and gloves and winter coats and were walking out of the garage. I had almost forgotten to take the notepad that Hailey had given me earlier, so I returned to the stack of newspapers to retrieve it, remembering to turn off the space heaters that had kept us warm and walked quickly out of the garage, with gym bag and notepad in hand.

During the course of the morning's discussion, I had written only one or two words on the front page of the notepad – mostly to look like I was paying attention – but I had no concerns of forgetting anything that was said during that first meeting of *The Sunday School Detectives* – or at any of the detective meetings that followed.

You may wonder why I had such confidence in remembering what was spoken by *The Sunday School Detectives* that morning. The answer is quite simple – yet remained unknown to the others at the time – I secretly recorded all of our meetings.

CHAPTER 34

I quickly made my way from the Ryerson's garage to their house, and found that many of the kid's parents had already arrived to pick them up. When I entered the kitchen, I saw Mrs. R., and even though I wasn't much of a detective, I could tell that she had been crying. Mrs. Cotton offered to drive me home and I was quick to say 'yes', arriving at my Dad's house a few minutes later.

Resisting the urge to watch *The Wide World of Sports* – as I typically did on Saturday afternoons – I instead, found a spot on my Dad's living room floor and emptied the contents of my gym bag. Soon, ten or eleven audio cassette tapes tumbled out. Using the black tape recorder I had earlier pulled from my bag, I rewound each of the tapes – so they would all start at the beginning – and over the course of the afternoon, listened to each cassette, labelling each of them with the date and approximate time of each recording.

While my Dad was at work, I started transcribing the first cassette tape in the set – one of several tapes that Sneak had given me earlier in the day, when I had first arrived at his house. I pressed the big green PLAY button on my black cassette player and soon discovered the recording was from Sneak's meeting with his Uncle Charlie on Thursday afternoon after school.

Diligently writing in a faded light blue three-ring notebook that overflowed with pages – a notebook that resembled the notebook Hailey had used earlier in the day – I wrote the words as they came forth from the machine. I hit the REWIND button, starting the cassette again to make sure I transcribed the tape accurately.

"Hey Uncle Charlie," I heard Sneak say over the sounds of crackles and thumps – sounds occurring because the tape recorder was located deep inside my friend's gym bag.

"Hey Sneak," I heard his uncle reply, as I recognized other background noises: high pitched voices of kids from my elementary school who were chatting with friends as they walked home or waited to board their bus, while noisy bus engines idled nearby.

"Did you get a new car?" Sneak asked his uncle.

"I did. Nice catch...my other car had too many miles."

I started writing about my young detective friend the previous summer – a number of months before our first meeting with *The Sunday School Detectives* – on one of those long summer days when my friends and I had a lot of time to play G.I. Joe's or watch TV – or if you're Sneak Ryerson, to contemplate starting a detective agency in your garage.

It was during one of the days when Sneak was setting up his office that I confided in him. Technically, you could say I misled him at first – but I thought it was the best way to get what I wanted. "I want to be a detective," I confessed.

"You do?" my friend answered with a smile.

"I do," I told him enthusiastically. "I've been thinking about it for a while and I think I could do it."

"Okay," my friend said. "I guess if you want to be a detective, there's nothing to stop you. All you need is a mystery."

"Cool," I replied.

"Why don't we go look for one?" he suggested.

"That sounds great," I said with a laugh.

The day was a lazy Saturday afternoon during the middle of summer and we were both eager to find some relief from the July heat.

"Why don't we go get a malt at Wilson's and cool off?" Sneak proposed. "Maybe we'll find a mystery there?"

"Let's do it."

We were soon on our bikes, heading along the uneven Sandusky Street sidewalk, cycling the mile and a half to downtown Findlay.

"Before we go to Wilson's let see if there's anything else going on downtown," my friend suggested when we reached Main Street. Soon, we turned right, biking north a few blocks, passing several stores and banks before crossing Findlay's wide central street at the County Court House, then headed south to Wilson's.

The air conditioning at the famous sandwich shop was a welcome relief when we arrived and we quickly ordered our chocolate malts. We each paid for our malts and after receiving the chocolate desserts, we moved to the front of the restaurant and sat in swiveling orange covered stools in front of the restaurant's large plate glass window that faced the Elk's Club, a large brick building that reminded me of an ancient Roman temple.

"Okay, here's someone coming," Sneak said to me, pointing to a man walking up the sidewalk who was soon opening one of the restaurant's glass doors. "Why don't you put your detective skills to work and tell me what you observe about him?"

"Okay," I said confidently, positive that I had learned much already about observation and deduction from my friend.

I carefully studied the unshaven middle aged man as he walked into the restaurant. He wore an old tattered baseball cap, dirty jeans and dirty t-shirt and a pungent smell came into my nose when he stood near us while he waited in the long line that had formed in front of the cash register as people ordered their food. When the man eventually arrived at the counter, I noticed that he ordered quickly but then had a few words with the cashier who quickly gave him back some money.

The man was waiting for his food near the cash register when Sneak asked me about him again. "So, what can you tell me about him?" Sneak paused. "... through observation or deduction," he added with a smile.

"Well, he's obviously really poor," I began.

"And what would lead you to that deduction?" my friend asked.

"His clothes are filthy," I explained, "...which would tell us that he doesn't have any money to clean them or buy new clothes. His hands are dirty too, meaning he probably doesn't have a place to wash them. He smells horrible, so maybe he's a hobo riding the rails from town to town. His shoes look a little newer, maybe he just got those at the City Mission when he arrived in Findlay. That's what I would.... deduce," I concluded.

"Anything else, Pep?" my friend asked.

"Naw, what do you think?"

Sneak paused before replying, but soon spoke quickly and quietly as the man waited for his food at the counter.

"Well, I would deduce something very different," Sneak began. "The man's stubble on his face is one day old....meaning he shaved only yesterday. His fingernails are neatly trimmed and the dirt – as you call it – on his hands is green, indicating that he's been working with organic materials, like freshly cut grass from his lawn. His shoes are new, only a week or two old from *Finstermaker's*. We passed an identical pair in the window when we rode passed the shoe store a few minutes ago, and the price tag showed they were expensive. The hat he wears – although dirty and faded – is from a small boarding school in New England. He was also able to place his order without mistake, I'm pretty sure I heard him say '*two with*', indicating...?"

"Indicating two hamburgers with cheese," I replied with a scowl.

"Right, but also indicating that he is *from* Findlay – he knows that you are supposed to order the hamburger and cheese first, before moving up the line to say what he wanted on the *hamburg*. Outsiders never know how to order a Special."

"Yeah," I replied with another grimace. "But what about the smell?" I asked. "He smells terrible."

"The smell, I'm fairly certain, is not of a train engine, but is gasoline. If I'm not mistaken, it's actually a mix of gas and oil that the man likely spilled on himself when he was pouring it into his lawn mower – probably a LawnBoy, it's a mower that uses that kind of fuel mix."

"But what about his shoes, why is he wearing leather shoes with dirty clothes?"

"Well, I think he actually spilled most of the gas and oil on his old lawn shoes and didn't want to wear them in his car, so he probably put on the nearest shoes he could find to go to get his lunch. Those shoes he's wearing are his dress shoes that he probably left by the door at his house."

"Yeah but still, there was some problem at the cash register," I insisted. "That was another reason I thought he was poor. He got some money back or something...like he didn't have enough money to pay for everything and wanted some money back."

"I think the problem at the cash register happened because his mind is good with numbers," Sneak explained. "You know they only accept cash here, and I think he noticed a small error the cashier made when she calculated his order. So she gave him back some money – which he quickly put into the tip jar along with a few more dollars."

"Wow, how could I have missed all that?" I wondered.

"There's even more…but I'll add just a few more interesting things…."

"Thanks for sparing me too much embarrassment," I told him.

"If you go back through this week's paper, you'll see his picture."

"What…what for?"

"Because he was just promoted at the bank to Senior Vice President."

"Oh brother," I replied.

"And if I'm not mistaken, he is going to take his bag of food to that nice red MG convertible parked outside."

"What?" I asked as I watched in shock as the man grabbed his bag of food, exit the restaurant and then carefully open the door to a shiny cherry red convertible parked only a few feet away.

"I think the bank director would find it pretty funny he was mistaken for Boxcar Willy," my friend summarized. "Don't you think?"

"I can't believe how bad I did," I said dejectedly.

"I was surprised when you said you wanted be a detective, Pep. Are you sure you want to do this?" my friend asked.

"Not really," I replied. "Let's split an order of fries and I'll tell you what I really want to do."

CHAPTER 35

That afternoon over fries at *Wilson's,* I told Sneak Ryerson what I wanted to do with my life. "I want to be a great writer," I told him.

"Then why did you tell me you wanted to be a detective?" he asked.

"Because," I said after a pause. "I thought it was the only way I could hang out with you and do what I wanted to do."

"Which is what, exactly?"

"To write about you and the stuff you do," I explained.

"Write about me?" Sneak asked, surprised at the idea.

"Yeah," I told him, "I mean eventually I want to write about lots of other things, like movies, or travelling to different places, or maybe food or politics – there's this writer for the *New York Times* I like named Johnny Apple who writes about different things like that. But for now, I want to write about all the exciting stuff happening right in front of me…and that's the stuff you're doing!"

Sneak laughed. "It's not always exciting," he confessed. "Sometimes it's just reading the newspaper or interviewing witnesses."

"Sneak, come on," I continued. "You have a crazy gift for finding out answers to mysteries! And, well, I want to write about it. I want to be like Watson was to Sherlock Holmes."

"You know that's all made up, right?"

"Yeah, I know, but it would be cool to write down all the stuff you figure out – like knowing the bank vice president wasn't a hobo!"

"Yeah, that was fun," Sneak replied. "Did you really think he just came in on a train?"

"Yeah," I said sheepishly. "Obviously, detective work is not my thing."

"Well, let's just say you should work on your skills," he said as we both laughed.

"I mean, I don't want to step on your toes if *you* want to write about your cases, but you don't want to do that, do you?" I asked, hopeful that I knew at least that much about my friend.

"No, I don't have any desire to do that," he confessed.

"Right!" I exclaimed. "I mean, it seems like you're more interested in *solving* mysteries than *writing* about them. Right?"

"Right, I really just want to figure them out. It would be pretty boring for me to write down all the details of a case for a newspaper article."

"Well, that's what I'm interested in doing. And instead of thinking it would be boring, I think it would be pretty cool."

"I definitely wouldn't want to do it," Sneak concluded.

"So would you be okay with me writing about you and your cases?" I asked. "Like Boswell did for Samuel Johnson."

"Who?" Sneak asked.

"Did I stump you?" I said shocked. "I've stumped the great Sneak Ryerson, kid detective!" I said loudly as several people in the restaurant turned to look at me.

"Was Samuel Johnson involved in a crime?"

"No," I told him. "I don't think so."

"Well, no wonder I never heard of him," the young detective replied.

CHAPTER 36

Following our afternoon meeting over fries at *Wilson's*, I tagged along with my friend as he worked on solving mysteries that summer. One interesting case led us to the Hancock County Historical Society – where we went through boxes of old documents from the 1800's.

"Sneak! Look!" I exclaimed, while examining an old yellowed paper – among many other dusty old papers that we had placed on a heavy wooden table in the society's meeting room. "This isn't part of the case we're working on, but I think it shows there were Asians in Findlay back in the early 1800's."

"Asians here in the early 1800's?" my friend asked from the other side of the table. "That would be really interesting. I know there was a lot of immigration from Asia to California in the 1840's with the Gold Rush – but coming to Ohio earlier than that would be remarkable."

"Yeah, look at this," I said, holding up the document. "I think it's about an Asian restaurant, or some kind of store called S ANS KI CHEN."

"What?" he asked, as he moved to the stack of papers near me.

"KI CHEN," that definitely sounds Asian, I explained.

"It does," he said as he picked up the dusty document to examine it.

"The name is right here," I explained, pointing to a sentence.

After a moment, he turned to me and said, "Pep, you need to look at the rest of the document. It looks like the ink has faded on most of the page."

"I noticed that," I replied.

"But the letter "t" is no longer visible anywhere in the document."

I looked at the paper, puzzled.

"The printer used a typeset that has faded out the letter 't'," he explained. "It's not there anymore."

"So, it's STAN'S KITCHEN?" I asked.

"Yeah, I think so."

"Well, maybe Stan was Asian?" I said as we laughed.

After another failed attempt at detective work, I decided it would be best for my friend to do the investigating while I wrote about his exploits. During that summer, most of the mysteries my friend worked on were from people who heard about the young detective through friends or members of their family. While my friend investigated, I wrote a number of short stories about how Sneak had found lost pets, lost jewelry and how he had even figured out who had been stealing bikes around town (just by reading about the crimes in the newspaper). By the end of the summertime, Sneak's Uncle Charlie had asked him to work on the police department's cold cases and I trailed along with him to his interviews – mostly with elderly witnesses who had been victims of break-ins – and tried to help him as he dug through old and dusty case files.

After Sneak had solved several of the cold cases – leading to the apprehension and conviction of several criminals – I sent several of my stories to the editors of the area newspapers. The editors, in turn, sent reporters to write more detailed articles about Sneak. Although I was disappointed that they didn't publish what I had written, I was pleased to read the articles about my friend that described "*The Amazing Sneak Ryerson*" and a local consulting detective who was "just like a young Sherlock Holmes." I was happy that my writing had helped my friend and Sneak seemed pleased with the free advertising.

It was during that time that I discovered how difficult it was to be a reporter – in particular, how hard it was to take accurate notes. Sneak's interviews with witnesses – even the ones who claimed not to have seen anything – could last an hour or more, and I found it impossible to accurately write down everything the young detective asked a witness or everything a witness had said.

One day I was complaining about my difficulties to one of my Dad's co-workers, telling him about my hand cramps from writing so many words at such a fast speed and the lack of thoroughness in my witness interview notes. My Dad's co-worker was a young man, in his mid-twenties, who worked as a salesman alongside my father at a local appliance store. My Dad sold (or tried to sell) large appliances like refrigerators and ovens, while this younger salesman concentrated on selling electronics.

"Why don't you just record it?" he asked, after hearing my complaints on that slow summer afternoon when I stopped in at the store.

"Record it?" I asked.

"Yeah man, if you just record it you can have everything they talked about. Later, you can figure out the things that are important to put in your stories, you know, once the case is over."

"How's that?" I wondered.

"Well, once your friend solves the case – he can tell you what conversations were the important ones," my salesman friend explained. "All you'd need to do is rewind the cassettes to the part that was important and write down what they talked about. If there's stuff on the cassette that's not important – there's no need to write it down and your hand won't get all cramped up."

"That's great!" I replied enthusiastically.

"But, one piece of advice," he said to me in a serious tone. "Keep the tapes, just in case you need them later."

I thought the idea from my salesman friend sounded brilliant and soon I had a flat Panasonic tape recorder that I took with me to the interviews. After Sneak solved a case, just as my friend had advised, I transcribed the important parts of the witness' statements and used those for my stories.

But then, shortly afterwards, another problem arose.

"What am I supposed to do tomorrow?" I asked my salesman friend at the appliance store. "My Mom scheduled me to get a physical at the doctor's office – it's like a requirement now before starting school. I'm not going to be able to make it to an interview that Sneak scheduled at the same time. If I miss the interview, my whole story will probably be ruined!"

"Hey Pep, just ask Sneak to take the tape recorder with him," my friend told me confidently. "You don't have to be at all the meetings, right? Just ask your friend to hit the RECORD button and you can listen to the interview later."

"Yeah, I already thought of that," I told him. "I don't think it will work. Sneak can be so focused on the details of a case, I think he'll forget to turn it on. And if he forgets, I'll miss the whole interview!"

"Well, then, what you want is a *voice-activated* tape recorder," my friend told me confidently.

"Voice activated?" I asked.

"Yeah, it starts recording when it hears a noise."

"You mean it's off until someone starts speaking?" I wondered.

"Yep," he assured me.

"Cool," I told my friend. "How do I get one?"

"I can get you one," my salesman friend said. "Just take it to your friend tomorrow before your doctor's appointment. Just before you leave, all you need to do is press RECORD at the same time you press down on the voice activated button. If you use a long-format cassette, like a 120 or 150 minute tape, you should be able to get everything recorded."

"Aren't there 180 minute cassettes?" I asked.

"Yeah, but I'd stay away from those," he explained. "I've had a few issues with that kind. But you know, 120 or 150 minutes, that's two or two-and-a-half hours. That's a long time!"

"Yeah it is," I agreed.

"We've got a lot of long-format cassettes here at the store that you can try out – BASF, TDK, or Sony," he told me.

"Wow that would be great!" I exclaimed.

"Oh, and don't forget, when it's over and you get the cassette back, just pop the tab off the top of the tape so you don't record over it. Do you know how to take off that plastic notch?"

"Yeah, I know how to do that," I told him.

The next day, when I was at the doctor's appointment, Sneak went to the witness interview and brought along a gym bag filled with his detective gear: binoculars, magnifying glass, evidence collection bags as well as a new voice activated tape recorder that I had acquired for the interview. The next time I saw him, I got the recorded tape and gave him a blank cassette for the next interview he would conduct when I could not attend. The solution was perfect for me because I was able to hear all of his discussions with witnesses – without always being there.

After Sneak was grounded and our friends became *Sunday School Detectives*, I acquired more voice-activated tape recorders from my Dad's friend at the appliance store and gave them to each of the kids. Most of the *Sunday School Detectives* took the tape recorders with them when they were out collecting evidence or interviewing witnesses for our cases. Some of the things that were recorded were funny non-detective conversations – but most of what was recorded had to do with the cases we were working on.

Joel's cassette tapes were probably the most fun to listen to – as they recorded him humming or singing popular songs. Occasionally an argument about song lyrics would be recorded on one of his tapes and that was always fun to hear. "No, it's *I bless the rains down in Africa*," he earnestly said in one of his recorded conversations. "I don't know where you came up with those words you're using."

"No, that can't be right," came the reply from the person he was arguing with.

"Have you even listened to the song?" Joel asked. "It's I bless the rains down in Africa."

"I'd like to give you a one-way ticket to Africa!" the other person shouted angrily.

Several tapes recorded Joel explaining and re-explaining cars to people, especially the Ford Deuce Coupe and the Little Deuce Coupe – hot rods originating from the 1930's – that were the subject of a number of song lyrics.

Unlike Joel's tapes, Moscow's recordings were a challenge because his cassettes and tape recorders would frequently be broken when he returned them to me. His many falls from mopeds and bicycles and unicycles and even snowmobiles meant that I had to try to patch torn audio tapes together and replace broken tape recorders for his next adventure.

The girls mostly erased their non-essential conversations, so their recordings tended to be much choppier compared to the recordings by the guys. Their tapes were difficult to listen to, with muffled sounds lasting only a few seconds when they stopped the cassette and then rewound it for other audio to be recorded over.

After receiving a cassette from one of my fellow detectives, I would frequently rush home to listen to it – anxious to hear their interviews with witnesses or their conversations with other detectives. And then later, after we had solved the case, I would transcribe the parts that seemed important.

The recordings made by Sneak and Joel and the other *Sunday School Detectives* when they had meetings or interviews, were all made – of course – voluntarily. The recordings I came to regret – deeply and for many years afterwards – were those I made secretly, without telling my friends.

Initially, I had foolishly justified the idea because Sneak was slow in returning a cassette tape to me after conducting an interview. But as time passed, and my secret recordings continued, I barely remembered the initial reason I started.

Secretly recording my friends was wrong. It was a terrible mistake and something that led to a number of problems. I am very sorry for doing that and it should never have started. Once it had started, I should have stopped it immediately and told my friends. I had many opportunities to confess what I had done and stop what I was doing – well before all of the trouble started. But, unfortunately, I waited too long.

In addition to not telling my friends about the secret recordings, I also did not tell them about my salesman friend from the appliance store, who, I learned, not only sold electronics but turned out to be an expert in procuring and setting up concealed audio equipment. With his help, I acquired a number of small recording devices that we placed in areas where *The Sunday School Detectives* met – turning the spaces into virtual recording studios, filled with hidden microphones and tape recorders, known only to my salesman friend and myself.

The full consequences of my secret recordings were not realized until several years after *The Sunday School Detectives* formed. Most of those recordings, honestly, were pretty boring – as my friends discussed solutions to our cases. However, there was one recording – made just after our first meeting – that turned out to be one of the scariest.

I had activated the recording just before leaving the Ryerson's garage during our first meeting of

The Sunday School Detectives, then, a few weeks later I returned to pick up the cassette tape.

Knocking on the family's front door – on a Saturday morning in early April – I could see that Mr. Ryerson was sleeping in his recliner with a newspaper on his chest. "Oh, hey Pep," Mr. Ryerson said as he greeted me at the front door, with a newspaper in his hand. "Sneak and Jennie aren't here."

"That's okay, Mr. Ryerson," I told him. "I just forgot something in the garage."

"The side door should be unlocked," he said bleary-eyed. "You can go and get what you need."

"Thanks," I told him. "It will just take a minute."

"The garage will look a little different since the last time you were there," Mr. Ryerson explained as I was leaving the front porch. "With Sneak grounded from his detective's office, Mrs. Ryerson and I are parking our cars in there now."

Jumping off the porch, I raced to the back of their house and entered the garage from the unlocked side door. With the busyness of our investigations, I had nearly forgotten about the voice-activated cassette recorder, but on that Saturday I had decided to get the tape – curious to learn if Sneak was really following his parent's rules of not doing detective work. *He loves being a detective*, I thought, *I'm sure he's been doing some interviews or other stuff if he can get away with it.*

I was surprised at how dramatically Sneak's office had been transformed when I entered the dark garage. Sneak's metal desk, the green chalkboard and his office chairs had all been moved to the rear wall to make space for the Ryerson's cars. The tape recorder, to my relief, was still in its hidden location and I was able to quickly grab the cassette tape – replace it with a blank cassette – and quickly exit the garage.

I returned home and listened to the cassette on my tape player – hoping I could catch Sneak disobeying his parents and discover that he was continuing to do investigations. I was disappointed, however, when I listened to the audio – initially hearing only cars rumble into and out of their spots while garage doors opened and shut. After a number of minutes, I was happy to hear a few words from Jennie to her friend Mr. Knick Knack as she got out of a car, but the words soon faded. For a large portion of the tape there was nothing.

After fast-forwarding the cassette for several minutes, I soon discovered some voices were recorded near the end of the cassette. I quickly rewound the tape to where the conversation began and to my surprise, the voices on the recording were ones that I couldn't understand. I laughed when I first heard them and thought that either my friend from the appliance store was playing a joke on me or someone had left a foreign radio station on in the garage.

Even though it was confusing, I could definitely tell there was some sort of conversation – a verbal exchange between two men. But I could not understand any of it.

A few days later I played it for my Dad, who was very focused on trying to learn French, so I thought he could help identify the foreign language.

"It sounds Eastern European," he told me after listening for a few minutes. "Where did you get this?" he asked.

"I found it," I told him. "It's no big deal."

And I didn't think it was a big deal until a long time afterwards.

CHAPTER 37

It wasn't until much later – when some information came up in an investigation – that I remembered the tape from the garage. After some searching through the large cardboard box where I stored all of my cassettes, I eventually found the recording.

Knowing that I could not understand it, I got a ride to the campus of a nearby college and quickly took the tape to the foreign language department. "I believe this is Russian," the department secretary told me when she listened to it for a few minutes. "Or Ukrainian. I'm no expert on Eastern European languages, but I think it's either Russian or Ukrainian."

"My Dad thought it was Eastern European too," I told her.

"Let me get Professor Romanov to translate it for you."

"Thanks so much," I told her. "I didn't know where else to go."

Soon, we were joined in the department offices by Professor Romanov, a young professor in her early thirties.

"Where did you get this?" she asked after hearing a few words.

"I recorded it in my friend's garage," I told her.

"You need to find your friend quickly," she said in a thick Russian accent. "Your friend is in grave danger."

"That might be a little difficult. He's on vacation with his family."

"I don't care where he is," she said emphatically. "You must warn him now."

"Warn him of what?" I asked.

"Of the great danger he's in," she said with great emotion.

After making several promises that I would find Sneak as soon as I left the college campus, the young professor translated the conversation on the tape for me.

It was apparent, as we listened to the recording together – and she provided the translation –that two criminals had forced their way into the Ryerson's garage when the Ryerson's were away.

The professor told me that one of the criminals was named Vlad, short for Vladimir or Vladislav. Vlad seemed to be the leader of the pair and, she explained, appeared to be the more intellectual of the two. The second criminal was named Vasily, "not quite as smart," the professor told me, "but equally dangerous" she said ominously.

"Vlad, that lock was really easy to pick," were the first words of the conversation – spoken in Russian. "People can be so stupid with locking up their valuables."

"Yes Vasily, it was almost too easy," Vlad said in reply. "Could it be a trap? Do you see any security cameras or trip wires?"

"No, no cameras. No trip wires either. But you might be right, it could be a trap."

"Nobody's in the house, right?"

"Correct."

"Let's turn on a light then," Vlad commanded. "It's too dark in here."

The click of the light switch could be heard – only a few feet away from where I had hidden the secret tape recorder.

"Gardening tools?" Vasily said gruffly. "I thought this was a detective agency?"

"I did too. At least that's what the sign on the door said," Vlad said in Russian. Then in English he slowly pronounced the words, "SNEAK RYERSON DETECTIVE," quoting the engraved letters on the glass pane door of the garage.

"We could plant a bomb under those newspapers, over there," Vasily suggested as he walked toward the wooden box filled with newspapers – a box I had been sitting on only a few days before at our inaugural meeting of the *Sunday School Detectives.*

"That would be a good location," his partner said.

"Or, instead of planting a bomb, we could hide under the newspapers and jump out and scare him or something."

"That would be more difficult," Vlad replied with a laugh. "Seriously though, I think the best hiding place here would be up in the storage place above us."

"Like you say, 'Always take the high ground'," Vasily replied.

"Do I say that?" Vlad asked.

"You do, you do."

"If you say so," he replied with a laugh. "Let's look through the desk and see if there are any papers about Grigori."

Soon, the drawers of Sneak's metal office desk could be heard opening and closing.

"Yes, looking through the papers is good, but what about the bomb placement, we should figure that out while we're here," Vasily stated earnestly.

"Vasily," Vlad replied in an exasperated voice. "The boss told us just to look around. He would be upset if we blew the kid up."

"Or, maybe he would be happy?" Vasily replied with a laugh. "It's cold in here, why don't we turn on one of the heaters."

"Okay," Vlad replied, as sounds echoed throughout the garage of Vasily starting one of the space heaters. Soon, the sounds of another space heater being turned on could be heard as well as another desk drawer being opened and a set of file folders being removed and dropped on the desk. "This is interesting," Vlad said, reading one the contents of one of the folders. "There's some stuff here about some fires in the shape of circles. Maybe we could set a fire here and make it look like one of these."

"Let me look, let me look," Vasily said insistently while the sounds of him grabbing the papers were recorded by the secret microphone.

"You look at those...there," Vlad ordered. "I'll keep reading this."

"Okay, okay," came the response.

Soon I could tell that the two had moved locations to read through the files. The leader of the pair, Vlad, had settled into Sneak's office chair a few feet away from the desk, while Vasily had, like I had done only a few days before – ascended onto the stack of newspapers, still piled high within the wooden box – and found a comfortable spot to read the files.

"There's a lot of stuff here," said Vlad. "This kid keeps a lot of records. You find anything interesting?"

"Nah, not really," Vasily replied. "It's really getting hot in here, I'm taking my boots off, they've been hurting all day."

"Just don't leave them here!" his friend joked. "I wonder if the young detective should worry more about our bomb or about the smell coming from your boots?"

"They don't fit anyway." Vasily explained, ignoring his colleague's joke. "I'm not sure why. They fit when we left Peter." This was, according to the translator, how Russians referred to St. Petersburg – a city officially called Leningrad at the time.

Soon the sounds of paper shuffling stopped and the sounds of snoring could be heard – coming no doubt, from the box of newspapers and the office chair near the desk. (Hearing this, the three of us listening to the tape – the Russian professor doing the translating, the department secretary who had remained to listen to the translation and I, laughed loudly. I fast-forwarded the tape until the snoring stopped).

The noise of something loud falling on the floor woke the pair up. (I think it was the metal stapler that Sneak kept on his desk that was pushed off by the sleeping Russian who had his feet up on Sneak's desk).

"Hey, Vasily, Vasily," the leader of the pair said. "You awake?"

"I am now," his colleague said from the box filled with newspapers. "You ready to go?"

"Yeah, I'm tired of reading this stuff," Vlad replied.

"So, we're not planting a bomb today?"

"No, not today. The boss told us to wait, but I'm sure he'll want to do something soon. Let's get out of here. Don't forget to turn off the heaters."

"Okay. Don't forget your hat."

Soon, the two noisily gathered up the papers they had taken from the desk and placed them back into file folders and returned them to the metal desk. (They were put away in such a haphazard way that Sneak would later accuse Jennie and her friends of "messing up his files".)

After returning the papers and turning off the space heaters, the pair walked toward the door and ended their discussion with an ominous few words.

"Next time we're here, we get rid of him, right Vlad?"

"Right Vasily, next time *ubrat.*"

When the translation was complete, the Russian professor begged me again to immediately track down Sneak and warn him of the grave danger he was in.

"But this recording happened months ago," I told her.

"You need to tell him right away!" she warned.

CHAPTER 38

B efore my tapes were recording Russians, they were recording my friend Sneak Ryerson and his investigations – and on that cold Saturday afternoon on March 8th, 1980, instead of watching *The Wide World of Sports*, I spent the afternoon listening to tapes from *The Case of the Mysterious Circles*.

The first tape I listened to that afternoon was from Sneak's drive with his Uncle Charlie to the scene of the fourth crop circle fire. As I listened, I followed in my mind's eye the journey Sneak took from our school to the crime scene – southeast of downtown – with his Uncle Charlie. Soon, I was introduced in the audio recording to Deputy Curtis, who was stationed on the county road next to the scene of the fire. *It must have been so lonely for him,* I thought as I heard about the Deputy's assignment – *sitting in his patrol car all day guarding the crime scene.*

As I listened to the Deputy's questions, however, he seemed to me to be a little too clueless for an experienced sheriff's deputy. *It's almost like an act,* I thought. At other times, though, the deputy seemed a little too interested in Sneak's investigation, keenly interested in learning about the specific evidence that Sneak had already uncovered and how Sneak had been able to tip off the police that the fire was going to happen. *Does the Deputy know more about the case than he's letting on?* I wondered as I listened to their discussion.

My Dad arrived home later that afternoon – after a long day on his feet at the appliance store – and went quickly to the living room couch where he fell fast asleep. A few hours later we went to *Captain D's* for dinner, as we had the night before. The evening, however, was very different than many of the other evenings I spent with my Dad. Usually, Dad and I would go to dinner at *Captain D's* or another nearby restaurant and sit in silence – like we had done the night before – my father depressed, while I tried to think of things to cheer him up.

On that Saturday night, however, when we sat down to eat our fried fish and hush puppies, I started to describe my day. "You wouldn't believe what happened to me this morning," I began.

"What was that?" my father asked gloomily.

"I got invited to be in a group of investigators!"

"Investigators?" he asked, perking up in interest at the news.

"Yeah, we're going to be called *The Sunday School Detectives*, it's going to be pretty cool."

"The Sunday School Detectives? Is this with your buddy Sneak Ryerson?"

"Well, yes and no," I told him. "He basically started it with Hailey Cotton, but he won't be part of it."

"Hmm," my father replied, now even more interested in my words. "Sounds like there's more the story."

"There is," I told him. "A lot more."

And so, for the remainder of our time at *Captain D's* I told him the story of *The Case of the Mysterious Circles* and how I and the other kids were recruited to be detectives because our friend, the amazing Sneak Ryerson, was grounded and couldn't conduct the investigation on his own.

In my retelling, I tried to describe the case in way that was similar to how Sneak had explained it to us earlier in the morning – even using his questions on the chalkboard:

What is the mystery?
When did it happen?
Who did it happen to?
What evidence has been gathered?
What really happened?
Why did it happen?
Who did it?

It helped that right before going to dinner with my Dad, I had listened to the tape that recorded Sneak explaining the case – and answering each of these questions – while we were in his garage earlier in the day.

Throughout the evening, as I was telling the story, my Dad would stop me – sometimes mid-sentence – to ask a clarifying question. "So, you don't think this Julian Davis fellow is the guy who's starting the fires?"

"It couldn't have been him," I replied in a serious tone as I told him about Julian's air-tight alibi at *The Twin Palace* cinema.

"So what about that car in the cemetery?" he asked a few minutes later. "Sneak or someone got a description of the car, right?"

"Nope, not according to Sneak. He was too busy trying to hold on to the bumper of the car while he was leaving the cemetery and trying to get the note in the front seat."

"I just don't get why someone would do this?" he asked a few minutes later. "It seems like someone is going to a lot of effort for nothing really – I mean those fields should be fine later in the spring. The farmers should be able to grow their crops without any problem. Why would someone even do this?"

I replied to him with Sneak's answer that it was likely someone in the F.E.E.T. group seeking publicity.

"Do you really think his parents will keep him grounded?" Dad asked me a few minutes later. "I mean, Sneak's helped so many people. It would be a shame if he couldn't keep doing what he's good at."

"I think he's going to be grounded for a really long time," I explained.

"Well, that's too bad," my Dad replied somberly. He paused briefly then said, "So, I guess that means it's your turn to step up."

"Step up?" I asked.

"Yeah, you get to step up and be a detective and help solve cases with the other *Sunday School Investigators…*"

"…Detectives," I corrected.

"Right, *The Sunday School Detectives*," he said, correcting himself. "I, for one, hope you're able to figure out a whole lot of cases together. Unfortunately, I don't know anything about that stuff…but let me know if I can help. You know your Mom and I always want to support you in your interests."

"Thanks Dad," I said with a smile. "I'll let you know." It made me happy to hear him use the words "your Mom and I" together in a sentence – he didn't always do that.

After dinner we went to the *YMCA* where I continued my explanation of the case. The *Y*, as we called it, was crowded that night, with a weight lifting tournament in the East Gym, next to the racquetball courts. We stayed and watched the lifters for a few minutes before going to the *Y's* West Gym which was available for kids and families to play. We shot some basketballs on one of the hoops for almost an hour before descending the stairs to the locker rooms and then going to one of the Y's indoor swimming pools. Spending time with my Dad, playing basketball and goofing around in the swimming pool, was really enjoyable for me – and a happy memory in a youth that was not always happy.

By the time we returned home, I had finished telling my Dad all the details of the case and he had returned to his normal depressive mood. We changed clothes – I, in my pajamas, and Dad in warm wide whale corduroys and heavy sweater – and he soon went to the kitchen to read from several old French textbooks and dictionaries that he had laid out on his narrow kitchen table, while I listened to more of the cassette tapes in the living room.

In spite of his deep depression, I loved my Dad and found him to be an interesting guy. The story of his life, I found to be somewhat sad. I learned that when he was growing up, his older parents were somewhat impersonal and distant. And I also learned that as a youth he had envisioned himself as an intellectual – reading and studying as much as he could – but he dropped out of college after only two years to follow my Mom back to her hometown of Findlay. He said in the subsequent years, that he felt like his life had passed by – "like a movie" – without him ever accomplishing anything of any importance or significance. He said he felt like he could have done so more with his life, but was stuck – in a sense – in Middle America. By the time I was helping Sneak and *The Sunday School Detectives*, my Dad had started spending nearly all of his free time trying to learn French – with hopes of visiting – or even moving to France someday. As far as I knew, he had never even visited France – the closest he had come was working in a French restaurant in Toledo – but somehow the far-away Gallic country held sway over his imagination.

"Où est l'encrier? Où est l'encrier?" he repeated several times that night while studying his textbooks at his small metallic kitchen table.

"What does that mean?" I asked him from the living room.

"It's a question," he explained. "Where is the inkwell?"

"The inkwell? What's that?" I exclaimed.

"You know, if you have to write with a feather.... ink pen. You keep the ink in an inkwell. Then you dip the feather pen into the ink to write on a piece of paper. A lot of the school desks had a built-in holder for them. *L'encrier est sur le bureau.*"

"Wow, how old is that textbook you're reading?" I asked.

"It's pretty old."

"We don't have inkwells in school anymore."

"Yeah, I know," he told me.

"You didn't have an inkwell did you?"

"No."

"Did Grandpa have an inkwell in school?"

"We'll have to ask him," my Dad replied. "I think he….ah, probably did."

I could tell he seemed less attentive and guessed that he had returned to reading one of his books.

"Why don't you get a newer book?" I asked loudly.

"Maybe," he replied. "I got this one from…from a pretty neat used bookstore in Chicago. Maybe I can find a newer one when I go back sometime."

"Maybe something from this century, in the 1900's!" I said with a laugh.

Still later in the evening, after I had brushed my teeth and turned off my bedroom lights and hopped into bed, my Dad entered my darkened bedroom to "tuck me in", as we called it.

"*Bonne nuit,*" he told me in French – *Good Night.*

"Can you tell me a story?" I asked in the darkness, just as I did nearly every night I stayed at his house. "And don't forget 'zee stinky cheese," I said with a smile.

"Sure, I'll tell you a story," he said as he sat down on the edge of the bed. "Let's see...I've got so many different ones," he said with a laugh. "Is there one you'd like to hear?"

"How about *Pierre and his Two Sisters?*" I asked, referring to the story I had heard many, many times but with a number of variations.

"Okay, I think I know that one," he said laughing. "Well, once upon a time," my father began, "there lived a family – in the Kingdom of France."

"What city did they live in?" I asked knowingly.

"They lived in the city of Paris – sometimes called the City of Light."

"And where exactly in the city?"

"The family lived in the city's Sixth Arrondissement."

"I thought it was the Fifth," I said with a smile, teasing my father.

"Fifth? No, I must have been mistaken if I told you that before. The district where this story starts is definitely the Sixth Arrondissement."

"Okay, okay."

"So, the family lived in the Sixth Arrondissement...."

"And what was their last name?"

"The family's last name was DuPont, like the chemical company."

"I thought their last name was de Gaulle – like the French President."

"de Gaulle? No, no, I must have been mistaken if that's what I told you before, their last name was definitely DuPont."

"Okay."

"So, the DuPont family had five people. There was the father – *Monsieur DuPont*, as they'd say in France. And there was *Madame DuPont*. And there were three children."

"Three children," I said seriously. "Well, at least that's still the same since the last time you told the story!"

"Story?" he asked. "Did I say this was a story? It's not a story, it's all stuff that really happened!"

"Well, you could still tell a story from stuff that really happened," I replied thoughtfully.

"I guess you could! So I guess we're both right! Now where were we?"

"You just said there were five people in the family: Monsieur de Gaulle...

"Hey, don't confuse me, I know I said DuPont."

"Right," I replied with a laugh. "You said there was Monsieur DuPont, Madame DuPont and their three children."

"Yes, three children. There were two sisters and a younger brother."

"What were the sister's names?" I asked with a smile.

"Collette and Chantelle, of course."

"I think one time you said that one of the girl's names was Monique."

"Monique?" my father chortled. "Absolutely not." He paused for a moment. "Well, come to think of it, they may have had a *friend* named Monique, but she was definitely not a sister."

"Another time I think you said one of the sisters was Michelle."

"Michelle? No way."

"And then another time you said it was Suzanne."

"No, not Suzanne. The girls' names were….what did I say just now?"

"Collette and Chantelle."

"Right, Collette and Chantelle were the girl's names."

"Which one of the sisters was the older one?" I asked him with a smile.

"Collette, of course," he replied authoritatively.

"Last time you told me it was Chantelle," I said, again with a smile, which he probably could only partially see in the darkened bedroom.

"Well, I must have been wrong last time – I can do that sometimes – it happens when you get older. The older sister is definitely Collette."

"Okay, I'll remember that for the next time you tell the story," I said with a laugh.

"And the boy's name was Pierre. That was definitely the boy's name. I haven't changed that have I?"

"No, you haven't changed it, it's always been Pierre," I added.

"Good, because Pierre was definitely the boy's name," my father said seriously.

"That's why the story's called *Pierre and his Two Sisters*, right?"

"Right," my father agreed. "Anyway," my father continued, "every morning the sisters and their brother left their house in the....what district did I say?"

"Sixth..."

"Right, every morning they left their house in the Sixth Arrondissement to go to their school in the Fifth Arrondissement – which is where a lot of schools are located. Those details are pretty much how I told the story before, right?"

"Pretty much."

"So anyways, on their way to school every morning, the three would stop at the same bakery – a *boulangerie* as they called it in France."

"*Boulangerie*," I repeated.

"Yes, and each morning the three children greeted the baker and his wife. '*Bonjour Monsieur. Bonjour Madame*,' they all said to the baker and the baker's wife. And every morning the Baker's wife would respond by saying, '*Bonjour! Quelle belle journée.*' Which means '*Hello! What a beautiful day!*'"

(It had taken my father a long time to learn basic French phrases and I knew he was proud to use them in the story).

"When they arrived, Madame would get them seats together at a long counter," my father continued.

"Like *Miller's*?" I asked, referring to the famous diner, Miller's Luncheonette, located north of downtown.

"Well, yes – a lot like Miller's. Anyway, after she found them a place to sit…"

"Was the bakery busy?" I interrupted.

"Yes, very busy, that's why they needed Madame's help to find a seat. Anyway, after she found them a place to sit, she asked the children how their parents were doing and how their aunts were doing and how their uncles were doing and how their grandparents were doing."

"How were they doing?" I asked with a laugh.

"Oh, they were all fine. One of their aunts was recovering from a cold. *Elle fait froid*," he said incorrectly.

"That's too bad," I said.

"She's feeling a lot better now," my father explained. "Anyway, while the baker's wife was talking to the kids, the baker, who was dressed in a white uniform and had on a large puffy hat, brought Pierre and his sisters a small cup of hot chocolate and a piping hot croissant filled with chocolate."

"Mmmm," I replied.

"No kidding," my father added.

"Did they have to share the breakfast, or did they each have a cup of hot chocolate and a hot croissant."

"Oh no, they didn't have to share," my father explained. "The baker brought each of them a cup of hot chocolate and a croissant."

"That's good," I said, remembering another version of the story where the three had argued about sharing a croissant and hot chocolate.

"Well," my father continued. "Just as the kids were finishing up their morning snack, the baker gave Pierre a long list of supplies that the bakery needed by that afternoon."

"What was Pierre's job?" I asked – already knowing the answer.

"Well, Pierre's job was to go to different shops and get all of the supplies the baker needed. He was what they might call a *garcon de courses* – an errand boy. Every morning the baker would give the list to Pierre and then Pierre would read the list back to the baker. 'One large piece of dark chocolate,'" – my father said in a heavy French accent as he continued the story trying to sound like Pierre the errand boy – "'one bag of flour, one bag of sugar, one bag of truffles and a round of stinky cheese,' Pierre said, reading from the list."

"'Zat is correct,' said the baker." My father's voice now turned deeper, with an even thicker accent as he tried to sound like a French baker and continued the story. "'Can you get all of those things today?'"

"'Yes,' Pierre told him, 'I will return to the bakery with all of these things for you.'"

"'You are a good boy,' said the baker, 'but you can sometimes be forgetful.'"

"'I won't be forgetful today,' Pierre replied."

"'Just don't forget 'zee stinky cheese,' the baker reminded the boy," my Dad saying these words with a smile in the deep voice of the French baker.

"The baker's wife then begged him, 'Pierre, Pierre,'" – my Dad intoned in a high-pitched feminine voice – "'please, please, please don't forget 'zee stinky cheese.'"

"'Okay, okay,' Pierre would say, 'I won't forget 'zee stinky cheese.' "

"'And remember,' the baker told him. 'We close at four thirty this afternoon, so we need everything by then."

"'Okay, okay, I'll get everything by then,' Pierre told his boss."

"When the kids finished their food they got their coats and their French hats – called *berets* – and told everyone goodbye."

"'*Au revoir Madam*,' Chantelle said, which means *good bye*."

"'*A la prochain*, Chantelle,' Madame replied – *until next time*."

"'*A bientot!*' Pierre said, which means *see you soon*."

"'*Adieu*,' Collette added."

"...to you and you and you," I said with a laugh.

"Yes…to you and you and you," my Dad said. "Then, one of the three noticed that their stop at the bakery had made them late for school, so they rushed out the door of the bakery and raced down the street – hurrying to get to school on time." My father paused for a moment. "French schools, if you remember, are different than schools in America," he explained. "While you kids get out at two or three o'clock in the afternoon, the students in France usually have class until four in the afternoon."

"Wow, that's a long time to be in school," I replied.

"Yes, but they get a long *two* hour lunch break."

"That would be nice," I said. "I'd probably take a nap during that time."

"Well, I think that's what they do in some Spanish speaking countries – it's called a *siesta*."

"Cool."

"Anyway, Pierre and his sisters arrived at their school and after they had been there for their morning classes, they were ready for their long lunch break – and it was during this time, when they had their two hour break, that Pierre had planned to do the shopping for the baker."

"Because he had to get all his supplies by four thirty in the afternoon," I added.

"Right. And so, when school let out for lunch, Pierre walked outside with his list in his pocket ready to do some shopping – but as soon as he walked out

PEP STILES

of the school building he saw his sister Collette and
then their other sister…"

"Chantelle," I added.

"Right, Chantelle," my father said as he continued the story.

"'Bonjour, Pierre,' they said to him when he
walked out of school."

"'Bonjour, Collette. Bonjour, Chantelle. I'm
going to get supplies for the baker,' Pierre told his
sisters."

"'Oh, don't do that now.,.' Collette insisted. 'Do
your work later. Let's go have some fun this afternoon.' "

"'But I told the baker I'd get his supplies,' Pierre
told his sisters."

"'You can get that stuff later,' Chantelle told him."

"'Yeah, get it later,' Collette said to her brother."

"Well, the afternoon was a bright and sunny
Spring day," my father explained. "And the three
children wanted to enjoy the great day. 'Let's play
hide and seek in the garden,' one of the sisters
said."

"'Okay,' Pierre agreed. So, the three kids went to
one of the best gardens in the world - the Tuileries
Garden – which is a huge garden next to the Louvre
Museum, filled with a lot of statues and trees – and
they played hide and seek until they were tired from
running around."

"Is that all they did during their lunch break?" I asked, knowing that there would be more to the story.

"Well no," my father explained. "After they got tired of playing hide and seek, the younger sister…"

"Chantelle," I added.

"Right, Chantelle said, 'Let's go over to the Eiffel Tower'."

"'But I've got to do my shopping,' Pierre said."

"'Oh, that can wait,' Chantelle told him."

"'Well, I guess I'll have time later,' Pierre told his sister. So the three walked around the big tower in the center of the city."

"'Let's go to the top!' Chantelle said."

"'But I've got to do my shopping,' said Pierre."

"'Oh, that can wait,' Collette told him."

"'I guess I'll have time later,' Pierre told them. So, they all got in an elevator and went to the top of the Eiffel Tower and saw the great view of the city of Paris – and they pointed to their house in the…"

"Sixth," I replied.

"Right, Sixth Arrondissement and then they pointed to their school in the Fifth Arrondissement. And then they pointed to all the other famous landmarks…the Louvre Museum, the Arc de Triumph, and other places."

"That sounds cool," I said.

"I'd say so," my father explained.

"Is that all they did?" I asked.

"Well no, after they came down from the tower, Pierre said, 'I should do my shopping now', but Collette said, 'I like going on the carousel.' And Chantelle said, 'I do too!' And Pierre told them, 'I guess my shopping can wait.' So, they all walked over to the carousel next to the Eiffel Tower. And after they bought their tickets, they jumped on the wooden horses and rode around and around."

"Did they just sit on the wooden horses?" I asked – knowing that my father had read a story about French carousels.

"Well, no." my father explained. "The operator of the carousel gave each of them a stick when they entered the gate to the ride, and then when it started going around, the kids used the stick to grab metal rings that were on a long pole just outside of the ride."

"Did they get any rings?" I asked.

"Yes, each of them got some rings before the carousel stopped."

"How many?" I asked in the darkness of my room, imagining the colorful carousel spinning around downtown Paris with smiling kids riding around and around on a bright Spring day.

"I think Pierre got three. Collette got four and Chantelle got five rings."

"Cool," I replied. "So, is that all they did?" I asked again.

"Well, by that time they were getting pretty tired and hungry, and Chantelle said, 'Let's go get some food!' "

"'But I've got to do my shopping,' Pierre said to his sisters."

"'Oh, that can wait,' Collette told him. 'You can do that later.'"

"'Okay, I guess it can,' Pierre said."

"So they left the carousel and went to one of Paris' most famous cafés – it was one of those cafés that has a big awning and a bunch of tables outside the restaurant next to the sidewalk."

"Is that where they sat?"

"Yep, they sat outside – because the weather was so nice. And as people walked by on the sidewalk they'd look at who was eating – because a lot of famous people used to go there to eat."

"Like who?" I asked.

"Well, there were a lot of famous writers like Ernest Hemingway and famous artists, like Pablo Picasso."

"Cool. Were any of them at the restaurant that day?

"Well, I think Hemingway was there in the morning and Picasso had a dinner reservation."

"Oh," I replied, imagining a writer carrying his typewriter into the restaurant as a man with his easel and paints ate at a table nearby.

"So, like I said," my Dad continued, "the kids sat at a table outside the café and soon they were surrounded by waiters in black coats and black bow ties who brought them water and sliced bread."

"Wonder bread?" I asked with a laugh.

"No, not Wonder Bread – French," my Dad explained. "The waiters brought them French bread. And eventually, the head waiter came to their table and took their order – and each of them got something called *quiche* – which is like an omelet in a pie crust."

"That sounds pretty good," I said.

"Yeah, it does."

"Could you make one for me?"

"Maybe not quiche, but I could make an omelet for you before Church tomorrow morning. How does that sound?"

"Good, real good." I replied, envisioning a great breakfast. "So what happened next to *Pierre and his Two Sisters*?" I asked.

"Well, after they ate their lunch at the café they paid the waiter and then they hurried back to school for their afternoon session."

"Did they get back in time?" I asked – imagining the three running across sidewalks and streets.

"I think they were a few minutes late," my father explained.

"Oh."

"So, they were in school through the afternoon and then at four o'clock the bell rang and they headed out of class."

"What did Pierre do then?" I asked knowingly.

"Well, with all the stuff the kids were doing at lunchtime he sort of forgot about his job. But when he walked out of school at four o'clock he put his hand in his pocket and felt the piece of paper with the list of things he was supposed to buy."

"Yikes," I said.

"Definitely. So, as he was walking out he saw his sisters and said, 'Collette and Chantelle, I forgot to get the supplies for the baker! Can you help me go shopping?'"

"'Sorry, I can't today,' Collette said, 'I've got my piano lesson this afternoon.'"

"'And I'm meeting some friends at a café.' Chantelle said. 'Sorry we can't help you.'"

"'But, I have to get a lot of stuff!' Pierre said."

"'Sorry,' Chantelle said. 'We have other plans.'"

"'You better hurry, because the bakery closes in thirty minutes,' Collette told him."

"So the two sisters walked away and Pierre began running down the street as fast as he could. Soon, he got to the first shop and bought a big bar of chocolate. Then he went to the next store and bought a big bag of flour and then got a big bag of sugar."

"What about the truffles?" I asked.

"Truffles?"

"Yeah, there was a bag of truffles on the list. Did he have time to get those too?"

"Oh yeah, well that's where he went next. He went to the truffle store and got a big bag of truffles."

"Good," I told my Dad. "I was hoping that he wouldn't forget those."

"No, no, he had time to get them," my father told me. "So, anyway, after he got those supplies he ran as fast as he could to the baker's shop to deliver it all to the baker before he closed his shop at four thirty."

"Did he make it?" I asked.

"Well sure he did," Dad explained. "Pierre was a really fast runner."

"That's good."

"So, he got to the *boulangerie* with all of his bags just before the baker closed his shop," my father explained. 'You got here with only a minute left,' the baker told Pierre."

"'I ran really fast,' Pierre told the baker as he showed the bags to the baker and his wife.

"'So, I see you got my bar of chocolate,' said the baker as he went through the bags."

"'Yes,' said Pierre, happy at all the shopping he had done that afternoon."

"'And I see you got my bag of flour.'"

"'Yes monsieur,' Pierre replied."

"'And I see you got my bag of sugar.'"

"'Yes monsieur,' said Pierre."

I interrupted, "And the bag of truffles, don't forget that."

"Right," my Dad agreed. "'And I see you got my bag of truffles,' the baker said to Pierre."

"'Yes monsieur, I got your truffles,' Pierre told him."

"'Oh no!' the baker said when he had gone through all of the bags. 'Where is 'zee stinky cheese! Pierre, did you forget 'zee stinky cheese again?'"

"He did," I said.

"'Oh Monsieur baker, I'm so sorry, I forgot 'zee stinky cheese,' Pierre said. 'I didn't have time to get it.'"

"'But I told you more than once this morning, not to forget 'zee stinky cheese!', the baker said loudly." (As did my father in the retelling.) "'How could you not remember 'zee stinky cheese?' the baker asked Pierre. 'I told you just this morning, 'Don't forget 'zee stinky cheese!'"

"'But it's stinky', Pierre said. 'Why do you want stinky cheese anyway?'"

"'Its real name Pierre,' the baker said, 'is *epoisses* – that's the name of the stinky cheese – it is what Napoleon himself called *The King of All Cheeses*.'"

"'But why do you like it?' Pierre asked."

"'It is Madam's favorite,' the baker explained."

"'Yes, but why does she like 'zee stinky cheese?' Pierre asked the baker. 'It's stinky?'"

"'Madam requested it!' the baker said sternly."

"'Yes, but *why*?' Pierre asked."

"'It is because of where she's *from*,' the baker finally explained."

"'Ah, where's she's from,' Pierre said, 'Like a special place like Normandy or Provence?'"

"'No, it's not like that,' said the baker. 'She's not from those places.'"

"'Oh, maybe she's from a big city like Paris or Lyon?'"

"'No, no, that's not where she's from either,' the baker explained."

"'What you do you mean,' Pierre asked. '…when you say, she likes the cheese because of where she's *from*?'"

"The baker was quiet for a moment and finally said to Pierre, 'You see, she grew up on a farm and she misses the smell of the barnyard.'"

At this joke, both my Dad and I laughed loudly – even though he had told it many times before in his retelling of the story of *Pierre and his Two Sisters*. Once we were done laughing, my father continued.

"'I will try to remember 'zee stinky cheese tomorrow,' Pierre told the baker."

"'I hope you bring it tomorrow,' the baker told Pierre. 'It would make Madam very happy.'"

"'I will try not to forget 'zee stinky cheese again','" Pierre said.

"'You are a good boy,' the baker said. 'Just don't forget 'zee stinky cheese.'"

"That's a good story," I told my Dad, knowing that the story had come to an end.

"Yeah, it is. I guess the moral of the story is..." my father paused for a moment, "What is the phrase... work before pleasure. You know, get your work done first before doing fun stuff."

"Or buy 'zee stinky cheese before going to play hide and seek at the park," I said with a laugh.

"Or...don't trust French girls wearing berets who don't want you to do your work," my Dad replied with a laugh. "Wow, hey," my Dad said with a jolt, quickly standing up and turning on the light in my darkened bedroom. "I just thought of something! Give me just a minute."

I sat up in my bed, moved my pillows to prop up my back and rubbed my eyes, wondering what he was talking about.

Soon, I heard my Dad opening his books on the kitchen table and noisily paging through them.

Something about France, I thought to myself.

A few minutes later he returned to my bedroom with a piece of paper.

"You know how I told you earlier today that I didn't know anything about detective stuff?" he began.

"Yeah," I said, confused at what he might soon be telling me – because he had mentioned to me several times that he had no experience in working with detectives or cases or investigations when I was telling him about *The Sunday School Detectives* and *The Case of the Mysterious Circles* earlier in the evening.

"Well, our bedtime story reminded me of one thing I've learned as I've been studying French – and I just realized it might come in handy for your detective work."

"What's that?" I asked sleepily.

He handed me a torn piece of paper and I noticed he had written the following words in pencil:

CHERCHEZ LA FEMME

"Do you know what it means?" he asked.

"Something about a wife, maybe?" I guessed.

"That's pretty good!" he said enthusiastically. "You're pretty close. I guess in all of my studying, I've taught you a thing or two! Wife is one way of translating the word *femme*. This is not about a wife, but it could be, I guess. In this case, the word *femme* means woman."

"Okay," I said pensively.

"The phrase '*Cherchez la femme*' means 'look for the woman'," my Dad explained. "I remember reading somewhere that mystery writers use it a lot in their books when a man is accused of doing something wrong – and the reason he did it is because of a woman."

"Look for the woman," I repeated while looking at the paper. "So, it's another way of saying '*blame the woman*?'"

My father let out a loud and long laugh – something that he rarely did.

"No, it's not a way of saying 'blame the woman'," he said seriously. "It's just a way of saying – the guy did something because of a woman." He paused for a moment. "I guess if you think about our bedtime story and a detective was trying to figure out why Pierre didn't get 'zee stinky cheese you could said '*Cherchez la femme*'."

"Look for the woman?" I said.

"Right! Well, in Pierre's case it was not exactly a woman – it was two girls, his sisters."

"So, it's like, 'blame the girls because Pierre didn't get the cheese'?" I asked.

"No, it's not about blame," my father explained. "If you think about the story, the girls probably would have gone off to the garden and the Eiffel Tower and where else?"

"…the carousel and the café," I added.

"Right! They would have probably done what they did with or without Pierre, but Pierre decided not to go shopping because he wanted to go with his sisters to all of those fun places. So, '*Cherchez la femme*'."

"Look for the woman," I translated before pausing. "You could say that for the baker as well," I added.

"The baker?" my Dad asked.

"Yeah, if you were wondering why the baker wanted 'zee stinky cheese in the first place, you could ask..." I looked at the paper again, "*Cherchez la femme.* The baker wanted the cheese because his wife missed the smell of the barnyard."

We both laughed.

"Right! You're absolutely right about that Pep," my father exclaimed. "Both Pierre and the baker were affected by women. I think the phrase could explain the actions of a lot of young and old men!"

I looked at him with a puzzled expression on my face.

"For me, if you'd ask me why, back in Junior High School, I wanted to play the saxophone. What do you think?

"Look for the woman?"

"Yep, there were two girls...they were both saxophone players and I thought it would be pretty neat to sit next to them. So I started playing the saxophone too."

"How did that work?"

"Well, I wasn't very good," he said with a laugh. "But, I did get to sit next to the girls for a while."

"That's funny," I replied.

"Or, if you ever wondered why I quit college, and moved to a different city?"

"Look for the woman?"

"Yep," my Dad said, as his voice began sounding remorseful. "I met your Mom, and I wanted to be close to her, and she lived here in Findlay."

"Hmm."

"…and then you came along," he said. "So I guess it was a good decision to be here."

At this comment, we both paused – I, knowing that he probably did not mean what he said, having experienced firsthand his great sadness and hearing all of his depressive talk about 'wanting to be somewhere else' – and him, pausing after seeing the look on my face.

"Well, I guess that's my contribution to your detective work," he finally concluded. "It won't help you on every case…but it might come in handy sometime."

"Okay, thanks," I said with a yawn as I looked up at him. "Don't forget 'zee stinky cheese."

"Don't you forget 'zee stinky cheese either," he replied as he turned off the light in my bedroom.

"*Bonne nuit Pep*," I heard him say, just as I was falling into a deep sleep.

CHAPTER 39

I n a spaceship located at what seemed to be the edge of the galaxy, Commander Klaxon stood behind a bank of blinking lights and dials barking orders to his crew. He was small in stature and green. His face looked like Greedo from *Star Wars* and he had a hat like Marvin the Martian from *Looney Tunes.*

"Prepare for the invasion," he said to one of his alien soldiers.

"Yes commander," came the reply.

Suddenly, a green lieutenant approached, saluting the Commander when he arrived.

"Commander, I have word from Findlay," he explained.

"Findlay?"

"Yes, commander."

"Go on," the Commander said in a dark and evil tone.

"There's a problem with our landing area," the lieutenant said.

"What kind of problem?"

"They've got Sneak Ryerson on the case. He's working on solving the mystery."

"We've got a detective of our own!" the Commander barked. "Send in Sne Kissiim."

Suddenly, another green character entered – looking a lot like my friend Sneak, but with a green face and dark green hair that fell into his eyes.

"Yes Commander, you requested me?" the alien detective asked.

"We have a problem with one of our landing areas."

"Where Commander?"

"Findlay."

"In Hancock County?"

"Yes, there seems to be some sort of mystery to solve."

"There's no mystery," the alien detective said. "We'll land our spaceships at our locations in the flat cornfields around the city, then set up the vacuums to collect all of the Earth's oxygen. The earthlings won't know what happened until it is too late. They'll be out of oxygen and we'll have enough to fuel our spaceships to travel to more systems."

At the explanation, both the alien detective and the alien commander let out loud sinister laughs.

So, that's it! I thought. *That's the reason for all of the circles. They're going to take all of our oxygen! I've got to call Hailey and warn the others! I've figured it out.*

"Our plan seems to be coming together," the commander said. "Why don't we check with our spies?"

Immediately, two girls wearing flat black hats appeared.

Their wearing berets! I thought.

"Collette, Chantelle, glad you could join us," the Commander said.

"We flew in from the Eiffel Tower," the girls said in unison.

"The Eiffel Tower?" the alien detective asked.

"Yes, it's got rockets on the bottom to travel through outer space," one of the girls said.

So that's why it's shaped like that! I realized.

"Are we ready to collect the oxygen?" the commander asked.

"Yes, we are ready," one of the girls replied.

"Thank you Michelle."

Her name's not Michelle, it's Chantelle, I thought.

"We'll take all of the oxygen soon," the Commander added. "Hey, what's he doing here?" the Commander asked when he saw me. "Pep has heard our plans!" he yelled as he tried to grab me with one of his green tentacles.

"Get him! Guards arrest that earthling!"

Soon the alien commander and the alien detective and the two alien spies wearing black berets were reaching out, trying to grab me. "You're not going to get me!" I yelled. "I know all about your plans to take our oxygen, I've figured it all out, you won't be able to get away with it….plus, you don't even know the girl's names, it's Chantelle, not Michelle!"

The girls looked at each other.

It all makes sense now, I thought. *It's about the oxygen. They're going to take our oxygen. I've got to call Hailey, she can call the other detectives.*

My heart was racing as I thought about how the aliens needed to be stopped.

I need to call Sneak's Uncle Charlie too. He can get the police and maybe the Army….or the Air Force.

My mood was ecstatic at having figured out the mystery. *I've figured it out!* I thought, feeling so happy.

It's all about the….oxygen?

Stopping the….aliens?

They're coming from outer space, they want our…

It took me a few moments to grasp where I was – still in my bed – and to realize that I had been dreaming. There were no space aliens trying to get me or attempting to land and get our oxygen….or at least I didn't think so.

CHAPTER 40

I was up early that Sunday morning, excited to hear what the other detectives had learned during their investigations from the previous day. As promised, Dad made me an omelet, and after breakfast we dressed in our "Church clothes" – nearly identical grey dress pants and blue dress shirts, blue blazers and red ties and went to church.

We arrived at the Church building a few minutes before Sunday School was to start and pulled into a parking spot just as Joel and his parents were arriving. My Dad and I waited as Joel and his parents got out of their car, and after my Dad and Joel's Dad shook hands and we greeted Joel's mother, I quickly told Joel and his parents about my dream about the space aliens and the crop circles.

"Wow, you sure have an over-active imagination," Joel's mother commented.

"Did you have a banana before going to sleep?" Joel's father asked, interested in my account. "I've read about some experiments on that."

"No, I don't think so," I explained.

"Banana?" Joel said with a smile. "One banana, two banana, three banana four…," he sang, in an early morning rendition of the theme song from the *Banana Splits* show. "Tra la la, tra la la la…," he continued, as I laughed.

"Joel David Hemlinger," his mother soon scolded. "We're walking into church! You'll have to sing about other things now."

"Yes, Mom," Joel said while looking down and humming the rest of the *Banana Splits* song.

After walking up the large stone stairs and passing the greeters who handed out the bulletins for the Church services, Joel and I separated from our parents – after saying goodbye to them – and quickly ran up a flight of stairs to our Sunday School classroom.

The room for our grade (a combined 5th and 6th grade class) was on the top floor – next to large wooden closets holding the robes we wore for the Children's Choir – and filled with kids sitting on metal folding chairs seated around two long folding tables. Most of the kids who were part of *The Sunday School Detectives* were in our class that morning – except for Moscow, Jennie and Michelle who were in different classrooms for younger kids.

Professor Telson was our guest teacher again that Sunday and greeted all of the kids he knew by name. As there were kids who were not part of *The Sunday*

School Detectives, he didn't make any references to *The Case of the Mysterious Circles* or our budding detective agency or our meeting the previous morning. Instead, the Professor talked about the *Trinity* – how God is one being, but also three persons – the Father, the Son and the Holy Spirit. "Co-eternal and co-divine", I remember him saying about the three persons of the Trinity.

After our Sunday School class, we joined our parents who had been at their own Adult Sunday School classes – or who had spent the time chatting with friends, as my father had. We met in the church basement for a brief "coffee fellowship" time and ate donuts and drank hot chocolate and played tag through some empty classrooms while our parents stood talking with friends while drinking freshly brewed coffee from small white Styrofoam cups. Afterwards, we made our way upstairs with our parents to attend the hour-long church service.

Since all of the *Sunday School Detectives* attended the same church – and the church consisted of several hundred people who had many opportunities to talk to each other – I would guess that by the time the final note of the closing benediction was sung – a song that sounded a lot like *Edelweiss* from the *Sound of Music* – most members of the Church had heard about Sneak's plight and the start of *The Sunday School Detectives*.

After the service, after waiting – for too long, in my opinion – for my father to say goodbye to people – Dad and I made our way outside to his car in the parking lot and then drove to get lunch.

I was anxious to meet with the other detectives and find out what they had learned – but was annoyed when my Dad stopped at a gas station to fill the empty tank of his blue 1973 Chevrolet Impala.

"Fill 'er up," he told the gas station attendant seriously, "and check the oil."

"Dad…" I implored. "We need to get to lunch."

"I don't want to run out of gas going there," he explained.

When we arrived at *Friendly's* – a restaurant near the mall – I saw that the other Sunday School Detectives were already there – seated around a large circular table at the back of the restaurant. Sneak, I noticed, sat gloomily with his parents and Mr. and Mrs. Cotton, a few tables away.

Meanwhile, I was happy to see that my Dad was joining my Mom at a large booth. Even though they were separated, they still seemed to get along – and, probably like a lot of kids whose parents separate, I had hoped they'd get back together some day. They sat with Michelle's parents – while Joel's Mom and Dad and Lisa's parents sat at an adjoining table – united after a waitress lowered an opaque plastic window that slid down between the two booths.

"Sorry," I said when I arrived, pulling up a chair next to Jennie. "My Dad took forever getting out of church and then we had to stop and get gas."

The table, I noticed, was crowded, but we all had room to sit. The other kids already had their drinks – mostly waters – and long plastic menus in front of them. Jennie was to my left. To her left was Joel while Moscow sat to his left. To my right was Michelle, and next to her was Cressida and then Lisa. Hailey sat directly across from me between her brother to her right and Lisa on her left.

"We were just laughing at the rumors we heard at church this morning," Hailey explained, as many of the other young detectives were smiling.

"Someone told my Mom that she heard that Sneak was *sick* and wasn't going to be doing detective work for a while," Lisa said.

"I heard someone say…" Michelle began.

"Someone asked our Mom if Hailey was sad," Moscow interrupted with a wide grin, "because her *boyfriend* got grounded," he added, elongating the word boyfriend for dramatic effect.

At this comment, Hailey blushed. "He's *not* my boyfriend," she insisted, as her face turned a bright red. "He's a boy and a friend, but that doesn't make him a boyfriend."

"Right, sure, whatever," Moscow said with a smile. "Just let me know when I should call him my brother-in-law."

"Well, there *is* a way he could be your brother-in-law," Hailey responded seriously, as we all listened intently.

"How's that?" Moscow asked.

"Well, if you married Jennie, then Sneak would be your brother-in-law," she said as her serious look quickly changed to a wide smile.

At this comment, it was Jennie's turn to blush. "Eww! Hold on! Hold on!" she gasped.

"Let's order some food," Moscow said, quickly changing the subject. Soon he took a big and loud slurp from the long straw that went into his large glass of root beer. "I'm starving and have hockey practice this afternoon."

"You look like you're going to the gym too, Pep." Lisa asked me, looking at the gym bag I brought with me into the restaurant.

"Uh, yeah," I lied – deciding not to tell her that a voice-activated tape recorder was hidden inside.

With perfect timing to address our group's restlessness and need for food, our waitress, Patsy, approached the table to take our order. She was warm and friendly and started taking orders first from the kids she knew: Jennie, Hailey and Moscow – who were her customers every Sunday afternoon – before moving to the others at the table.

It was one of my first times at the restaurant, so I ordered simply: chicken strips with coleslaw, but others ordered a variety of food, hamburgers and cheeseburgers, fish-a-majig sandwiches, while Moscow and a few others ordered the clam-boat special.

Every time someone ordered the clam boat special, Joel would begin singing, "*Don't Rock the Boat*" – the 1974 song by a band called the *Hues Corporation*. A few times, people would respond by singing, "Don't tip the boat over" – but a lot of other conversations were happening at the same time, so most kids continued talking – which, I think, disappointed Joel because he couldn't get more people to sing along with him.

"Okay, let's talk about the case," Hailey interjected after Pasty had left. Unfortunately, a number of us were still talking to people seated next to us, so Hailey had to ask again more loudly. "Guys! We don't have all day – let's talk about the case." Quickly, our attention turned to Hailey. "What have we learned since our meeting at the Ryerson's yesterday morning?"

For some reason I felt like she looked right at me – maybe she did – maybe not, but I stammered out an answer. "I...uh....I haven't really done anything," I explained, not wanting to reveal my secret recordings to the group and how I had spent several hours transcribing the tapes of our first meeting.

"Me neither," Jennie answered to my relief – quickly taking the attention away from me. "We went out to our grandparent's farm last night, so I couldn't really talk to Sneak about the case, but he's only a few booths away, so I could probably get him to answer a question if we had one."

"With your parents and Hailey and Moscow's parent's sitting right there?" Joel asked. "I don't think so."

"Well, maybe." Jennie answered.

"I didn't do anything either," Michelle explained with a frown. "Jennie and I talked about a few things, but we just played at her house after everyone left yesterday."

"Oh, and Mr. Knick Knack didn't do anything either," Jennie added. "In case you were interested."

"I was wondering about that guy," Moscow said with a grin. "So, did anybody do anything? This might be a short meeting."

"Well we did some….investigation yesterday," Lisa began as she glanced at her cousin next to her.

"Yes," Hailey added knowingly. "Lisa and Cressida had an interesting adventure yesterday."

"What happened?" Michelle asked with great interest.

"I had my brother, Brad, drive Cressida and I over to Joel Davis'….," Lisa continued.

"Hey!" Joel interjected.

"Sorry, I don't know why I keep doing that! Brad drove us to *Julian* Davis' apartment building," Lisa clarified.

"You did not!" Jennie exclaimed. "Did you get to meet him?"

"Yes, we did, actually." Cressida said in a quiet voice.

"How did you work it out....to meet him?" Michelle asked.

"Well," Lisa continued. "Yesterday morning, someone said something like 'you just can't just go up to his door and see him'. But after I heard that, I started thinking...kids do that a lot...that's exactly what we do! We go up to people's houses and try to sell something like something from the Girl Scouts..."

"Or something from Campfire Girls," Jennie said.

"Bluebirds!" Jennie and Michelle said at the same time, while smiling at each other – because they were in the same Bluebird group – led by their mothers.

"Right," Lisa replied. "So, I was thinking...Cressida and I already have to do a fund raiser for school – we're selling candles and have a big brochure with pictures and an order form and everything. So, I just had Brad take us over to Julian's apartment building and we went door to door."

"No way!" Jennie said, astonished. "That's so smart."

"We started at a different door," Lisa explained. "You know, so it wouldn't seem like we were just going to his door."

"That's smart too," Jennie added.

"Did he answer?" Michelle asked.

"Yes, he did," explained Lisa. "He seemed really nervous, and he left his building a few minutes after we came to the door."

"Wow, maybe you spooked him," Moscow said.

"Did he buy anything?" I asked.

"Maybe," Lisa continued, answering Moscow's question instead of mine. "We tried to follow him, but he had already driven away by the time we were able to get Brad's attention and get into Brad's car."

"So, you had wanted to see him face to face – to see if you had ever seen before – had you?" Hailey asked.

"No, but Brad said he'd seen him around. He thought it might have been just at the *Twin Palace.* Brad likes to go to the movies."

"I might have seen him there too," Moscow said. "We go there sometimes."

"Anyway, there was one really interesting thing I wanted to tell the group, and maybe try to tell Sneak, if we can," Lisa continued.

"What's that?" I asked.

"Well, remember how Sneak described his adventure at the cemetery?"

"Yeah, that was pretty cool," Moscow replied. "I need to talk to him more about how he did that."

"But he got in big trouble for it," Hailey clarified.

"Well," Lisa continued, "Do you remember, that Sneak said because it was dark, he couldn't see anything?"

"Right," Joel replied quickly. "He said it was so dark and the car was going so fast, he couldn't even see what kind of car it was or even see the driver's face. Remember, how his Uncle Charlie was all over him about that?"

"Yeah...," Jennie said with a frown.

"Well, there was one thing he said he could see, do you remember?" Lisa asked.

"The envelope?" I replied.

"Okay, I guess there were two things that he could see," Lisa continued. "He could see the envelope and he could see what the driver was wearing."

"I remember," Michelle said. "He said he could see the driver's brown winter coat."

"Right," said Lisa. "And that's what I wanted to tell Sneak today. There was a problem when we saw Julian Davis leave his apartment yesterday afternoon."

"What?" Jennie asked.

"His winter coat was light blue," Cressida explained softly.

CHAPTER 41

"Light blue?" several of us said in unison, as we continued discussing the case while waiting for our food at *Friendly's*.

"But....but, that's not possible," Joel added.

"Didn't Sneak say he saw Julian when he followed him out of the cemetery?" asked Moscow.

"No," Lisa said. "I even double-checked my notes to make sure I remembered exactly what he told us. He said that he couldn't see the driver when they left the cemetery. All he saw was his brown winter coat."

"And that's not what Julian Davis was wearing when you saw him leave his apartment yesterday?" I asked.

"Right," Lisa continued. "He was wearing a light blue winter coat."

"And you're sure it was him?" Joel asked. "Could it have been someone else leaving the apartment?"

"No, I don't think so. Cressida and I got a good look at him when he left and even Brad saw him leave too. That's when Brad said that he thought he recognized him from the movie theater."

"Yeah, he left in a light blue winter coat," Cressida confirmed.

"But it doesn't make any sense, does it?" Joel said.

"No," I confessed.

"Two coats, anyone?" asked Moscow.

"I'm not sure," replied Joel. "He works at the movie theater. He's not going to have a ton of money to buy two winter coats. The girls here," he said pointing to the girls around our table. "They're into fashion and stuff and probably have a lot of different winter coats, but I only have one winter coat, how about you guys?"

"I just have one," I confessed.

"Me too," Moscow added. "Well...," he began saying, unsure of where to continue the conversation with this new evidence.

"So...," Hailey began, "we have two detectives who have seen Julian, so they can recognize him... if they see him around town. And we have evidence that he has a blue winter coat."

"Light blue," Lisa corrected.

"Okay, light blue." Hailey added. "Did you learn anything else?" she asked Lisa and her cousin.

"No, that's about it," Lisa concluded.

"Okay, is there anything else that anyone has learned since we met yesterday?"

"Well, I went to the newspaper and you were going to go to the Library," Joel replied.

"Right," said Hailey.

"Why don't you go first....maybe your investigation was better than mine," said Joel.

"Well, I didn't find too much," Hailey confessed. "But I can go next," she said before pausing to collect her thoughts. "I spent a couple of hours at the library doing research on crop circles. What I learned is that in the last twenty years, there haven't been any reported in Hancock County – besides the ones we're investigating."

"Hmmm," someone said.

"And I learned that what we're investigating aren't technically really even crop circles – in the traditional sense."

"How's that?" Jennie asked.

"Well, in most places, crops like corn or wheat are in fields and pushed down to form circles or interesting shapes. The articles I read, said those kind of crop circles started in England – the first ones were reported in the 1600's. In the last few years a lot of crop circles have happened there, but they've also appeared in lots of other places, like Australia and Canada. In some cases, people have been caught pushing down the crops with their feet or with big boards tied to a rope – to make the pattern. In other cases, it just happens overnight and people think they're made by U.F.O's."

"Technically, you'd say they're made by aliens, sis." Moscow replied. "U.F.O.'s are what they fly around in up in the sky."

"Okay," Hailey continued, "Some people think that *aliens* are making them."

At this comment, I thought of the crazy dream I had the night before about aliens taking over the world to steal our oxygen and wondered why it was so vivid and clear.

"So, really not much to add," Moscow said curtly.

"Yeah, unfortunately," Hailey replied. "I did look into the shape as well – you know, the three circles from each of the fires."

"Did you learn anything about those?" Michelle asked.

"Well, it was funny, when Professor Telson was giving his talk this morning in Sunday School about the Trinity – he said that Christians have used three overlapping circles to represent the Trinity. It reminded me about the shape of the crop circles we're studying, but the circles in our investigation don't really overlap like they do in Professor Telson's picture he showed us this morning – they are separate. I spent some time in the library trying to learn more about the shapes, but I couldn't find anything."

"Probably engines from a U.F.O.," Moscow added glumly.

"That's it exactly!" Hailey replied as many of us laughed.

"Well, it could be," Moscow said. "Joel told me that Pep had a dream about aliens last night. Maybe they've started controlling our minds."

"They've definitely taken over yours!" Hailey said to her brother.

Instead of immediately replying, Moscow simply began staring at his sister with a stoic expression. "Take me to your leader," Moscow said after a brief pause in a robot-like voice. Slowly and mechanically he stretched out his arms in front of him. "Take me to your leader," he said again before breaking into a laugh.

"Well, I found out some interesting stuff at the newspaper," Joel added enthusiastically – as our attention moved away from Moscow and his funny alien voice. "Maybe I should go next?"

"Sure," Hailey said with a smile. "I'm all done with my report from the library."

"I guess I got a little bit more than you did, Hailey," Joel began.

"That's great!" Hailey said enthusiastically. "What happened?"

"I got to the office before it closed and the reporters who were there were really great."

"What did they say?" Jennie asked.

"It wasn't really what they said, it was what they gave me," Joel explained. "I got some articles about the F.E.E.T. group and two pictures."

"Cool," I replied.

"The pictures are of the F.E.E.T. officers," he said as he pulled two black and white photos from a large yellow envelope. "One picture is from January, at the beginning of this year – so only a few months ago – and the other picture was taken about a year before that."

I looked quickly at the black and white pictures as they were passed around the table, seeing that the photos displayed a group of about eight or nine serious looking twenty-somethings sitting in chairs or standing behind those who were seated. Both pictures looked like they were taken in a common area of a dorm or perhaps a large living room. Many wore traditional late 1970's garb – bell-bottom jeans or painter's overalls – while a few of the guys had long sideburns, which was common for the time.

"Those guys look like a barrel of fun," Moscow said glumly. "I'd probably join their group...if I was having a hard time falling asleep!" He added with a flash of anger.

"Moscow!" his sister exclaimed. "Why are you being so mean? They're not *all* guilty of starting the fires."

"That would be interesting," Joel added.

"What's that?" I asked.

"If they all did it!" Joel replied.

"Like *Murder on the Orient Express!*" Jennie exclaimed.

"What?" Michelle asked.

"I saw it on T.V. once with my Dad, it had a really crazy ending," Jennie told her friend.

"I don't think it was *all* of them," Lisa said seriously. "It would be too hard to keep it a secret with so many people involved…we're in Findlay after all. But one or two of them setting the fires…I could see that. Plus, Sneak said he thought it was a young person who set them…you know, to haul the gasoline."

"And drive the motorbike!" I added.

"Moscow, you didn't say why you got so out of sorts when you saw the picture," Hailey asked her brother. "Normally, you just make fun of me."

"I don't know," he said sullenly. "I guess just sitting here looking at these guys in the picture and then looking over at Sneak sitting over there….just made me angry. I mean, we're over here, having fun, making jokes, talking about a cool mystery – but it's a mystery that Sneak really should be solving. He's so good at this stuff, but instead of being here with us – helping us trying to figure this out – he's over there, sitting with our parents. It just makes me mad at these F.E.E.T. guys. If it wasn't…if it wasn't for them – probably somebody in one of these pictures –," he paused for a moment as he looked down at the pictures on the table, "…then, Sneak wouldn't be grounded."

"I didn't know we'd be talking about sad stuff again," Jennie said with a frown.

"Think about it Jennie," Moscow continued. "If it wasn't for one of these bozos, Sneak wouldn't have even needed to go to the cemetery that night to catch them. He wouldn't have had to lie to your parents about where he was going on those nights he was doing a stakeout and he wouldn't have been bumper hopping from the back of one of their cars. It just makes me mad at what's been going on."

"What's going on," Joel sang from the chorus of the Marvin Gaye song, as the others continued their conversation. "What's going on…"

"Yeah, I'm feeling blue about it too," Lisa added.

"Me too," said Michelle.

"Me three," Jennie whispered.

"One of the things we can do to help Sneak," Hailey said encouragingly – trying to force some cheeriness to our table, "…is solve the case, right?"

"Yeah, I guess so," her brother agreed. "Let's try to solve the case, because Sneak can't," he added hopefully.

"That sounds good to me," said Lisa.

"Me three," Jennie said again as a few of us chuckled.

"Hey, which one is Julian?" Michelle asked when the pictures arrived in front of her.

"It's this guy," Lisa said pointing to a mousy looking young man with dark hair and thick glasses. "Here he is in this picture – sitting in the front – and he's right here in this other one."

"Check out the back," Joel said pointing to the photographs. "Their names are written on the other side. Let's make sure the guy you saw at the apartment is the same guy in the picture."

"That's a good idea," Hailey told him.

"Well that's who we saw at the apartment building," Lisa explained. "...and the name on the back says he's...Julian Davis." She then quickly looked on the back of the second photograph. "Yep, and the other picture lists that as his name too."

"Okay, so we definitely know that's him," Joel summarized.

"So, besides the photos, did you get anything else from the newspaper?" Hailey asked.

"No, not much else," Joel replied. "Here's a few articles you can all look at," he said pulling several small newspaper articles from the manila envelope and placing them on the table for us to read. "They are mostly notices about when the F.E.E.T. group had their meetings," he said. "They've been meeting in a classroom at the college."

"How often do they meet?" Lisa asked.

"Looks like they get together once a month," Joel explained.

We were quiet as we passed around the newspaper clippings and read them closely for clues.

"There is not much here," Lisa summarized. "It's just dates and times."

"Right, not really helpful," Joel replied.

"So, do we have any other evidence from yesterday?" Hailey asked.

"Nope," a few people said.

"So does anybody have any ideas?" Hailey asked.

"About what?" Moscow asked, looking towards his
sister.

"About what we should do next," Hailey explained.
"Even after all of our work yesterday, it doesn't seem
like we have any new...," she paused as she searched
for the right word. "Clues," she continued. "I guess
that's the right word for it....I'm still pretty new at
this," she said in an exasperated tone.

"Well, we could...," Michelle began. "Sorry, I just
thought of something and then forgot it. I can't think
of anything good."

"Me either," Jennie added.

"How about you Joel?" Hailey asked. "Can you
think of any new clues that came out of your visit to
the newspaper?"

"No, not that I can think of," Joel said. "The
reporters I talked to all seemed to think that the
F.E.E.T. group was just a bunch of goofy kids – you
know college kids, or kids about that age – looking
for something to do."

"Had they heard of Julian Davis?" Lisa asked.

"No, none of the reporters I talked to," Joel
replied. "The sports reporter was in the office – you
know – listening in as I talked to the other reporters

– and he said the F.E.E.T. guys all seemed like a bunch of 'knuckleheads'."

We laughed.

"Knuckleheads, huh?" Moscow said. "That's a funny word."

"Okay, let's focus," said Hailey, trying to sound positive. "So, Joel got some good information from the newspaper – two photos of the group and some articles about their meetings – but nothing more to go on." She paused for a moment. "Lisa or Cressida, how about you? Anything else from your visit to Julian's apartment?"

"I can't think of anything else," Lisa said as Cressida whispered into her ear. "And neither can Cressida." She paused for a moment. "I was going to make sure Sneak knew about us seeing Julian in a light blue winter coat…maybe that might mean something to him. But, I'm not really sure what else we can do at Julian's apartment…it's illegal to break-in."

"Now, that's an idea!" Moscow said with a smile.

"No!" Hailey scolded.

"I was just joking," her brother said.

"And we can't really follow him," Lisa continued. "I asked Brad, but he said he didn't want to. He has to work at Dietsch's after school. Plus, he said we'd probably just wait around all day to see if Julian left his apartment and then once he left, lose him in traffic."

"Well that stinks," Michelle replied.

"I'll bet I could keep up with him on my bike," added Moscow, "...it's a three speed."

"Maybe around downtown," replied Lisa. "But not when he gets going fast on a road like Tiffin Avenue."

"Yeah, you're right about that," Moscow admitted with a frown.

"Anyone else have any ideas?" Hailey asked again – still working hard at keeping the discussion positive and productive.

"Yeah," Moscow said, "I was thinking we could try to follow the evidence – that's something Sneak would tell us to do."

"I like the sound of this," Joel said.

"What evidence were you thinking we should follow?" asked Hailey.

"So, you know, like, whenever anyone touches anything, they leave fingerprints," Moscow continued.

"Right!" Jennie replied.

"And, we know that Sneak went bumper hopping on the back of someone's bumper," Moscow explained. "...maybe not Julian Davis' car because he had a different winter coat, but probably someone in one of these pictures," he said while picking up one of the black and white photographs and then quickly dropping it on the table. Then, he paused dramatically, before continuing. "So, all we would need to do," Moscow paused again, "is go to each of their cars and dust the bumpers with that fingerprint dust – like they do on the police detective shows – and we'd know right away who's bumper Sneak was holding on to."

"Hmm," Joel said loudly. "I hadn't thought about that."

"I like it!" Michelle exclaimed, giving a thumbs up sign towards Moscow.

"I think there's just one problem with that idea, Moscow," Jennie said.

"There may be more than one problem," Lisa said skeptically.

"Do you remember how cold it's been?" Jennie asked.

"Yeah," Moscow replied.

"Well, I'm pretty sure Sneak would have been wearing gloves," Jennie explained.

"Ah, man!" Moscow said, frustrated.

"We could ask him – but I'm pretty sure it was *really* cold on those nights he was out there in the cemetery," Jennie continued.

"Yeah," said Moscow. "You're probably right."

"Fiddlesticks, is what my Mom would say," Jennie replied.

"Mine too!" Michelle added, smiling at her friend.

"Okay, so Sneak was probably wearing gloves and we can't go around to the bumpers of everyone's cars pouring out fingerprint dust," Hailey concluded. "Any other ideas?"

We sat silently for a moment.

"We're sorta' stuck," Lisa said.

"Workin' on mysteries without any clues," said Joel.

"Maybe," Michelle offered tentatively. "Well, forget about it."

"What?" Jennie asked.

"Go ahead Michelle," Hailey encouraged. "We're kind of out of ideas."

"Well, I was just thinking – what if Professor Telson was here? What would he tell us to do?"

"He'd tell us to read a big theology book!" Moscow said with a laugh. "Or, answer questions about swans or something."

"What do you think he'd want us to do, Michelle?" Joel asked seriously.

"I think he'd tell us we should pray about it, don't you think?" Michelle explained.

"You mean like, right here?" Moscow asked.

"Maybe?" Michelle replied with a shrug.

"I think that's a great idea," Joel responded. "We need some help – we're pretty stuck. Maybe God can help us."

"Okay, can someone say a prayer?" Hailey asked.

"I'll do it," Cressida said, as several of us stared at her with our mouths agape – astonished that the girl who had a hard time talking in front of other kids would not have a problem talking to God.

Soon, we quickly bowed our heads.

"Dear Lord, please help us," Cressida said in an almost whisper. "We want to be able to solve the case and help Sneak, but it seems like we've run out of clues. Please be with everyone here and keep us safe. In Jesus name, amen."

"Amen," we said in unison.

"Okay, well," Hailey started again. "Did anyone get any ideas while we were praying?"

"About what, exactly?" Michelle asked.

"About what we should do next," Hailey explained.

"I did," said Moscow. "I got an idea. It just came to me as we were praying."

"What was it?" Hailey asked.

"I realized that the case isn't about tracking down *all the cars* of the F.E.E.T. people is it?"

"What do you mean?" Joel asked.

"It's just the opposite, right?" Moscow continued. "Think about what Sneak told us about the clues he got. I thought it was really cool when he was telling us about the *motorbike* – you know the one where he took those casts of the tracks?"

"Yeah, but Uncle Charlie said it might be those kind of tires on a different bike," Jennie added.

"Sure, maybe it could be a different bike," Moscow continued. "But, I was thinking, what if it is really – you know – what if it really is a Yamaha that they're using to set the fires – the 1978 model, like Sneak said. If they've been running it through some fields, there's a chance the owner took it in to a shop to get it serviced – so we could check with the mechanics in town to see if they remember it and could tell us who brought it in. That way, we don't have to check *all* of the cars of the F.E.E.T. people – we'd just have to look for *one* motorbike."

"That's actually a really good idea," Hailey said. "It wouldn't take too long to call the mechanics in Findlay."

"There might be one problem," Lisa interrupted.

"What's that?" asked Moscow.

"What if the owner took it down to Lima or up to Toledo to get it worked on? That would be a lot more repair shops to call."

"Yeah, it would," Moscow replied disappointedly.

"Moscow," Hailey said, "Would you mind calling the shops here in Findlay? And if nothing turns up, maybe you can tell us what to say and we can all start calling places in Lima or Toledo...or, if that doesn't work maybe we could call places in Columbus or Detroit."

"To widen the search perimeter," Jennie said as many of us laughed.

"Where did you hear that?" Hailey asked.

"I guess on T.V. – I don't really know what that means."

"It means we're going to keep searching for a motocross bike," Moscow explained.

"Yeah, but, they might not have even taken it into a repair shop," Lisa added. "They might have fixed it on their own. Or, they could have taken it to some place really far away. It's going to take us a really long time calling all those places…and it may not even pan out."

"Yeah, I hadn't thought of that," Moscow added. "The bike's only two years old, they might not even need to bring it in."

"Well, it's a start," Hailey said encouragingly. "At least we can tell the repair shops to be on the lookout for it," she added optimistically.

"Yeah, but it might take a long time to find," Moscow said dejectedly.

"Okay, well that's a good start," Hailey continued. "Does anyone else have any ideas – from when we prayed? Checking for the motorbike is good – is there anything else we could do this week?"

The cause for what happened next – I've considered for quite a while. I'm not sure if it occurred because I thought Hailey had looked directly at me – like she had done earlier – or, because I wanted to show the other kids that I was just as smart as they were. While they had been talking about the case, I had simply sat quietly – listening to the others share their great ideas with Hailey – and feeling more and more like an observer to the discussion instead of a participant. Maybe there was something or someone else that was prompting me that morning – maybe it was the Lord working "in mysterious ways", as Professor Telson might have told us. Maybe God decided to show mercy on a bunch of kids who were trying to figure out a complicated case. Whatever the cause – "it blew the case wide open" – as my friend Sneak Ryerson would later tell me.

Hailey's last words to us contained two questions that lingered in the air for a few moments –like mist hovering over a cold river, I later thought. "Does anyone else have any ideas?" she had asked. And "Is there anything else we could do this week?" she had added.

Before Hailey had finished her last question, I was already reaching into my green gym bag that was stuffed under my chair and pulling out a small folded piece of paper – a paper that I had put there earlier in the morning.

"W…well," I replied to Hailey's question with a stammer, after quickly looking at the crumpled paper. "My Dad always says, '*Cherchez la femme*'."

CHAPTER 42

The momentary silence from my fellow detectives – amid the rattle and clank of pots and pans and silverware being handled in the nearby kitchen – seemed to last forever. I immediately felt uncomfortable, quickly wishing I had not shared the French phrase that my Dad had taught me the night before.

"What?" Jennie asked quickly.

"Cherchez la femme," I replied. "My Dad always says, '*Cherchez la femme*'."

Michelle grimaced and Lisa looked visibly perplexed as they tried to understand the words I was saying.

"Chair say what?" Moscow soon asked, as the girls began giggling. "My chair ain't sayin' nothin'!' he exclaimed while leaning his ear down towards the back of his seat. When he said this, the younger girls broke into loud laughs, hardly able to stop themselves while the older kids chuckled.

Did I say it wrong? I wondered as I quickly looked at my Dad's handwritten note. *No, I think I said it right. That's the right way to say it,* I thought. *Cherchez la femme.*

"Chair say la fez?" Moscow added, as he put a napkin on his head while the girls continued to laugh.

"It's probably nothing," I added, "just forget about it."

Moscow leaned his head down again, getting his ear closer to the back of his seat.

"Chair say you need to watch more *Ten Speed and Brownshoe,*" he said loudly with a broad smile, referring to a new T.V. detective show starring Jeff Goldblum and Ben Vereen.

At this comment, even I laughed along with all the kids at the table – as we were all familiar with the ABC network's many commercials promoting the new television program.

"Okay Moscow," his sister scolded. "That's enough. Let's hear what Pep has to say."

"It's....it's nothing really," I stammered. "I probably shouldn't have brought it up."

"What does it mean?" Lisa asked. "We don't get it."

"It's nothing," I explained.

"No really, we want to know," Lisa protested.

"Forget about it," I added.

"Oh come on Pep," Lisa continued. "You started it – you must have thought it was important when you said it."

"Okay, fine. The words are *Cherchez la femme*," I said slowly, pausing for a moment after saying the words and holding up my Dad's note with the words written on it, so the entire group could see it.

"What language is it?" Jennie asked as she looked at the note.

Looking to my right, I could see Cressida whispering something into her cousin's ear.

"It's French," Lisa explained. "Does it mean, '*look for clues*'? That's what Cressida thinks it means."

"Close!" I replied happily – relieved that Cressida had made my words seem less strange to the rest of the group. "It means, '*look for the woman*'."

"Look for the woman?" Moscow asked, with a surprise look on his face.

"Look for the woman," Joel repeated, as his mind raced as he tried to think of a suitable pop song to reference. He initially drew a blank but a few moments later he began singing *Lady* – the 1973 song by *Styx* – which really had nothing to do with the phrase I had shared with the group.

"So, what does chair-say la femme mean?" Lisa asked me.

"Well, it means like….*sometimes things happen because of a woman*," I explained.

"So, things happen because of a woman," Moscow repeated.

"Yeah," I replied.

"So, it means, like, '*blame the woman*'," Lisa scoffed. "Just like Adam did in the Garden of Eden with Eve, right? That's what everyone wants to do…blame the woman!"

"Hey Pep, what's the big idea?" Jennie said heatedly.

"No, no, no," I protested nervously – instantly feeling uncomfortable as the skin on my forehead and upper lip began to sweat and feel warm – as I uneasily pondered how best to react to the girls' objection of my idea. "It's not like that," I told them. "It's not a way to say 'blame the woman'. It's just a way to say that a lot of times guys do stuff because of a woman." I paused again trying with all of my might to remember the exact words my father had used in explaining the idea. "It's like my Dad playing the saxophone," I finally told them.

"I didn't know your Dad played an instrument?" Joel asked as he quickly stopped singing, intrigued now that the discussion had turned to music. "Is he any good?"

"No, he hasn't played for a long time."

"Oh," Joel replied.

"What does that have to do with the case?" Jennie asked.

"Nothing, really," I told her. "It doesn't have anything to do with the case, but I think you'll get it if I explain it this way," I said quickly, before pausing briefly to catch my breath as my heart raced. "So, my Dad played the saxophone, in like High School, or maybe Middle School. Anyway the reason he joined the band was because two girls were *already* playing the saxophone – and he wanted to sit next to them. So you see, *cherchez la femme*....look for the woman. The reason he was in the band was because of them."

"But those were girls, not women, right?" Joel added. "So, it's like *cherchez the girls*."

"Hmm," Jennie pouted.

"I don't get how it's not another way to say *blame the woman*," Lisa complained.

"Well, it's like...," I began again nervously – unsure of how else to describe the idea, then paused for another few moments. And then, miraculously, I remembered the story of *Pierre and his Two Sisters*. "It's like a story I heard," I continued. "...about a kid who worked for a baker, but he didn't do his work because he wanted to go to the park and go on some adventures around the city with his two older sisters – so, look for the woman – *cherchez la femme*."

"So, were his sisters girls too?" Joel asked. "Is it like *cherchez the girls*, again?"

"Sounds interesting," Lisa replied – in a way that made me think that she didn't find it very interesting at all.

We sat for a few moments in silence, collectively looking down at the table, staring at our drinks of fizzy soda and root beer as well as the glasses of water that were near us, while some looked at Joel's treasures at the center of the table – the newspaper articles and the two large glossy black and white photographs next to the long manila envelope that Joel had brought them in.

"Well, *cherchez la femme*," Joel said dejectedly while looking down at the table.

"*Cherchez la femme*," Moscow added, lifting up his glass of root beer in a toast, while looking at the others.

Sitting there, I felt miserable.

Why did I bring up such a stupid thing? I wondered. *You can hardly pronounce it*, I said to myself, recalling how I had stumbled in saying the French words each time I said the phrase. *I probably even looked weird saying it*, I thought. I was reminded of my appearance a number of years later when I read a book by P.G. Wodehouse, who described the appearance of one of his characters that, "there had crept a look of furtive shame, the shifty hangdog look which announces that an Englishman is about to speak French." *Did I have that strange look too, when I was trying to speak French?* I wondered.

You can hardly explain it, I thought at the time, remembering how poorly I had described the idea. *You don't even know what it really is*, I summarized. *You are so stupid*, I added as my thoughts turned darker.

From now on, Pep, just keep your mouth shut. Don't ever do anything like that again.

"Pep," Hailey had said in a strong voice while looking down at the table before she turned her gaze to look straight at me.

As she said these words the rest of the detectives at the table were quiet, looking at her, waiting for her to speak.

For me, her pause seemed to last forever. I knew that Hailey had always spoken nice words to me – even when I had said things that weren't the smartest – but for a moment, although brief, I thought she might ask me to leave the group – I thought she might tell me that I was so dumb, so slow, so out of it, that I had no business of being in the same group with such brilliant young detectives.

Maybe she won't ask you to leave, I thought next, *but maybe she'll ask you not to say dumb things like that ever again.*

I dreaded the next words that she was about to say.

Will she ask me to leave? I wondered. *Or, tell me not to say anything?*

But, then, incredibly, I saw a wide smile break out on her face.

"Pep," she said smiling brightly. "You're a genius!"

CHAPTER 43

"A....a genius?" I asked, surprised at hearing Hailey Cotton's description. That word, *genius*, was not a word that I had *ever* used to describe myself and one that I had never, ever heard anyone else use to describe me.

"Sis, what are you talking about?" Moscow asked, staring at his sister and sounding annoyed.

"Look at the pictures," Hailey explained pointing at the two pictures of the officers of F.E.E.T. – two photos that we had left undisturbed for several minutes in the middle of the restaurant table.

"We already did," Moscow replied. "We passed them around, remember?"

"Yeah, but look at them closely. What's different between them?" Hailey asked as she held them up.

The young detectives seated near Moscow and his sister peered intently at the photos. Sitting on the other side of the table, I couldn't see them once Hailey had picked them up – only the cursive-written script indicating the names of the people in the photographs, written lightly in pencil on the back of each of the photographs.

"They're wearing different clothes," Joel said with a laugh. "I guess that's a good thing."

"That would be weird if they were wearing the same clothes a year later!" Moscow scoffed.

"Hey! I see it too!" Lisa said suddenly. "I think I know where you're going with this, Hailey."

Jennie had moved from her chair and stood between Moscow and his sister. Suddenly she exclaimed, "Ah! I can't believe we didn't notice that before."

"What? What?" Moscow asked grabbing one of the pictures. "I don't see it! Do I have to cross my eyes or look away really quickly, or something?"

"No, just look at the people from last year to this year," his sister told him.

"They're the same people, right?" Moscow said. "Their haircuts are a little different and they're standing in different places but it's the same guys, right?"

"Not quite," Lisa added.

"Oh wow," Moscow replied in a surprised voice. "I can't believe we didn't notice that before."

"What?" Michelle asked – still sitting next to me, and like me, was unable to see the photos. "Tell us!"

"There's a girl in last year's picture," Moscow explained quickly. "But she's not in the newer one."

"A girl?" Michelle asked. "I thought it was a group of all guys?"

"Yep," Lisa said, grabbing the photos from Moscow. "Look Cressida," she said pointing to a young woman in the older photo. "It's like Pep said, just look for the woman!"

"Pep, tell us again how you say it?" Hailey asked.

"*Cherchez la femme*," I explained, exhaling deeply – relieved that I had actually helped the group, instead of looking foolish.

"*Cherchez la femme!*" Joel repeated.

"*Cherchez la femme!*" came the reply from the others at the table as several kids raised their plastic glasses and toasted each other with a clink.

CHAPTER 44

The other detectives wanted to look at the picture, so it took a few moments for me to finally get a good look at the young woman that everyone was talking about.

When the photo from the previous year was eventually passed to me and I could study it more thoroughly, I could soon see why we had all nearly missed her. The reason was that she was barely visible in the black and white photo – being partially hidden – standing behind two taller guys.

From what I could tell, the woman was young, in her early twenties and wore blue jeans and a flowered shirt – common for the late 70's – and had bright, wide eyes and long blonde hair.

"So what's her name?" Joel asked, as I quickly turned the photo over, reading the list of names on the back.

"Alice....Alice Williams," I said, finding the only female name located near the end of the list of names written in pencil.

"She'll tell us what's going on," Hailey said confidently. "I'm sure of it."

"She seems nice...in the picture anyway," Jennie added, after studying the young woman's face.

"Why don't a few of us girls pay her a visit....and hopefully she'll tell us what she knows," Lisa added.

"Sounds good," I replied – wishing I could tag along on the interview as well.

"Let's see if she's in the phone book," Hailey suggested.

"I'll go check," Jennie volunteered.

"Me too," Michelle replied – and soon the two young girls were racing towards the pay phone located near the back of the restaurant – near the door to the rest rooms – only a short distance from our table.

"Well, I guess while you girls are getting clues from that girl..," Moscow told his sister.

"Alice," Joel interrupted. "They'll go ask Alice."

"Right, Alice," Moscow continued. "I'll start making calls to motorcycle repair places. It shouldn't take me very long to call the places here in town – then if that doesn't pan out, I'll let you know that we need to start calling places in Lima and Toledo."

"Okay," Hailey replied. "Thanks Moscow, let us know if you need our help."

"Long distance might cost a lot," her brother explained. "But hopefully I can get an answer from a shop here in town – without having to call places far away, like Detroit or Columbus."

"You know," I said confidently – flush with self-assurance from my previous statement that had helped us find a potential witness. "A lot of places have what's called a *toll free number* – it starts with an 800."

"Yeah, I've heard of that," Lisa replied.

"How it works," I told them assuredly, "if you know their regular number, when you dial them *toll free*," I said adding air quotes with my fingers, "all you need to do is dial 800 first and then add their number."

"What?" Lisa questioned.

"Yeah, so let's say, their number is 424 – 7150."

"That's the number for the Police Department," Moscow said.

"Right," I replied. "But let's say that's the number for a motorcycle repair shop – and then they decided to get a 'toll free number'," I said again while making air quotes with my fingers. "Anyway, all you need to do is add 1 and then 800 to their phone number. So it would be 1-800-424-7150 and you get the same place – but you don't have to pay long distance."

"I don't think it works like that Pep," Lisa explained.

"I'm pretty sure it does," I told her.

"I think you'll need to double-check that," Hailey said.

Just then, the younger girls returned from checking the phone book.

"She's in the book!" Jennie exclaimed with a smile.

"Yep, we found her," Michelle added giving us a thumbs up sign.

"Does anyone have a quarter?" Hailey asked. "We'll give her a call and see if we can meet."

As she was finishing her question, Patsy, our server, arrived with our food and our discussion came to an abrupt end.

"Let's call her after lunch," Cressida suggested as we ate heartily on fried clams, cheeseburgers and chicken strips. After we finished the main meal, Patsy took our orders for dessert and many of the kids ordered ice cream. I asked my parents if I could have the large *Jim Dandy* sundae – a banana split-type dessert served in a giant glass bowl and filled with vanilla, chocolate and strawberry ice cream along with several bananas. To my surprise they both agreed – I was happy to see them agree on something together, even if I could not eat it all.

Sneak I noticed, also ordered dessert – a large Peanut Butter Cup sundae – but let much of the ice cream melt as he stared quietly into the soupy remains at the bottom of his glass. He looked miserable and I felt sorry for my friend – sitting there, on the other side of the restaurant with his parents and Mr.

and Mrs. Cotton – unable to investigate and look for clues. He would be happy, I thought, to learn that we had made some progress on the case. We had some good "leads" as he would say. I knew that he'd laugh when he heard that one of the leads came from my Dad's bedtime story called *Pierre and his Two Sisters*! It was definitely a much different approach to finding clues than the brilliant methods Sneak employed.

CHAPTER 45

The next day – a Monday – started like most others. I woke early – as I usually did on school days – and watched some T.V. before walking to the bus stop. I didn't have to wait long for Bus Four to arrive and quickly joined Sneak and Jennie and a few other kids who were already on board. I sat with my newly-grounded detective friend, as I usually did on my rides to school, but that morning we rode in silence – my friend being unusually somber and morose.

The morning at school went by quickly and I joined my young detective friend for lunch, seated along long metal tables in the school gym. The gym was a large room that served as the school's cafeteria and auditorium, with an elevated stage located at one end of the room, opposite from the line where the school lunches were served. Sneak and I were joined by a few other guys from the neighborhood who also noticed that our detective friend was unusually downcast.

While at lunch, a few other kids stopped by to ask some questions – having heard about some sort of "club" that was starting with detectives from our Sunday School. I answered their questions when they approached us, while Sneak remained somber – not responding to their questions – instead slurping loudly from the straw of his chocolate milk container and quickly eating the peanut butter sandwich he had hastily grabbed from his *Emergency!* T.V. show themed metal lunch box.

In the afternoon, I returned to my Mom's house on Bus Four and thought about transcribing more tapes – but instead fell quickly onto her orange and yellow flower printed couch in the living room and watched old black and white episodes of *Gilligan's Island* and *Lost in Space*.

I hope we don't get Lost in Space with this case, I thought as I lay on the couch watching the show and thinking of *The Case of the Mysterious Circles. I wish there was a robot warning us of danger if we get in trouble.* "Danger! Danger, Sneak Ryerson!" I said to myself.

Later in the afternoon, Hailey Cotton stopped by the house to get a tape recorder. The previous day – before we had left Friendly's – I had asked her if she would record her interview with Alice Williams – the girl we had discovered in the F.E.E.T. photo – and Hailey had agreed. I spent a few minutes showing her how the voice activation system worked and offered her my faded green gym bag as an easy way to carry the tape recorder. "Oh, that's okay. I'll find something else to put it in," she told me, as she looked at my gym bag. I realize now that it was not exactly the most fashionable accessory to carry for a girl who was trying to look nice.

"Will you meet with her today?" I asked, referring to the girl in the black and white photo.

"Yes!" Hailey replied enthusiastically – seemingly glad to change the subject from my old school gym bag. "She was free to talk today, so Lisa, Cressida and I are going to go over to her lab around dinner time."

"Her lab?" I asked.

"Yeah, she's a graduate student – I think in Chemistry – and works in a science lab at the college – so we're going over there after she takes a test this afternoon."

"That sounds interesting," I replied – wishing again that I had been invited to join them.

"It should be *really* interesting," Hailey said with a smile. "I hope she's able to tell us a lot about the science experiments she's doing....and the F.E.E.T. group too."

"Yeah, and maybe she can tell you why she was in the photo from a year ago, but not in the photo from January," I replied.

"Right!" said Hailey. "That's a question I want to ask her, too."

Our conversation suddenly came to an awkward halt – I wasn't the best at talking with girls at the time and Hailey had run out of things to tell me about the case.

"Well, thanks for the tape recorder, my Mom's waiting in the car," she said before turning to go.

"Okay, hope you get a bunch of clues," I told her.

"Me too," she replied with a smile before quickly turning and walking down the stairs of my Mom's front porch. I soon walked outside and waved to Mrs. Cotton who sat in the idling tan station wagon in the driveway, and then returned to the house. After closing the thick wooden door that stood between the cold air outside and the warmth of the house, I returned to the orange and yellow couch and watched another episode of *Lost in Space*.

CHAPTER 46

That evening, my Mom made an early dinner of Chef Boyardee pizza. After I helped her clean up the dishes, she drove me to the barber shop to get my hair cut. "It's just too long," she told me at dinner. "I brought some needlework," she said on the way to the barber's – pointing to a bag sitting between us on the front seat of the car, "just in case the line is too long."

"It probably won't be too busy on a Monday night," I told her as we drove the short distance to the barber shop located next to the mall.

The car briefly slowed due to traffic on Tiffin Avenue and eventually turned off the busy road at the local Burger King, then turned into the mall's parking lot. The parking lot at the back of the mall was shared with *Cinema World* – the city's largest movie theater with six screens – and as we drove by the long white building, I was reminded that our chief suspect, Julian Davis, worked at a movie theater nearby.

My mother parked the car near the mall entrance – near, I learned later, to where our case's culprit had parked only a few days before, to ensure he wasn't being followed as he made his way into the mall. Walking quickly in the cold night air, we saw only a few customers near the mall entrance and no customers waiting at the barbershop – a small shop that was attached to the mall but had a separate entrance. When we entered through the glass door – we quickly saw the two barbers – one located on the right and the other on the left of the entrance. Larry, located to the right of the entrance, was busy cutting the hair of an older man, while Dan, on the left side of the entrance, sat in his chair talking on the shop's telephone – its long black cord stretched its full distance from the phone's base located on a small platform in the center of the shop next to the cash register, fifteen feet away.

"Hey, I'll have to call you back," I heard Dan say when we walked in. "Okay, I'll talk to you later about the race."

My mom and I stood near the silver metallic coat rack and cash register located in the center of the large room, waiting to be greeted. "Well, if it isn't Pep Stiles!" Dan said as he walked towards us after hanging up the phone. "Seems like we just saw your old man in here a week or so ago," he said with a laugh. "Isn't that right Larry?"

"Yep," Larry, the older of the two barbers, replied slowly.

My Dad liked to keep his hair short and was often in Dan and Larry's shop.

"I'm not too busy tonight kiddo," Dan told me, as he chewed a large piece of bubble gum. "I can take care of you, unless you'd prefer Larry." Dan's gum chewing, constant talk of cars and racing, as well as his thick moustache, reminded me a few years later of Burt Reynolds in the movie *Cannonball Run*. Dan, I thought, could have been a perfect stand-in for the actor except that his hair was much lighter in color than the famous movie star.

"Going with you sounds good," I replied to Dan as I made my way to his chair.

My mother, who had followed a few steps behind me, greeted the barbers and stayed for a few minutes to explain how she wanted Dan to cut my hair. She should have simply said "bowl cut" – as that was the look I had been sporting for many years, with a straight cut about a half-inch above my eyebrows, a scissor cut around my ears while the sides and back of my head were cut short. Looking back at my school pictures, I've noticed that through most of my elementary years my hairstyle was nearly identical to Moe's bowl-cut from *The Three Stooges*. My mother, after giving her directions, had quickly dropped the idea of waiting and doing needlework in the barbershop, and instead decided to leave me with the barbers in order to shop at the mall before the stores closed for the night.

"See ya' Mom," I told her as she left.

"Did I tell you about my latest race?" Dan asked, after I was seated in his chair and we watched my mother through the shop's large plate glass window walk quickly to the mall's entrance. Without waiting for me to respond, Dan began telling me about the latest cars he was racing and – although it was many months away – soon told me about his plans for the annual *Demolition Derby* in September.

"Someday I'm going to get your Dad out there and drive a crashed up car!" he said with a laugh.

"I'd like to see that!" I said enthusiastically – thinking that the excitement of driving a car into other cars would surely have a positive effect on my father's depressed mood.

While he cut my hair, Dan continued talking about cars and races – discussing the differences between Stock Cars – which I didn't know much about – and Funny Cars – which I also didn't know about – and other types of drag-racing cars, before changing the subject and talking about Ford Mustangs – one of his favorite types of cars – and how I could tell the year a Mustang was manufactured by looking at the taillights.

"So, that's how you can tell a '64 say from a '68," he summarized about halfway through my haircut.

"You're gonna' see more spacing between the three rectangular taillights of the '68 model compared with the '64…but if you're talking about a Shelby, then that's a totally different story."

Suddenly, he stopped cutting my hair and paused his monologue on cars – struck by another thought. "Hey Pep, I just remembered. We had a guy in here just the other day asking about you and your friends."

"Me and my friends?" I asked.

"Yeah, he was askin' all kinds of questions," Dan explained, while still chewing his bubble gum.

"What kind of questions?" I asked.

"Well, he wanted to know if I knew you and Joel and Moscow," Dan said with a laugh.

"And what did you tell him?" I wondered.

"I told him, 'Of course Larry and I know you guys – we cut your hair!'"

"Yep," I replied, while my thoughts churned through different ideas of who exactly the person might be and why he was asking questions about my friends and I.

"And then he was askin' about your buddy Sneak Ryerson and if I had heard that he was grounded."

"Grounded?" I said with a startle – surprised that the news had travelled so quickly since the weekend. *It's only Monday! And that just happened on Saturday morning!* I thought, shocked at who might have been asking these questions.

"I told him I hadn't heard about it," Dan explained casually, as he restarted snipping my hair with his scissors – unaware of my growing concern. "You know, we hear most of the scuttlebutt about you kids, but I hadn't heard that one yet."

"Was that yesterday?" I asked, thinking that the person might have heard the news after our Sunday church service – as many of the people in our Church likely had.

"Naw, we're not open on Sundays," Dan replied. "That's when I like to work on my cars."

"Ha!" I heard Larry say from his barber's chair. By then, Larry had finished cutting the hair of the older gentleman and without any other customers to serve, was now sitting in his chair reading a newspaper – which covered his body from the waist up.

"What are you laughin' at?" Dan asked his older co-worker.

"You work on cars!" Larry said with a guffaw from behind his paper. "Be honest with the boy, you don't really work on your cars. You just invite your mechanic friends to come over to your house and keep them company while *they* work on your cars."

"What!" Dan replied in mock indignation.

"Admit it, you really don't know how to repair cars, you just have your friends come over and have them do all the work so you can keep driving those old junkers to your races and the crash up derby."

"I do some stuff on the cars," Dan protested.

"Fill up the gas, maybe," said his co-worker from behind the paper.

Dan was unusually quiet as he continued cutting my hair, but now had an annoyed look on his face. "Larry's smelled too many of my fumes at the drag strip," he said to me in a whisper.

"So, it wasn't Sunday when the guy came in," I asked after a moment's pause.

"Naw, not Sunday," Dan replied. "Must have been Saturday. Isn't that right Larry?" Dan said, looking towards his co-worker. "Hey Larry...."

"Yeah," the voice replied through the newspaper.

"It was Saturday that we were getting all those questions about Pep and Sneak and the other kids... and we heard about the new detective group, right?"

The new detective group! How could someone know about that on Saturday night? I wondered anxiously. *We just decided to create the group on Saturday morning!* And then I paused for a moment, thinking of a simple explanation. *Maybe it was someone's Dad,* I hoped.

"Yeah, it was right before closing time," Larry, the older barber explained.

"Did he say how he heard about the group?" I asked tentatively.

"No, but he mentioned you guys were joining a couple of girls to start a new detective agency because Sneak was grounded. Is that right?" Dan asked.

"Yeah," I replied softly.

"Well, I hope your new group goes well," Dan paused for a moment. "Are the girls cute?" the barber asked with a smile.

"Now, Dan," Larry interjected. "It sounds like they are embarking on a professional endeavor instead of a social one – not something where Pep would be thinking about those things."

Larry, I remembered, served as a voice of moderation in the barbershop – having to remind patrons that he had daughters in High School – and didn't put up with certain topics or language.

"Right," I replied quickly. "I'm not thinking about girls," I said nervously. "It's a professional endeavor... like Larry said."

"Okay, okay," Dan replied with a smile, as he began cutting my hair again. "I won't ask any more questions about the girls."

"So, who....who was it that was asking all of the questions?" I asked tentatively, trying to hide my shock and concern.

Maybe it was just Uncle Charlie or Professor Telson? I hoped. *Maybe they were just making conversation with the barbers. Maybe it was Mr. Cotton? Maybe it was my Dad,* I thought – before remembering that we had spent Saturday night together at *Captain D's* and the YMCA. "Was it like Joel or Moscow's Dad?" I asked Dan.

"No. Ah, who was that?" Dan asked himself, perplexed by my question. "He was a young guy…"

"Yeah?" I asked anxiously.

"…and he told us about the fires you were investigating and then he asked us all those questions about you kids. Hey, Larry…"

"Yeah."

"Who was it that was asking all those questions? Whenever he comes in I call him Casanova, because he's named after that movie star…Tony, something…the one who has the really good Carey Grant impression."

"It's…." Larry replied before stopping.

"Tony…Tony," Dan said, struggling to remember the name.

"Anthony," Larry replied from behind the newspaper.

"Yes, that's it," Dan concluded. "It was the Sheriff's Deputy, Anthony Curtis."

CHAPTER 47

My mind raced as I took in the news. *Why would Deputy Curtis know all about The Sunday School Detectives and ask the barbers questions to learn more about us?*

Then it struck me – and I was shocked at the discovery I had made. *Deputy Curtis must be the one setting the fires and sending the information to Julian Davis! It makes sense,* I told myself, *he knows all about the case.*

And then I remembered how strangely he had acted when Sneak saw him at the crime scene – and I had heard him on the recording. It seemed like he was *acting.* It was as if he was pretending like he didn't know what was going on – but really did know what was happening with the case. On top of that, he was asking Sneak a number of questions, trying to understand what Sneak knew about the case. *No wonder he asked Sneak all of those questions,* I reasoned. *He wanted to know if he'd been caught!*

It all made perfect sense to me.

So, it must have been the deputy that was starting the fires, I concluded. *He must have been the one who made Julian Davis write the letters to the newspaper – so that people would suspect Julian and not him!*

I paused for a moment.

It was brilliant, I thought. *All along, people like Sneak and The Sunday School Detectives were chasing Julian Davis and the F.E.E.T. people, when instead we should have been investigating Deputy Curtis!*

But, what reason did Deputy Curtis have to start the fires? I wondered.

It took me a moment but I quickly came to an answer.

He must have wanted to get a promotion, I reasoned. *He probably wants to become the Hancock County Sheriff himself – like most deputies would want – instead of just being assigned to some really bad assignments, like waiting all day along a lonely stretch of highway. Instead, he wants to be sheriff!*

It makes sense, I thought. *He probably figured if he could be on a case where the big T.V. networks came to town and all the newspaper reporters were covering it, he could act like he was able to "catch" Julian Davis – which really wouldn't be catching him at all – but if he could do that, he would be famous. People would be talking about him all over Findlay and northwestern Ohio and beyond. And he could move from being a Deputy to being the sheriff of all of Hancock County whenever he wanted to.*

Wow, I thought. *That is crazy. That's a pretty devious way to get ahead.*

Soon a sense of pride filled my thoughts.

I've got to let the other Sunday School Detectives know that I've solved the case. It's going to be so cool to tell them, I thought, imagining myself standing in front of a group of cheering fans receiving a medal for my great detective work. *Maybe it would come from Uncle Charlie – or the Mayor of Findlay – or maybe Hailey Cotton or Lisa or Cressida would put the medal around my neck as I stood on a platform – maybe at the band shell at Riverside Park, that would be a good place – in front of everyone in town – as they clapped for me just like the last scene from Star Wars. Maybe I'll let out a Wookie growl,* I thought as I smiled while still sitting in the barber's chair. *Or maybe I'll just joke about that – teasing the mayor that I'd do that when I got my medal – as he shook my hand in congratulations and said "On behalf of a grateful city, let's show Pep our appreciation" and the crowd clapped and cheered wildly.*

And then another thought struck me – one that was more concerning. I realized then, that I needed to quickly let the others know what I'd discovered – not just to brag about solving the case – but let them know because of their safety. *If he's asking all those questions about Sneak at the barber shop,* I reasoned, *maybe Sneak is in danger! Deputy Curtis has already set four fires in some fields – I wouldn't put it past him to set fires at our houses!*

I paused for a moment, remembering that the Deputy had known that Sneak was grounded and wouldn't be part of the group. *If he knows all about the guys and the girls in the group, maybe it's not Sneak that's in danger, maybe it's all of The Sunday School Detectives!*

Suddenly, convinced of the imminent danger to myself and the group – I realized I couldn't wait to tell the authorities – I needed to let them know immediately – I needed to quickly tell Uncle Charlie what I had discovered and ask him to get his fellow police offers to find and arrest Deputy Curtis.

My heart raced as I pondered these many ideas while Dan continued cutting my hair – taking, it seemed, longer than normal – having just moved from the sides around my ears to the hair above my eyebrows.

"So, did you notice if Deputy Curtis was wearing a winter coat?"

"Well, everyone comes in here wearing a winter coat…'cause it's winter, kiddo," Dan replied, occupied with the haircut.

He paused for a moment.

"Hey Larry, did you notice Tony Curtis wearing a coat?" Dan asked his co-worker while pointing to the metal coat rack in the middle of the large room.

"Yeah, I think so," the older barber replied. "I think it was brown."

"Yeah, I do too," Dan concluded. "It was a brown winter coat."

My body jolted when I heard the news.

"Hey, watch it kid," Dan said with a laugh. "I don't want to nick you or anything."

"That's pretty good," I said rapidly, referring to my haircut, quickly looking in the mirror as Dan continued cutting. "So, I've got to go…now."

"I'm not done yet," Dan told me, as he stepped back from the barber's chair.

"No, no – it's okay," I told him anxiously, as I pushed on the black cape that surrounded me. "I need to go now."

"But, I still need a few more minutes," Dan protested.

"I need to go now!" I said anxiously.

"Oh, okay, I'll help you down," Dan replied, likely thinking that I needed to use the bathroom. "If you've got to go, you've got to go," he said quickly as he removed the barber's cape and lowered the chair.

I hopped off the chair and grabbed my own coat from the coat rack – not having time to explain to my barber friends that I needed to quickly warn the other Sunday School Detectives of the great danger we were all in.

"Hey, where are you goin'?" I heard Dan ask as I raced out of the barbershop. "I'm not done yet…"

CHAPTER 48

Leaving the barbershop, I frantically raced through the mall looking for my mother. Instead of doing her needlepoint, she had decided to go shopping – and now I was desperate to find her.

I raced through the larger stores first – Sears, then J.C. Penny and then Britt's, a discount store located at the end of the mall – but could not locate my mother. I quickly retraced my steps and walked through some of the smaller shops selling women's clothes and even a craft store – but still did not see her.

I eventually made my way back to the Barber Shop as she was walking out.

The barbershop closed at seven o'clock and behind the plate glass window I saw Larry reaching up to turn off the large neon blue "OPEN" sign while Dan was turning off the electric barber's pole next to the door.

"Where have you been?" I asked exasperatedly as I met my mother at the door.

"Oh my...," she began when she looked at my hair. "Dan said you left before he was done. I was at a shoe store, where have you been?"

"I was looking all over for you," I said breathing heavily from my race around the mall.

"Why were you looking for me?" she asked.

"I found out some new stuff about the case."

"The case?"

"Yeah, the case that the Sunday School Detectives are working on. I need to talk to Sneak's Uncle Charlie. You remember him, right?"

"Of course I do, but why do you need to speak with him now?"

"He'll know what to do," I told her. "He needs to arrest someone."

"Arrest someone?"

"I'll explain it later," I told her.

"Okay, well I paid for your haircut, but Dan told me there's more to do and I would definitely agree," she said looking at my half-cut hair. "We could go back inside and have him finish it up...there's still a few minutes left before they close."

"That can wait," I told her quickly as I walked rapidly to the car. "Come on Mom, we need to hurry."

And soon we were on our way to Uncle Charlie's house.

CHAPTER 49

My mind was flooded with thoughts as we arrived at Uncle Charlie's house on Winterberry Drive – located only a few blocks from the mall. If I were a better detective, I would have noticed the additional cars in his driveway – one in particular would have caught my eye – but I was in such a rush to get to the large wooden front door, I didn't notice it. My mind was flooded still, as I entered a few feet into Uncle Charlie's living room, not noticing the type of coat that was resting on one of the plush blue chairs near me. Instead, I was almost breathless with excitement as I rushed to get the words out of my mouth, standing in the doorway. "Hey Uncle Charlie," I said rapidly as Sneak's uncle held the door open and invited me in. "I....I found....something...some new evidence...I know who it is....that set the fires....you're not going to believe it...but I think Sneak and us... and Hailey...and the other Sunday School Detectives are in danger. You aren't going to believe it...it all makes sense…Julian's got a blue winter coat… but he's got a brown winter coat and he knows all about the case….it's cause it's the Sheriff's Deputy…. Deputy…Anthony Curtis."

"Anthony Curtis?" Uncle Charlie replied, not understanding any of my previous words because I had spoken them so incoherently. "Well, Deputy Curtis is right here, tonight," he told me.

"What?" I asked, stunned by the news.

"Deputy Curtis, is here tonight having dinner with us, I'll introduce you to him," Uncle Charlie explained. "Hey, Anthony," the tall police captain bellowed as he turned towards his dining room. "Come on out here, there's someone I'd like you to meet."

CHAPTER 50

Earlier that evening, while my Mom was still fixing our Chef Boyardee pizza and planning my trip to the barber shop, the older girls from *The Sunday School Detectives* – Hailey, Cressida and Lisa, along with Hailey's mother, Mrs. Cotton – were making their way to the biology lab where Alice Williams worked.

The lab was located within the college's Science Building, a tall three-story building near the Old Main in the middle of campus. The group used a large map – located on the lobby wall of the Science Building – to find the third-floor lab and decided to take a nearby flight of stairs instead of an elevator on the other side of the building.

The three Sunday School Detectives, along with Mrs. Cotton, soon entered the open door of the lab off the third floor hallway and quickly discovered that the laboratory was large and well-equipped – filled with glass cylinders and containers, Bunsen burners, microscopes and other scientific equipment. Near the entrance to the lab were several Geiger counters – operated to make sure experiments using radioactive materials were not spilled.

The girls were surprised to see that Alice wasn't the only one working in the lab in the early evening – in fact, the area buzzed with activity as several researchers in white lab coats hunched over microscopes observing samples under glass slides, while others used their dexterous thumbs hidden under latex gloves to work blue handheld pipettes to first fill and then dispense liquids and compounds into petri dishes and small plastic tubes located in centrifuges.

After their initial greetings with the professor who ran the lab, the girls and Mrs. Cotton soon met Alice who, like the other researchers, wore a long white lab coat, plastic safety glasses and latex gloves.

The girls recognized Alice immediately from the picture and she greeted them warmly, quickly inviting the girls and Mrs. Cotton to sit at a small table in the hallway outside of the lab and join her in drinking some hot tea that she brewed in a small orange metal tea kettle.

"So what does everyone do in there?" Hailey asked looking over at the entrance to the lab, after the detectives and Alice and Mrs. Cotton were seated around the table.

"Well the lab is focused on studying an insect called a cabbage looper," Alice explained in a friendly tone as she poured cups of hot tea for Mrs. Cotton and the girls. "It's found all around the U.S. and Europe and Asia too. Maybe you've seen some of the posters we've put up around the Science Building describing our research?"

"I don't think so," said Lisa.

"Ah, well, we use the scientific name on the posters," Alice explained with a smile. "We don't say *cabbage looper*. Instead, we use the scientific name – *Trichoplusia ni*, it's sometimes called *T. ni*. – like we have on that poster over there," she said, pointing to a nearby wall.

"Ah," Lisa said. "Tiny."

"Well, something like that!" Alice replied with a laugh as she and the others took sips of hot tea. "So anyway, I'm getting my Master's Degree in Biology – and this is where I work part-time!"

"So, what exactly is *T. ni*?" Hailey asked – interested in learning more from the young researcher.

"Well, it's actually a couple of things. Most people think of it as a moth...that's where it gets its name, because the markings on their wings look like a Greek letter *ni*." Alice replied.

"A moth?" said Hailey.

"Well, it doesn't start out as a moth. It starts as an egg, then larvae, then pupae, and then it becomes a moth," Alice explained.

"Is it pretty like a butterfly, with lots of different colors?" Cressida asked.

"Well, no, it's kind of grey looking with dark brown wings."

"Oh," came Cressida's disappointed reply.

"We do a lot of different tests on them here in the lab – that's what you saw the researchers working with, when you saw them put materials in those little plastic tubes for the centrifuge or onto slides for the microscope."

"Ick!" Cressida exclaimed.

"You get used to it," Alice continued. "The food they eat can be pretty smelly. But it's kind of cool to do the research. We test their cell lines and try to figure out why they go from one state to another – you know, how they transform from larvae, to pupae to moth."

"I thought moths were caterpillars too?" Lisa asked.

"Well, we call caterpillars *larvae*, but it's the same thing."

"So how do you grown them?" Hailey asked. "Or, raise them? Or, whatever you do to keep them going? Do you have to put them on a farm or something?"

"We do it all here in the building," Alice explained. "We keep the moths in empty ice cream containers in the basement. And the containers are all lined with green construction paper."

"Why's that?" Lisa asked.

"So the moths think that it's…" Alice began.

"Leaves, right?" Hailey interrupted. "They think that the green construction paper are leaves."

"Exactly," Alice continued. "We use green construction paper so the moths think they are laying their eggs on leaves. Then, I pull the paper out and cut it up into small squares and staple the small sheets of paper to the bottom of a lid. Then I put the lid on top of a smaller container with some food that I've made – that's probably the smelliest of everything that I do – and then in a few days those eggs turn into *larvae* – caterpillars – and eat the food I've made for them. And then they turn into pupae and then moths."

"That's really neat," Hailey replied – interested in many things, including science.

"Would you like to see the area where we keep them?" Alice asked. "It's kind of dark and smelly, but you might like it."

"Sure," Hailey said enthusiastically.

"Not me," Lisa said with a grimace.

"Me either," replied Cressida.

"Oh, come on, let's go check it out," Alice suggested. "It's not too bad."

"Well, I guess we could just go for a little while," Lisa agreed.

"I'm going to finish my tea," Mrs. Cotton told the others.

Soon the girls followed Alice down the stairs to the basement of the Science Building, while Mrs. Cotton finished her tea.

When the girls reached the basement they found themselves at the beginning of a dark and long hallway, lit only by a few dim overhead lights located near the hallway entrance.

"Come on it's not too far," Alice said.

"Wow, it's dark," Hailey admitted.

"Did you hear that?" Lisa asked quickly. "I don't think we're alone down here."

"I think I heard that too," Cressida said.

"What?" Alice asked.

"It sounded like someone was following us," Lisa explained.

"There's all kinds of echoes and noises down here," said Alice. "The building's heating and cooling pipes are down here and they make all kinds of sounds. Plus, I think there's an electrical box that clicks a lot too. I work down here all the time, it'll be okay. Your eyes will eventually adjust."

The girls continued walking in the near-darkness, carefully taking one unseen step after another.

"How much further?" Lisa asked.

"It's just up ahead," explained Alice.

"Why's it so dark?" Cressida questioned.

"Well, the *T. ni* and a lot of the other things we raise down here are nocturnal," Alice replied. "So, we want them to think it is night."

"I'm getting freaked out," Lisa told the others. "I can hardly see anything."

"Me too," Cressida said, as the girls continued slowly down the darkened hallway.

"Hey watch it," Alice said as the girls bumped into her, not knowing that she had stopped walking. "It's just right here," she explained as she opened a large metal cabinet filled with large ice cream containers.

The girls stared at the dozens of containers stacked in the cabinet – as a putrid smell coming from the cabinet filled their noses.

"So this is where I work a lot," Alice explained, "These are the containers with the moths and the green construction paper. You can see where I've written the dates on top so I know when I last pulled the eggs. And over here is where we keep the smaller cups with the pupae and their food."

"Why's it so smelly?" Lisa asked.

"Well, the food is pretty smelly," Alice admitted. "And this is like their bathroom too."

"Eww," Lisa replied.

"Okay, someone is definitely behind us," Cressida said. "I can hear their footsteps."

"I don't think so," said Alice. "Don't you hear those noises from the furnace? I think that's what you're hearing," she said – as the girls heard several loud mechanical noises nearby.

"No, really there's someone else here," Cressida replied. "Really."

"Who do you think it is?" Hailey asked.

"Maybe Julian knows we're on to him," Lisa said, "and he wants to stop us before we tell the police."

At this comment Alice laughed. "Julian....Julian Davis?" she asked. "Are we talking about the same person? He wouldn't hurt a fly...or a moth. You don't have anything to worry about from him."

"I don't know about that," said Lisa. "I definitely feel like someone else is down here."

"It's just the building, really," Alice said, just as Cressida felt a cold hand on her shoulder.

"Hi kids," they heard a voice say, but by then the three girls had already turned – screaming – and raced down the long and dark hallway towards the stairs leading them to safety.

CHAPTER 51

The girls were out of breath after running up the four flights of stairs when they returned to the hallway outside of the lab. "Where's your Mom?" Lisa asked Hailey as the three girls sat down at the empty seats around the small table.

"I don't know," Hailey replied. "She said she wanted to finish her tea. Maybe she went into the lab to get some more, or talk to the professor we met earlier?"

"That was so scary," Lisa continued.

"What happened down there?" Hailey asked. "I just started running when you grabbed me. Was someone there?"

"Oh, yeah," Cressida explained. "I heard someone behind me and then I felt this cold, creepy hand on my shoulder. It was so scary."

"Wow," said Hailey.

"Could it have been a ghost?" Lisa asked.

"A ghost!" Hailey protested. "There's no such thing as ghosts!"

"Well, what was it then?" Lisa asked. "I couldn't see anything."

"I don't know," Cressida continued. "But I've never been so scared in all my life."

As the girls caught their breath, Hailey poured them more tea from the orange metal kettle while they waited for Alice to return.

Soon they heard laughter coming from the nearby stairway and saw Alice walking up the stairs carrying a long black tray filled with small containers. Walking a few steps behind Alice, to their surprise, was Mrs. Cotton.

"We were hoping you'd have sense enough to come back here!" Alice told them as she walked towards the door of the lab with her tray of containers. "Let me drop these off and we can talk some more."

"You girls almost knocked me over," Mrs. Cotton explained, as they looked at her with quizzical expressions.

"When did we almost knock you over?" Lisa asked.

"Downstairs, in the basement," Mrs. Cotton explained. "I told you I wanted to finish my tea. But I was only a few minutes behind you. I wanted to see how Alice took care of the moths. I was pretty good at science back in my day," she added with a smile.

"That was you that grabbed my shoulder?" Cressida asked.

"Well, I wasn't trying to grab your shoulder....but I put my hand up because I couldn't see anything in front of me. Who did you think it was?" Mrs. Cotton asked.

The girls laughed as they smiled at each other with knowing looks.

"I'm so relieved it was you!" Lisa exclaimed as she turned to Mrs. Cotton. "I thought it was...well, never mind."

"I'm glad we didn't actually run you over, Mom." Hailey said with a smile.

"Me too," Cressida added.

"Well, it was pretty dark in that hallway," Mrs. Cotton admitted.

A few minutes later, Alice returned from the lab and joined the girls and Mrs. Cotton at the small table in the hallway.

"So, I know you didn't come here to talk about moths...," she began.

"No," Hailey replied.

"Definitely didn't come here to talk about the moths," Lisa added.

"Like I said on the phone," Hailey explained. "The reason we're here is to find out more about F.E.E.T."

"Ah, yes....Findlayites Entertaining Extra-Terrestrials," Alice said with a laugh as she rolled her eyes. "I admit it. I was part of that group."

"So what can you tell us about them?" Lisa asked leaning forward.

"Well, it's a group I wish I hadn't joined," she said remorsefully. "But I'd be glad to tell you more about it."

"How long has it been going on?" Lisa asked.

"The group was started a few years ago by an older couple – they've moved away – I think to a college in Indiana. Everyone said they were like Hippies or something."

The girls laughed.

"Anyway, kids from our college have basically led the group since the founders left," Alice said before pausing for a moment. "I joined the group a few years ago – around the same time Julian joined."

"Julian Davis, right?" Cressida confirmed.

"Right, Julian Davis," Alice continued with a regretful tone. "When I joined, I thought it would be really fun – but it didn't turn out that way."

"What about Julian," Lisa asked. "What can you tell us about him?"

"Well, he seemed basically normal when I met him. We had a lot of fun at first – but then things changed....he changed."

"How?" Hailey asked.

"Well, F.E.E.T. became like an obsession for him. He got so into it. Like, he spent all day long working on the group. He even quit school to focus on it.

And, at first, he tried to recruit people like crazy – at lunches or dinner in the dining halls here on campus, or sometimes he'd even go out to the mall to try to get people to join. And, you probably know, he's been writing letters to the newspaper for a while."

"Yeah, we've heard about those," said Hailey.

"So, what's the purpose of the group?" Lisa asked bluntly. "I don't really get it – there's no such thing as aliens – so why have a group?"

"Well, for me, I've always loved science. I like biology – like what I'm doing here. I can't remember if I told you, I'm getting my Master's Degree in Biology. But, I also like astronomy and I like to think about space and what is out there…you know, beyond our solar system. And I guess that's what I liked about F.E.E.T. When I joined it was a place where we could talk about our ideas about space and other life forms – and we had some great discussions. We watched some fun science fiction movies too. And in theory, I liked the premise of the group – I guess I still do."

"What's the premise of the group?" Hailey asked.

"Well, I think the best way to explain it is to think about it in reverse," she began.

"In reverse?" Lisa asked.

"Right," Alice continued. "Think about it…if you were going to travel to a different planet, would you want to be greeted by a welcoming committee or would you rather have people be afraid of you and ask you to leave without getting to know you?"

"Well, a welcoming committee, I guess," replied Lisa.

"Yeah, welcoming committee," Hailey agreed.

"Well, our group thought the same would be true for aliens if they came to visit us here on earth. So we thought F.E.E.T. would be that welcoming committee for them."

The girls smiled and were surprised by who asked the next question.

"But, what if they weren't nice?" Mrs. Cotton asked, interested in the discussion that the younger women were having. "What if the aliens wanted to take over the planet.....like....you know, *Invasion of the Body Snatchers* or something like that, and didn't 'come in peace'?"

"That's a great question," replied Alice. "And one that we debated a lot in our F.E.E.T. meetings. But ultimately, most of us came to the conclusion that the probability was that the aliens who came here would be friendly – they would want to learn from us, or want us to learn from them – instead of being bad aliens. If there are superior life forms out there, we thought we'd really be able to learn so much from them – like curing diseases or even how to expand our minds to know more things. Plus, we figured if bad aliens came to earth, their technology would be so much better than ours, we probably couldn't stop them even if we wanted to."

"That makes sense," said Mrs. Cotton.

"So why did you leave the group?" Hailey asked. "If you were having such great debates, why aren't you in it anymore? We saw you in the picture from a year ago but didn't see you in the group picture from last month."

"Yeah, I quit before the latest picture," Alice explained. "It had a lot to do with Julian," she continued. "I really liked him...you know...he's kind of cute."

At this comment the girls giggled.

"...and I thought," Alice continued, "it was really great that a person could be so energetic and passionate about something. I mean, he was really into the group. But then, things started to really change."

"Like quitting school?" Hailey asked.

"Well, no, not that," Alice said with a laugh. "He quit school a while ago. It's...it's going to sound crazy when you hear it, but I'll tell you anyway."

"What was it?" Lisa asked.

"Julian thought he was being contacted by aliens."

CHAPTER 52

The girls and Mrs. Cotton all reacted with surprise when Alice explained that Julian Davis believed that he was being contacted by aliens.

"Like, *real* aliens?" asked Lisa. "From outer space?"

"Yeah, he really thought he was being contacted by aliens," explained Alice.

"But why would they contact him?" Lisa asked. "Of all the millions of people on earth, wouldn't you think the aliens would contact President Carter, or someone like that?"

"Yeah, hopefully him and not Brezhnev...," Mrs. Cotton murmured to herself, "...or Billy."

"Well, you might think that," Alice replied in a serious tone, "...that aliens would contact political leaders. But you have to remember that Julian is the President of F.E.E.T – a group that is dedicated to welcoming aliens to earth. So, when he was contacted he sort of reasoned – and a few of the other members did too – that if there was someone an alien would contact, why wouldn't it be the president of our group instead of the President of the United States?"

"Makes sense," one of the girls said.

"But how did the aliens contact him?" Hailey asked. "Was it like a mental telepathy sort of thing, or a radio signal or something?"

"No," Alice explained. "They sent him notes."

"Notes, like letters?" Lisa asked.

"Yep," Alice continued. "Most of us told him it couldn't be from aliens – they were written in hand-writing just like you or I would have. But he became more and more convinced. You see the letters were all in code and Julian's really smart and it didn't take him too long to decode them."

"That's neat," said Lisa.

"I think that was part of it….one of the reasons he believes it so strongly," Alice added. "Because he's in on a secret that no one else is."

"What did the letters say?" Cressida asked.

"They were pretty crazy," Alice explained. "They claimed to be written from an alien – who was originally from outer space – but got trapped here on earth."

"So he…or it…is like trapped here?" Lisa confirmed.

"Right," Alice continued. "And because of the way the alien looked….and other alien limitations… he wanted Julian to do some things for him."

"So Julian really thought an alien from outer space was sending him letters?" Lisa asked incredulously.

"Yes," replied Alice. "And at the beginning, a few of the leaders of F.E.E.T. did too. Some, I think were just playing along because they thought it was a joke. But most of us are scientists – or would like to be scientists someday – so we told him not to trust the letters. You know....the lack of evidence was overwhelming. I mean Julian couldn't meet with the alien or talk with the alien, he just had to go on the letters that he was getting. Anyway, at the beginning of it all, Julian shared the letters with us, but then as more and more of us became skeptical of the letters, and some people were even laughing about it and making fun of him about them, he began to get more...you know...secretive."

"What did the letters say?" Lisa asked impatiently. "What was Julian supposed to do?"

"Well they said that Julian should get ready."

"Ready?" Cressida asked.

"Right, because the alien had been able to contact his 'friends' – I guess you could call them – from outer space and they were going to be landing a bunch of spaceships."

"You mean like landing them all around the world?" Cressida asked.

"No," explained Alice. "The letters said that they'd all be landing here...around Findlay. The letters said that Hancock County would be their spaceship's landing area."

"Wow," Hailey replied.

"They said it was because it is so flat around here..." Alice continued.

"The Great Black Swamp that was drained...," said Mrs. Cotton.

"Right," Alice agreed. "So because it is so flat, the alien said it would make a great place for an alien landing area."

"That's crazy," Lisa said.

"Even crazier, was the name of the alien," Alice continued. "The letters were all supposed to be from an alien with the name of..."

"Wait!" Lisa interrupted. "He had a name?"

"Oh yeah," Alice explained. "The alien's name was *Peggu*...or sometimes the alien called himself *The Great Peggu*."

"The Great Peggu?" Mrs. Cotton asked.

"Yeah, it was kind of weird," said Alice. "Peggu said that he had somehow gotten trapped here on earth, but now a bunch of his fellow aliens were coming not just to rescue him but to take over."

"And Julian believed all of this?" Hailey asked.

"Yeah, all of it," explained Alice. "Eventually, I told Julian that someone was just pulling his leg. But he didn't believe me. I mean there was stuff in the letters about getting in contact with *The Mothership* and stuff that seemed to come straight from science fiction movies...stuff that seemed totally made up."

"What about the other leaders in F.E.E.T?" Lisa asked. "Was there anyone else who believed the letters?"

"Well, like I said, there were a few people that at least acted like they did at first. But over time, nobody else believed him either. And that was sad – you know, I think if maybe Julian had someone else he could talk to, things might be better for him. But, after a while, he was the only one who believed the letters were real – and then he just sort of distanced himself from the group. He made it really hard to be his friend. One of the last times I talked to him, he was really angry."

"Why?" Hailey said.

"He was mad that I didn't believe him. He said that the Great Peggu was real and was really going to send spaceships...and I was the crazy one for not believing it."

"Wow," said Lisa.

"I didn't like that he was so angry with me," explained Alice. "Plus, it seemed like he had gotten really fearful and paranoid – thinking that governmental agencies are watching him."

"The government?" Lisa asked.

"Yes, like the CIA and FBI. He thought for sure they were trying to capture *The Great Peggu*...and the best way to find the alien was to follow Julian."

"I guess that hasn't happened yet," Lisa observed.

"No, not yet," said Alice. "At least as far as I know." She paused for a moment. "It's just sad – the whole thing is sad, you know, the way that Julian's changed because of those dumb letters. I really liked him. I admired how passionate he was about the group – how he was willing to make some sacrifices to try to get other people to join. But now he's so different."

The girls were quiet for a moment, before Alice spoke again.

"He wrote a long manifesto that he gave to the rest of the F.E.E.T. leaders before he fired us."

"Fired you?" Cressida asked with a startle.

"Yeah, it was funny – I hadn't been to any meetings for a while. But he sent each of us a letter with a long *manifesto* – as he called it – sixteen pages long, that explained why *The Great Peggu* was so important, and that if we changed our minds we could probably get powerful positions in the new government that the aliens would create. He said if we didn't believe it, we would be fired from the group."

"I think we'd like to read that manifesto, right girls?" Hailey said as she looked at her friends.

"Definitely," Lisa added. "It might have more clues in it."

"Sure," replied Alice. "I can get it for you. I have it at my desk here at the lab. You can have it, I don't have a need for it."

"Is there anything else you can tell us about Julian or the F.E.E.T. group?" Hailey asked.

"Well, like I said, I haven't been very involved for a while because of Julian's weird behavior. That last time I talked to him was when the fires started – at the end of January."

"Yes, the fires," said Hailey. "We wanted to talk to you about that too."

"That's when I really regretted being part of the group."

"Why's that?" Lisa asked.

"Well, once the fires started, I knew that somehow Julian was involved and I figured something illegal was happening – but I didn't know what. That's when I called Julian at his apartment and tried to reason with him – telling him that the things he said about Peggu – that he had a green face, so he couldn't go out in the daytime, but roamed around Findlay at night and that an alien was even writing letters – just all seemed too preposterous. I tried to tell Julian that there were so many other more advanced communication techniques….but he didn't want to listen. He was so angry with me that he hung up after a few minutes."

"Wow," replied Cressida.

"Wow, is right," Lisa added.

"There just wasn't any evidence for the things he was talking about," Alice explained. "And that was the last time I talked to him. Let me go get Julian's manifesto for you," she said as she walked quickly to the lab.

CHAPTER 53

While the girls were talking to Alice outside the biology lab, I was across town standing in Uncle Charlie's doorway, shocked at the words he had just spoken to me. A short time earlier, while at the barber shop, I made the startling discovery that a Sheriff's deputy – Deputy Anthony Curtis – was behind the fires, but when I went to tell Uncle Charlie, I made the dreadful discovery that Deputy Curtis was actually having dinner at Uncle Charlie's house.

What is he doing here? I thought, shocked and confused by the news I had just heard. *What am I doing here?* I wondered. *I'm definitely a goner,* I thought, as I imagined our culprit coming to get me. I quickly looked behind me, thinking of an escape route. My best bet, I imagined, was running straight to my Mom's waiting car and driving away. *Why is Deputy Curtis here with Uncle Charlie?* I wondered again. *Deputy Curtis is with the County Sheriff's Department but Uncle*

Charlie is with the City's Police Department – they work at different places. Why would they be together?

And then another shocking thought flashed through my mind. *Is Uncle Charlie involved in these crimes, too? Is Uncle Charlie working with Deputy Curtis? As I thought this,* I pictured, for a brief moment, the two of them – not even knowing exactly what Anthony Curtis looked like – driving through fields at night on a Yamaha motocross bike and setting fires in the shape of circles.

But then I paused for a moment. *That doesn't seem like Uncle Charlie, does it? Pep,* I said to myself, *you've known Sneak's Uncle Charlie for a while now. Being involved in a crime doesn't seem like something he would do, is it? A*nd quickly my mind began processing the many things I knew about the police captain and his family.

The newspapers, I remembered, used Uncle Charlie's full name and title – Captain Charles William Foster, Jr. – when they quoted him in articles describing his work with the Findlay Police Department. His family, however, I knew still called him by the names they had used when he was much younger – "Charlie", "Young Charlie" and sometimes "Bud", which was a common nickname in the Midwest for boys named after their fathers.

Knowing the family well, I knew that Uncle Charlie and his older brother and younger sister

(Sneak and Jennie's mother), were raised on their family's farm – one that I loved to visit when Sneak invited me in the summertime. The family farm was located east of Findlay, between the town of Arcadia and the city of Fostoria and was where Sneak's grand-parents – Charles and Lee Foster – still worked and lived. Uncle Charlie's older brother, Oren, lived on a nearby farm, and carried on the long family tradition of working his family's land.

It was interesting for me to learn that the Foster's were some of the first settlers in the area, having arrived in Ohio from Pennsylvania in the early 1800's. Early members of the family had helped found sev-eral towns and villages in Hancock County, while later, another relative – also named Charles William Foster, Jr. – became Ohio's 35th governor in 1891. The family, however, was already well known and beloved in the area, well before the governor took office. In my research, I learned that when the towns of Rome and Risdon merged in 1854, the residents decided to give their new municipality a name that would honor Charles William Foster, Sr., the governor's father, and decided to name their new city: Fostoria.

Unlike his older brother, who had joined his father on the family farm immediately after graduat-ing from Arcadia High School, Uncle Charlie longed for adventure and excitement and when he went off to college, he joined the Reserve Officer Training

Corps – known as the ROTC – and spent four years training to become a non-commissioned officer. After college, he put his training to use with three tours of duty in Vietnam.

My career as a reporter and editor has allowed me to interview a number of people in our community about their service to our country in the Army, Navy, Air Force, Marines or Coast Guard – and ask questions about their experience during wartime. When talking with Uncle Charlie, however, I found he didn't talk much about the combat he saw in Vietnam – which was similar to many of the veterans I've interviewed for newspaper articles over the years. The horrors seen in combat and the toll that the war took on many soldiers was difficult for many of them to speak about or even put into words. Instead, Uncle Charlie, like many of the other veterans I've interviewed, talked a lot about the great friendships that were formed during the conflict. "We were closer than brothers," he told me once. "We fought for each other and died helping each other – it's hard to explain to people who weren't there."

Invariably, my interviews with Uncle Charlie would turn to the subject of his wife – who all of my friends called Aunt Marie – a woman Uncle Charlie met while he was stationed in Vietnam as an American G.I. (One time, after I had written in an article that the term G.I. — a common term used for

American soldiers – stood for 'Government Issue', Uncle Charlie set me straight. "I was always told by my friends that it was for '*General* Issue' he explained – because getting thrown into some of those battles made us feel like a throw-away General Issue can of soup," he said with a laugh.)

It was easy to see why Sneak's Uncle Charlie was attracted to Aunt Marie – a woman short in stature and full of energy and enthusiasm. The two married a few years after they first met, in what was known then as South Vietnam. Eventually, Aunt Marie came to America and lived first on military bases with her husband before they moved to Findlay. In my later research, I learned that Congress had created a special visa – "K Visa's" in 1970 – that permitted South Vietnamese spouses of soldiers to move to the United States. After relocating to Findlay, Aunt Marie found that she was talented in selling cosmetics and other products – and my Mom was a frequent guest to their house for "cooking shows" where appliances and cookware were demonstrated, while Aunt Marie would stop by our house with cosmetics.

Throughout my youth, Aunt Marie was my "go-to person" for many of my school reports. If I was assigned a paper on world culture, I'd ask Aunt Marie, and she would tell me about Vietnamese food or society or their respect for their ancestors, or their use of ancestor altars and even bamboo, telling me, "When the bamboo is old, the bamboo sprouts appear." If I had a modern history paper, I'd ask Aunt Marie and she would help me understand the reasons behind the Cold War and the War in Vietnam – and share some of things she experienced during the conflict. (As of this publishing, she and Uncle Charlie still live on Winterberry Drive – and she frequently calls me to offer advice on how I could improve my weekly newspaper columns).

In addition to talking about Aunt Marie in my interviews with Uncle Charlie, he also liked to talk about her family. One of the proudest accomplishments of his life, he told me several times, was helping – through much difficulty – get Marie's family out of the war-torn country – only a few weeks before the fall of Saigon on April 30, 1975. After emigrating, Marie's brothers and sisters spread out to places all around the U.S., while her parents and a great-aunt lived only two doors down on Winterberry Drive.

For some of my school reports I had interviewed Aunt Marie's parents– the Vo's – as well as her great aunt. The transition to America, they had told me, was difficult. But, they loved America and our freedoms, and yet at times, found themselves homesick for their Vietnamese family and friends as well as the food of their homeland. The fast-paced American culture was challenging – as was their new economic status.

"We used to have four or five maids," Mrs. Vo once told me. "Now, I'm the maid."

"I thought I was the maid!" Aunt Marie interrupted. "I'm the one who runs the vacuum."

"Well, maybe," Mrs. Vo said with a smile. "I love America, but it's taken some time to adjust."

Mr. Vo, who had been a government official, was also happy to be in America and spend his retirement years with his family. Interestingly, Uncle Charlie's parents – the Foster's – had warmly welcomed their extended family members to the U.S. and after the Vo's had moved into their house on Winterberry Drive, invited them to help them with their large garden behind their farmhouse. While helping, the Vo's introduced the Foster's to a number of Southeast Asian vegetables and herbs – which they grew alongside large tomatoes and carrots and rutabagas in the garden. It was common in the summertime, I was told, for cars to slow down while passing the farm on the Township Road, as drivers did a double or triple-take, surprised to see several elderly people tending the distant garden – along with tall Uncle Charlie or Mr. Ryerson behind a rototiller – all wearing *nón lá's*, the traditional cone-shaped hats frequently worn in Asia – now worn to protect the gardeners from the bright Ohio summer sun.

When Aunt Marie and the Vo's arrived after the fall of Saigon in 1975, Findlay had only a few refugees from Southeast Asian countries such as Vietnam, Cambodia and Laos. Findlay, Ohio it seemed, was not a place that many immigrants sought out – unlike other places in the U.S. A few years later, however, by early 1980, several other groups of immigrants had arrived in our city – in particular some from the Soviet Union, and that will be another interesting story to tell.

After many of these thoughts flashed through my mind, I found it unlikely that Uncle Charlie was involved in the fires with Deputy Curtis. *It just doesn't seem like something Uncle Charlie would do*, I concluded.

"Hey, Anthony," the tall police captain bellowed again, over other loud voices and the clattering of dishes in the dining room. "Come on out here, Anthony! Pep Stiles is here and I'd like you to meet him."

"Pepper! Pepper!" I heard young voices yell from the dining room and soon Uncle Charlie's two children – four year old twins, a boy and a girl – raced to me at the door.

"Pepper! Pepper!" they yelled as they jumped up on me to give me hugs.

"Hey Trey! Hey Lilly!" I said as the kids surrounded me.

"Where's Sneak and Jennie?" one of them asked, inquiring about their cousins.

"It's just me tonight," I explained, as I thought how strange it must have been for them to see me without their cousins – in the past they had always seen me in the company of Sneak and Jennie when we rode our bikes to their house or played at their grandparent's farm in the summertime. "I just stopped by to see your Dad," I told them.

"Give me five!" Trey said after he had given me a hug and I dutifully slapped his hand.

Moments after the kids arrived we were soon joined by Aunt Marie – who greeted me enthusiastically. "Pep!" she said with a smile. "Would you like some dinner? We just finished, but have a lot left over."

"No thanks Aunt Marie, I ate earlier."

"Your hair is…." she said quickly, without finishing the sentence, and quickly changed the subject. "There's a lot of Vietnamese noodles you could have."

"No, really, I'm…uh…okay," I told her, distracted by two people walking behind her.

While she was talking, I noticed that a young man and an older woman followed Aunt Marie into the living room. The young man, in his early twenties with a boyish face – who I took to be Deputy Curtis – smiled widely. He was joined by a woman, who walked next to him. She was older than the deputy, and I guessed was in her mid-thirties – and was someone, like the young man, whom I had never met before that night.

"Let me introduce you," Uncle Charlie said with a smile. "This is Deputy Curtis, of the Hancock County Sheriff's Department."

"Nice to meet you," the young deputy said with a grin as he shook my hand.

Seeing Deputy Curtis, and his fake smile, made me feel nauseous – knowing that I was in the presence of such an evil person. *How could he have started all of the fires?* I wondered as my mind raced. *He's just trying to get Julian Davis in trouble – so he can be the sheriff.*

"Pep, you don't look so well." Uncle Charlie said as he saw the color fade from my face. "Maybe you should sit down."

"Can we talk somewhere…alone?" I asked meekly.

"Alone?" Uncle Charlie asked.

"You know, like in private."

"Well, sure," Uncle Charlie agreed. "Let's go to my office."

"Is your Mom outside Pep?" Aunt Marie asked, also surprised at my appearance.

"Yeah, she's in the car," I explained.

"I'll go out and get her," I heard Aunt Marie say as she dashed outside into the cold night to find my mother. "You do not look so good."

CHAPTER 54

"I think you need a tall glass of water," Uncle Charlie told me as I followed him first into his kitchen for the glass of water and then to his office – a small room located next to the kitchen. The wood paneled walls, I noticed, were covered with framed photographs of Uncle Charlie in combat fatigues standing next to other soldiers – some American, while others wore uniforms from other countries – France, Australia and South Vietnam, I learned later. In addition to the many framed photos, one of the walls held numerous framed medals and military decorations with different colored ribbons, next to an antique gun and sword.

"Cool," I said – mesmerized by the memorabilia on the walls.

"I don't let too many kids in here," Uncle Charlie explained. "This stuff is too expensive – and too important to me – to get messed up."

On one side of the room was a small wooden desk neatly organized with a few papers, while on the other side of the room were two leather chairs.

"Why don't you have a seat, Pep, and tell me what's going on," he told me pointing to one of the chairs.

Can I trust him? I wondered again. *Should I tell him what I've learned?*

"It's him," I whispered, hoping my voice was not carrying beyond the open office door.

"Him? Who?" Uncle Charlie, asked loudly – at least at a volume higher that I would have preferred.

"It's Deputy Curtis. He's the one behind it all."

"Behind what?"

"Behind the crop circles," I explained. "He's the one who's been setting the fires and writing the letters to Julian Davis. Plus, he's been trying to get information about us."

"About who?" Uncle Charlie asked.

"About me and the other Sunday School Detectives."

Uncle Charlie stared at me intently before showing a slight smile and asking, "Why in the world would you think Deputy Curtis is involved?"

"Well, from the facts of the case," I said, trying to sound as much like a professional investigator as possible.

"And what facts are those?" Uncle Charlie asked.

"Well, the fact that he's been asking a lot of questions about us at the barber shop and wears a brown coat."

"A brown coat?" Uncle Charlie asked.

"Yes," I replied in a serious tone. "That's the same kind of coat Sneak saw when he was following the guy at the cemetery….and we learned yesterday that Julian Davis, the guy who *was* our main suspect – wears a light blue coat. So, it just all adds up."

Just then, my mother followed Aunt Marie into the small office.

"Pep, are you okay?" my mother asked. "Marie told me you weren't looking well. Why don't we go home now?"

"Mom, I'm fine." I told her. "I'm feeling better now."

"It looks like we're interrupting dinner," she added. "Why don't you get your things and go… now," she said sternly, letting me know she "meant business" – as she'd call it.

"I'll bet it gave you quite a shock to see Deputy Curtis – your prime suspect – here at my house," Uncle Charlie said, ignoring my mother's impassioned pleas to leave.

"Yeah," I replied. "Do you believe me?" I asked. "I'm pretty sure he did it."

"Well, Pep," Uncle Charlie replied with a smile. "There's a lot more going on with this case than you're probably aware of. Why don't we go out to the living room and sort this out?"

CHAPTER 55

Back at the college, the girls had just received Julian Davis' sixteen page "*Manifesto*" from his friend – and former F.E.E.T. member – Alice Williams, who was now anxious to get back to her experiments in the biology lab where she worked.

"Wow, this is long," Lisa complained, as she leaned over Hailey and Cressida as they all tried to read the pages at the same time – still seated at the small table outside of the lab. "What did you think of it?" Lisa asked Alice.

"I only got through the first couple of pages," Alice admitted, while putting her hands in the wide pockets of her white lab coat. "It didn't really make sense to me."

"I'm struggling with this too," Hailey confessed. "Julian's using a lot of words I've never seen before... I mean, I don't really know what they mean. They seem to be words from philosophy or something like that."

"He did take a few philosophy courses," Alice added.

"I think he's trying to explain his ideas about God," Cressida summarized. "But I'm getting pretty lost too."

"Hey, how about this for an idea," Lisa began with a smile. "Isn't the seminary close by?"

"Yeah, I think so," replied Hailey.

"We've read a lot of stuff in his paper about God, right?" suggested Lisa. "Stuff that we don't really understand. Why don't we see if Professor Telson could help us with this?"

"Do you think he's working this late?" Mrs. Cotton asked.

"Maybe," said Lisa.

"It'd be worth a try," Hailey explained. "I don't think we're going to understand this on our own." And soon they agreed that they should find Professor Telson to help them understand Julian's sixteen page paper.

After saying their goodbyes to Alice Williams, the four quickly exited the college's Science Building, and rode in Mrs. Cotton's tan station wagon the short distance to the seminary.

When they arrived, the three detectives along with Mrs. Cotton were happy to find the seminary building unlocked and quickly made their way up the stairs – passing the auditorium on the first floor, classrooms on the second floor and easily reached the third floor that contained a number of offices for the school's professors.

The hallway was empty but they soon found the door to Professor Telson's book-filled office open and the Professor seated, reading an old red leather bound book while hunched over his messy desk.

"Professor Telson?" Hailey said as she knocked on the doorframe.

"Well, hello, hello," the young professor said as he quickly stood and greeted the four visitors.

"We're not interrupting you, are we?" Hailey asked as she and the others entered the messy office.

"No, no, I was just reading this fascinating book I found in the library today," he explained while holding up the book in his hand. "It's called, '*Aramaic Papyri of the Fifth Century B.C.*,'…fascinating stuff," he said with a smile, "…written in 1923." The girls, Mrs. Cotton and Professor Telson paused in silence for a moment staring at the book. "It's a good distraction from what I should be doing," he said quickly. "Grading papers!" he explained with a smile. "So, how is everyone?"

"Good," Hailey replied.

"Yeah, we're good," Lisa answered in a tired voice.

"So, how can I help you tonight?" the professor asked.

Lisa was the first to respond. "Well, we were wondering if you could read this paper?" she said while holding up Julian's manifesto and passing it to the professor.

"And tell us what it's all about," Hailey added. "We're looking for clues for the case – you know the one we talked about on Saturday morning – *The Case of the Mysterious Circles.*"

"Ah, yes, of course," the professor replied. "How's that going?"

"Well, we're tracking down as many clues as we can," Hailey explained. "And we thought maybe this...this...manifesto...might have something we could go on."

"Where did you get this?" Professor Telson asked as he first studied the outside of the document – reminiscent of how an archeologist might study the outside of an ancient vase or fragile manuscript.

"From a friend of Julian Davis," Hailey explained. "You know, we talked about him on Saturday morning at the Ryerson's – he's the one who's been writing the letters to the Editor."

"Right, right," said the professor. "I don't think I could have recalled his name...I can be a bit absent minded at times, but I remember that now that you say it. So, would you like me to read this now?"

"If you can," replied Hailey.

"Well, sure, it's not a problem. Not a problem at all."

"It might take you awhile to get through it," Mrs. Cotton interrupted. "Why don't we just leave it with you and you can call us with your answers…tomorrow or the next day."

"Well, that would be fine," said the professor. "But, I think I could tell you pretty quickly what's in this document, it should only take a few minutes."

"A few minutes?" one of the girls said. "I guess we could wait that long before we went home."

"Sure, but unfortunately, I don't really have room in this small office for everybody to sit," the professor explained as the group looked at the stacks of papers, academic journals and books that covered the office floor and the blue cloth covered chair that was opposite his desk. "There's a sitting area with a few chairs just down the hall. Why don't we go there? Let me grab my yellow notepad."

"Sounds good," said Lisa.

The girls and Mrs. Cotton waited a few minutes for the professor to find a blank yellow legal pad in his messy office, but were soon sitting in leather seats around a glass coffee table located in a small alcove along the quiet third floor hallway – passed only occasionally by quickly walking students who were taking night classes that evening.

"Interesting," the professor said as he read the title and author's name out loud. "A MANIFESTO ON THE METAPHYSICS OF ALIENS, by Julian Davis."

The professor then quickly flipped to the second page of the stapled document.

"Hmmm….interesting….interesting," the Professor said to himself as he quickly scanned the second page and moved on to the third page and then the fourth.

"Wow, you're reading that pretty fast," Lisa observed.

"Oh, I taught myself to speed-read a few years ago," the professor explained. "It comes in handy with some of those boring Ugaritic texts."

"Speed reading," Hailey said. "Evelyn…someone."

"Right," the professor replied. "I always want to say Evelyn Underhill, but that's not right of course."

"Of course," Hailey said – unsure of who the professor was referring to.

"Would you like some tea?" the professor asked, pointing to a nearby hot water dispenser.

"Tea?" Lisa replied with a frown. "We've had a lot of that already tonight," remembering the several cups that Alice Williams had poured for them outside the biology lab.

"Thanks, but I think we're okay," Mrs. Cotton said.

"Alright. Well, I should be done reading this in just a few minutes," the professor replied before he resumed his scanning and quickly flipped through the remaining sheets of the sixteen page document.

"Well that was interesting," the professor said when he finished his reading and put the document down on the small glass table in front of them. "Very interesting."

"So what did it say?" Lisa asked. "Were there any important clues?"

"Well, I don't know about clues," said the professor. "You're the detectives around here. I'm just a lecturer in theology!"

"Maybe it would help if you explained how Julian's ideas are different than ours," Hailey added. "We've all been going to church for a long time, so we're pretty familiar with what we believe. Maybe you could explain how his ideas are like or different than our beliefs?"

"So a compare and contrast question!" the professor exclaimed with a laugh. "I make my students do that!"

"That might be good for us tonight," Lisa added.

"Well, I definitely can do that," the professor said as he dropped Julian's manifesto on the table and reached down and grabbed his yellow legal notepad. A few moments later, the professor began drawing shapes on the first page.

"More circles?" Lisa asked when she saw the professor drawing.

"Are you drawing the three circles, like Sneak did, to show us what the fires looked like?" Cressida asked.

"No, no, I'm just drawing two," the professor explained. "Here, look," he said as he held up the notepad.

"For Christians," the professor continued, "I think it's helpful to explain our view of the world by using two circles like this," he said pointing to the shapes before writing a word in each of them. "In the top circle we could put the word 'CREATOR' while in the lower circle we could put the word 'CREATION'."

"So as you could guess," the professor continued, "for Christians, in our view of the world, we believe in a God who is the *Creator* and Sustainer of His *Creation*. So, if you think about the Bible, the very first verse in the Bible presents this view of the world. And what's interesting is that this perspective in the Bible doesn't waver or change from that very first verse all the way through its many pages to its end. Have you learned the Bible's first verse in Sunday School?" the professor asked.

The girls were silent for a moment.

"I've got this one," Mrs. Cotton said with a smile. "I know what it is," she said clearing her throat as the others turned to her. "In the beginning, God created the Heavens and the Earth."

"Exactly!" Professor Telson said encouragingly. "That's the very first sentence in the Bible. God created the heavens and earth. Like I mentioned, God's described as our Creator and Sustainer in the Bible from the very beginning all the way to the end. Even in the New Testament, we learn that Jesus was actively involved as our Creator and Sustainer as well. So we have a belief in the Creator," he said pointing to the top circle.

"And," the professor continued. "We read in the Bible that there is a Creation – a heaven and an earth – that God created," he said pointing to the lower circle. "So these two things are not the same, right? There is a Creator and there is a Creation, and they are different. This is what we call the *Creator –Creation distinction*, meaning that the Creator and the Creation are different."

"Right, they're different," Lisa said. "But doesn't everyone believe that?"

"Well, no." the professor explained in a serious tone. "Some religious views, if we were to draw them as circle drawings, would look very different than this. Many would have just one circle."

"One circle?" Lisa asked.

"Right, there might be a couple of reasons for that. One reason is because some people deny God's existence. So for them, for their drawing, there wouldn't be a circle even labelled 'Creator', just one labelled 'Creation'."

"Ah, got it," Lisa replied with a knowing look.

"There are other religions that just have one circle," the professor continued, "not because they deny the Creator but because they don't see a *distinction* between the Creator and Creation like we do. Some Eastern religions believe that we are all gods of some sort, as do some contemporary ideas about spirituality. So if we were to diagram their view it would have one circle, not two, while the circle might be labelled something like 'Creator dash Creation', again all in one circle."

"Ah," Hailey replied.

"That's really helpful," Cressida added.

"So, what about Julian?" Lisa asked, while looking at the long manifesto that rested on the table. "What does he believe? Is he one circle or two?"

At this comment, the girls laughed, as it sounded funny to think of religious beliefs in those terms.

"He seems pretty out there," Lisa added.

"Well," the professor explained. "He definitely has a two circle view. Even though he uses a lot of big words in his paper, he definitely writes about a Creator and Creation."

"So, he's a Christian, like us?" Hailey asked.

"Well, not exactly," Professor Telson added. "Someone can have a two circle view – as we've been calling it – and not hold Christian beliefs."

"How's that?" Lisa wondered.

"Well, like you've learned in Sunday School," the professor explained, "we don't just hold general concepts. We have some very specific beliefs about the *nature* of our Creator and the nature of Creation. So, as you try to understand Julian's view – or other views you encounter – it's important to ask, 'what do they think about the *nature* of the Creator and Creation?"

"What do you mean by that?" Hailey asked.

"Well, for Christians, we believe that God – our Creator – is a God who has revealed himself to Creation. Even though He's infinite and all-powerful and sovereign – and all of the other attributes that we talk about in Sunday School – He is still, to some degree *knowable*. We're told in the Bible that all people know God to some degree, they just suppress that knowledge. And we're also told in the Bible that God has made a covenant – a special relationship – with his people – and part of that covenant promise is that He's given us the ability to know Him."

"That's cool," Cressida added.

"And it's not just revelation about Himself," Professor Telson added. "In addition to making Himself known, Christians believe that God – our Creator – saw our plight as humans and came down in a personal way to Creation. He saw that we needed help, and so the Father send His Son Jesus to live among us and die for our sins."

"That's cool too," Cressida replied.

"It is, it is," The professor continued. "So, we have very specific ideas about who God is and what He has done."

"So, I'm guessing that's not what Julian believes," said Hailey.

"Well, no it isn't," the professor explained. "For Julian, and quite frankly, a lot of people, they believe that there is a Creator and Creation just like we do. But what they believe about the nature of the Creator is very different from what we believe. Julian and many others think that the Creator is virtually unknowable, so instead of a God who reveals Himself – their idea of the Creator is someone, or something, who hides himself from people."

"So it's almost like there is a barrier between the Creator and Creation," Lisa said. "Can I draw on this?" she asked as she grabbed the yellow legal pad.

"Sure," the professor replied and soon Lisa drew a line between the two circles.

"You've got it exactly right, Lisa," said Professor Telson. "That's exactly how I would diagram Julian's beliefs."

"Or, you could put the circles really, really far apart from each other," Cressida added.

"Right, that would explain it too," the professor said.

"So does Julian think there's *any* way for us to know the Creator?" Hailey asked. "Or does he think it's just impossible?"

"Well, that's where his paper got kind of interesting," the professor explained. "I should note that most of his paper was pretty straightforward – even though he used a lot of long philosophical words

– and most of it wasn't really new. In history, there's been a group of people – called Deists – who, like Julian, have rejected the specifics of the Bible but have come to the conclusion that there is a Creator. And there's been a lot of debate among them if the Creator is an interventionist or non-interventionist – meaning does he involve himself in creation or not. Julian falls on the non-interventionist group – believing that the Creator isn't really involved with our lives. But that point's been made many times over the years by Deists. Where Julian's paper gets interesting is his contention that if we could work with aliens to build really big computers, there would be a chance for us – both the aliens and earthlings – to know God. Otherwise, God is essentially unknowable."

"So, the line would disappear with aliens and computers?" Lisa said, pointing to her line between the two circles.

"That's it in a nutshell," the professor explained. "His contention is that some aliens have already come to earth and that a lot more will be arriving soon…"

"That lines up with what Alice told us at the lab," Lisa interrupted.

"Yep," said Hailey.

"And," the professor continued, "Julian believes that the aliens will be bringing these massive computers with them on their spaceships. And those computers could then be programmed to help us understand who God is."

"So, without the computers we're pretty much in the dark?" Lisa asked.

"That's what he believes," the Professor replied shaking his head. "I probably don't even need to tell you that his beliefs are really, really different than what we believe about God."

"No," Hailey said, as the professor continued.

"We believe that because of God's great love and grace, He has made Himself known to us. He's given us a great resource that is reliable and trustworthy to help us understand who He is and what He's done for us...and to help shape our views. It can all be found in...."

"The Bible!" the girls said in unison.

Hearing this, Mrs. Cotton let out a loud laugh. "Well, Professor Telson, it looks like you've done a good job of training these girls on the answer to that question!"

"It's an answer to a lot of his questions," Hailey said with a smile.

"I guess it is," the professor said with a laugh. "I guess it is."

They paused for a moment.

"Well, there you have it," the professor summarized. "I don't know if it will help you with your case – but at least you understand where Julian Davis is coming from. You know about his views – which shape his decisions and actions. Hopefully that helps."

"Thanks Professor!" Cressida said enthusiastically. "We couldn't really understand his paper."

"Yeah, Julian should have written his manifesto with easier words if he wanted more people to get it," Lisa added.

"That's a good lesson for Christians to remember," the professor replied. "We need to write and talk in ways that other people can understand. Because Julian's ideas are so different than ours, I guess I'm glad he's kept it so confusing!"

"The circle picture, you know, showing how we see a difference between the Creator and Creation is helpful," Hailey added. "Did you come up with it?"

"Oh, no," replied the professor. "There was a professor by the name of Cornelius van Til, who…" the professor suddenly stopped mid-sentence, interrupted by a ringing phone, originating from somewhere down the quiet hallway.

"My office is the only door that is open down there," the professor explained as he looked down the long corridor towards the ringing noise. "That must be my phone ringing. It's strange…no one ever calls my office this late at night, let me go check. I'll be right back."

Soon the professor was walking quickly to his office.

"We probably should be going," Mrs. Cotton said to the others. "I think you've learned what you needed to from Professor Telson."

"I'm not sure what clues there are in the paper," Lisa added. "But, like the professor said, at least we know what Julian's views are."

"Yeah, that might be helpful in our investigation," Cressida added – in an uncommonly talkative tone.

The four soon stood and gathered their purses and notebooks along with Julian Davis' manifesto and the yellow legal notepad that Professor Telson had left on the glass coffee table and soon began walking toward the professor's office.

A few moments later, the professor came out of his office and approached Mrs. Cotton and the girls, his face serious and grim.

"That was Mrs. Willingham – from church," the solemn professor explained. "She's part of the prayer chain and said that there's been an accident…Sneak's been hurt."

CHAPTER 56

"It's Deputy Curtis. He's the one behind it all," I had confessed to Uncle Charlie earlier in the evening – convinced that the young deputy had started the fires. And then I had nearly fainted when I heard that Deputy Curtis, my chief suspect, was in Uncle Charlie's house that night for dinner.

In Uncle Charlie's home, away from the culprit and the others, my mother and Aunt Marie doted on me with a second glass of cold water, and then a glass of 7-Up, some saltine crackers and a blanket – trying to restore my spirits – as they made me rest in one of Uncle Charlie's plush leather chairs in his small and orderly, wood paneled office.

While I was recuperating, I had the chance to make my case once again to Uncle Charlie, a tall police captain, who lowered himself to my level to patiently listen to me.

"So, we know that the guy Sneak followed out of the cemetery had a brown winter coat," I began. "But we learned this week that Julian Davis has a blue winter coat – a light blue coat, so it probably wasn't him. And who do we know that has a brown coat?" I asked without waiting for an answer. "Deputy Curtis."

"Hmmm," the tall police captain said as he rubbed his bushy mustache. "Interesting theory."

"And then," I continued. "When I was at the barber shop earlier tonight, I found out that none other than Deputy Curtis was asking a bunch of questions about me and Joel and Sneak…like he was trying to find out stuff about us. Plus, he knows all about *The Sunday School Detectives*. I mean, our group just got started on Saturday morning, and he knows that Sneak is grounded and who all the members of the group are. He's guilty, Uncle Charlie. It's got to be him!"

"Well, Pep, those are interesting ideas," Uncle Charlie said in a serious tone. "Why don't we go out to the living room and sort this out?"

Soon, I found myself following Uncle Charlie out of his home office and into his living room to meet the man I was convinced was the culprit in our case.

"Deputy Curtis," Uncle Charlie said as he entered the living room. "Pep has an interesting theory about the case – that case of the crop circles."

I looked down at the floor as Uncle Charlie made this statement – not seeing if his face looked serious or if he was smiling. *I hope he's not making fun of me*, I thought.

"That's great," the young deputy said enthusiastically. "We'd love to hear what it is."

We? I wondered. *What does he mean by that?*

"Pep, I don't think I got a chance to introduce you two properly," Uncle Charlie continued. "You see, the county sheriff has personally assigned Deputy Curtis here to help lead the Task Force to investigate the case. Anthony, maybe you can tell him about the clues you've found in your investigation first," Uncle Charlie said while looking at the young deputy. "Then Pep can tell you about his ideas."

"That's great!" the deputy said again enthusiastically. "Hey Anna," he said in a loud voice to the woman on the other side of the living room who was finishing a loud and old-fashioned game of *Simon Says* with Trey and Lilly – Uncle Charlie and Aunt Marie's children. "Could you come on over here with us?" the deputy asked. "We're going to talk about the case."

She's going to talk about the case, too? I wondered. *I don't even know who she is?*

"Pat your head," the woman said to the children – in a voice that reminded me of Mary Poppins. "Oh, no, Simon didn't say that."

"Ahh," Trey cried. "Again, again! Let's do that again!"

"Sorry kids, that's all for now," she said to the children with an accent I failed to place. "I've got to do some work," she explained as she turned and joined us on one of the plush blue chairs in the living room.

"Again! Again!" Lilly insisted. "I almost won!"

"No, *I* almost won!" Trey asserted.

"No, *I* almost won!" Lilly insisted as the adults began to laugh.

"Kids! Knock it off!" Uncle Charlie commanded.

"Kids! Come in here!" Aunt Marie commanded from the kitchen. "Come and help Pep's Mom and me in the kitchen. Papa needs to talk about work with his friends."

"Awe, Mom!" one of them complained.

"Come on, you need to get a snack and then get ready for bed!" she told them as the kids quickly scampered out of the living room to join their mother and my Mom in the kitchen.

"I don't think I had a chance to introduce you earlier," Uncle Charlie said to me after the children had departed. "This is Anna Baxter, she's an investigator with the State Fire Marshal's office."

"The state Fire Marshal?" I asked. "What's that?"

"We investigate fires….and explosions…by helping local police and fire departments."

"And sheriff's departments," Deputy Curtis added.

"Right, and sheriff's departments!" Inspector Baxter said with a laugh. "I came up here about two weeks ago…and already they've got me working undercover!"

Undercover? I wondered.

"Is it alright to tell him?" the deputy asked Uncle Charlie.

"About?" Uncle Charlie asked.

"About what we learned at the mall," the deputy replied. "On Friday afternoon."

"Sure, I think he'll keep it confidential," Uncle Charlie said seriously, "at least until everyone is caught. You won't say anything will you, Pep?"

"No, I won't say anything," I promised – keenly interested in what I was about to hear.

"We tracked him to the mall," Inspector Baxter said in her funny accent. "We had done that before – but we had been such a long distance away we couldn't see exactly what he was doing. On Friday I had this pram – what do you call it?"

"Baby carriage," Deputy Curtis explained.

"Right, I had a baby carriage that I pushed around near the mall entrance."

"By the barber shop," Deputy Curtis explained.

"Right, but then he moved his car," the woman explained. "So I took the pram back to our van and hustled over to the other entrance."

"I didn't get out of the van," Deputy Curtis described, "because I was worried he would see me."

"Anyway, he went to a bench," Anna explained.

"Near *The Toggery*," Deputy Curtis added.

"And after he had looked around to make sure no one saw him," the woman continued, "he picked up a letter from under it. Then, he literally ran into me on his way out of the mall."

"Wow," I said.

"Anyway, we definitely know he's getting letters from someone and not just making the stuff up that he sends to the newspaper," Deputy Curtis explained.

"Wow," I said again.

"And he probably already knows about the next fire," the Deputy continued. "We're expecting something big to happen again in the next few days."

"You don't know that for sure," Uncle Charlie interjected.

"So, who exactly were you following?" I asked quickly, while Deputy Curtis and Investigator Baxter responded with strange looks.

"Julian, of course," Anna replied.

"Julian Davis," the deputy replied. "We thought you knew that already."

"Well, I did...I did," I replied nervously. "I just wanted to make sure we were all talking about the same person."

"So what is your theory?" the deputy asked. "We've got Julian....we just need to know who he's getting his information from."

"You don't exactly *have* Julian," Uncle Charlie added.

"Well, sure we do Captain Foster!" Deputy Curtis said adamantly. "He tried to evade us at the mall and we saw him get a note from under a bench! It's definitive proof that he's involved in the conspiracy."

"That would be pretty hard to prove in court, Anthony," Uncle Charlie interjected. "Right now, you've just observed him picking up a piece of paper at the mall. That's not illegal! My kids pick up stuff from the floor of the mall all the time…mostly quarters near the Arcade, but that's not illegal. The only thing Julian's guilty of is wearing his roommate's coat!"

"Right…I'm glad he gave that back to me," the deputy said.

"You're his roommate?" I asked incredulously.

"Yeah, me and four other guys," the deputy explained. "We've actually been roommates for a couple of years. It's a crazy coincidence. I couldn't have imagined that Julian would be involved in something like this – but, he's been acting really weird the past few months."

"And he didn't say what he's been doing?" I asked.

"No, he doesn't really talk to us very much. He's a pretty quiet guy and keeps to himself."

"Oh don't describe him like that!" Uncle Charlie said. "That's what they always say about…"

"Introverts?" Inspector Baxter asked.

"Oh, don't worry about that," Uncle Charlie concluded.

"Well," Deputy Curtis continued. "He doesn't spend too much time in the apartment. He just takes off for long amounts of time."

The four paused for a moment.

"So Pep," Deputy Curtis asked. "What's *your* theory? What clues did you find?"

"Well, we – *The Sunday School Detectives* – learned that Julian has a light blue coat, but when Sneak Ryerson, one of our detectives, was following a suspect, the suspect was wearing a brown winter coat."

"That was probably mine," Deputy Curtis admitted. "Julian's been borrowing different coats from each of us at the apartment – he must think it will be harder for law enforcement to follow him."

"Because of that," I said sheepishly, "I had actually thought that you were involved." I paused for a moment to see the Deputy react with a surprised look and then laugh.

"I don't think I'm smart enough to pull off this crime," Deputy Curtis admitted. "To be honest, I'm not really sure what the arsonist is trying to do."

"Make circles," Inspector Baxter said with a laugh.

"Plus, I heard you were asking a lot of questions about us at the barber shop," I added.

Deputy Curtis laughed again. "Oh yeah, right," he explained. "I did ask Dan and Larry a bunch of questions."

"Why were you asking the barbers questions about the kids?" Uncle Charlie asked. "That would make anyone who heard about it suspicious of you."

"Well, you and I had talked on Saturday afternoon," the deputy explained to Uncle Charlie, " – after your meeting at the Ryerson's house. So, when I went to the barber's shop that afternoon, I just started asking Dan and Larry a bunch of questions about the kids. I thought the idea of a bunch of kid detectives was pretty neat. I wish I could have done that when I was younger – the most excitement I ever had was playing Little League baseball games and talking to my friends about 'cow tipping'."

"Well, it sounds like you've done a lot already with your investigation," I added. "Hopefully we won't get in the way."

"No, no, I don't think so," the Deputy said with a smile.

"We might actually need their help on this, Anthony," Inspector Baxter said seriously. "We still need to figure out where Julian is getting his information from."

Just then, the air was pierced with the sound of a telephone ringing in the kitchen. From the muffled sounds, I could tell that the phone was answered by Aunt Marie.

"Charlie...the phone's for you...it's work!" she said loudly from the nearby room.

"I'll be right back," Uncle Charlie said as he dashed from the plush blue chair and raced towards the kitchen.

"So do you mind if I ask where you are from, Inspector Baxter?" I asked. "I'm guessing South Africa."

"Heavens, no," she replied with a laugh. "...nothing that exotic. I'm originally from England, but I live in Columbus now – well technically Reynoldsburg – that's where the Fire Academy is located."

"Ah, got it," I told her. "I couldn't place your accent."

"Yes, well I've been in the states now for a number of years, but I can't drop the accent entirely. I've actually met a few other Brits while I've been in Findlay. One was a Scotsman who I met at *The South Side Six*. And I met another gentleman who was waiting for his pizza at the *Rocking U Outpost* – he was from near London."

"I can't remember, do they have seats there?" I asked about the restaurant.

"Oh, at the Outpost? No, it's just takeaway," she explained. "The gent was really friendly – had been transferred to Findlay for work. Oh, and then, interestingly two of the farmers who were victims of the fires – had connections to England. One was born in Salisbury – I interviewed him last week, Rusty, I believe his name was, came here when he was a young lad. And then Randy, his grandmother was from Portsmouth."

"In our research we heard that England has a lot of crop circles," I added, as I tried to learn more from the inspector.

"Well, there are. But what we're investigating here, aren't really crop circles," she explained. "We're investigating fires in the shape of circles. Traditionally, crop circles, like you'd find in England or other places," she continued, "are shapes that are made in fields that actually have crops in them – like wheat or maize here in the states. But you're right, in England we've had a lot of crop circles, there were some in Gloucestershire, and a lot in Wiltshire – near Old Sarum – and Hampshire."

Soon, I could hear the brusk voice of Uncle Charlie in the kitchen. "Captain Foster here. When? Where? Where are they now? I'll be right there."

Suddenly Uncle Charlie returned to the living room – his face ashen with a grave expression.

"We've got to go!" he said briskly to Deputy Curtis and Inspector Baxter. "There's been an accident – my nephew's hurt."

CHAPTER 57

Sneak hurt? I wondered. *What is going on?*

"Get your things," Uncle Charlie said quickly to Deputy Curtis and Inspector Baxter. "I'll give you the details when I meet you at the scene downtown. We'll need to drive separately. It's going to be a long night. I'm going to go change into my uniform."

He paused, as he looked at me and the scared expression on my face.

"It will be okay," Uncle Charlie said to me earnestly. "Why don't you and your Mom go home now, and we'll let you know later how Sneak's doing.... but you may not hear from me until the morning... maybe sooner, I'm not sure. It will be okay, Pep."

Turning to Inspector Baxter and Deputy Curtis, the police captain explained, "We've got to get over to a park – it's just on the other side of downtown, then go out to the hospital."

The hospital! I thought as my mind raced.

"Is Sneak okay?" I asked – worried about my friend.

"I don't know," Uncle Charlie said, "I'm sure we'll find out soon. What I do know is that waiting around here isn't going to help matters. Let's get going," he said and gave a twirl of his finger – a similar move, I learned later, that he had given to numerous helicopter pilots on their departures from the landing zones – "the LZ's" – in the war. "Say a prayer for your friend," he said to me as he left the room.

I went to the kitchen and found my mother as the two adult investigators quickly grabbed their coats.

"What's going on?" my mother asked me quietly, trying not to disturb the young children who had just been sent to their bedrooms and were being "tucked in" by Aunt Marie.

"Sneak's been in some sort of accident."

"What?" she said surprised. "What sort of accident?"

"I don't know," I told her. "Let's go home and I'll call Jennie or Hailey."

We quickly went to the front door and left without saying another word to Uncle Charlie, Deputy Curtis or Inspector Baxter. Soon, the three raced passed us as my Mom and I were walking to her car and we watched as their cars peeled out of the driveway with screaming sirens and flashing lights.

"Let's go," I told my Mom when we reached her car, but then I paused for a moment, gathering my thoughts before opening the car door. "This day stinks," I summarized.

"Yes, yes it does honey," my Mom answered. "Let's remember to say a prayer for your friend."

CHAPTER 58

For Sneak and Jennie Ryerson, the day had unfolded much like any other. The kids rode Bus Four home from school and raced down Decker Avenue to their house. They watched the *Munster's* on T.V. – without arguing about who should select the show – and then had an early dinner.

As with most Mondays, Mr. Ryerson arrived home from work early and ate quickly – to ensure he would arrive at his Monday Night Bowling league on time. And like most Mondays during dinner, the kids teased their father about returning home from the bowling alley smelling of cigarette smoke.

"Why are you so smelly when you come home?" Jennie asked.

"It's not me!" their non-smoking father protested with a smile. "It's the other guys!" he told them.

During dinner, Sneak told his parents about a letter he had received earlier in the day's mail.

"It's from a potential client," he told them, "...
one who wants to meet with me."

"Steven, we said you couldn't do any investigations," Mrs. Ryerson said.

"I know, I know," said Sneak. "I know I can't do
the work, but the letter doesn't have a return address
on it...or a phone number. So, I don't have any way to
let them know I can't take the case. I was just going to
go over to Rawson Park – where they want to meet –
and tell them I can't do the investigation. I was going
to give them Hailey's phone number in case *The* uh...
what's the name of the group?"

"*The Sunday School Detectives*," Jennie added with a
frown – knowing her brother already knew her name
of the group.

"Right, in case *The Sunday School Detectives* wanted
to take the case."

"What do you think, Dad?" Mrs. Ryerson asked
her husband.

"It sounds okay," Mr. Ryerson said. "As long as
you aren't investigating."

"I won't," Sneak insisted. "I promise."

"I've got to get to the *Sportsman*," said Mr.
Ryerson – referring to the bowling alley on the north
side of town.

"And I've got to get to Naomi Circle," Mrs.
Ryerson added – referring to a women's group at our
church. "I'm running late as it is. I don't think I'll

have time to take you over to the park and bring you home."

"It's okay," Sneak explained. "I can just ride my bike. It will only take a few minutes to get over there, and then a few minutes to tell the person that I can't take the case and then a few more minutes to bike home." He paused. "Plus, even though it's cold, I'd like to get out for a while."

"That's fine," his father told him. "Be safe."

"Okay," Sneak told his parents. "I'll be able to stay on the sidewalks – they're mostly cleared off. What's Jennie doing tonight?" he asked.

"You don't have to watch her," his mother told him. "I'll take her with me to Circle tonight – there's childcare at church and Michelle will be there."

"Yay!" Jennie replied with a smile. "I'll bring a few dolls. Mr. Knick Knack might be bored, so he might decide to stay at home and watch T.V."

When six forty-five approached that evening, Mr. Ryerson got into his small Chevrolet Chevette and left for the bowling alley, while Jennie and Mrs. Ryerson hopped into *The Maroon Monster* – the family's long red 1976 Chevrolet Impala station wagon – and left for Church. Sneak, meanwhile, went to the garage to find his bike.

The garage was unusually dark and lonely that evening, but it took the famous detective only a few moments to find his three-speed Raleigh bicycle. He began by cycling down Decker Avenue to Osborne Avenue and then followed the sidewalks along Sandusky Street. When he reached downtown Findlay, Sneak turned north at Main Street, then turned west on Main Cross Street, passing the large County Courthouse, the Continental Cablevision offices and the Post Office as he rode next to the red-bricked Junior High School he would be attending in the Fall. Soon, Sneak passed The *Rocking U* – a cowboy and western themed pizza parlor – and then the famous downtown branch of *Dietsch Brothers Ice Cream* – closed, as everyone knows, because it was a Monday. The route was one that he knew well – his family frequented many of the businesses in the area – and it was the same route he had recently used for his nightly stakeouts at the nearby cemetery.

Riding down West Main Cross Street, the young detective flipped on the headlight attached under the handlebars – illuminating his way on the dark sidewalks – and cautiously traversed over bumpy railroad tracks before passing the West End Tavern and St. Michael's Church. Soon, he arrived at the intersection of Western Avenue and after crossing the street, turned right and rode on the narrow sidewalk a short distance before seeing the signs for the park on his left. Two large green wooden signs read: "CITY OF FINDLAY, RAWSON PARK", while a smaller white sign read, "MAPLEGROVE and ST. MICHAELS CEMETERIES" – indicating the rear entrances to the cemeteries.

Turning left on River Street, the young detective entered Rawson Park and quickly passed its yellow "Park Entrance" sign, as well as two empty tennis courts and a cold metal swing set on his right.

I must be the first one here, Sneak said to himself as he scanned the empty parking lot for vehicles. In the distance, he could hear the voices of several kids playing but as he rode toward the park's baseball field, the evening was eerily quiet.

I wonder who wants to meet with me? It seems a little strange to be so confidential, but maybe they are scared. Or, just immature.

It should be over in a couple of minutes, he told himself.

CHAPTER 59

Sneak Ryerson rode his bicycle slowly around the lonely parking lot as the seven o'clock meeting time approached and then passed. *Mr. X,* Sneak said to himself with a laugh. *That's a funny name for a client. I wonder what he wants to talk about?* The young detective waited, but the lot, however, remained empty. Eventually, he looked at his watch again while thinking, *Mr. X isn't coming* – noticing that the time was now seven fifteen. He considered riding out to the nearby sidewalk, but decided to circle the lot once more, riding near the park's deep bowl-shaped basin – frequented by local kids after heavy snowfalls for its great sledding – and then approached the baseball field again.

When he was about half-way into the long parking lot next to the baseball field, Sneak was surprised to suddenly hear the sound of a speeding car – one that had gathered speed after coming out of its hiding place next to a nearby house on River Street.

The sound of the revving motor had first caught the bicyclist's attention – but then he heard the screeching, spinning wheels.

In a moment, the car was racing towards him and Sneak began pedaling as fast as he could.

What's that guy's deal? Sneak wondered as he tried to move away from the middle of the parking lot. *Maybe he can't see me because of the darkness.*

The crash was quick and immediate – crushing the bicycle into a mangle of tires and metal – and flipping Sneak forward as he tried to point the bike away from the speeding car when it hit his back tire.

The car sped past the bike and rider and then slowed at the end of the parking lot.

"What's the big idea?" Sneak yelled as he quickly assessed his injuries while he lay on the cold asphalt. His body ached from the crash but he sat up quickly, glad that, although he was scratched, he did not seem seriously injured.

His stomach, however, began to churn as he saw in the darkness, the car slowly turn around at the end of the parking lot and face him again. And soon it began to increase its speed.

It's heading right toward me! Sneak shuddered in disbelief.

"Hey, hey!" Sneak began yelling. "I'm down here, you ran over my bike! Hey, you're coming right at me. Watch out!"

His eyes widened as he saw the car speeding towards him and he realized then that it was no accident that the car had hit his bike. *He's trying to get me,* he thought as the car came closer. *He's trying to run me over!*

The young detective wanted to run, to spin to his right where the safety of a curb and a baseball dugout were only a few feet away. To his left were the houses on River Street where, if he escaped in that direction, he could find shelter and ask for help.

He wanted to run – safety awaited in either direction – but he couldn't move. He quickly discovered that his legs were trapped under his smashed bike.

"Hey!" he continued yelling. "Hey, watch out!" he yelled again as he quickly tried to free his legs from the pretzel of tire tubes, chains and handlebars that ensnared him.

"Lord, please," he cried out in a desperate prayer.

Seeing the car rapidly approach, the young detective continued to grab and grasp at his feet, trying desperately to get free.

"Jesus, I need your help right now," he cried out as the car was nearly upon him.

CHAPTER 60

The hit to Sneak Ryerson was swift and hard, moving his body sideways towards the curb of the parking lot and the baseball dugout.

His feet, he found, had escaped the bicycle that had only moments before been wrapped in a tangle of bent tires and handlebars.

It took the young detective several moments to realize what had happened. *That hit should have come from in front of me,* he said to himself while he was still in midair moving towards the nearby curb. *The car is still coming from in front of me – but something hit me from the side. What's happening to me?*

Sneak landed hard upon the grass near the baseball dugout as the full weight of much of his body and a weight on top of him drove his shoulder into the ground.

Moments later he heard the speeding car crash into his mangled bike and then speed away, spinning its wheels as it exited the park, while a voice above him yelled at the speeding driver. "Up your nose with a rubber hose, man!"

"What?" the young detective said as he looked up, trying to determine what – or who – the heavy and loud object was that was on top of him.

"R...R...Roger?" the young detective exclaimed instinctively as he lifted his head from the frozen ground and saw the bushy hair and smiling face of the boy he had known from school several years before. "I think you broke my shoulder!"

"You're lucky it's just your shoulder," the boy said as he rolled off the young detective and sat up. "If I wasn't around, I think everything on you would have been broken."

It took a few moments for the young detective to collect his thoughts and attempt to understand the events that had just occurred. "Roger, what are you doing here?" the young detective finally asked, trying to make sense of the situation.

"I live here," Roger explained. "Well, not at the park. I live in that house, just over there, near the back entrance to the cemetery."

"But I haven't seen you at school," said Sneak, remembering their encounter in third grade when Sneak had identified the tall boy as the one who had taken a silver toy Amtrak train engine and cars that another student had brought to class. He was thinking of asking, "Did you get kicked out of school?" but thought it better not to ask.

"I haven't gone to Whittier in like three years," Roger explained.

At this comment, Sneak felt bad for not noticing that his fellow student was no longer enrolled at his school – and for not discovering what had become of the boy. His detective skills had failed to notice that, he thought remorsefully.

"Where have you been?" Sneak asked, still groggy.

"It's not like I'm playing hooky or somethin'. We've moved around a bunch since I left."

At this, Sneak imagined some of the challenges the boy must have faced if he'd "moved around a bunch" in a period of three years.

"...but now we're here. Do you know where Adams Elementary School is? Over on Washington Street?"

"Yeah," the young detective replied.

"That's where I go now," Roger explained.

Soon, the two were quiet in the cold and darkness of the park – looking at the empty parking lot.

"Man, that was a close one," Roger finally said.

"Yeah," the young detective agreed. "My shoulder is killing me," Sneak grimaced in pain while holding his right shoulder.

"That guy was trying to run you over, wasn't he Sneak?" Roger asked.

"Yeah, I'm afraid so," replied Sneak.

"Well, I got a good look at him," Roger said, "... before I tackled you like Mean Joe Green would do to Roger Staubach and we did that pile driver into the grass."

"I think you saved my life," Sneak explained. "Where were you?"

"I was just walkin' home and heard you yellin'. I didn't know what was goin' on until I got closer and saw you stuck under your bike."

"Thanks man," Sneak told him gratefully. "I thought I was a goner."

"I felt the front of his car hit my foot," Roger told him. "I thought I was a goner too."

"Are you okay?"

"I'm scraped up, but I mostly landed on you," the tall boy explained, as the two laughed – relieved that they had escaped such terrifying danger.

"We need to call the police," Sneak explained. "Could you go do that? I don't think I should move until I can get looked at by an ambulance."

"Okay, sure." Roger told him. "I'll be right back."

"Could you bring some blankets too?" Sneak asked. "I'm freezing out here."

"Uh, sure. I'll be right back." Quickly, the tall boy ran off to his house to call the police. "424 – 7150," the boy chanted as he ran – having memorized the police department's phone number during elementary school with the other kids.

The darkness and cold soon engulfed the young detective as he lay back on the cold ground of the city park. *Who would want to do that to me?* he wondered. *It must have something to do with the crop circle case – that's the only active investigation going on right now. But why? We must be getting close. Our investigation must have scared them,* he concluded. *But it's not really my investigation anymore....because I'm grounded!*

Dazed and unsteady, the young detective shut his eyes – trying to think about the case and the dangerous driver – but his mind, he found, had a hard time doing that.

CHAPTER 61

"Sneak! Sneak!" the young detective awoke, startled, to hear Roger yelling. The tall boy, he saw, was leaning over him – his eyes wide with concern.

"Ugh," the young detective moaned, as he winced and grabbed his shoulder again.

"I think you passed out," the tall boy said. "I'm glad you woke up – I was worried for a minute."

"Are you bleeding?" Sneak asked, seeing blood on his rescuer's coat.

"It's just a little scrape," the tall boy said. "I'll be okay."

"The cops will be here in just a minute," Roger explained and almost on cue the sound of sirens could be heard in the distance. "So, what were you doing out here?" the boy asked as he placed a blanket around the young detective. "I mean it's freezing cold – most people don't just ride their bikes to a park in the dark…on a winter night."

"I was supposed to meet someone," Sneak explained.

"I hope it wasn't that dude driving the car."

"I think it was," Sneak replied and then paused for a moment. "I guess he didn't want to meet with me!"

"Well, like I said, I got a good look at him," Roger added. "Plus, I know what his car looks like too." He paused for a moment as the sound of the sirens grew louder. "I hope they catch that jerk – he could have really hurt you."

"Yeah, I know," Sneak said with a wince, as he continued to tenderly hold his shoulder.

"Do you think it's broken?" Roger asked.

"I don't know, but it sure hurts," Sneak said with a grimace.

When the paramedics arrived, they quickly placed Sneak on a wooden stretcher, put him in their ambulance and then sped down South Main Street to the city hospital. Sneak, by this time, was alert and talkative – telling the paramedics all about the case.

The ambulance quickly turned onto East Pearl Street and the young detective was rushed into the Emergency Room area – located on the north side of the hospital. He was quickly seen by a nurse and doctor in the Emergency Room who – after seeing his initial X-rays – diagnosed him with a dislocated shoulder and gently put it back into place.

A police officer had followed the ambulance to the hospital and stayed with the boy in a curtained area and took the young detective's statement as he waited with him. With his functioning left arm, Sneak was able to pull the note from his pants pocket and give it to the patrolman, as the officer noted that Sneak had gone to Rawson Park to meet "Mr. X" – a potential client – and then was hit by a driver who had attempted to run him over.

By then, Sneak was alert enough to explain where his parents were that evening, and soon patrol cars were dispatched to the *Sportsman's Bowling Alley* and our church to inform Sneak's parents of the accident and request that they meet their son at the hospital. They arrived about the same time – although Mrs. Ryerson was delayed for a few minutes in reaching her son because she had to talk with the staff who insisted that Jennie sit in the waiting room – as she was not old enough to go back to Sneak's hospital room.

"It's okay, Mom," Jennie reassured her mother. "Mr. Knick Knack can wait here with me, he didn't want to stay at home and watch T.V., so he's been with me the whole time." Soon, the young girl, with her pigtails bouncing back and forth, cleared two plastic seats of magazines to make space in the waiting room for herself and her imaginary friend. "It's okay, Mom," she said again. "Go and see how Sneak is doing."

"I hate to leave you here," her mother replied.

"Go, it's okay," the young girl said, motioning her mother to walk to the examination rooms. "I'll just play with Mr. Knick Knack."

Mr. and Mrs. Ryerson were relieved to find their son in good spirits when they arrived at his room and hugged him as gently as they could, avoiding the blue sling that held his right arm.

"Steven, I told you not to ride your bike at night," his mother scolded. "I should have known something like this would happen. You need to be more careful."

Soon, however, as Sneak began to tell them about the night, they stood aghast that someone would intentionally try to hurt their son with a car and sought to understand all that had happened at the park. After some time of waiting, his parents eventually walked with their son as he was taken by wheelchair to have his shoulder and chest further x-rayed. And then they waited for the results.

Later, the Emergency Room doctor arrived and spoke to Mr. and Mrs. Ryerson in clipped, short sentences while Sneak laid back on his hospital bed. "Well, I've talked to the radiologist and looked at the x-rays," he said to Sneak's parents. "I don't see any breaks to the collar bone or shoulder," the doctor told them. "He's going to be sore for a while. He arrived with a dislocated shoulder and we did a reduction.... to put it back in place when he arrived. It needs to be immobile for a while to reduce the swelling, but it should be fine. And, some of his ribs are bruised as well. He doesn't seem to have any internal bleeding or injuries. So, considering the circumstances, he's one lucky boy."

"I'm not sure how much luck had to do with it," Mr. Ryerson said with a smile, remembering how his son had told his parents that he had prayed before being rescued from the oncoming car.

"Well, whatever it was – he could have been hurt a lot more than he was," the doctor continued. "From the information his friend told the paramedics, it sounds like he received a concussion from the fall – so I'd like to keep him here under observation until the morning. Just to make sure we didn't miss anything going on internally...and to monitor his concussion symptoms."

"I'm feeling a lot better," Sneak said weakly.

"That's fine, it's fine for him to stay the night," his mother said, while rubbing his left arm. "That's fine with us."

Back at Rawson Park, the police had taken Roger's statement when they arrived and lauded the boy for his bravery. Uncle Charlie soon arrived and was quickly briefed by the officer in charge.

A crowd of neighbors had gathered near the scene – curious to see the many police and fire vehicles at the nearby park with their red and blue lights illuminating the dark night sky.

Many of the neighbors were also questioned by the police – none of whom had seen the driver or the bicyclist that was nearly run over.

Uncle Charlie was soon introduced to Roger and thanked him for saving his nephew's life.

"I just saw him stuck there," the boy explained to Sneak's uncle – while Deputy Curtis and Inspector Baxter listened nearby. "He was trapped under his bike. And then I saw that car coming towards him. It didn't look like he'd have a chance."

Having come so close – inches really – to the vehicle that had attempted to run over Sneak, Roger was able to give a clear description of both the car and driver to the first police officers that had arrived on the scene – and reiterated his description to Uncle Charlie and the others. With that information, the officers had called their fellow law enforcement officers to quickly set up road blocks around the city and issue an *APB* – an All Points Bulletin – over the radio to apprehend one Julian Davis.

CHAPTER 62

S neak Ryerson heard the news shortly after he arrived at the hospital as he was waiting to be taken to his x-ray. It had come in over the squawking radio on the belt of the police officer who was guarding the curtained area where he waited – an APB for Julian Davis, said the dispatcher's voice, explaining that Julian was wanted in connection to an aggravated assault with a motor vehicle. Possibly armed and dangerous.

Julian Davis? Sneak wondered while sitting in a wheelchair, still nursing his shoulder. *Julian's just a letter writer. He's not an arsonist and probably not even the ring leader of this criminal group. He probably has no idea what's going on. Why would he turn violent? Up until now he could have argued that he didn't know anything about the fires. I know nothing!* Sneak said to himself – as he remembered his father's imitation of Sargent Schultz from the T.V. show *Hogan's Heroes.*

His co-workers at the movie theater gave Julian alibis for all of the fires. We couldn't pin anything on him – until now!

Sneak was perplexed.

After concluding his investigation at the park, Uncle Charlie arrived at the hospital – talking first to the officer who had been with Sneak that evening, then he talked to the doctors in the Emergency Room – before entering the room with a warm, "Hi guys!" to the Ryerson's.

"Oh, Bud," Mrs. Ryerson said as her older brother hugged her and she began to cry. "I'm so glad you're here. I was so scared when the officer came and got me at church. I prayed all the way over here."

"Well, it looks like the Lord was pretty gracious tonight," her brother concluded. "Sneak's friend was at Rawson Park at just the right time, that was amazing," he paused briefly before continuing. "So, how's the patient doing?"

"I'm okay," the young detective said quietly – having moved from the wheelchair to a hospital bed before his uncle arrived. "I can't believe I rode into that trap."

"Don't you worry about that now," his uncle explained as Mrs. Ryerson returned to the chair where she had been sitting while her brother moved closer to his nephew's hospital bed. "We'll have time enough to talk about that later. I've got your friend's statement and the statement that you gave to the officer who's been with you here and that's plenty for me to go on. Is there anything else about the attack you can tell me about?"

"Attack?" Mrs. Ryerson asked suddenly. "Is that what you're calling it?"

"Nothing more than what I told the officer who took my statement, it just happened really fast," Sneak explained to his uncle, ignoring his mother's question.

"That's okay," his uncle told him. "If you remember anything else, call me, okay?"

"Okay," said Sneak.

Uncle Charlie returned to his sister, putting his hand on her shoulder. "Sis, I'm sure we'll pick up our suspect soon, Findlay's not that big of a place, right?" he said reassuringly. "But, you've got to understand… this guy, Julian Davis, he's dangerous. And with him on the loose, we need to make sure he doesn't try to do anything else to Sneak, right? So, I'm going to station an officer here tonight, okay? You're going to be okay with that, right, Sis?"

"Sure, Charles," Mrs. Ryerson replied as she took a tissue and wiped the tears from her eyes. "It's okay to have someone here. I…I just can't believe someone would want to hurt Steven. It's unfathomable."

"Yeah, I was surprised when I heard it myself," her brother told her. "But it will be okay, you hear what I'm saying, Sis?"

"Yeah," she said looking down at the hospital room floor.

"It will be okay," he said again. "We're going to get this guy. And we're going to get the guys he's working with too. And we're going to put them in jail for a long time. Do you hear me?"

"Yeah, okay," said Mrs. Ryerson. "I don't know what came over me," she added. "It will be okay, I'll regain my composure in a few minutes."

"Have you talked to Mom and Dad yet?" her brother asked.

"Yeah, I called them a little while ago," Mrs. Ryerson explained. "I didn't want them to hear the news from someone else."

"That's good, that's good," Uncle Charlie told her. "So, why don't you all try to get some rest, okay? It's been a crazy night. Try to get some sleep."

"Sure," Sneak replied to his uncle. "We can do that, right, Mom?"

"Of course we can, Steven" Mrs. Ryerson said in a calm voice.

"In the meantime, I'm going to go get this guy," Uncle Charlie concluded.

"Okay," Sneak replied as he watched his uncle shake his father's hand and hug his mother one more time.

"Be safe," his sister cautioned as her brother left the room.

CHAPTER 63

S neak Ryerson had a hard time sleeping that night,
and long after midnight – around one thirty in the
morning – according to the loud ticking clock on the
wall – while his father slept soundly on a small couch
located a few feet away from his bed in the small hospital room and his mother paced the hallways and
prayed in the hospital chapel – the great detective
got out of bed and walked to the room's wide glass
window that overlooked South Main Street.

The street, two floors below, shined in the soft
orange glow of a nearby streetlight and was quiet
except for the rare sound of a car or truck that
occasionally rumbled by. Years later, Sneak would
become accustomed to the loud streets in the big
cities of Europe and Asia – with loud police sirens
and honking horns, which drivers immediately used
if those in front of them were slow. Findlay, he always
remembered, was not like that. Sirens and personal
car horns, they learned in Findlay's driving schools,

were to be used in emergencies – to warn a child away from a street if they were too close to a moving car or to warn another driver of oncoming danger – not for the examples he had seen as an adult in other cities, like prodding moving traffic or petty things like getting the attention of a worker at a restaurant's drive-through window. Findlay was quiet. Findlay was peaceful. At least it was that night.

I should be tired, the young detective thought. Yet, he couldn't sleep, his mind was still processing the experience of nearly getting run over by a car and the many questions that followed. *Why didn't I realize it was a trap?* He wondered. *That was so foolish riding my bike into that ambush. I could have been killed.*

He paused for a few minutes and began to focus his great mind on a topic he had considered earlier that evening – knowing that the medication the doctors and nurses had given him earlier would make the task even more demanding.

To help focus his thoughts, he quickly turned away from the window and pressed the small plastic RECORD button on a small tape recorder that sat on his bedside table.

"So, why did Julian do it?" he asked softly as the cassette began recording. "It doesn't make any sense. What was his motive?"

Motive. Sneak had been wrestling with the concept since he had arrived at the hospital – and had been drawing a blank. He was well aware of the quote by one of his heroes – Sir Arthur Conan Doyle – who explained that, "the bigger the crime, the more obvious…is the motive".

"What is Julian's motive in this case?" Sneak asked again in a quiet tone – trying not to wake his father on the nearby couch.

Regardless of how he phrased it on the tape recorder or turned the idea around in his mind, Sneak could not come up with an adequate answer. He paused for a few moments, then turned to something he hoped could help – a small paperback book that he had asked his father to bring to the hospital earlier in the evening.

His father had been initially reluctant to retrieve the book and his tape recorder from home, but Sneak's sister, Jennie, had been waiting patiently in a nearby waiting room for much of the evening and when their parents realized that Sneak would be spending the night in the hospital under observation, Mr. Ryerson had agreed to take Jennie home to stay the night with Mrs. Helen Nelson, the Ryerson's elderly next door neighbor.

"Mr. Knick Knack loves all of her pets!" Jennie said enthusiastically when she heard the news, reminding her father and mother of their neighbor's dog named Ginger and several cats and other animals. "He'll be so happy we get to spend the night at Mrs. Nelson's!"

Mr. Ryerson let out a loud sigh when Sneak had asked him to retrieve the book and tape recorder earlier in the evening. "Sneak," Mr. Ryerson had told his son, "I'm just going to drop off Jennie at Mrs. Nelson's and get you a clean pair of *gacchi's*," he explained, using the family's unique name for men's underwear.

"But I really need that book," Sneak pleaded. "Do you think you could bring it?"

"Fine, as long as I can find it quickly," his father replied – and Sneak told him exactly where it could be located in his bedroom.

"Oh, and my tape recorder, I'll need that too," Sneak had added.

"Fine," his father said reluctantly. "I guess I do need to spend a few minutes at the house, anyway, to get a few newspapers and magazines to read here at the hospital this evening."

In the dim light, after a few moments of staring at the cassette tape spin slowly around and around inside the black tape recorder, Sneak grabbed the book – that he had earlier placed on the small table next to his hospital bed – and flipped through its pages, hoping for some inspiration. The book was a novel called *Crime and Punishment* – written by the famous Russian writer Fyodor Dostoyevsky – a book that Sneak had purchased only a few weeks earlier. Even though it was new, the young detective had quickly become fascinated with the story and it soon became one of his favorites – a book that he would read and re-read many times.

The novel's main character, he remembered as he flipped through the pages, was Rodion Romanovich Raskolnikov – who Sneak called *Triple R* – because, even though he was a brilliant young detective, even he had a hard time remembering a name like Rodion Romanovich Raskolnikov.

As Sneak turned the pages, he was surprised to see that *Triple R* shared much in common with Julian Davis, the main suspect in *The Case of the Mysterious Circles* and the young man who had tried to run him over with a car only a few hours before. Both, Sneak noticed, were twenty-three year olds. And both, interestingly, were recent college drop-outs. And both, it seemed, were engaged in some very serious crimes.

"I wish I had a book that told me all about Julian Davis," Sneak lamented into the tape recorder as he continued scanning the pages of *Crime and Punishment.* While looking over the pages that described in dramatic fashion *Triple R's* planning and execution of a horrible crime, Sneak appreciated afresh how the author used the book to explore the depths of the criminal mind. "Maybe this will help me figure out why Julian is involved in all of this," he said softly. "Crimes just don't happen by accident, there's always a reason. Sometimes, there's even more than one reason. In the novel," he added, "there are probably five or six different motives that describe *Triple R's* crime."

Sneak had read in his Dad's newspapers about the recent riots at the New Mexico State Penitentiary – a disturbance that had happened a month before – and his thoughts turned to *poverty* as a motive – an explanation that was popular among many newspaper stories at the time. Later, as an adult, Sneak would laugh when he read a quote by Aristotle who had written that "poverty is the parent of revolution and crime" – knowing, as he did, that crimes had many other parents – not just lack of money.

"Is it because Julian's poor?" Sneak considered, still speaking softly into the black tape recorder. "Is his lack of wealth the reason he's involved in this crime?" he wondered. Sneak paused for a moment before answering his question. "Probably not," he replied. "He has a job at the movie theater. He probably doesn't make a lot of money, but he probably doesn't need a lot either. His job probably pays the few bills that he owes."

He paused again before his mind turned to another motive that Dostoyevsky had explored, although it was one that Sneak had a hard time putting into words. When he was older, he would realize it was a philosophy called *utilitarianism* – doing things because of the 'greater good'.

"One of the reasons *Triple R* thought he should commit the crime," Sneak said softly into the tape recorder, "was because he thought it would be the best thing for society. His victim was a pawn broker, what was her name?" he wondered, as he flipped through the pages. "Oh, yeah," he replied after finding what he was looking for. "Her name was Alyona Ivanovna, and she had taken advantage of a lot of people because of her work. Because she had done a lot of bad things, *Triple R* felt he was justified in committing a crime against her. He thought it would benefit all of humanity if he killed her," Sneak said with a shudder.

At this thought, the young detective became angry as he reflected on his own situation. "Did Julian Davis think society could really benefit if I wasn't around?" he said loudly, forgetting that his father slept only a few feet away. Hearing the noise, his father rolled to his side on the small couch – as the newspapers he had been reading earlier, loudly crunched beneath him. Sneak paused for a moment to confirm that his father had not wakened before he continued. "How could running me over with a car benefit society?" he wondered as he spoke in a softer tone. "I've just tried to help people," he said strongly, before pausing again. "If this was the reason for Julian's actions," Sneak concluded, "we're dealing with someone who's really off their rocker."

Next, his thoughts turned to the acquisition of *power* as a motivation for crime, remembering in the story that *Triple R* wanted to be a great man like Napoleon.

"So, is it power? Is that Julian's motivation?" he asked. "That's probably not it," he answered, quickly dismissing the idea. "How could power be a motive for a twenty-three year old ticket taker who works at a movie theater? He hasn't really tried to do anything to get power, other than be the President of F.E.E.T., right?"

Moving through his mental list, his thoughts turned next to *family pressures*, remembering that sometimes people do things for the sake of their family. "If I heard the officer's radio correctly," Sneak said softly, trying not to wake his father, "Julian's parents still live in *Upper*," he said, referring to the community of Upper Sandusky, located about thirty miles to the south – where local police officers were dispatched to look for Julian Davis. "I haven't heard of any issues with his family, but maybe the kids – *The Sunday School Detectives* – could check that out."

The young detective paused for a moment, waiting for the words to come into his racing mind. *"Pressures from society,"* he said next, as he remembered that some people explain criminal motives by pointing to larger cultural forces. "So, what if society somehow made him do it?" he asked. "Because of *capitalism* or something like that?" As soon as he finished saying these words he started to quietly laugh. "I don't think any of the judges at the Hancock County Courthouse would accept that as a defense," thinking of several of the older judges he had met at the historic courthouse and nearby courtrooms. "Telling them that society made him do it, wouldn't go over too well."

Flipping through the novel he remembered that Dostoyevsky looked at many different factors for *Triple R's* crime – even *Triple R's* frustrations with being a writer. (As a journalist, this is a frustration that I know well). "Could Julian's work at *The Twin Palace* or being the President of F.E.E.T. push him to commit a crime?" Sneak asked. "Was he so frustrated at taking tickets that he just lost it?" The young detective wondered before he paused for a moment. "There's no evidence to indicate that – but I guess it's possible."

He paused again – this time, his mind again flush with anger.

"Anything seems possible at this point!" he said, throwing the book down on his hospital bed as his father stirred on the nearby couch. "That's the problem!" Sneak said a little more quietly. "It could be any of the reasons I've been considering, or something completely different."

The process was humbling – making him turn once again to God.

"Dear Lord," Sneak prayed. "Thank you for saving me tonight from Julian's car. Help me figure out what is going on. My brain doesn't want to function like it usually does. Help me focus on this and solve the case. Amen."

As he was praying, the young detective was reminded of two additional motives that he had read about in *Crime and Punishment* – those of *atheism and pride*. While it was certainly true, he knew, that Christians could be prideful, in the story Sneak remembered those two motives seemed to be connected. "Is it because Julian is prideful and doesn't believe in God?" Sneak wondered. "Was it his arrogance and unbelief?" he asked, rephrasing the words.

Quickly the young detective's mind remembered some of the discussions that Professor Telson had with our Sunday School class. "I remember," Sneak said softly, "Professor Telson telling us about the ancient Greeks and Romans – and one philosopher who said that *man is the measure of all things*," he said quietly, quoting the Greek philosopher Protagoras.

"Man is the measure of all things," he said again. "Professor Telson told us that this old idea has never really gone away. It's used by people – like *Triple R* – to claim that there isn't a God who has set up, you know, absolute truth, but instead affirms that people are the ones who judge things by their own ideas." With this, Sneak let out a laugh as he admitted, "This is totally opposite of what Christians believe. I remember Professor Telson telling us about a book by C.S. Lewis called *God in the Dock* that talked about people putting God 'in the dock' as they'd say in England – or on trial, because they think they're the ones who have the final authority to judge things. People think that they can judge God, instead of having a view – like we have in Christianity – that it's actually God who is judging us. Professor Telson reminded us that it's God who's the one who has final authority over our world – not us. He's the Lord – not us. It's people who are on trial – not God."

The young detective paused for a few moments.

"So what was Julian's motive?" he wondered again thinking through all of the ideas that he had considered. "Was it something like poverty, or pressures from society, or his atheism, or pride?" He paused for a moment after asking these questions. "I don't know," he finally admitted as he picked up Dostoyevsky's novel again from his hospital bed and continued flipping through the book's pages, hoping to discover the answer.

"Why do people stupefy themselves?" another Russian writer, Leo Tolstoy, had asked many years before. For Sneak Ryerson, as he thought about Julian Davis and the case, the answer remained a profound mystery.

CHAPTER 64

While the famous young detective was pondering criminal motives late into night in his hospital room, Julian Davis – the young man who had nearly run Sneak Ryerson over with his car – was also having difficulty sleeping.

Where did that other kid come from? he wondered, as he thought about the events of the evening, huddled under a metal table in the darkness of the Science Building. *I came so close to taking out that Sneak Ryerson kid. The Great Peggu will be so angry I didn't finish the job,* he thought before pausing for a moment. *Who was that other kid?* he wondered again, as his mind recalled the tall, bushy haired boy who raced across his path in the parking lot and grabbed Sneak Ryerson, pushing him out of the way of his speeding car.

The spookiness of the basement, with its dark shadows, strange noises and putrid smell of moth food had been off-putting to the girls earlier in the evening, but the eerie sights and sounds did not bother Julian Davis. He was filled with excitement, anxiously awaiting what would happen next.

Earlier that evening, immediately after fleeing Rawson Park – with wheels spinning at great speed through the parking lot – Julian raced to his apartment, grabbed a few clothes and quickly stuffed them into his tan duffle bag. *This is silly*, he thought immediately after he packed the bag. *They'll have uniforms for me where I'm going next.*

After packing his clothes, he quickly reached into a hiding place he had created months before inside his mattress and grabbed two stacks of papers. He looked quickly at the first stack and carefully placed them into his duffle bag between two shirts. The second stack of papers, he held tightly in his hand. Then, after throwing his duffle bag over his shoulder he raced down the stairs of his apartment building.

I won't ever have to worry about Anthony or the other roommates after today, he realized as he exited his building. *Catch you guys on the flip side,* he scoffed as he thought of them.

Upon reaching the ground floor, he dashed to the side of his apartment building where he threw open a lid to one of the many metal trash cans that lined the side wall and dropped the papers he was carrying, covering them with a dark trash bag that was already in the metal bin.

I only have a few minutes until the police get here, he thought as he made his way to his car and tossed his duffle bag into the back seat.

But then he remembered one additional item and raced back to his apartment to find it.

It took a few moments of scanning the bookshelf in his room before finding the small paperback book – one that had been invaluable since his encounters with *The Great Peggu* – and then he rushed back to his car.

He was in and out of his apartment in only a few minutes and his heart raced as he drove through downtown Findlay, trying to stay within the speed limit. He turned north onto Main Street and soon passed the large historic courthouse.

The other boy had seen him – he was sure of it – they had locked eyes for a fraction of a second when the bushy haired kid ran in front of his car.

They'll be on to me soon, he thought.

For a brief moment he thought about fleeing to Canada, knowing that it would be easy to cross the border – either by car in Detroit, or by boat near somewhere like Port Clinton – and it would be easier still, he knew, to return to the United States once the spaceships arrived.

He was passing the college and some of his favorite fast food and pizza places, when he began convincing himself not to go to Canada. *I'd miss their arrival,* he thought remorsefully as he imagined the alien spacecraft arriving. Plus, he did not want to miss the surprised looks on the faces of the many people who had doubted him. He pictured them – Alice and the other *former* F.E.E.T. officers – mouths open, as they stared up in amazement at the giant spacecraft that would be filling a quickly darkening sky.

"That Julian Davis was right all along," he imagined them saying. "Why didn't we listen to him?"

They won't know what to do when all of the spacecraft arrive, he thought as a smile crept on his face. *But I won't be able to see the look on their faces if I'm all the way up in Canada.*

As he drove further north, he reached the Dark Horse Restaurant near the city limits, and saw that traffic had slowed. Flashing lights of a police car, he soon noticed, were in the distance near the Dow Chemical plant.

"Probably a road block," he said to himself.

It was then that he realized that he had only one place to go – having distanced himself from his family in Upper Sandusky and his friends in F.E.E.T. – his only hope, he knew, was *The Great Peggu.*

"*Peggu* will know where I should hide until the spaceships arrive. If I can just make it until tomorrow night," he said to himself, "*The Great Peggu* can save me."

But for tonight, he thought, *I need to go somewhere where no one else will find me. Somewhere really out of the way.*

Then the idea hit him. Last year, Alice had shown him where she worked – the busy biology lab on the third floor of the Science Building and the area where she raised moths in the darkness of the basement, and soon Julian turned his car around and raced toward the college campus.

The F.E.E.T. President parked his car in the heart of a large and crowded parking lot filled with the cars of students who lived in nearby dorms and campus apartments and he quickly made his way to the Science Building. After trying two doors, he found that a third – near the loading dock – was open, and he quietly walked down the stairs to the basement. The lights were dim as the twenty-three year old made his way to the area where Alice raised the moths and after stumbling for a few moments in the darkness, he found an area under an old metal table to hide.

The hall was dark and the noises that had scared the girls earlier in the evening continued – hissing and coughing noises from the pipes and loud clicks from an electrical box. Several times in the night Julian thought that someone else was in the basement with him and he tried to remain as still as possible as he rested his head on his duffle bag and bent his legs close to his body – trying to take up as little space as possible.

Maybe The Great Peggu has found me down here! he thought once and hopefully cried out, "Peggu, Peggu is that you?" but received no reply.

As the night wore on, he tried to get some sleep but his mind kept racing, thinking about the momentous events that would happen the following night. *I'll finally get to meet him!* he thought. *But The Great Peggu will be disappointed,* he knew, because he had not done as he had been instructed. He tried – he had lured that pesky kid detective to the park and had heard his bike crunch under his car – but in the rearview mirror had seen that the boy with the bushy hair had been successful in getting Sneak out of the way – with only seconds to spare.

I can explain it to Peggu, Julian thought. *Sorry,* he corrected himself. *I can explain it to **The Great** Peggu.*

As he shut his eyes in the darkness of the long hallway – while the electrical panel clicked and the noises from the heating system creaked – Julian Davis imagined his future. *Vice Regent, that's what Peggu told me,* he said to himself. He liked the sound of that. *Vice Regent of an entire galaxy. It will be so great,* he continued. *Correction....I will be so great.* He paused for a moment before thinking of how he would be introduced:

Vice Regent Julian Davis

He liked how that sounded, so he practiced saying it softly in the darkness of the hallway.

"I'd like to introduce you to *Vice Regent Julian Davis*," he said softly, imagining being introduced to a large and important crowd amid great cheers and loud applause.

My friends will be so surprised, he thought. *More than surprised. They will be in shock.*

"You're a Vice Regent of an entire galaxy?" he imagined Alice and some of the F.E.E.T. people saying with mouths agape.

He paused again for a moment as he thought of his response.

"Yes, I am the Vice Regent, you should have listened to me," he imagined himself saying as a reply.

Dealing with them will be one of my first acts as a Vice Regent, he thought. *I've got to punish them for not believing me,* he concluded. *Otherwise, what will all the other creatures in the galaxy think? You can't just say stuff like they've said against a VICE REGENT. They said I was crazy for thinking an alien would contact me. They said I was stupid for reading all of his letters. They'll see. But what should their punishment be?* He wondered. *Expulsion? Hard labor? Death?*

Soon, Julian's thoughts turned to his meeting with *The Great Peggu*, scheduled for the following evening. I *wonder what he will sound like?* he wondered. *Obviously he can write, all of the letters he's sent me show that he can write in English, but can he speak English? And what will Peggu's native language sound like? Will I be able to understand it? ....with some practice maybe,* he concluded. *And what exactly will he look like?* he wondered. *I know he's got a green face – he's told me that already in a letter – that's why he doesn't go out in the daytime. But will it be ugly like a monster's? Or, will his face look like a human's – just green? Does he have ears that can hear me talk?* He wondered – again uncertain how the two would communicate. *Probably,* he concluded. *But, most important of all, I know he's got that incredible intelligence. Learning all the things that he and the other aliens know will be so cool.*

He paused for a moment, before considering his new role again.

I wonder how soon it will be before they make me Vice Regent? he asked himself. *Will it be like right when the spaceships arrive, or will they wait a little while?* he wondered. *The actual timing shouldn't really matter. Vice Regent of at least one galaxy or maybe even two, that's what The Great Peggu told me,* he reminded himself. *Think of all of the people and the things on those planets and solar systems that will have to listen to me,* he thought with a smile. *They'll all have to do what I say.*

Ju-li-an, Ju-li-an, Ju-li,an, he imagined them chanting over and over.

And with these thoughts – late into the night – the motive for committing his crimes was clear, although, it was one that Sneak Ryerson, the great young detective, had failed to understand and had dismissed quickly. When thinking about the young ticket taker, Sneak had dismissed the motive of *seeking power* almost instantly, just after it had come to his mind. "How could power be a motive for a twenty-three year old ticket taker who works at a movie theater?" he had asked. "He hasn't really tried to do anything to get power, other than be the President of F.E.E.T., right?"

The young detective, however, had failed to understand how seductive and addictive the promise of power could be on a young and impressionable mind. *I'm going to be famous*, Julian said to himself again and again, late into the night. *Vice Regent of at least one galaxy or maybe even two, that's what The Great Peggu told me.*

When *The Case of the Mysterious Circles* was finally over, and all of the facts were brought to light, the brilliant young detective would realize he had dismissed Julian's real motive too quickly. "Even a ticket taker wants power," he remorsefully told me afterwards. "I missed it."

"Could you have caught him sooner?" I asked. "You know, if you would have figured out Julian's motive earlier?"

"Maybe," the young detective told me. "We'll never know about that. But," he paused a long time before finishing his sentence, "it's a mistake I don't want to make ever again."

CHAPTER 65

While the police were rushing to the scene of the crime and my friend was getting treatment for his injuries, I was returning home from Uncle Charlie's – desperate for information, knowing only that there had been an accident and that my friend, Sneak Ryerson, had been hurt.

I spent much of the rest of the evening on the telephone – dialing frantically on the phone in my mother's kitchen – trying to connect with others who could give me the information I so desperately desired.

I first tried the Ryerson's, hoping that Jennie or one of her parents were home, but the phone simply rang and rang. I tried and tried but no one answered. One time during my many attempts, I found that their line was busy – giving me hope that someone was home – but when I tried again, it rang and rang again – and I concluded that someone else must have called their house at the same time I had tried.

Eventually I stopped calling the Ryerson's house and instead tried Hailey Cotton – reaching her, providentially, on my first attempt. Hailey told me that she and the other girls had just returned from Professor Telson's – after they had met with Alice Williams at her biology lab. She explained that they had heard about Sneak's "accident" – as we called it that night – from the professor who had received the news from Mrs. Willingham – our Church's youth choir director. Mrs. Willingham, Hailey told me, also led the Church's *prayer chain* – a phone calling list for sharing prayer requests – and had called the professor to ask him to pray for Sneak and his family. Sadly, Hailey did not know any other news about Sneak's accident and after we hung up, I grew more and more distressed and worried for my friend. *Is he going to be okay?* I wondered. *What will I do if he doesn't make it?*

I was so desperate for news, that after talking with Hailey, I found Mrs. Willingham's phone number in the Church Directory and called her. After a brief greeting and my rapidly fired questions about my friend, she told me that she had found out about "Sneak's accident" while at church earlier that night. The police, she told me, had interrupted her Naomi Circle meeting and requested that Mrs. Ryerson go immediately to the hospital.

"The police!" I said with a jolt – knowing that Uncle Charlie had been notified, but had not considered that other police officers would be involved.

"Yes, I guess the accident was serious," she told me in a solemn voice.

I asked if she had any other information, but she did not.

"I'm going to call the hospital," I informed my mother after I hung up the phone with Mrs. Willingham.

"Don't do that," she told me. "You'll hear from your friend soon enough."

"But this is bad," I told her. "I think….well, do you think Sneak's going to be okay?" I asked.

"I don't know Pep," she told me. "We don't really know much about what's going on. It seems like we'd hear from our Church friends if he was in critical condition, don't you think? We'd probably be invited to a prayer vigil or something like that."

"I don't know," I told her nervously. "I'm really worried."

"I know you are honey," she said as she gave me a hug. "You can pray for him, sometimes that's the only thing you can do." And so, we said a brief prayer for my friend.

Soon, though, I was overwhelmed again with worry and distress and called my Dad to tell him the news.

"Wow, I'm sorry to hear that," he said in his sad and quiet voice.

"Do you have your scanner on?" I asked him, knowing that he would occasionally sit in his living room listening to a scanner that picked up police and fire dispatches – sometimes providing some exciting news in our otherwise quiet city.

"No," he told me. "I've just been sitting at the kitchen table going through my French books."

"Could you turn it on and tell me if you hear anything about Sneak?" I pleaded.

"Sure," he replied "I'll let you know if I hear anything. N'est pas," he added.

Shortly after I hung up the phone with my Dad, I went to bed and quickly fell asleep, exhausted by the events of the day.

The call arrived at my mother's house – long after I had gone to sleep – from one of her friends from church who described Sneak's injuries and explained that the family hoped that the young detective would be discharged from the hospital in the morning.

"That's such good news," my mother told her friend. "Pep will be so glad to hear that."

CHAPTER 66

The next morning was Tuesday, March 10th, and my mother woke me early to tell me the good news about Sneak's prognosis. "That is so cool," I told her – relieved that his injuries were not worse than I had imagined. "Should I call the hospital?" I asked her.

"Why don't you wait until he's home," she advised. "Wait until he's ready to see visitors."

"Probably after school, right?" I asked expectantly.

"Well, let's wait until we hear from Mrs. Ryerson," she cautioned. "You better get ready for school."

Jennie was already on Bus Four when I climbed the stairs of the yellow school bus. She was already telling the account of her famous brother's "accident" to eager listeners, but, seeing me, she quickly retold the details of what she had initially told the others. She told us, in dramatic fashion, how a car hit her brother's bike as he was riding it in the parking lot of Rawson Park and that a bigger boy – she didn't remember his name – pushed her brother out of the way just before the car returned to try to run him over.

I was shocked – as were the other kids – at hearing Jennie's news. I had worked with Sneak on interviewing crime victims around Findlay, but had never imagined that my friend would be a victim of a crime. My thoughts turned quickly to the safety of our friend. *Who would want to hurt Sneak?* I wondered. *Could it have anything to do with The Case of the Mysterious Circles?* And then, my thoughts turned to the others in our group. *If someone is out to get Sneak, are the other detectives in danger too?*

School flew by for me that day while my emotions were like a roller-coaster – happy that my friend was okay – but shocked and saddened that someone would want to harm him. Once school had ended and I arrived home, I immediately called Sneak and his warm voice saying, "Sure, come on over," was all I needed to hear to rush to his house.

I ran the few blocks from my house near the Blanchard River to his – while my green duffle bag filled with cassettes and a tape recorder flopped awkwardly in my hand. While I ran, I hummed the song *Singin' in the Rain* – which, in retrospect, seems funny because it wasn't raining and I wasn't singing – just humming. *Our friend Joel*, I thought as

I ran, *would be happy that I was humming a song today. That's something he would do.* I was overjoyed at the prospect of seeing my friend and couldn't wait to see him and tell him how happy I was that he was okay and to learn more about the events of the previous evening.

I quickly arrived at the intersection of Decker and Osborne Avenues but instantly slowed when I saw a black and white police car idling in front of the Ryerson's house – four houses down from the yellow DEAD END sign.

I apprehensively approached the house, but Sneak, however, was at his front door to greet me. "He's a friend of mine!" he explained with a shout while he stood on his front porch waving to the officer in the patrol car with his left hand. His right arm, I noticed, was in a blue sling. "It's okay Pep," he told me as I slowly approached him on the porch. "It's okay to come up."

"It's great to see you," I exclaimed greeting him loudly while patting his healthy left arm and shoulder. "I was so worried after I heard about your accident."

"It was no accident," Sneak explained while we remained on his front porch. "Our suspect was out to get me."

"Our suspect?" I asked.

"Yeah, our suspect in *The Case of the Mysterious Circles*, Julian Davis."

"What?" I replied quickly, surprised by the news.

"He was definitely trying to get me. He hit my bike and then he turned around to try to run me over."

"Wow," I replied.

"The police haven't caught him yet, so Uncle Charlie's assigned an officer to guard the house until they get him," he said as he motioned to the police car parked with one set of its tires in the Ryerson's still-frozen front yard while the other set of tires rested on the narrow stone-covered street.

"Wow," I said again, looking at the black and white patrol car. "I guess it's good that he's here today. But what about the others in our group. Do you think the other *Sunday School Detectives* are in danger?"

"Probably not," Sneak replied quickly. "I doubt Julian knows about the rest of the group yet. You guys just started on Saturday – that was only a couple of days ago. He probably remembered me because I went to interview him at his work – you know, at *The Twin Palace.* And then he must have seen me bumper hopping off his car last week at the cemetery."

"Makes sense," I told my friend.

"But, you bring up a good point."

"What's that?" I asked.

"We need to solve this case quickly, before anyone else gets hurt."

"Yeah," I said meekly – unsure of how that could happen.

"Why don't we get out of the cold," Sneak said motioning to the door as I followed him inside. Going through the open doorway, I saw that Mrs. Ryerson and Jennie were only a few feet away. I greeted Sneak's mother first, who was sitting on their long orange living room couch sipping coffee with a serious look on her face. Jennie, I noticed, was on the green carpeted floor of the living room with her head on an orange pillow – with a second pillow beside her – watching an episode of the *Munsters* and laughing at the television characters.

"Hey Jennie," I said as we walked near her.

"Oh, hey Pep," she replied. "Watch out for Mr. Knick Knack, he's watching the show with me this afternoon."

"Oh, uh, hey Mr. Knick Knack," I said to her friend.

"Mr. Knick Knack says *hi*," Jennie told me.

"Let's go upstairs," said Sneak, as we passed his mother.

"Uh, sure," I told him. "Maybe we can play with your *Johnny West* guys," I added.

"Maybe," Sneak said loudly. "Plus," he said in a softer tone when we reached the stairs, "we can check out what my uncle brought."

"What?" I asked.

"I think he forgot I was grounded," Sneak explained.

As we made our way upstairs, I asked Sneak a question that had been bothering me throughout the day – something sparked by Jennie's account of the previous night's events. "So why were you at Rawson Park, anyway?" I asked.

"It was an ambush," he told me in a serious tone. "I should have figured it out…but I walked…or biked right into it," he explained with a laugh. "I got a note in the mail from someone called 'Mr. X' who said they wanted to hire me to investigate a case. I went over there to tell him that I'm grounded and he needed to talk to Hailey, instead."

"So you couldn't call him?" I asked.

"No, there was no phone number or return address," he explained.

"And who was it that pulled you out of the way in the nick of time?" I asked my friend. "Jennie said it was a boy but couldn't remember his name."

"It was Roger, you know from Whittier."

"Roger! The guy you caught taking the model train set?"

"Yep," came the reply. "One and the same."

"Wow, I haven't seen him in a while…."

"Well, I was definitely glad to see him last night," Sneak said with a smile.

"What was he doing at the park?"

"Just walking home. He heard me yelling when I was trapped under my bike."

"Wow," I said, amazed at the events that had taken place. "So, he lives over there now?"

"Yep, right next to the park," Sneak added.

We soon arrived at Sneak's bedroom located on the second floor of the Ryerson's house and I noticed, to my surprise, that the room was covered with papers. Nearly a hundred white letter-sized papers were strewn across the room, covering his blue bedspread, blue carpeted floor, the top of his wooden dresser, his book shelf, as well as the top of his metal office desk. "What is all this?" I asked as I picked up a piece of paper and read words and numbers that I could not understand.

44 of, 86 principle, 211 it, 192 and, 107 that, 92 inversely, 139 not, 34 Smith, 269 was, 232 matter...

"It's code," replied Sneak. "And it's pretty ingenious."

"Wow," I said again. "I don't understand it."

"It's from Julian Davis' apartment," the young detective told me. "They're copies, of course. The originals are with the police, but apparently our suspect threw them away in a trash can when he made his escape last night."

"But what do they say?" I wondered.

"Well that's what I've been trying to figure out all afternoon. My mind's still a little fuzzy after last night, but if I can't figure it out, I was thinking that maybe you and the other Sunday School Detectives can crack the code? I've invited the rest of the group over too."

"That's great," I said enthusiastically, as I looked at a second piece of paper. "I can try to start working on it until they get here. What do you want me to do?"

"There's a couple of ways to decipher it. One way is to look to see if any of the words are repeated. If you could do that, I think it would be helpful."

"Sure," I said again as I began scanning the papers for similar words. "So, why do you have these?" I asked after a few minutes.

"Well, Uncle Charlie told me that he and the other police detectives were having a hard time deciphering them," he explained. "So he brought the copies over here when he came to check on me this afternoon."

"That's cool," I told him. "I guess you're right – he forgot you're grounded from doing this sort of thing."

"I'm hoping that maybe my parents will let me take a break from being grounded – just for this case," Sneak said seriously. And then he added, "Pep, I really want to catch this guy."

"Me too," I told my friend as we began taking the papers with similar words out of the bedroom and into the nearby narrow upstairs hallway and then placing colored construction paper on the top of each stack with a description of what we had found.

We continued sorting and stacking the papers with the incoherent words and numbers for nearly an hour before the young detective told me, "I'm ready for a break…you've heard about my adventures from last night, why don't you tell me what you've been doing lately. Jennie told me a little bit about your lunch with the other detectives on Sunday. Maybe you can give me more details?"

"Sure," I replied enthusiastically and we soon made our way to the Ryerson's kitchen and split a bottle of *Pepsi* and ate some cold *Reece's Peanut Butter Cups*. With Mrs. Ryerson in the basement, I felt free to share the details of our discussion from Sunday – explaining that Cressida and Lisa had gone to Julian's apartment and had seen Julian in a light blue coat, while Hailey had gone to the library to study crop circles and that Joel had acquired two photos and several articles from the newspaper.

"You're going to love hearing how we figured out there was a girl to interview," I said to my friend with a smile, before telling him about my Dad's French phrase: *cherchez la femme.*

When I had finished my story, he asked with a laugh, "So, Hailey discovered the young woman in the F.E.E.T. photo because of a story your Dad told you the night before?"

"Pretty much," I said with a smile.

"Well, that's good," he told me, "That's real good, Pep. I'm sure that's blown the case wide open – having someone involved in the group to interview – you really didn't have too many clues to go on without that."

I told him that I didn't know what the girls had learned from their visit at Alice Williams' lab – only that Hailey told me that they went to Professor Telson's office afterwards.

"That is also very interesting," he replied, as we both wondered about the reasons for their visit to the professor's.

"That's basically it," I told him, "except that I thought Deputy Curtis was involved."

"What!" my friend exclaimed. "Why is that?"

And soon I was telling him about the conclusions I had made the previous night after talking with Dan and Larry at the barber shop.

"I was wondering why your hair…"

"My what?" I asked.

"Oh, never mind about that," Sneak told me. "So you thought Deputy Curtis was involved in the case, because of some questions that he asked at the barber shop?"

"Right!" I said. "Well that and because of his brown coat. You know the girls said that Julian had a light blue coat. So, it was beginning to add up."

"Hmmm," he replied. "So once you discovered that he had a brown coat and was asking questions at the barber shop, you probably went over to my Uncle Charlie's to tell him the news, right?"

"Right!" I said again – surprised that he knew exactly the actions I had taken. "I went straight to your Uncle's, but I couldn't believe it," I added with a laugh. "When I got to your Uncle's house, Deputy Curtis and another investigator were there having dinner with your Uncle Charlie and Aunt Marie."

"Another investigator?" he asked, intrigued at the news.

"Yeah, her name is Inspector Baxter," I explained. "She's from the state fire marshal's office."

"Interesting," the young detective replied.

"They didn't really have much to say," I told him. "But I was pretty shook up after I saw Deputy Curtis, so I hung out in your uncle's den for a while until I felt better. That's a pretty cool room."

"Yeah," Sneak agreed. "I've only been in there once or twice. So did you talk to Deputy Curtis and Inspector Baxter once you felt better?" he asked.

"Yeah, I still think Deputy Curtis might still be involved – but you know he denied it. Anyway, it turns out that he's one of Julian's roommates..."

"His roommate!" Sneak exclaimed.

"Yep, and he claims that Julian would take his brown jacket so it would be harder for the police to follow him."

"Well, that's one explanation," said Sneak.

"But they were able to follow him!" I said enthusiastically. "They followed him to the mall and saw him getting another letter."

"Could I listen to what they told you?" he asked as we returned to his room. "Do you have the tape from last night?"

"Sure, let me find it," I said as I searched through my green duffle bag.

Soon, the young detective sat back in his chair – staring at one of the encrypted pieces of paper that he held in his left hand – as he listened to my discussion with Deputy Curtis and Inspector Baxter on my tape recorder.

"Interesting," he said as I played the tape. "Could you rewind that last section again?" he asked, and I dutifully replayed the part of our discussion when Uncle Charlie was called into the kitchen to answer the phone call.

"I was pretty shook up," I said. "You know, to hear your Uncle Charlie tell us that you were in an accident. Do you want to hear that part again?"

"No, I've got some things to think about," he told me – as he stared again at one of the encrypted papers. "Would you mind helping me find something in my files?

"Sure," I told him. "What is it?"

"I need to find the list of victims, you know the farmers that had fires in their fields – Inspector Baxter mentioned she met a few of them. The list is in one of these file folders," he said as he pulled out two large manila envelopes from his desk drawer – the contents overflowing with handwritten notes and other pieces of paper. "I gave a more organized set of files to Hailey when she took over the case, but here are some of my original notes."

I eventually found the paper listing each of the names of the farmers who had been victims of the crop circle fires and was about to read them to the young detective when we heard the doorbell ring.

CHAPTER 67

"It's okay, they're our friends," we heard Jennie Ryerson yell to the police officer from the open front door when several Sunday School Detectives arrived – as Sneak and I hurried to the living room to meet them.

"That was nice of your Mom to give all of us a ride," Lisa said to Hailey when they entered, as Moscow, Cressida and Michelle followed closely behind them.

"Well, the gang's almost all here," Sneak said as he looked at the Sunday School Detectives gathered in his living room. "I guess we're just missing Joel."

Mrs. Ryerson had gone to the front porch to talk with Mrs. Cotton, so Sneak explained, "I asked my Mom if you could come over to wish me well, but I think we're really close to solving *The Case of the Mysterious Circles* too. So, maybe everyone can explain what you've learned and we can figure it out together?"

"Sure," Hailey said enthusiastically, "We learned a lot last night."

"Why don't we all go upstairs," Sneak said as he pointed up. "My room's pretty messy, but Mom won't notice we're talking about the case if we're up there."

"Sure," Hailey said again. "But we want to hear about what happened to you last night, too. We're really glad you're okay," she said with a warm smile.

"Yeah, it sounded like you were in a bad accident," Michelle added.

"Yeah…well it wasn't an accident," said Sneak. "I can tell you about that first," he added as the Sunday School Detectives quickly followed the young detective to his room.

When we arrived, the others were amazed at the volume of paper that filled Sneak's bedroom, but the young detective promised the others that he would explain the papers later as he cautiously took a seat in his chair at his metal desk – being careful not to hit his right arm in the sling against the metal arms of the chair.

Soon, he was telling the Sunday School Detectives about his encounter with Julian Davis.

"I can't believe someone would want to hurt you," Lisa said angrily. "That's so uncool."

"No kidding," Michelle said with a frown.

"What's surprising to me," Hailey said seriously. "Is that Julian didn't need to do it, right? We've talked about how he's had perfect alibis for all of the other crimes. All of the people he works with said he was working at *The Twin Palace* when the crop fires started, so he didn't need to do anything – you know, he could have just let the others commit the crimes, but for some reason he showed his true colors last night."

"Right!" Sneak said enthusiastically. "I was thinking the same thing. And it got me wondering, why would he do that?"

"Well Deputy Curtis and Inspector Baxter thought something big was going to happen…and Julian almost running over you seems to prove that," I said to my friend.

"Who are those people?" Hailey asked, and soon I told my friends about the conclusions I had made the night before at the barber shop and my meeting with Deputy Curtis and Inspector Baxter at Uncle Charlie's house – and their account of following Julian to the mall.

"I was wondering about your hair…" Lisa began.

"What?" I asked.

"Oh, forget about it," she replied. "It's not important."

We paused for a moment before Sneak began. "So, from what Pep and Uncle Charlie have told me today, I don't think the police know much more than we do. They thought something big was going to happen because they saw Julian Davis retrieve the letter at the mall. And now, because he tried to run me over last night they're on the lookout for him."

"He's such a turkey," Jennie said with a frown.

"No kidding," Michelle added.

"Right," Sneak concluded. "But I don't think the police have any other leads to go on. I was thinking if we put our brains together we might be able to figure this out. So Hailey," Sneak continued. "Why don't you tell us what you and the others learned last night when you interviewed the girl from F.E.E.T? Pep told me that after you met with her you went over to Professor Telson's afterwards."

Hearing these questions, Hailey, Lisa and Cressida soon explained what they learned at Alice Williams' lab the previous evening. The girls, I found were very descriptive – explaining the lab where Alice Williams worked as well as the dark and creepy basement where she took care of the moths, in addition to the information she provided about Julian and the F.E.E.T. group.

They soon described Julian's great enthusiasm for F.E.E.T. and how he had been contacted by an alien named *The Great Peggu.*

"Like a real alien?" Moscow asked his sister – who, bored by the earlier discussion, had been trying to juggle some items from Sneak's desk. "For real?" he asked.

"Yeah, well he thinks it real. It's sort of sad," Hailey explained. "Alice, his friend, thinks he's being manipulated by someone. She doesn't think it could be an alien at all."

"Take me to your leader," Moscow soon intoned in a robotic voice. "I come in peace. I come in peace."

"*The Great Peggu*," Sneak replied – ignoring Moscow. "A lot of things are starting to make sense now," he said seriously. "So what did this *Great Peggu* tell him?"

Soon the girls were recounting Alice's description of the letters that Julian had received and how Hancock County would be a landing area for the spaceships.

"Interesting," Sneak said when they concluded. "So why did you go to Professor Telson's afterward?" he asked.

"Because of this," Lisa said as she held up Julian's *Manifesto* and gave it to Sneak, who immediately began reading its contents.

"It had a lot of *stuff* we didn't understand," Cressida said softly. "Stuff about God and aliens."

"So, you went to Professor Telson's to have him explain it to you....," Sneak added.

"Right," Hailey admitted with a smile.

"I can see why you went there," Sneak acknowledged after reading only a few sentences. "This is really hard to understand. Did the professor explain it?"

"He did!" said Hailey. "I know you've got a lot of paper around here, but do you have some blank paper we could use?"

Sneak quickly gave her a piece of colored construction paper from his desk and soon Lisa was drawing a two-circle diagram representing a Christian view of the world and another diagram with a line between two circles to represent Julian's view.

"So this is like what we believe," Hailey explained, pointing to the two circles representing a Christian view. "We think there is a Creator..."

"So, like God," Lisa added.

"...and Jesus," said Cressida.

"And then there is Creation," Hailey explained as she pointed to the second circle.

"Like our world," Lisa added.

"And the two are different," Hailey continued. "That's why there are two circles. The Creator is not the Creation. God makes Creation. And the Creation is not the Creator. They're separate."

"That's interesting," Jennie added, as she and Michelle and I – and Moscow – saw the circles for the first time.

"The professor said that the Bible explains this idea from the very beginning," Cressida added as we looked at the diagram. "From the very first verse in Genesis."

"In the beginning God created the Heavens and the Earth," Michelle said quickly.

"Hey, good job!" Jennie said encouragingly to her friend.

"Our Mom remembered that verse last night, Moscow," Hailey added.

"Cool," her brother replied.

"So, I'm guessing Julian Davis doesn't have this view?" Sneak asked.

"No, his view is more like this one," Lisa explained pointing to another diagram that she had drawn that had two circles with a line between them. "He thinks that it's almost impossible to know anything about the Creator – unless we get help from aliens and build really big computers."

"Aliens, again?" Moscow asked. "Take me to your Creator! Take me to your Creator!" he said in a robotic voice as we all laughed. "I need a computer. I need a computer."

"That is really interesting," said Sneak.

"Yeah, I thought Professor Telson did a good job explaining it to us," Lisa said.

"We were at the professor's office last night when he got a call from Mrs. Willingham," Hailey explained, "– asking him to pray for you because you were in an accident. We were really, really worried about you Sneak."

"Yeah, we said a prayer for you before we left," Cressida explained.

"Thanks," Sneak said awkwardly – not liking the fact that everyone's attention was now focused on him. "I really appreciate it."

"So what are all these papers doing here?" Lisa asked bluntly. "You said that once we told you about what we've been learning, you'd explain these papers to us. Do they have anything to do with our case?"

CHAPTER 68

"These papers," Sneak explained to the Sunday School Detectives that were gathered in his room, "...are in code."

"Code?" asked Moscow, intrigued by the idea.

"Yeah," the young detective continued. "They're from Julian Davis' apartment building. We think he threw them away when he made his escape last night."

"Wow," Jennie added. "How did you get them?"

"I got them from Uncle Charlie. The police have been trying to decipher them since last night, but haven't been able to crack the code yet. So, he gave them to me to try to decipher."

"Wow," Michelle said as she picked up one of the papers and tried to make sense of the words and numbers.

"Do you think these are letters to Julian from the alien?" Jennie asked as she picked up another piece of paper from the floor. "What's his name again?"

"*The Great Peggu*," Hailey added.

"I think it's a good deduction Jennie," Sneak said. "It's likely that these were the letters that Alice Williams was telling you about – the letters that Julian was getting from the person calling himself *The Great Peggu*. He must have taken the deciphered letters with him – the ones where he learned about the alien landing and all that other stuff."

"Wow, these are letters from an alien!" Michelle said, impressively holding one of the papers loosely between her fingers. "Do you think they have cooties or something like that because they're from outer space?"

"Cooties?" Moscow asked loudly. "I never heard of aliens having cooties."

"Well, these are just copies of the letters," explained Sneak. "These aren't the original ones. Uncle Charlie told me that the police department just got a new Bell and Howell copier – so he made the copies on that."

"Sneak, I think the technical name for the machine is *duplicator*," Lisa said.

"Or, *mimeograph*," I added.

"Ditto Machine," Cressida corrected. "I think that's what it's called."

"Well, not exactly," said Sneak. "Anyway, these are copies of the letters from Julian's apartment building."

"I don't get it," Lisa said, as she picked up one of the papers. "They're just words and numbers."

"Right, it's in code," said Sneak. "It's pretty ingenious.

"So how do you think it works?" I asked. "I forgot to ask you that before."

"Well, I'm pretty sure that these numbers refer to page numbers in a book," explained Sneak.

"A book?" Jennie asked. "What kind of book?"

"Well, it could be any kind of book, really," her brother clarified. "That's what we need to figure out. The important thing for the code to work, is that it was a book that both the *sender* of the letter and the *receiver* of the letter had in common. The sender would need the book to write the code, and the receiver would need the same version of the book to read the coded message."

"Hmm," Jennie replied. "So, it could be like a dictionary or something?"

"Yeah, maybe," said her brother. "You'll notice that each of the numbers have words next to them. So, what would happen, I'm pretty sure, is that when Julian saw the number, he would go to that page in the book and then follow an agreed upon rule to find the real word. The *real* word that he needed to know – to make the translation – was probably the word that was so many words away from the word listed on the paper, so maybe like three words to the left or three words to the right. To make it more complicated, they might have special rules for odd or even pages."

"I didn't know it was like that!" I protested, growing angry at the seemingly impossible prospect of deciphering the papers. "This is going to be impossible to figure out! How could we ever know what book they used? It could be any book, right? And there's like thousands of books! Why did you have me spend like an hour looking through these letters? That seems like such a waste of time."

"Well, you're right about that first part Pep," my friend told me. "It could be any book, or they may have even used a couple of different books – like a different book for each day of the week, I've read about that being done before. But in English, or most languages, there are common phrases that are used in a lot of sentences, like the words '*the*' and '*and*' and '*a*'. So, I don't think it was a waste of time for us to look through them."

"Hmm," I replied angrily. "This just seems totally impossible."

"Well, maybe if the other's took a look at them, we might find something," the young detective said hopefully. "Since my accident last night, I don't think my brain is working as well as it usually does."

"Sure," Hailey replied with a smile. "Why don't we take a look at the papers?"

"Okay," Michelle said as the other Sunday School Detectives soon began flipping through the papers.

Meanwhile, I was feeling quite agitated at the difficulty of reading the encoded words. *I've spent nearly an hour sorting through these papers!* I thought. Soon, I became even more angered to see my stacks get resorted and moved by the others. *We don't even know what book to use to break the code!* I fumed. *We might not even have the book to look at once we figure out if that really is how the code works!* It was too much for me to take.

While the others were flipping through the papers on the floor, I found the paper within the file folder that contained the names of the victims that Sneak had asked me about earlier. "Here you go," I said angrily to my friend. "Randy and Sarah Baker to the South, Dick and Rita Sullivan to the East, Russell and Margaret Crenshaw to the north, and Lee and Deloris Williams on the eastside of Findlay."

"Okay, thanks," the young detective said, still sitting in his chair as he held up an encrypted note that one the detectives had just given him.

The minutes that followed were a flurry of activities as the detectives sounded like an unorganized game of "Go Fish".

"Does anyone have any 116's?" Cressida asked softly.

"I do!" Moscow exclaimed. "Just one 116 on my page."

"What's the word next to it?" Cressida asked in her soft voice.

"It's," Moscow said.

Cressida waited for a moment before asking, "It's what?"

"It's," Moscow replied.

"It's what?" Cressida asked again.

"The word is *it's*," Moscow said with a smile. "That's the word."

"Ah, okay," Cressida said, "Let's put that in this stack."

Soon the stacks that Sneak and I had created earlier in the evening had changed into very different shapes – moving even further out of his bedroom and into another hallway that led to a nearby bathroom as *The Sunday School Detectives* worked on deciphering the code.

After sorting and stacking for quite a while, several of us were getting tired, and shortly Jennie and Michelle went downstairs. "Let's play with my dollhouse, I got some new toys for it," I heard Jennie say as the two left a stack of papers.

Soon, I went downstairs too, to get a glass of water and discovered that Mr. Ryerson had just returned home from work.

"How long is the patrol car going to be here?" he was asking Mrs. Ryerson as they stood in the living room and looked out the front window.

"Until they catch that Julian Davis character," Mrs. Ryerson said with a worried look. "I hope they catch him soon."

"Yes, definitely," he replied.

"With all that's been going on," Mrs. Ryerson continued, "I haven't had a chance to go to the grocery. I'm going to go now. We can eat later tonight, right? Why don't you hold down the fort while I'm gone? Michelle's playing with Jennie in her room and the rest of *The Sunday School Detectives* are upstairs with Steven. I thought it would cheer him up if they came over."

"But he's still grounded," Mr. Ryerson said in a serious tone.

"But George, he was in that horrible accident last night. Let's let him do a little investigation tonight – you know it will cheer him up – then we can make sure he takes a break tomorrow."

"Fine," Mr. Ryerson replied as he saw me in the kitchen getting a glass of water. "Oh, hey Pep," he said. "Are you making much progress on the investigation?"

"Not much," I told him.

As we were talking, the doorbell rang and Mrs. Ryerson went to the front door as Mr. Ryerson and I followed.

"Ma'am. Sir," a tall patrolman in a blue uniform said as he greeted Mr. and Mrs. Ryerson at the door.

"I've been the officer stationed outside your house this afternoon," he explained.

"Thanks for being here. We appreciate it." Mr. Ryerson replied.

"We've just had a reported sighting of Julian Davis near The Fern Café," the patrolman explained. "I'm one of the closest patrols to that location, so I'm going to go check it out. It may be nothing, or it may be the break we've been waiting for."

"That's great," Mrs. Ryerson told him.

"Call our office if you see anything suspicious around here. Okay?"

"Sure, that's fine. We've got a house full of kids. I don't think much is going to happen to Steven while they're here," Mrs. Ryerson explained.

"Alright. I'll be back as soon as I can," the patrolman said reassuringly.

As the policeman was leaving, our friend Joel came bounding up to the porch singing *Band on the Run* by Paul McCartney and Wings – his mother having just dropped him off in the driveway.

"Hi Mrs. Ryerson, Mr. Ryerson," he said with a smile as he stopped singing. "My mom told me that you've invited all of *The Sunday School Detectives* over to cheer up Sneak. Can I come in?"

"Well, sure, come on in," Mr. Ryerson said warmly. "All of the kids are upstairs."

"Hey Joel," I said greeting my friend. "I'll go upstairs with you, there's a lot you need to know about," I told him.

Turning behind me, I noticed Mr. Ryerson had gone to his recliner to begin reading his newspapers while Mrs. Ryerson grabbed her coat and keys for her trip to the grocery store.

CHAPTER 69

Joel was quick and I had a hard time keeping up with him as he went bounding up the stairs to Sneak's room. "Joel!" several of my fellow detectives cried out when they saw him.

"Get well soon, Get well soon, Get well soon, Get well soon," Joel began – when he saw Sneak at his desk chair – singing a modified version of the theme song to *Welcome Back, Kotter.*

"Good one," Sneak said.

"Hey Sneak, you look different with your arm in a sling! But you don't look as bad as I thought you would," Joel said as he finished singing. "Wow, there's a lot of paper here!" he said, surprised at the many stacks of paper the filled Sneaks' bedroom and nearby hallways.

"We think it's all from *The Great Peggu,*" Hailey explained.

"Who?" Joel asked.

"*The Great Peggu,*" Hailey said with a smile.

"An alien," Moscow said matter-of-factly.

"That's the alien who's been writing Julian Davis," Lisa added. "We know he has a green face and doesn't show himself in the daytime – at least that's what Julian told his friend Alice."

"Yeah, and they're getting ready for an invasion," Cressida added. "*The Great Peggu* told Julian that Hancock County would be like the landing pad for their spaceships."

"Wow," Joel said surprised. "That's crazy. But, it goes along with what he's written to the paper, right? And by the way, he's sent in another *Letter to the Editor.*"

"What?" one of us asked in a surprised voice.

"Yep, the police have asked the newspaper not to print it because Julian's a fugitive and everything, but I got a copy for us to read."

Soon we all gathered around Joel as he read us the Letter to the Editor.

To the Editor,

This will be my last Letter to the Editor. I wish people would have listened to me when I warned all of you of an alien invasion, but you did not. Soon you will see that the seeds you have sown will be crushed. We are all angels becoming gods, pips that will develop into great beings, people who are gods

*in embryo. But you have not listened, now you will
be burnt with that knowledge forever.*

Sincerely,
Julian Davis

"Man, that's weird," Moscow said as Joel finished
reading the letter. "That guy is really messed up."

"Joel, how did the letter arrive?" Sneak asked.
"Did anyone see Julian Davis drop it off?"

"No," Joel explained. "The newspaper called the
Police Department as soon as they found it, because
Julian's a fugitive. I think it was slipped under the
door, or something like that, nobody saw him drop
it off. They weren't even sure exactly when it was that
he dropped it off."

"Hmm," Sneak replied as he leaned back in his
chair.

"Hey, do you want to see something cool," we heard
Moscow say to Jennie as he noticed that she and
Michelle had rejoined our group upstairs.

"Sure," Jennie said with a smile.

"Okay," Moscow said as he placed three shiny
quarters on an open space on the blue carpeted
floor. "I'm going to do a cool trick and make these
quarters disappear."

"Really?" Jennie asked.

"Yep," Moscow exclaimed. "It only works if there is a good audience, so if you want to sit there," he said pointing to a place nearby for Jennie to sit.

"Okay," Jennie said.

"And Michelle if you could sit there."

"Sure," the young girl said.

"And what about Mr. Knick Knack?" Jennie asked.

"Oh, yeah, he can sit right there," Moscow said. "And your doll," he said pointing to a doll that Jennie had brought from her room, "she'll probably want a front row seat."

"Of course," Jennie said as she placed her doll next to the quarters.

"Okay, it's a pretty cool trick, are you ready for it? You have to watch pretty closely." Moscow instructed.

"Okay, I'm watching," she said with wide eyes.

"Me too," said Michelle.

"Mr. Knick Knack is watching too," Jennie added.

"Great," Moscow replied.

"What are you doing?" Lisa asked from another side of the bedroom.

"I'm going to make these three quarters disappear," Moscow explained.

"Oh, okay," said Lisa as she returned to the papers.

"Okay, get ready, set," Moscow said before pausing. "Oh, wait a second. Do you want to say a magic word or anything before I make the three quarters disappear?" he asked Jennie.

"No, that's okay," she replied. "Just let me see them disappear and then I'll guess how you did the magic trick."

"Okay," Moscow said as he reached down with his left hand, picked up the quarters and then put them in his pocket. "Ta-da!"

"What?" Jennie asked.

"That was weird." Michelle observed. "You just put them in your pocket."

"That's not a magic trick!" Jennie complained.

"Oh yeah," replied Moscow. "Well your doll thought it was."

And to the girls' amazement, Jennie's doll that had been sitting next to the quarters was gone.

"Good one Moscow," I said with a smile as I noticed the young magician held the doll behind his back with his right hand.

"You'll probably have to give me *four* quarters to get your dolly back," he said as he took the doll and held it high above Jennie's head.

"Hey, come on give it back," Jennie said as she jumped up trying to reach her doll.

Soon Moscow ran from the bedroom to the hallway with the doll held high, while Jennie and her friend Michelle followed. As he ran he sang a modified version of the song *The Itsy Bitsy Spider*. "The itsy bitsy spider went up the water spout. Down came the rain and washed the spider out." As he sang these words he opened the palm of the hand holding the doll and dropped the doll down behind his back and then caught it with his other hand – briefly showing the doll to Jennie. "Out came the sun and did something else." As he got to the chorus of the song he sang loudly, "Where is Jen's dolly? Will she bring it home? Here is the dolly, hope she doesn't cry alone!"

"Hey come on!" Jennie protested as she tried to get her doll. She then jumped and jumped trying to reach the doll while Moscow held it up above his head as they ran back into the bedroom. "It's mine. It's for me. For me! Your magic trick didn't have anything to do with making the three quarters disappear," she protested. "It was just about taking my doll!"

"Say what?" Sneak asked from his chair at his desk. Moments before, he had been closely studying one of the papers and now, interestingly, he was keenly interested in the plight of Jennie's doll.

"What!" Joel said with a laugh as he was helping the others sort through more papers, literally answering Sneak's question.

"Jennie, you're brilliant," her brother told her.

She smiled broadly while she continued jumping up. "I don't know why, I just want my doll back."

CHAPTER 70

S oon Moscow tired of making Jennie jump for her doll and returned it to the young girl and she and Michelle returned to sorting the papers.

"Hey Joel," Sneak asked a few minutes later, as he pondered the case from his chair at his desk in his bedroom. "Do you think there are still some reporters working at the paper tonight?"

"Well sure," Joel told him. "They work pretty late most nights. Do you want to talk to one of the crime reporters? With all of the stuff going on with Julian Davis, I think they're waiting as long as possible to go to print."

"No," Sneak told him. "I'd like to talk to the Business reporter."

"Oh, sure, I can probably get him on the phone, he may not be at the office this late, but there are people who could find him," Joel explained.

I watched Joel make a phone call and then wait for a few minutes until he was connected and soon, I heard Sneak talking to the reporter on his tan colored touch-tone phone in his bedroom. "And his business is called what?" I heard him say, "Okay, thanks you've been a great help."

Unfortunately, I couldn't hear Sneak's conversation because the other Sunday School Detectives had continued their process – like a game of *Go Fish* – of shouting out numbers and words from the papers that were strewn across the bedroom and hallway.

"Does anyone have any with page 112?" Cressida asked.

"You've already asked for that," Lisa said loudly above others. "How about 42's?"

"I've been looking for 223's," Joel replied. "Anybody got any of those?"

"Jennie and I are looking for 35's," Michelle added.

Soon, I heard the young detective ask Joel to connect him with another person from the newspaper – this time the writer who edits the obituaries. *Why is he focused on that now?* I wondered. *If he's looking for an obituary, he can probably go out to his garage and find all of his Dad's old newspapers from the last month or two in that old box of papers out there.*

By this time, I was beginning to feel angrier and angrier at my friend – the *supposedly* brilliant young detective. He was having all of us look through papers – that he knew had no chance of being deciphered – all the while he was spending time talking to people from the newspaper. It all seemed like a waste of time.

Suddenly, Hailey's voice rose above the others.

"Hey! Everybody! Stop! Stop! I found something!" she exclaimed. "You're all going to want to see this!"

Hearing this information, her brother stopped trying to do a trick of balancing a horse from Sneak's *Johnny West* set on one leg and Sneak quickly got off the phone with the newspaper's obituary writer.

"What is it?" Lisa asked.

"It's a paper that isn't like the others," she explained. "I didn't notice it at first, because it has some numbers on it – but it's not the same. It's not like the other ones we've been looking at. The others usually have a word, then a number and then a comma, but this one is different."

We soon huddled around Hailey as she read the letter.

VERSE RE
2,000 pound in battle
10 – 3
Eight before One
Turrets 3

"Great job Hailey!" Sneak exclaimed. "You're right! This paper is different than the others," he added while Hailey held the paper up for all of us to see.

"Nice," Michelle said as she gave a thumbs up sign to Hailey.

"This one is not encrypted like the other papers here," Sneak advised. "It's not referencing page numbers. It's just a simple code," Sneak told us.

"VERSE RE? That's weird," I said.

"I've read about codes like this before," said Hailey. "Sometimes, the first line gives you a clue on how to read the rest of the words. So, in this case, we should read the rest of the words in…."

"Reverse!" Jennie shouted. "What do you think, Sneak?" she asked her brother.

"I think that's a good start," he replied.

"2,000 pounds in battle?" I asked. "That's pretty weird."

"Is it like fighting something heavy?" Moscow asked as he made a punching motion with his arms.

"Or maybe the reverse of war is peace?" Cressida asked with a quizzical look.

"Maybe," Sneak said. "I think once we get it, then we should put it in reverse."

"So another word for battle is…" Hailey began.

"War!" cried Jennie.

"What is it good for!" Joel said as he began singing a few lines of the 1970 song.

"I'd go with war," Sneak said.

"Okay, but in 2,000 pounds?" I wondered.

"That's a ton," said Hailey.

"Ton of War?" I said.

"Tug of war, maybe?" Moscow said.

"What if you reversed the order?" Sneak added. "Remember, that's what we got from the first line."

"War of ton," I said.

"It doesn't say '*of*'," Lisa corrected, "It says '*in*'."

"War in ton?" I asked.

"War in ton?" Jennie asked as well. "That doesn't make any sense."

We were quiet for a few moments thinking of what the clue might mean.

"Sometimes if I say stuff quickly it makes sense," Michelle said. "War in ton, war in ton, war in ton," she said quickly. "I still don't get it."

"Could it be Warrington Avenue?" Hailey asked.

"That's not very far away from here," Joel replied – having stopped singing. "That's probably it. So what else does the clue say?"

"Ten minus three," Lisa said.

"If we flip it around, it's 3 minus 10," Cressida explained.

"That's equal to negative seven," Hailey calculated.

"What if it's not a minus sign," Sneak said. "What if it's just a dash?"

"So 3 *dash* 10?" said Hailey.

"That could be a date, right?" Lisa asked. "Like the three stands for March? And the ten would be for….the tenth?"

"That's today's date!" Cressida said loudly.

"So something's happening today on Warrington Avenue?" Michelle said excitedly.

"And eight before one?" I asked.

"If we flip it around, it's one before eight..." Hailey said.

"That's seven!" Jennie said, as her friend Michelle gave a thumbs up sign.

"Could it mean that something is happening at seven o'clock tonight?" Lisa asked.

"That's only a few minutes from now!" Moscow exclaimed.

"And turrets three...if we flip it around, it could be 3 turrets...or towers," said Hailey.

"But what's going to happen at seven tonight at the three towers?" I asked.

"That's where the next fire's going to be!" Sneak replied. "We've got to get over there as soon as possible!"

"But where are we going? And what are we going to do when we get there?" I asked.

"To save Julian Davis, of course," the young detective replied.

CHAPTER 71

With the recently discovered clues, *The Sunday School Detectives* were a bustle of activity – as kids called their parents, telling them not to pick them up at the Ryerson's house but instead to meet them on Warrington Avenue – and then rushed downstairs to grab coats and other belongings that they had left in the living room when they had entered the house.

In the midst of Sneak giving the other detectives directions about calling their parents – I noticed the young detective quickly write some words on a small piece of paper – made difficult since his writing hand was in a sling – then fold it and then hand it to me.

"Put this in your pocket, Pep – just to see if I'm right," Sneak directed.

"What is it?" I asked.

"It's the name of the person we're going to try to catch tonight."

"I thought we're trying to catch Julian Davis?" I questioned.

"Well, we're probably going to catch him too, but there's a bigger fish we're going after."

"Well, okay," I said shaking my head as I put the small paper into the front pocket of my Wrangler jeans.

"You'll know when to look at that," he told me with a smile as we made our way down the hallway and down the stairs.

My mind raced, as I thought of the potential suspects. I first thought of my prime suspect from yesterday, Deputy Anthony Curtis – he acted like he was unaware of what was going on – but my mind still thought he was guilty. *It was interesting too that he had a perfect alibi for the time Sneak was hurt. He was at Sneak's Uncle's house eating dinner!*

I wondered too about Inspector Baxter as well as Uncle Charlie. Was there more they weren't telling me?

And what about Julian Davis? Maybe he was just making up the whole Great Peggu thing to make people think he was crazy and not as involved in the crimes as he really was. He could have planned the whole thing, right?

And what about the victims? I wondered about them as I ran down the stairs. *Inspector Baxter said one of them named Randy had a grandmother in England – so he would have known about crop circles.*

I had no idea how to narrow down the list of suspects from that list, yet it seemed like my friend Sneak

Ryerson – the great young detective – had done just that. With only a few phone calls to the newspaper he was able to confirm his suspicions and even write down the name of the person on a piece of paper that I was carrying in my pocket. I was amazed at his abilities as I hurried down the stairs.

And how about you, dear reader? Do you have a suspect in mind? You've been given the same information that the great young detective received. What do you think the solution is to the *Case of the Mysterious Circles*?

If you have an idea, write it in the space below:

_____

_____

_____

_____

CHAPTER 72

Soon, Sneak Ryerson and the other Sunday School Detectives gathered in the Ryerson's living room. "Where's the policeman that was stationed outside?" Sneak asked when he looked out the front window.

"Ah, I forgot to tell you," I said contritely, "He went to find Julian at The Fern Café. There was a report that he was over there."

"Ah, okay," the young detective said with a grave face. "Well, I guess we're probably the closest ones to saving him now. Can you call the police and tell them where to meet us?" he asked me.

"Sure," I said with a smile. "424 – 7150," I chanted as I went to the Ryerson's phone in their kitchen.

"Dad! Hey Dad!" Sneak yelled, waking his father who was napping in his recliner – surrounded by his many newspapers and magazines.

"Yeah, uh, what is it?" he asked groggily.

"We need you to take us over to Warrington Avenue. It's almost seven – we need to get over there quickly. We don't have enough bikes and we can't run there fast enough."

"Uh, okay," he said, shaking his head, still waking up. "Who needs to go over there?"

"We all do," Sneak said, looking around the crowded living room. "I had all the kids call their parents to pick them up over there, instead of getting picked up here."

"Uh, okay," his father said again.

"I thought the patrolman who was out front could get over there quickly, but he left, so we're probably the closest ones. We've got to hurry."

"Okay," his father said again.

"Where's Mom," Sneak asked impatiently. "We can all fit if she drives the station wagon and you drive the Chevette."

"She's uh…not here," he told his son.

"Where is she?"

"She went to the moon!" he said with a smile, using a familiar family joke.

"Come on Dad," Sneak said urgently. "Where is she?"

"She went to the grocery store," his father told him.

"Ah…" said Sneak. "Well, I guess we'll all have to go in the Chevette." He paused before saying loudly, "Let's go everybody, we're going to have to squeeze in."

Soon we were in the driveway, crowding into the Ryerson's small red Chevette. Three of us boys – Moscow, Joel and myself – scrunched down in the far back of the car under the glass hatchback, while three of the girls – Lisa, Cressida, and Hailey – joined Sneak in the back seat, trying not to hurt Sneak's shoulder and arm that remained in the sling. Jennie, meanwhile, sat on Michelle's lap in the front passenger seat, along with – she reminded us, her imaginary friend – Mr. Knick Knack.

"It's a good thing it only takes a minute or so to go over there," Mr. Ryerson told us after we had all squeezed into the small four-door subcompact car. "Or else I would never have agreed to this."

We soon arrived at a quiet set of buildings – a large seed barn with offices on Sandusky Street –and pulled into the empty parking lot. The small car, I soon noticed, was dwarfed under three tall silo towers in the night sky – across from the entrance to Warrington Avenue.

"There's lot of doors around this place," Sneak told us as we exited the small car like clowns at a circus. "Our best bet to catch him is to spread out around the building."

"But, we don't have any walkie-talkies or anything," Moscow noted. "How will we talk to each other?"

"I've got an idea," Hailey told us. "Let's make a circle around the building and make sure we stay within shouting distance of each other. That way, if someone needs help we can hear them and be able to go help them out."

"Sounds good," Sneak said. "Hailey, why don't you go to the front of the building – that's probably where the police will show up when they arrive. Pep, why don't you and I go into the building from this side here. It looks like the door is open."

"Ah, I don't think so," his father replied seriously. "I'm not letting you trespass into a building."

"But I think Julian Davis is in trouble," Sneak protested. "He's going to need our help."

Just then a shout was heard from within the building.

"Okay," Mr. Ryerson said. "*We'll* go in there, together. You're not going in there by yourself."

"Okay, thanks Dad," said Sneak. "You coming Pep?"

"Ah, yeah, I guess so," I said tentatively.

"I want to go too," Moscow said, sensing the adventure that awaited inside.

"We don't have enough people to surround the building," Sneak told him. "We need you to catch a bad guy coming out."

"Aw, man," Moscow said dejectedly. "Why does Pep get to go?" he asked.

"Because he's going to write about it someday," the young detective said authoritatively while my heart filled with happiness at that thought.

"You promise to write about me too?" Moscow asked.

"Sure," I replied.

"Okay, let's spread out," Hailey commanded as she and the others left to circle the building.

The three of us – Sneak, his father and I – entered the dark building slowly, unsure of what was ahead and soon found ourselves in a dark hallway, lined with office doors.

"This is just the office," Sneak offered. "They're probably farther back, near the silos."

"I wish I would have brought my flashlight," I lamented.

"Me too," replied Sneak, knowing that we had left our duffle bags filled with detective gear at his house because we didn't have room in Mr. Ryerson's small car.

As our eyes became more accustomed to the darkness, we progressed quickly through the office area and into the area where the three silo towers hovered overhead.

"Help! Help me!" we heard a meek voice calling.

CHAPTER 73

While Sneak, his father and I were entering the dark corridors of the office, the other Sunday School Detectives circled the building. Hailey and Jennie went to the front of the building, while Moscow walked beyond them, waiting at an exit on the building's east side. Lisa and Cressida waited in an empty field near the exits at the back of the building, while Joel and Michelle waited at an exit on the west side of the building – not far from where Sneak and I, along with Mr. Ryerson, had entered the office.

"So we're supposed to just wait here for the bad guys to come out?" questioned Michelle as she waited with Joel in the darkness, near the small red car.

"Yeah, I guess so," said Joel.

"What are we gonna' do?" Michelle asked.

"I like to sing when I don't have anything to do," Joel admitted.

"You like singing all the time!" Michelle laughed.

"Well that's true," Joel acknowledged and he soon began humming the famous guitar introduction to the song *Smoke on the Water* by Deep Purple. "Da,da,da," he paused, "Da,da,dada. Da da, da, dada."

"Come on Joel," Michelle protested in the darkness of the cold night. "That's too scary, don't sing that."

"Too scary?" Joel asked. "Really?"

"Yeah, sing something less scary."

"Okay, I'll try," Joel agreed. "I can do something different."

He paused for a moment and began singing, "It's Friday night and the lights are low," – the first few words in the song *The Dancing Queen* by the band *ABBA*.

"That's still too scary," Michelle protested. "I need something a lot less scary than that."

"*Dancing Queen* is too scary?" Joel asked.

"Yeah," Michelle said, her voice quivering. "It's so dark out here, I need something that's not scary at all."

"Fine," Joel replied. "Just don't tell anybody about this," he said, as he began singing a song that he knew Michelle would not find scary.

"Thanks Joelsie," Michelle said when she heard the song.

Inside the building, the shouts of "Help! Help me!" continued and we continued racing through the corridors to find the source – Mr. Ryerson led the way, followed closely by his son while I trailed a short distance behind.

Soon, we found a young man tied to a wooden chair.

"It's...Julian Davis!" I said, recognizing his face from the F.E.E.T. photos that Joel had displayed at our recent meeting.

"Yes, quite," Sneak said as we quickly approached.

"Let's get him untied," Mr. Ryerson said, looking at the ropes the bound the young man. "I think I smell smoke."

"I saw him! I saw him!" Julian said excitedly as the three of us worked on untying the many knots that bound him.

"Who?" I asked, as I worked to untie the knots near his right hand, while Sneak and his father worked on the knots on his left side. The knots, we found were tied very tightly and our efforts at untying them were made even more difficult by the darkness of the building – and Sneak's right arm still held tight by his sling.

"*The Great Peggu!*" Julian replied excitedly.

"Who?" Mr. Ryerson asked, surprised by the funny sounding name.

"*The Great Peggu!*" Julian said again enthusiastically. "I finally saw him, but he tricked me into sitting in this chair and then he tied me up! I don't know why he would have done that. Maybe he's coming back for me and didn't want me to leave?"

"I'm smelling smoke now," I said as a pungent smell began to hit my nostrils.

"Keep working the knots," Mr. Ryerson said. "I should have brought my pocket knife," he lamented in an exasperated tone. "This would have been so much easier."

"There's a lot of knots here," I told him.

"Let's just keep working the knots, boys." Mr. Ryerson continued. "If it seems like the fire is getting close and we haven't freed him, we'll have to drag him *and the chair* out with us."

"I think we can get it Dad," Sneak said as he continued untying. "Say a prayer for us Pep, if you can."

"Lord Jesus, help us," I said as I worked the knots. "We need your help."

"Got it!" Sneak exclaimed as a section of the rope came loose. "I think this might do it," he said as he pulled the rope back and Julian Davis was free.

"Let's get out of here," Mr. Ryerson commanded. "Where there's smoke, there's fire."

"What about *The Great Peggu*?" I asked.

"Hopefully one of the other detectives has stopped him," said Sneak as we ran towards the exit.

CHAPTER 74

Mr. Ryerson, Sneak and I raced back through the dark corridors – holding Julian Davis by his arms. We followed the path we used to enter the building, staying ahead of a fire that we were sure had been set behind us. I was beginning to picture acrid smoke beginning to descend upon us and I began to cough and wheeze as I imagined it hitting my nose and lungs.

"Keep going boys!" Mr. Ryerson shouted to us. "We don't have much further to go!"

I was panting hard by the time we reached the long dark hallway filled with office doors. We had run a long distance – much farther than I was used to – and my physical strength suddenly left me. I paused briefly and then went down on my knees while the others continued down the hallway.

"Wait!" I heard Sneak yell. "Where's Pep? He's not with us."

"Pep!" I heard Mr. Ryerson scream. "Pep! Pep!"

"I'm...back...here," I shouted. "Go on without me."

I shut my eyes briefly and a wave of exuberance filled my thoughts. *We got him!* I thought excitedly. *Julian Davis tried to run over Sneak last night with his car, but we've caught him. He's going to go to jail for a long time. And I'm....I'm...* Quickly, my thoughts became unfocused and confused. I looked down the long dark corridor knowing that I needed to go forward – sensing that more answers awaited outside the building – yet I was unable to move.

Soon, I felt Mr. Ryerson's arm around my shoulder.

"We're not leaving without you," he said reassuringly. "Do you have asthma? It sounds like you're having an asthma attack."

"I...don't...know," I said haltingly.

"Let's get outside and get some fresh air," Mr. Ryerson said as he pushed open two heavy double doors and I felt the cold air sting my face and hands.

"That fresh air feels really good," Sneak confessed.

"Yeah!" I said, as I continued my labored breathing.

"I saw him! I saw him!" Julian Davis was saying again. "Why would he trick me and tie me up? I don't understand." Julian's face, I remember, was one of absolute confusion – uncertain as to why months of anticipation had ended so differently than he had planned.

"Let's go to the front of the building," Sneak suggested. "That's probably where the police and fire trucks will arrive first."

And soon we were walking with Julian Davis towards the front of the building – our hands holding tightly to his arms. "Hopefully, someone got him," I heard Sneak say.

"Who?" Julian asked.

"Your *Great Peggu*," Sneak told him.

CHAPTER 75

"This is the door the bad guy will come out of, I'm sure of it," Jennie had said authoritatively, when she and Hailey first arrived at the front of the building.

The front of the large building, they noticed, was used for loading and unloading trucks, and contained a large stone covered driveway, while the western edge of the area was littered with stacks of large wooden pallets, piled high with netting and rope, for tying down shipping containers to long flatbed trucks.

"How are we going to get him when he comes out?" Hailey asked, looking at the large open area in front of the building. "He'll have a lot of space to run."

"Could we just stand by the door and grab his legs when he comes out?" Jennie asked.

"That might be hard for us to do," Hailey admitted. "We might be able to hold on for a little while, but it seems like someone could get away pretty easily if we were just holding on to their ankles."

"Hmmm," Jennie said perplexed by the problem.

"Hey, look, over here," Hailey said as she studied the many ropes and nets on the side of the dark parking lot. "We could use this netting over here," she explained. "This could stop him – at least for a little while – until the police arrive."

"I like it," Jennie said. "But there's only one problem."

"What's that?" her older friend asked.

"Well, the exit to the building is over there, and the nets are way over here."

"Yeah, well about that…." Hailey said to Jennie. "I was thinking you could kind of get him to come over here to this area…"

"How'm I supposed to do that?" Jennie asked with a gulp.

"Maybe you can make him chase you?" Hailey suggested.

"Chase me? What if it's really an alien that comes out of that door? And you want him to chase me?"

"Well," Hailey said. "Yeah? I guess that was what I was thinking. Do you have a better plan?"

They paused for a moment.

"No, I guess not," Jennie said dejectedly. "I guess we'll need to get him over here to get the ropes or a net on him. But if he's tall, you won't be able to throw it over his head, could you?" Jennie asked as she looked at the heavy ropes.

"How about this for an idea?" the older girl suggested to her friend. "I'll take hold of the netting and climb up on one of these wooden pallets," she said pointing to a stack of wooden pallets that rose high into the air. "Then, if you can get him to stand right below it, I can drop it down on him and then he'll be covered."

"So, you'll be like twenty or thirty feet up in the air and I'll be down on the ground with the alien monster?" Jennie asked.

"Well, yeah, do you have a better plan?" asked Hailey.

"I'm not going to ask you any more questions," Jennie said with a laugh. "Because I'm not liking how the answers turn out with these plans of yours!" And soon both of the girls were laughing.

"Okay, if you can help me up I'll grab the net and start climbing," Hailey said seriously and soon she was climbing the tall and unstable wooden pallets while holding onto a heavy net.

"That looks like something your brother would do," Jennie said to her friend, as she saw Hailey climbing higher and higher up the wooden pallets.

"Oh yeah," Hailey explained. "He's not going to like that he missed out on this, but we don't have enough time to go get him."

The rickety pallets moved back and forth as Hailey first rose five feet above the ground, then she climbed to a place about ten feet up, then twenty, then twenty-five, then thirty feet above the ground – while Jennie remained far below her.

They waited a few minutes in the darkness before Hailey called down to Sneak's sister. "You doing okay down there Jennie?"

"Yeah, I'm okay, I'm going to go stand by the door in a few minutes. How are you doing?"

"I'm okay, but this netting is pretty heavy," Hailey replied. "I'm not sure how much longer I can hold it."

"I'm sure he'll be out soon," Jennie told her friend as she looked up into the dark sky – unable to see her friend in the darkness of the night.

"How will I know when to drop it?" Hailey asked. "It's so dark, I can't even see you down there."

"I'll give you a signal, would that be okay?" Jennie asked.

"Sure, that sounds good," Hailey said from her perch far above the ground. "When he's right below me give me a signal."

They paused for a moment.

"What will your signal be?" Hailey asked.

"I'll say....I'll say, 'Roller Derby'," Jennie explained.

"Uh, okay."

"No, I'll say *Roller Derby 123*."

"Okay, why will you say Roller Derby?" the older detective asked.

"It just sounds cool," Jennie said with a nervous laugh as she looked up in the darkness. "Have you ever heard of Pinky Tuscadero?"

"Fonzie's girlfriend on *Happy Days*?" Hailey asked.

"Yeah...she likes pink stuff...and I do too...like Pink Jeeps...and my bike is pink...and my doll house is pink, too. And I think Pinky likes Roller Derby's too."

"I think it's *Demolition* Derby's that she likes," Hailey replied, but as she said these words she saw a door open at the front of the building. "Shhh," she told her friend. "I think someone's coming."

"Okay," Jennie said in a loud whisper. "I'll get closer to the building."

Soon, in the darkness, they saw the door open wider and a dark figure step out.

In a moment, Jennie raced to where the figure stood and confronted him. "Ahh, hey! Hi!" Jennie said bravely, catching the creature by surprise as it walked quickly on the gravel driveway.

Jennie was surprised as well, seeing the great ugliness of the creature's green face.

"Arrg," the creature said as it advanced towards Jennie as she turned and ran toward the wooden pallets.

But soon Jennie noticed the creature wasn't chasing her at all, but going in the opposite direction from her – just as Hailey had feared – heading towards the wide open driveway in front of Warrington Avenue.

Thinking quickly, Jennie screamed, "Mr. Knick Knack he's running straight for you! You'll be able to catch him in just a minute!"

With these words, the creature stopped and changed directions – this time heading straight for Jennie.

Jennie had initially stopped to entice the creature in her direction and in seconds it seemed, the creature was in pursuit of her – only a few feet away, as Jennie had yet to build any momentum in her run.

Pigtails flying, Jennie soon arrived near the side of the driveway where the tall stack of wooden pallets and ropes were stored.

"Roller Derby 4-5-6!" Jennie yelled as the creature chased her – now, only a few feet away.

Jennie, now fearing she would be caught, looked desperately to her friend atop the pallets – but Hailey remained shrouded in dark shadows.

"Roller Derby! Roller Derby! 4-5-6!" Jennie yelled as the creature came close to grabbing her shoulders. "Hailey throw the net! Throw...the... net!" she yelled as she heard a crash behind her while she sped away down the dark sidewalk along Sandusky Street.

"Hey, hey!" she heard a deep voice shout, as the creature thrashed about under the net – only to get more and more wrapped up in the rope and netting.

"Hey Jennie! Jennie!" she heard Hailey yell. "Come back! Can you help me down?"

But Jennie had sped away.

CHAPTER 76

Soon the night air was filled with the sounds of sirens from police cars and fire trucks, who converged – as Sneak had predicted – at the front of the building.

Uncle Charlie was one of the first to arrive and greet his brother-in-law, nephew and myself.

"We would have been here sooner, but we were dispatched to the *north* end of Warrington Avenue... it took our guys a few minutes to realize we needed to be here...at the *south* end, where the silo towers are. What's going on?" he asked.

"We...caught...him!" I said jubilantly with heavy, labored breath. "This...is...Julian...Julian Davis," I said while holding tightly to the F.E.E.T. President's arm.

"Nice work boys," said Uncle Charlie. "Take him away," he said to a police officer who was standing nearby. Soon, the officer took Julian Davis from me – placed handcuffs on him – and then moved him to the back seat of a patrol car.

"There's another perpetrator," Sneak told his uncle, "calls himself *The Great Peggu*. He started a fire inside. If I can talk to someone from the Fire Department, I think I can give them a pretty good location of where the fire is."

"Sure let's go," Uncle Charlie said as he and Sneak raced over to a fire truck and talked to the firefighters who were setting up their equipment.

"Pep, it looks like there's a big commotion going on over there," Mr. Ryerson said to me as he pointed to several police officers near the front of the building. "Let's go check it out," he said with a smile.

When we arrived at the front of the building, we soon noticed that Hailey and Jennie were with the group of police officers, surrounding a large net. "He's in here," I heard Hailey say. "He can't run away now."

Meanwhile, hearing the sirens, Lisa and Cressida had begun walking from the back of the building towards the front and soon heard Joel singing.

"...and we'll find a place to where there's room to grow...," they heard Joel sing.

"Hi Joel, Michelle," Lisa said when she and Cressida approached – as Joel abruptly stopped his song. "Let's go check out what's going on at the front of the building, I don't think anyone's coming out this way."

"Sounds good," Joel replied quickly.

As they walked to the front of the building, Lisa asked. "So why were you singing *We've Only Just Begun* by *The Carpenters*?"

"I wasn't singing that," Joel protested. "I only sing rock and roll songs."

"I'm pretty sure it was *The Carpenters*," said Lisa.

"Yep, *We've Only Just Begun*," Cressida said.

"Fine," Joel said, dropping his head. "I was singing it because it's not as scary as the other songs I know."

"It was pretty good," Michelle admitted.

"Yeah, I liked it too," said Lisa.

"I thought it was great," Michelle added as she smiled.

Eventually, all of *The Sunday School Detectives* – including Moscow, who had spent a dull, uneventful time on the east side of the building – arrived at the front of the building to find Hailey and Jennie, along with myself and Mr. Ryerson and a group of police officers, surrounding the thrashing creature caught in the net.

"That was *so* boring!" Moscow complained as he approached the large group. "There is nothing going on!"

"The more you thrash around, the more you'll get tangled up," a young policeman was saying. "Just stop moving and we can get you out."

Soon, even more police officers arrived, along with Deputy Curtis of the County Sheriff's Department and Inspector Baxter of the State Fire Marshal's office.

"So, what do we have here?" Deputy Curtis asked.

"I think someone really interesting," I replied, having finally caught my breath, but unsure of exactly who – or what – we would find under the netting.

"Hailey got him!" Jennie said enthusiastically. "She dropped the net from way up there," she said pointing up to a high wooden pallet.

"Okay, okay…" we heard a voice say. "I'll stop moving around."

Carefully, several officers untangled the ropes and netting that covered the monster and soon we saw a creature with an ugly green face.

"*The Great Peggu!*" Michelle said in horror.

"He's really alive!" Jennie said frightfully, as she grabbed her father's hand. "I was so scared when he chased me towards Hailey, I almost ran all the way to the Fairgrounds."

"Wait, what?" her father asked perplexed.

"I don't think he's really an alien," Hailey explained. "Look at his hands and his arms and his legs. They don't look alien to me."

"He's wearing a mask!" Moscow exclaimed when he saw the human features.

Soon, a police officer moved towards the creature and placed the creature's arms behind his back and put his hands in handcuffs and then quickly moved to take off the green mask.

"Hey, wait a minute," Deputy Curtis said. "Don't you think you should let the detective who caught him do the honors of taking off the mask?"

"Okay," the policeman said with a smile.

"Why don't you do the honors?" Inspector Baxter said encouragingly to Hailey. "You caught him right?"

"Well, I guess it would be okay," Hailey said as she reached up and removed the ugly green mask. Just as she did this, two flashes appeared that momentarily blinded Hailey in the darkness. After blinking hard several times, she saw two newspaper photographers taking pictures of her removing the mask.

CHAPTER 77

"Old man Crenshaw?" Moscow Cotton said loudly when he saw that the mask had hidden the face of an older gentleman – known to several of the detectives.

"Moscow!" Hailey scolded.

"Sorry, I should have said *Mr. Crenshaw*," Moscow said correcting himself. "You're *The Great Peggu?*"

By this time, I noticed that Uncle Charlie and his nephew had joined the group of police officers and *The Sunday School Detectives* that surrounded the suspect.

"But why?" Deputy Curtis asked.

"You won't get me to talk," Mr. Crenshaw sneered.

"He wanted to get rid of the competition," Sneak explained. "He owns a seed company on the north side of town, there's only two of them here in Hancock County, so he thought if he could burn this one down – he'd have a..."

"Monopoly," his uncle interrupted.

PEP STILES

"Right, a monopoly." Sneak added.

"I would have been able to get away with it too, if it wasn't for you meddling kids," Russell Crenshaw, the man in handcuffs said in a deep voice.

"Dad, it's just like *Scooby Doo*!" Jennie said proudly as she looked up at her father.

"Let me advise you of your rights…," we heard Uncle Charlie say as he held his notepad out and began walking with Mr. Crenshaw to his patrol car and quickly put him into the back seat. "Nice work kids," he said as he stood near his car. "This wasn't an easy case."

By then, many of the parents of *The Sunday School Detectives* had arrived and were standing next to their children.

"The fire's out," the fire chief announced as he approached our group. "It didn't get much of a chance to burn. He probably planned on it starting slow so he could get out of here in time. I'm glad we caught it when we did, the fire could have been pretty bad."

"Wow, I'm glad the silos didn't catch on fire," Lisa said. "That would have been really bad."

"Me too," Joel added.

"Me three," Michelle said.

The fire chief then explained, "We've got to clean up some things around here, and use this parking lot for our hoses. So we'll need you kids to move out."

"Okay," a few of us said.

"It's getting late," Uncle Charlie added – still standing by his car. "I can get your statements tomorrow, if I need to."

"Okay," a few of *The Sunday School Detectives* replied.

"Let's go Jennie," Mr. Ryerson said to his daughter, who was holding tightly to his hand. "You've had a pretty busy night, plus we need to take your brother home – he's injured and still grounded."

"Ah, Dad," Jennie Ryerson complained. "Can't I stay out here a little bit longer? I just saw a reporter take Hailey aside and ask her about how she caught Mr. Crenshaw."

"No, we need to go," Mr. Ryerson said, and soon I saw the three Ryerson's get into their red Chevette and drive away.

My mom soon approached and asked if I was ready to go home.

"I guess so," I told her. "This has been a crazy night."

Then, as I saw the Ryerson's turn out of the parking lot and onto Sandusky Street to drive home, I remembered the paper that Sneak had given me earlier in the evening and I quickly pulled it out of the front pocket of my Wrangler jeans. Unfolding it, I was stunned to see the name that Sneak had written: *Russell Crenshaw.*

CHAPTER 78

The next day was Wednesday, March 11th, and the morning paper had a large picture of Hailey Cotton on the front page holding Mr. Crenshaw's mask with the headline, "GIRL DETECTIVE NABS ALIEN IMPOSTER" with a few paragraphs about the case. I took the paper to school to talk with the kids about our adventure.

After arriving at school, I discovered that it was our Annual Picture Day and in the afternoon, all of the kids from my class walked to the stage in the cafeteria and stood together on a tiered platform and got our class picture taken with our teacher, who stood on one side of our group and our principle who stood on the other. Unfortunately, with all of the excitement of the previous two nights, I had not returned to the barber shop to fix my hair – I had left Dan's chair before he was finished with my haircut – and that year's picture was very memorable, with one half of my head cut in a standard bowl cut – with hair cut about two inches above one eyebrow – while the other side of my head was left uncut and hanging low, touching an eyebrow. It was an interesting look – *The Half-Bowl*, as I called it in later years.

After school I went to Sneak Ryerson's house, where we decided to play with his massive collection of *Army Men* in his room.

"So how did you figure it out?" I asked, as we set up the two-inch tall green plastic toy soldiers in rows across from each other.

"It ended up being pretty easy," he told me as he set up his pieces, hampered still with his right arm in the blue sling.

"Elementary, huh?"

"Well, it wasn't at first," he told me. "We all knew that Julian was involved...but we didn't know who else."

"I thought it was Deputy Curtis!" I said with a smile.

"Yeah, I hadn't considered him," the young detective said. "But because you went to Uncle Charlie's with your suspicions we got a big breakthrough in the case."

"A breakthrough? What do you mean?" I asked doubtfully.

"It was on the recording...at his house," Sneak explained.

"Oh, yeah, I figured you would think it was interesting to hear your Uncle announce that you were in an accident," I said as I continued setting up a row of soldiers.

"No, it wasn't exactly that," Sneak told me. "It was what Inspector Baxter told you."

"Inspector Baxter, from the State Fire Marshal's office? She didn't tell me anything – except that she followed Julian Davis to the mall with a baby carriage and met some people from England at places like the *Rocking U Outpost.*"

"Exactly," said Sneak. "That helped me narrow down the list of suspects."

"How'd you do that?" I wondered.

"Well, you told me that Hailey reported to the group that there hadn't ever been any crop circles reported here in Hancock County, right?"

"Right, that's what she learned at the library."

"So a local person probably would not know much about them, right?"

"Right," I said skeptically.

"But someone from England, well, they would have heard a lot about crop circles. And if they were thinking about committing a crime – they would probably turn to something they're familiar with."

"That makes sense." I replied. "Weren't there, like, four people from England she met. And like two of the guys who were victims of the fires?"

"Right, one had a grandmother from England. But the other was from Salisbury."

"Salisbury? Why's that important?" I asked as I set up a plastic green officer holding a pair of binoculars.

"Well it's important because it's only about two miles from *Old Sarum* – that's where Inspector Baxter said a lot of crop circles were reported. So someone from there would definitely know a lot about crop circles."

"And what did she say his name was?" I asked, as I positioned a plastic tank on Sneak's desk. "I can't remember."

"She called him Rusty, that's one of the reasons I asked you to read me the names of the victims – to see who she was talking about."

"Oh, yeah," I replied, remembering how I had angrily read the names to him.

"That's when things really started to make a lot more sense," the young detective told me. "And that's when I deduced that it was likely Mr. Crenshaw. It made sense that he would start the first fire on his property, you know, to see if it would work before setting the others."

"But I don't think his name was the one I read first in the list," I said, thinking about the list I had angrily read.

"You didn't," the young detective explained. "You actually read them in a different order. But I remembered that the first fire was started on the *north* side of the city. And that's the property that Mr. Crenshaw owned."

"But, I don't even remember the name *Rusty* even being in that list. I remember the name Randy, but not Rusty."

"Well, there was a farmer named Randy, but you read out Mr. Crenshaw's full name."

"What?" I asked, as I moved a toy soldier holding a bazooka.

"You gave the property owners full names – Russell and Margaret Crenshaw – along with all the others. When I heard that, it made sense who Inspector Baxter was talking about. She said she had talked to Rusty about growing up in England – Rusty's a nickname for *Russell*. Russell Crenshaw was the person she identified as being from Salisbury, England – near the site of all of those crop circle fires."

"But that doesn't really prove anything, right?" I suggested. "That just shows that Russell or Rusty... or whatever his name was....was from Old Sardum, England..."

"Old Sarum," Sneak corrected.

"...where there were a bunch of crop circles."

"And remember, it was his property that was the first to have a fire," he reminded me.

"Still...," I said.

"Remember how that first property was different than the others?" Sneak asked.

"How's that?" I wondered.

"Well, that's the one property where I didn't find tracks from the motorbike."

"Right," I agreed. "But I thought I heard you on the tape tell your uncle that was because the arsonist was getting sloppy – he made the tracks in the other places but not the first one."

"Well, that's what I thought at first," Sneak explained. "But, then after Mr. Crenshaw became a suspect, even the missing tracks made sense."

"How's that?" I wondered.

"Well, think about why they needed that moto-cross bike?" my friend asked. "They used it to get in and out of a field really quick, so the farmers nearby wouldn't hear them. But if he's setting fire to his own property…"

"He doesn't need to be real quick," I answered. "And he doesn't need to be real quiet about it either."

"Exactly!" my friend said, as he continued setting up more toy soldiers. "He didn't need the motocross bike on his own property!"

"So, that was it?" I asked. "It all had to do with where the guy was from in England?"

"Well, no," said Sneak. "But it helped to narrow down the list of suspects. And, then, when the girls came back with the information about *The Great Peggu* – that clinched it."

"Clinched it? How was that?" I asked, setting up a plastic radioman behind my long line of plastic soldiers.

"Well, think about it. That name *Peggu*…it's clearly fake. I think I've read that name only one other time in a book about India, but how many people are from India that live here?"

"None," I replied.

"Well not too many," Sneak continued. "So, it was more likely that someone was writing a similar name when they came up with the name Peggu as their alien identity. And what name is similar to Peggu?" the young detective asked me.

"Pegg-o?" I guessed. "Er, Pegg-er, uh, Pegg-y?" I finally guessed.

"Right! Peggy. I'm guessing he had been writing the name Peggy a lot and decided to change it to make that his identity as an alien. And you know what Peggy is a nickname for, right?"

"No," I replied as I was setting up a soldier holding a minesweeper.

"It's Margaret. Sometimes people use the name Peg. But a lot of times they use the nickname Peggy if someone is named Margaret."

"So, someone was writing the name Peggy over and over and came up with the name *Peggu* for a space alien?" I asked.

"Right, and why would someone be writing the name Peggy, over and over again?"

"I don't know," I said, exasperated by my friend's questions.

"Well, if someone was related to Peggy and then Peggy died, and so they had to write thank you notes to people who had given gifts or flowers or donations or something like that. That would be one reason, right?"

"I guess so," I replied.

"That's when I checked with the writer of the newspaper's Obituary Page, and they confirmed that Margaret Crenshaw died back in the fall – only a short time before Julian Davis was contacted by *The Great Peggu.*"

"So you're saying that from Inspector Baxter's description of someone who lived in England named *Rusty* and the alien's name being similar to *Peggy* – you were able to figure out that their real names were Russell and Margaret?"

"Well, pretty much."

"So if Russell and Margaret Crenshaw hadn't used the nicknames *Rusty and Peggy* you wouldn't have figured it out?"

"Maybe," the young detective said with a smile. "I guess we'll never know that answer."

"Wow, it's weird how people are always using nicknames instead of their real names isn't it Sneak."

"Yeah, Pep, it is," my friend replied.

"Well," I continued as we were finishing setting up our Army men, "that all makes sense of *who* was contacting Julian Davis, but *why* was Mr. Crenshaw setting the fires and pretending to be an alien in the first place? Last night you said it had something to do with his seed company?"

"Right, that idea came from Moscow playing with Jennie's doll."

"What?" I asked as I stopped setting up of the plastic soldiers to focus on my friend's answer.

"Well, do you remember when Moscow told Jennie he was going to make three quarters disappear and then while her attention was on the magic trick, he took her doll?"

"Oh, yeah, I remember. That was funny."

"That's when it struck me. The four crop circles have really just been a diversion. Nothing of value has been damaged…except, I remembered a small shed with seeds at the last fire."

"A diversion?"

"Right, they were used to set up Julian Davis…to make everyone think he's guilty," the young detective explained. "The real target were those big silos filled with seeds, where we were last night…"

"The three towers off of Warrington Avenue," I interrupted.

"Yep," the young detective confirmed.

"So tell me again why Mr. Crenshaw was interested in that…"

"Well, he owns a competing seed operation on the north side of town – that's something he didn't tell me when I interviewed him at his farm after the first fire. Remember, I interviewed each of the farmer's after the fires in their fields?"

"Oh yeah," I replied.

"Anyway, he thought that if he could get rid of those seeds at the silos near Warrington Avenue he'd...what's the expression...*corner the market* for all of Hancock County. My grandpa was just telling me that spring planting will be starting soon – and all of the farmer's around here will need seeds for that. So, Mr. Crenshaw thought he would be able to jack up the prices really high..."

"...since he would be the only one in the county that had any seeds," I said excitedly.

"Right," my friend agreed.

"So how did you figure that out?" I asked. "I didn't know anything about the seeds before last night. There wasn't any evidence about seeds in what we found out about the case and you said Mr. Crenshaw didn't even tell you he owned a seed company when you interviewed him!"

"Well, that was Mr. Crenshaw's biggest mistake, if you ask me," Sneak explained. "It was all from that last *Letter to the Editor* that he sent. You know, the one that Joel read to us."

"*Mr. Crenshaw* sent it? I thought that letter was from Julian Davis?"

"No, clearly it was from Mr. Crenshaw," the young detective said in a serious tone as he finished lining up a group of soldiers holding bazookas. "He wanted to make everyone think Julian Davis was involved – that's why he set the four other fires, and that's why he lured Julian to the building and tied him up and that's why he sent that last *Letter to the Editor*."

"But it was signed by Julian, right?"

"Well it was signed with Julian's name, but it was clearly from Mr. Crenshaw," the young detective explained. "Unfortunately for Mr. Crenshaw, he didn't know anything about Julian's ideas – like we did. He probably never even read Julian's *Manifesto*."

"His *Manifesto*?" I asked.

"Right, do you remember what the girls told us about Julian's...what does the professor call it? His view of the world?"

"I remember some of it," I admitted.

"Julian believed that God was pretty much unknowable..."

"Right, except if we got big computers from aliens, I remember that part," I interrupted.

"Exactly," Sneak continued.

"Yeah, I remember the two circles with the line between them too," I told him.

"Right, so his view is that we can't really know God unless we get help from aliens who have big computers, but if you look at that last *Letter to the Editor*, there were sentences in there that were totally different from what Julian wrote in his *Manifesto*. There was stuff like, 'all men are angels becoming gods' and 'people are just gods in embryo'. That's not at all what Julian believes. I still have a copy of that letter on my desk if you want to look at it," my friend said.

I quickly stood up and found the letter on Sneak's desk.

"Oh, yeah," I said as I scanned the letter again. "This last *Letter to the Editor* is really different from Julian's *Manifesto*. I didn't pick up on that," I confessed.

"Plus," Sneak continued. "Look at the allusions to *seeds* and *fire* – I'm sure that Mr. Crenshaw put those in the letter thinking that after the fire destroyed the silos, Julian would be blamed for it."

"I guess I missed that too," I replied. "The seeds you have sown will be crushed...you will be burnt with that knowledge forever," I quoted from the letter. "Wow, that's creepy."

"Yeah, and then to top it all off," Sneak concluded. "That last *Letter to the Editor* had the word 'pips' in it."

"Pips?" I asked.

"Yep," the young detective said seriously. "It was almost as if Mr. Crenshaw wanted to get caught."

"How's that?" I wondered.

"Well, 'pips' is a common English word for seeds…"

"That might be used by someone from Old Sardum," I added.

"Old Sarum," Sneak corrected. "I recognized it because the word *pips* is in the title of one of Sherlock Holmes' most famous stories."

"About crop circles?" I asked.

"No about orange seeds," the young detective replied with a laugh. "They were used as a warning to a British person who took papers away from America after the U.S. Civil War."

"It sounds complicated," I said.

"It is," said Sneak.

"So hearing about the seeds led you to call the business reporter?" I asked.

"Right, with all of the evidence pointing against him, I figured Mr. Crenshaw had something to do with seeds. And then the business reporter was able to let me know that Mr. Crenshaw was actually the owner of that seed company on the north side of town. It just confirmed that he was the one behind it all."

"Do you think he'll go to jail for a long time?" I asked.

"I don't know," the young detective told me. "Maybe he'll say that he was really sad after his wife died and it made him temporarily crazy, or something like that."

"Hmm," I replied, pausing for a moment. "Maybe. He went to a lot of work to make Julian Davis look guilty."

"Well at the beginning, Julian was pretty much an innocent victim," Sneak explained. "Until he tried to run me over with his car."

We paused for a moment.

"Okay, let's prepare for battle," I told him.

"Let's," said Sneak and soon we began making loud noises that sounded like explosions and shots being fired from guns as we took turns knocking over each other's plastic figures in his room.

CHAPTER 79

The next day was Thursday, March 12ᵗʰ, and the morning paper was filled with even more details of the case and news that Mr. Crenshaw had confessed to the crimes – setting all four of the crop circle fires, setting the fire at the seed silos near Warrington Avenue, as well as tying up Julian Davis and pretending to be *The Great Peggu.*

In addition to arresting Mr. Crenshaw and Julian Davis, the newspapers reported that the county sheriff's department also arrested two workers from Mr. Crenshaw's seed company for helping him with the crop circle fires. After their arrest, they confessed to where they had hidden the motorbike they used to create the fires – a 1978 Yamaha DT 400 – just like Sneak had described.

That evening, all of the *Sunday School Detectives* were at Children's Choir in our Church's Chapel and Mrs. Willingham greeted each of us with a smile. When Sneak arrived – his arm still in a sling – she told him how glad she was that her prayers were answered and that his injuries were not as serious as they could have been.

"You had a lot of people praying for you," she explained to the young detective.

When Hailey and Moscow arrived, she congratulated Hailey on capturing the 'bad guy' and told her, "We were proud to see you in the paper!"

"I had a lot of help," Hailey explained.

"It was pretty boring," Moscow added.

Soon Mrs. Willingham started practice as she usually did, "Okay, let's begin. Palm Sunday is coming up, we have a lot to do," and soon she dropped her baton with a loud "BAM!" on her metal music stand to get our attention.

The next day, Friday, March 13th, school went incredibly slow as I anticipated the evening. Math, then science, then reading all dragged on and on until the end of the school day finally arrived.

After taking Bus Four to my mother's house, I went with her on a few errands – including a visit to the fabric store at the mall, which was always challenging – because it was always so boring for me – and then to the barber shop for Dan to fix my haircut. Eventually, we returned home and I raced to the Ryerson's house.

Even though Sneak was grounded, Mr. and Mrs. Ryerson had agreed – after a number of pleas from their daughter Jennie – to have a party celebrating the end of *The Case of the Mysterious Circles*.

I arrived with my clip-on metal roller skates rattling around in my duffle bag and soon made my way into the house and quickly greeted Mrs. Ryerson, Mrs. Cotton and Mrs. Hemlinger, who were preparing food in the kitchen.

"The other kids are downstairs," Mrs. Ryerson told me and I quickly ran down the wooden stairs to find the other Sunday School Detectives roller skating to multi-colored lights in the basement. At first I thought a disco light was spinning, but instead I discovered that Sneak had made multiple blue and purple and yellow and green liquids bubble in beakers above the Bunsen burners in his forensics lab.

The song called *December, 1963* by the Four Seasons played loudly from Jennie's red and black ladybug shaped turntable as the kids laughed and spun and glided on their roller skates across the uncarpeted concrete floor. "Oh What a Night!" Joel sang loudly as the others laughed and skated.

"Pep!" the kids yelled when I arrived and I quickly found a place to put on my roller skates.

Moscow, I noticed was trying to do a roller skating trick – laying back while sailing under a model train set – located precipitously close to the floor. He fell once, but on his second attempt sailed under the table without crashing.

I quickly put on my skates as Lisa put on another '45 record with the song *Y.M.C.A.* by *The Village People* and we skated in wide clock-wise circles around the basement while spelling out each letter with our arms – raised high amidst the multi-colored lights.

"This is so fun!" I said to Sneak as I went racing faster and faster in circles.

Lisa decided next to "slow things down" – as she put it – and played the song *How Deep is Your Love* by the *Bee Gees*. With the start of the slow tune, the boys scattered towards the ping-pong table, as some of us tried to play the game while still on roller skates while a few others sat nearby on the cold floor and played a game of *Paddle Pool* – a fun game that used paddles attached to a small plastic playing area and hit plastic ping-pong sized balls into other player's goals.

We soon returned to the make-shift roller rink as the song, *You Should Be Dancing* by the Bee Gees came loudly over the record player and we remained skating as Lisa continued to play faster songs.

"Joel!" I yelled above noise of the music and laughter from the other *Sunday School Detectives*. "This disco music is so cool! I'll bet we're skating to this kind of music when we graduate from college!"

"Uh…" he replied, not knowing how best to answer me.

I was drenched in sweat after several more loud songs were played and after having skated many, many circles around the basement floor, and I welcomed the news that dinner and dessert awaited us upstairs. We quickly took off our skates – some of the detectives had 'real' roller skates, while several, like me, just had metal clip on's that went over our shoes – and we quickly went upstairs to the Ryerson's dining room.

Mrs. Ryerson, Cotton and Hemlinger had made a large pizza for us, and they poured us Pepsi and Root Beer at the dark wooden dining room table – after we had washed our hands, and waited for our meal to be served.

"Here's to solving *The Case of the Mysterious Circles*," Moscow said as he raised his glass of root beer. "I was pretty bored over at the seed place, but I'm glad some of you others weren't."

"Me too," Joel said.

"Me three," Michelle said with a smile. "That reminds me, I really liked that song *We've Only Just Begun*. Don't you like it too, Joelsie?" she asked Joel.

"Joelsie?" I asked.

"Yeah, that's the name I came up for him while he was singing *The Carpenters* to me at that seed place. "

"Hey come on," Joel said with a frown. "I was just trying to help you out. You said you were scared."

"I'm just teasing," Michelle said with a smile.

"Nice job Hailey on getting the bad guy," Lisa interrupted with a smile.

"Everyone helped," Hailey explained quickly. "It wasn't all me – like the newspaper's made it sound like. You know that, right?"

"Oh yeah, we know that," Moscow said with a smile.

"I really think the Lord helped us," Hailey continued. "The Lord was really faithful. He really answered our prayers."

"Yeah, the Lord really helped you Sneak, over at Rawson Park," Jennie said. "You could have been really hurt."

"Yeah, and he helped us catch the bad guys," Lisa added. "Both Julian *and* Mr. Crenshaw."

"You know, I was just thinking about that," Sneak added. "I came across this paper that Professor Telson gave me," he said as he grabbed a yellow paper from a nearby table.

"What is it?" Lisa asked.

"It's a couple of verses about God's faithfulness," Sneak explained. "The professor asked me to read these and think about them before we got together again."

"Let me see," Jennie demanded.

"Here, I'll hold it up so everyone can see it," Sneak said. "It's just a couple of passages."

We looked at the sheet of paper for a moment, as he lifted it up.

Passages on God's Faithfulness
Matthew 11:28-30 - We read together
Exodus 34: 5-7
Psalm 36:5-9
Psalm 89:1-8
I John 1:9
Romans 8:38-39

"Maybe those would be good for all of us to read," Hailey suggested. "I'd be happy to write them down for us."

"Sure," Sneak replied. "I haven't had a chance to study them yet, but it would be fun to read them together."

"Yeah, that'd be cool," said Lisa.

We paused for a moment – reflecting on how God had helped us with the case.

"Well, I'm pretty happy I called it from the beginning," Jennie said smugly.

"Called it?" her brother asked.

"Well yeah, I totally called it," Jennie replied.

"How's that?" her brother asked with a puzzled look.

"Well, don't you remember when you were telling us about the case out the garage," Jennie began.

"Sure," said Sneak.

"And then I said, 'wouldn't it be funny if the person starting the fires was someone from the Farmer's

Market?' And sure enough, Mr. Crenshaw was from the Farmer's Market...we've seen him there selling his seeds."

"Yeah, but that's not really *calling it*," her brother explained.

"Sure it is," Jennie insisted.

"No, it isn't," her brother replied. "There's a lot of people who sell stuff over at the Farmer's Market. There's the guy who sharpens knives and there's the lady with the great sweet corn...."

"And that one farmer who sells the great tomatoes," Michelle added.

"Right, you can't really say that you *called it* if you didn't really know who it was," Sneak concluded.

"Sure I can," Jennie said with a smile. "I called it."

"No you didn't," her brother insisted.

"Yes, I did," Jennie replied.

"Well, all I know," I interrupted. "Is that capturing *The Great Peggu* was hot!"

"Well, when you're hot you're hot," Cressida replied in her quiet voice – saying the first part of a very popular expression.

"And when you're not you're not!" the rest of us said together amid laughs and smiles.

"Good one Pep!" Moscow said as he raised his glass of root beer.

CHAPTER 80

A few days after our party to celebrate the conclusion of *The Case of the Mysterious Circles,* one of the many people described in this book received a phone call. It was from a familiar caller – and a call the person had been expecting for several days.

"Do they suspect that you're spying on them?" the voice on the phone asked.

"No, *The Sunday School Detectives* don't suspect me," came the reply.

-Soli Dei Gloria

Made in the USA
Columbia, SC
03 June 2019